Wed to the Barbarian

Also by Keira Andrews

Contemporary

Honeymoon for One
Beyond the Sea
Ends of the Earth
Arctic Fire
The Chimera Affair

Holiday
The Christmas Deal
The Christmas Leap
Only One Bed
Merry Cherry Christmas
Santa Daddy
In Case of Emergency
Eight Nights in December
If Only in My Dreams
Where the Lovelight Gleams
Gay Romance Holiday Collection

Sports
Kiss and Cry
Reading the Signs
Cold War
The Next Competitor
Love Match
Synchronicity (free read!)

Gay Amish Romance Series
A Forbidden Rumspringa
A Clean Break
A Way Home
A Very English Christmas

Valor Duology

Wed to the Barbarian

Barbarian Duet Book One

BY KEIRA ANDREWS

Wed to the Barbarian: Barbarian Duet Book One
Written and published by Keira Andrews
Cover by Dar Albert
Formatting by BB eBooks

© 2021 by Keira Andrews
Print Edition

ISBN: 978-1-988260-61-7

This is a work of fiction. Names, characters, businesses, places, events and incidents are either the products of the author's imagination or used in a fictitious manner. No persons, living or dead, were harmed by the writing of this book. Any resemblance to any actual persons, living or dead, or actual events is purely coincidental.

Acknowledgments

Huge thanks to Leta Blake, Rai, Anara, and Lili for their encouragement and help in bringing Jem and Cador's story to life. xo

Chapter One

H OW DID ONE man possess *that* many muscles?

As the cleric expounded from the stone temple's center dais under a cloudless sky, Jem's gaze returned time and again to the wild strangers across the square courtyard. He'd never attended a spring summit, though he'd heard breathless tales two years before of the Northern barbarians who'd suddenly reappeared at the annual gathering.

As a boy, Jem had never quite believed the far-flung kingdom of Ergh actually existed. It was the stuff of legend, a cautionary tale—anger the gods at your peril.

The gods of wind, water, fire, and earth had conspired to sever Ergh from the mainland and banish it north for...something or other. Jem couldn't recall the exact nature of the offense offhand, but it was to do with one of the wars that had once plagued Onan.

Yes, the clerics had sailed across the forbidding Askorn Sea on occasion in attempts to lure Ergh back into the fold and restore balance to the world and whatnot, but that was all rather theoretical. Ergh had remained a fiction to Jem, even once his brothers returned from the spring summit with sneering reports of the barbarians who'd attended for the first time in centuries.

Yet here they sat! Almost two dozen people of Ergh in the very impressive flesh, right before Jem's eyes. They spoke the common language of Onan, although their accent was harsher.

The language was proof they'd once indeed been part of the realm in ages past.

They were led not by a queen or king or royal as they had been before Ergh was banished north, but by a chieftain—a title that Jem assumed applied to people of all genders. The current chieftain, Kenver, had apparently been in power for some time. He seemed to be a humorless man.

The delegates came in various descriptions, much like the people of Jem's home, Neuvella, and Gwels to the east and Ebrenn to the west. Skin from pale to dark, hair from silver to black, bodies lean to wide.

Yet they were unlike anyone Jem had ever seen. Although their number was fewer than the other delegations by half, the Northerners somehow seemed to fill their side of the temple to the breaking point. Instead of wearing silks, they were clad in animal skins all over, some with fur still attached despite the afternoon's heat.

Their legs were spread wide where they sat, their boots thick and heavy rather than smooth and sculpted. They had no weapons Jem could spot, but he imagined even the smallest person from Ergh could break his neck with a brutal snap. Let alone the larger delegates who very strongly resembled the murderous mountain warriors who kidnapped the heroine in Jem's favorite book.

Lowering his head as if deep in contemplation, he stared through his eyelashes at the chieftain's second son. Fur accents on coarse material sat atop wide shoulders, his muscled arms bare and a black leather vest covering his chest—barely—the same leather straining over thighs that were like tree trunks. This son looked around thirty years and had the same straw-colored hair and pale skin as his father and older brother.

The chieftain's daughter had dark skin and hair, cropped short like her brothers. Some delegates had longer hair that hung wild, not twisted and neatly sculpted like Jem was used to seeing. The chieftain's hair met his broad shoulders. Instead of a crown of jewels, he wore a headpiece of two curving white tusks.

From a distance, it appeared the second son's square jaw hadn't seen a razor for days. Did he smell as fierce and wild as he looked? Jem imagined musky sweat and dirt and ice. Did ice have a smell? If it did, the second son surely reeked of it. If Jem were pinned helpless beneath him, it would fill his senses...

He repressed a shudder of desire, fiddling with the silk collar of his green shirt. Where he sat, almost at the end of the front row on the southern side of the temple, he could examine the man while appearing to pay heed to the chief cleric's sermon, her hoarse voice echoing as she spoke passionately on something he was surely supposed to find profound. At least Jem was in no danger of falling asleep in boredom—not with all those leather-clad muscles to ogle.

Still, he shouldn't be eyeing the son of the Ergh chieftain at all. Hadn't he learned his lesson? If his brothers noticed, humiliation would undoubtedly follow. Jem shifted his gaze to the eastern side of the temple and the ruling family in the front row led by two queens, one his cousin.

There. They had a son who wasn't too tall or broad and apparently enjoyed sums and formulas, if Jem recalled correctly. He was much more appropriate for a mate. Much less likely to break out into roars of laughter if Jem approached with a bold invitation for later.

Not that he would. He almost snorted aloud at the notion, coughing to cover the aborted sound. Since becoming a man, he'd issued precisely one invitation to bed him and there would not be another.

On cue, the remembered humiliation of a feast a few years ago bloomed to life, sticky and cloying even as it cut deeply. Would Jem be ancient like the stooped and wrinkled cleric and *still* experience the shame and horror of that rejection as though it was yesterday?

It was his own doing. He should have known it was a trick. His two older brothers had always enjoyed tormenting him, but when they confided that a visiting soldier had expressed desire for him, Jem had been all too pathetically eager to believe it.

He'd been mad to consider even for a fleeting moment that a man of the soldier's bravery and strength would want *him*. No. Jem was too small, too weak, too quiet, too odd. He'd be lucky if any man would agree to take him for a spouse. He was a prince, so someone eventually would for political gain if nothing else, but Jem wouldn't be the one to make a proposal.

He squirmed on the stone chair. Even once the soldier had realized Jem wasn't jesting with his invitation, he hadn't been able to curtail his laughter at the absurdity of it all. At the absurdity of Jem himself, apparently. The man had then schooled himself and attempted a kinder refusal, but Jem had run into the night, wishing more than ever he could unfurl wings and fly into the endless sky.

The soldier had been one of the royal guard regiment from Gwels. One soldier each from the royal guards of Neuvella, Ebrenn, and Gwels now stood sentinel at the sole entrance and exit to the temple under a white marble arch. They wore shiny bronze helmets, and the soldier from Gwels this time was mercifully a woman.

Since arriving at the Holy Place the previous day, Jem had held his breath each time he spotted a royal guard from Gwels.

He might curl up and die with humiliation if he actually encountered the man who'd rejected him. The sooner he could safely escape home to his peaceful days with his birds by the lake and cozy nights with fanciful tales in the pages of his books, the better.

He wondered again if the tiny dillywig hatchlings had survived. They had only been beige, bald, sightless little lumps, their yellow beaks open in soundless protest at leaving the safety of the eggs that had been cracked too early. One of the groundskeepers had sworn to look after them in Jem's absence, and Jem hated not knowing the tiny creatures' fate.

He turned his head enough to peer at the tense Western delegates from Ebrenn. King Perran was a nasty piece of work. His back was straight and he kept his expression neutral during the sermon, but Jem imagined the cruel thoughts slithering through the king's head. His pale face was wrinkled and hair gray, but he was strong yet. His jeweled crown was so enormous Jem wondered how he could sit up with it atop his head.

His wife had died some years before after falling suddenly ill. There were still whispers that she'd been miserable married to the old man and her death had been murder. Others said it was by her own hand in her grief for her daughter, who'd been ill herself and had only lived a decade.

At the king's right hand sat his remaining child. Prince Treeve of Ebrenn had certainly grown up in the years since Jem had seen him. His shoulders were broad—though not as wide as the barbarian's—his skin and hair tawny, legs long in tight breeches and tall boots.

His glittering crown was less ornate than his father's, but the emeralds seemed to make his brown eyes sparkle with hidden depths. It was only Ebrenn's tradition that the children of royal leaders wore crowns as well, and Jem was relieved he didn't have to parade around in one. The emeralds suited Treeve, though. His teeth were white and straight, lips full—

And lifting into a smile as he noticed Jem's surreptitious stare! Jem barely resisted squeaking as he whipped his head too far to the right, garnering attention from the Eastern delegates. Cursing himself, he stared at the cleric on the pedestal, breathing shallowly. The last thing he needed was Prince Treeve mocking him. Jem got enough of that from his brothers.

Besides, for as long as Jem could remember, he'd been told Ebrenn was not to be trusted, and that the king in particular was treasonous and greedy. While much nicer to look at, his son was likely just as horrible. The king had boldly encroached on the border with Neuvella for far too long, one stretch of it through a disputed valley.

The anger of Jem's mother toward Ebrenn had deepened so much recently it worried him. Jem typically ignored all things royal and political, but he felt that if not for the presence of the clerics, Mother and Ebrenn's king might come to blows.

As it was, they gave each other painfully civil nods and smiles so brittle the slightest offence would surely shatter the peace. The threat of war had never been so real, even as they sat in the temple for a sermon on unity. Was land really worth it? Couldn't they share the valley in question?

His brothers would scoff and call him naïve, no doubt. This was just one of the reasons Jem preferred to stay home with his books and hatchlings. He dreaded getting involved in politics, never mind war.

Shifting, he tried to hide his wince at the numbness in his backside. He knew this sacred site, resting like a crown atop the mainland of Onan, was unchanged from the earliest records. He knew it was the holiest of land—chosen by the gods themselves, the clerics often reminded them. He knew he should be reverent and still and dutiful as he listened to the cleric's boundless wisdom.

But surely a few cushions wouldn't go amiss?

He gazed over at the Ergh delegates once more. Even the chieftain's daughter was a head taller than Jem and far more muscled. Many of the group looked as if they spent their days hunting wild boar on horseback with deadly spears, which was entirely possible since boar was apparently Ergh's main industry.

Legend had it when the gods had banished Ergh across the Askorn Sea, the mythical tusked boars had been trapped there. Indeed, they'd only enjoyed smoked boar again on the mainland since Ergh's return, and Ergh traded it only at a premium. Jem supposed slaying wild boar wasn't an easy task.

The chieftain's children certainly looked suited to wielding a spear. The eldest son was scarred and scowling and frankly terrifying. But the younger had a beguiling handsomeness to accompany his might. What did his full lips look like lifted in a smile? Was his laugh warm and low? Did Erghians laugh? It was wonderfully strange to actually behold them in the flesh. Flesh that was—

An icy blue glare met Jem's curious gaze, and he bit back a gasp as he whipped his head down. That the man he'd been ogling had looked straight at him was akin to a hero from the pages of one of his books suddenly appearing before him in his chamber.

Jem must not gawk at the Northerners as though they were exotic beasts captured from the mountains of Ebrenn. He reluctantly lifted his head and looked everywhere else but across the courtyard.

Ancient stones rose up around the temple, carved to represent the four gods of earth, wind, fire, and water. Birds chirped, their twitters and cries making Jem miss the ravens' long caws and the trills of the dillywigs high in the branches near the lake's edge.

Would the hatchlings be too cold or hungry without him there to care for them? Jem would spend hours in his aviary whenever injured or orphaned birds needed him, sometimes through the night. All he could do was hope for the best, but he wished he'd never had to leave.

Mother had always permitted him to stay home rather than attend boring summits, much to his siblings' annoyance. Even Santo had complained that Jem was spoiled, that Mother was too free with him, and that he should have official duties as a prince. Jem was a man now, so he grudgingly admitted it was beyond time he fulfilled his obligation to Neuvella. Still, he missed home and would be happy to never leave it again.

If he closed his eyes to the waning day, Jem could imagine golden light turning orange and pink behind green boughs across his lake, crickets tuning up for their evening concert in the long grasses. He could almost smell the perfume of summer roses.

He snapped his eyes open, the thin soles of his knee-high boots sliding on the stone floor as he shifted. As a prince of Neuvella, if he couldn't appear rapt with the proceedings, he at least had to look awake. He smoothed a palm over the soft fabric of his breeches, then picked at a loose thread by his knee. He wrapped it around the tip of his finger, making light circles on his golden-brown skin.

As he realized the cleric's pontificating had in fact come to a close, a strange, fraught silence settled in. Gooseflesh rippled over him, sudden energy crackling in the temple. Had the thrilling outsiders of Ergh caused a scene? Jem glanced up eagerly—and his heart jolted with sudden dread.

Everyone was looking right at him.

Jem snapped his spine straight and pulled back his shoulders, hearing his father's constant refrain to stand tall instead of always hunching over books or hatchlings. Delegates from all sides stared at him slack-jawed, and his mouth went dry as dirt.

Had he spoken of his boredom with the sermon aloud? Had he insulted the clerics? The gods? Somehow betrayed his lustful fantasies of the Northern son pinning him down in a wild frenzy of passion?

No one so much as whispered, and Jem didn't dare breathe.

Oh gods, what had he done? His heart thumped so powerfully he was certain every soul in the temple could hear it in the stunned silence. His skin prickled hotly. He had no choice but to speak since an invisible vise apparently gripped the tongues of all present.

He glanced at his beloved sibling Santo next to him. Santo's mouth turned down, sympathy in their kind brown eyes. Yet they remained mute.

To the courtyard at large, Jem asked, "Pardon?"

Of all people, it was the second son of the North who broke the silence. He growled with clear disgust. "Are you mad?" he barked at his father. "Marry? *Him*?" Then he somehow turned his withering, sneering gaze directly on *Jem*. "This..." His lip curled, and he motioned at Jem. "This..."

"Cador," his sister warned, eyebrows high.

"This *boy*?" Cador spat the word like the bitterest poison.

"I'm a man!" Jem exclaimed, hands fisting. The sputtered

response came reflexively after years of his brothers' teasing about his stature. His voice rose too high in indignation, and almost everyone burst into laughter, breaking the spell of shock.

Wait, what was that part about *marriage*?

Jem must've misunderstood. He *had* to have misunderstood. He was certainly not marrying anyone for the foreseeable future, let alone this barbarian! Especially not this barbarian who sneered at him in horrified abhorrence. Beside Santo, their brothers Pasco and Locryn seemed shocked. Locryn struggled to stifle giggles.

Santo shook their head. "Oh, Jem. I'm sorry."

"What's happening?" Jem's pulse thundered in his ears and he could barely hear his own question.

The ancient cleric's thready voice positively boomed now. "Cador of Ergh and Prince Jowan of Neuvella shall be wed. Ergh's chieftain and Neuvella's queen have welcomed this historic partnership that will symbolize their renewed fellowship and the unity of Onan. We shall all be one."

Jem so rarely thought of himself as Prince Jowan that for a mad moment, he hoped the cleric spoke of another. His parents stared straight ahead, and Jem had to lean forward on the horrible stone chair to glimpse their faces beyond Santo and their brothers, who had stopped laughing, at least. "Mother, Father!" There was a din of chatter now.

Mother! Jem wanted to scream. How could she of all people do this to him?

Father said nothing as usual—he didn't make the decisions and never argued with Mother. Face composed, Mother beheld him with her dark gaze, her eyes beaming with unspoken sympathy. "It is done. For the good of Onan and the pleasure of the gods." Jem hardly saw the sheen of tears before she blinked them away and turned her head forward.

Across the temple, the chieftain's son—Cador—seemed to be having a similar discussion with his father, who was stone-faced and clearly unyielding. There didn't seem to be another parent there. A thunderous expression creased the scarred face of Cador's older brother, and he argued with their father as well while the sister seemed to ignore them all.

Married? To this stranger from a place that might as well be from one of Jem's books? Married to a huge man with all those muscles that both enticed and terrified him? Good gods. No. This couldn't be happening. It simply couldn't.

He'd told his parents he'd prefer a male spouse or perhaps someone of an open gender like Santo. Santo was married to a wonderful man, and Jem's brothers were wed to women. His mother's sister had a wife, and across Onan, marriages had always bonded whoever chose to be joined, children adopted or born of unions, no matter which.

Choice playing a vital role. After being spurned by the soldier and retreating to his daydreams and the pages of his books, Jem had idly hoped to one day find a good man who was pretty and kind and enjoyed reading in the evenings. Certainly not this beastly barbarian who likely couldn't even read his own name.

Yes, it was true that Cador had stirred Jem's loins the way a hero warrior in one of his books might. It had been a harmless fantasy! A whim to pass the time while he'd been forced to sit through the sermon. Nothing more!

It was impossible.

Jem's mind whirled this way and that like a flock of dillywigs zigzagging through the sky. Tonight, he'd appeal to his parents. Santo would help. There had to be another way to unify with Ergh. Neuvellan weddings took place after harvest, which was months off. Jem would find a way to stop this. He'd run away if he had to.

If only he could fly. He missed his feathered companions from the lake with a pang of longing so fierce it stole his breath. He shot to his feet, the need to move shattering his rigid shock.

A fresh burst of nervous laughter echoed through the temple, to the obvious displeasure of the clerics. A voice behind him from his own people jeered. "Perhaps he's eager for it!"

"Gods, can you imagine?" someone replied in a low voice that wasn't low enough. "Look at those savages! I wager he won't survive the wedding night. His groom might break him in two!"

Laughter rippled out despite the clerics' admonishing glares, although Ebrenn's king did not look amused in the least, his expression thunderous. Jem's face burned as more voices around the temple gossiped, as if this was all a bit of folly and not his *life*. Standing there, willing himself to simply disappear, he glanced left and right.

The raised courtyard temple had only one entry under the marble arch, the path leading into the hillside, winding a twisting route that led to a flowered meadow and the low, sprawling stone home of the clerics.

The delegates slept in austere chambers in wings corresponding to their kingdoms. The Ergh wing had stood empty for lifetimes upon lifetimes. And now Jem was expected to *marry* one of them?

The archway to freedom was too far to make a run for it, but now that Jem stood, sitting again on the awful chair was too great a surrender. He kept his head high and walked calmly across the temple, putting one thin-soled boot in front of the other.

He didn't risk a glance toward the Northern delegates. His eyes stung, and if he burst into tears in front of everyone—let alone in front of the barbarians—he might wither up and die right then and there.

Whispers followed him into the twisting tunnel through the earth, flickering torchlight casting ghoulish shadows across his path. The murmurs faded, his own harsh breath filling the quiet as he broke into a run, passing a startled young soldier who guarded the exit into the purple meadow.

Jem yearned to crawl under his blankets and wake with all of this nothing but an unfortunate dream. Footsteps echoed on the stone floor of the path inside the hill, and he imagined the barbarian bursting out, hauling him over his wide shoulder like a sack of grain, and spiriting him away to the frozen North.

Jem ruthlessly quashed a traitorous pulse of desire.

Santo appeared in the meadow, and Jem barely resisted throwing himself into his sibling's arms. Brown skin glistening, Santo dabbed sweat from their forehead. They frowned at the low sun and urged Jem toward the southern wing of the guest quarters.

They kept their dark, glossy hair far longer than Jem, and lifted the curls from the back of their neck. "I've never known it to be so hot here at the Holy Place. Feels like we're back home," Santo groused.

"If only," Jem muttered. Santo complained about the heat most days, but loved their long hair, as did their husband, who enjoyed weaving it into elaborate patterns. Jem had always found it romantic, but at the moment, any notion of romance made his stomach curdle.

The clerics' headquarters wasn't a castle like the one Jem's family had lived in for centuries, the idea being that the Holy

Place was austere and simple and only there in service of the gods. Although it still had a grand dining hall and Jem suspected there were more comforts hidden in its maze of buildings.

In the cool stone corridor of the southern guest wing, a servant nodded to them serenely and offered to bring refreshments to the chamber Jem was using. Once they were alone inside with fresh water, tea, and a plate of little round cakes, Jem was only able to sip from his cup, the idea of sweets turning his stomach.

"I'm not marrying him," he announced, pacing back and forth by the narrow bed. On one pass, he bumped the side table and shot out a hand to save the tower of books he'd brought on the journey from toppling. "We know next to nothing of him or these people! They reappear after lifetimes and we're supposed to, to—*marry* them? *I'm* supposed to marry one of them? I don't even know him! And gods, look at him!"

Perched on the side of the mattress, the sleeves of their purple silk shirt rolled up, Santo sighed heavily. They wore tall boots and tight breeches like Jem's and ran their palms over the material, making a *shushing* sound. "Jem, you don't have a choice. The bargain has been struck."

"Then they can un-strike it. It's only spring. There are months until wedding season. Ergh can find fellowship with Neuvella and please the whims of the gods in some other manner."

Santo made a little sound of…what? Jem stared at them, hair standing up on the back of his neck at the miserable expression creasing his sibling's face. "What is it?"

"Well… The thing is that the wedding will be out of season. For the sake of securing this bond with Ergh." Santo held up their hands. "I only learned of any of this earlier today. I'm sorry. I tried to warn you, but you were off following the birds as usual."

"Out of season," Jem repeated, fresh dread sinking through him.

Santo bit their lip. "For the good of Onan?"

"When is this wedding to take place?" The fingers of dread closed into an iron fist in Jem's belly. "When?" His voice rose. "*When?*"

"Tomorrow."

His knees buckled, but he caught himself. Santo half rose, but Jem waved them off and dropped onto the bed beside them. He flattened his hands on his thighs, then dug in his fingers, the soft material of his breeches bunching.

"I don't understand," Jem whispered. He slumped against his sibling, and Santo wrapped an arm around him.

"It was the clerics' suggestion," Mother said from the open doorway. She strode in, gathering the bright silk of her long red dress aside before perching on the stone chair across from the bed in the narrow chamber.

Father entered behind her, closing the wooden door with a creak and loud thud. His dark hair was threaded with gray, yet his belly showed no softening of age. He clasped his hands behind his back and said nothing, waiting for his wife to speak.

Gold and silver rings glittered on her threaded fingers. Jem looked at his favorite, a silver bird with wings spread wide and green stones for eyes. As a child, she'd let him wear it on his thumb whenever he asked even though he'd lost it more than once and owed the eagle-eyed servants for finding it.

But Mother had never refused him anything, even when she should. Jem stared at her now, feeling like she'd slipped a fatal knife between his ribs.

"Darling, I've told you before that you won't be able to while away your days with books and birds forever. You've reached twenty years. I have been patient, allowing you the time you seemed to need. But you knew this day was coming."

Jem couldn't choke down the sputter of outrage as he straightened from his sibling's half-embrace. "No! I knew I would be assigned more diplomatic tasks, and that I'd wed eventually. I was never warned of *this* day. Of wedding that barbarian! *Tomorrow!*"

A perfect curl had escaped the elaborate, jeweled twist of hair around Mother's head and her golden crown, and she brushed it from her forehead. Their whole family had long, thick eyelashes, but she'd curled hers more for the summit, making her brown eyes even bigger. She blinked away a fresh glistening. When she spoke, her voice was placid.

"It is a blessing that Ergh has returned to Onan. We will be officially united once more under the eyes of the gods. It is an honor to play our roles."

"I'm to feel *honored* to be forced into marriage with that brute? A complete stranger? We know barely anything of Ergh and its people! I don't want anything to do with them." Jem fought another surge of panic. "It's not fair!"

His parents shared a glance. Father said, "No, I wouldn't call it fair at all. Only necessary. Your siblings are already married, and of all the royal children in Onan, you are the best candidate."

"My cousin of the East is of marriageable age!"

Mother said, "He is to wed the daughter of an important family in Gwels. He loves her and the match is made."

"What of, of—" He cast about. "Prince Treeve of Ebrenn? He is not wed!"

"You know the West's reputation. Their king does them no favors. That man is—"

"I know," Jem interrupted before his mother could launch into a listing of grievances. "Still, Treeve seems pleasant enough."

Mother's lips twisted. "Don't let his pretty face fool you. No one in that family is to be trusted." She raised her hand, and Jem glimpsed the marriage brand that had been seared into her palm in the shape of a crown. "You will wed Cador of Ergh tomorrow. There is no alternative. We know you prefer men, or else you could have married the chieftain's daughter. We all want this to be a good match."

The daughter would be no less frightening. Jem sputtered. "But why must we marry at all?"

"The clerics wish it," Mother answered. "They have toiled for lifetimes to make Onan whole once more. The gods wish it. The time has come. Bonds must be forged."

"But why?" Jem wanted to stamp his foot. He cleared his throat and lowered his voice. It wouldn't do to keep acting like a child. "We haven't needed them for so many years. We don't need them now. They can keep their wild boar and their furs."

Mother frowned. "Perhaps they need us, Jem. Ergh was cast out alone while we have been blessed by the gods and lived together in harmony."

Jem scoffed mightily. "You've argued with the West forever! You *just said* none of them are to be trusted! If it's not the border in the Valley of the Gods, it's the price of oil from deep in their mountains, or even the cost of a bushel of sevels."

Her jaw tightened. "You have no idea how much the king has raised prices. We need oil, Jem. To light our lamps and make our perfumes and lotions and all sorts of conveniences you've never thought twice about. Do you know how much Neuvella depends on our perfume industry? Ebrenn has only produced pale imitations that gather dust on shelves. While we grow every other ingredient and hold the artisanal knowledge, the oil only comes from those damn mountains."

He couldn't deny that he had never given any of it a moment's consideration. "All right, so admit it! You hate the king. If not for the clerics forever making peace, we'd have been at war years ago. Didn't you just threaten to cut off Ebrenn's supply of grain from the East because they're encroaching on the border? And didn't they promise revenge for... I don't even know what, but the king was snarling at you."

His parents couldn't deny it, looking decidedly uncomfortable. Santo stayed silent. Mother said stiffly, "It's true we've had our differences, especially with Ebrenn. Trade must be fair, and we must defend our border. But no one wants war."

Jem sighed. "Why can't you just live alongside each other in actual harmony? You'll defend what you say is the border—although the West disagrees. Then they'll act out this revenge, and you'll retaliate, and the clerics will warn us about angering the gods, promising drought or floods or hurricanes, or being banished altogether like Ergh. And you'll ease back for a time, until new tensions bubble up over who knows what. And you only cooperate so well with Gwels because that's Father's homeland and you must."

Mother shrugged. "Yes. That's precisely why the clerics arranged the marriage between me and a prince of Gwels." She gave Jem's father a tender look that he returned. "Though we were *most* displeased about it at the time, what a gift they bestowed on us."

Father took her hand, pressing their branded palms together. "The gods blessed us truly. Not only do we keep the peace between our lands, but our hearts are so full and—"

"Yes, yes, that's wonderful for you!" Jem snapped. "Can we get back to me marrying that beast who looks as though he'd just as soon murder me in cold blood than cherish me in the bosom of his heart?"

Mother arched a thin brow. "Weren't you just saying we should live alongside each other in harmony?"

"Well...yes." He cringed, waiting.

"What better way to find harmony with Ergh than by blending our families? If this reunification is to be a success, we must open our minds about the Erghians. They are not beasts. They are children of the gods as we are, and we must help them find favor again. Lift them up to—"

Jem groaned. "Enough, please." He didn't think Mother truly believed in the gods, but she could certainly spout the rhetoric when it suited her.

She gave him a genuine smile. "My darling. It's frightening, I know. But you may be pleasantly surprised. I know the Erghians seem..." Her delicate brows met as she apparently searched for words.

"Beastly?" Jem suggested. "Ferocious? Unkempt at best?"

Mother settled on, "Foreign. But we must open our hearts. As I said, we are all children of the gods. Children of Onan. The clerics assure me the Erghians are not so different from us. Cruder, perhaps. Wilder. But they are good, hardworking people, which I have seen myself since they have returned to the fold. Their ways might be...simpler, but there is value in that. And we can help them, Jem. We can enrich their lives and share our more modern methods. After all, it is Ergh that has sought to reconnect with us after all this time. We can help them build a better future."

"I suppose so," Jem muttered. Yet when he thought of *marrying* this wild stranger he wanted to run, as pointless as that was. Where would he even go? He'd only ever left home in a carriage and hadn't paid attention to directions because he'd had his nose in his books.

"Oh, darling." She stood and drew Jem to his feet. Even his mother was a few inches taller than him. Brushing back his short, wavy hair, she said, "I know this is sudden. I should have given you warning, but I worried you would run home."

"Could you blame me?"

She smiled. "No, my precious." Her smile faded. "But I have coddled you too long. Santo and your brothers have taken on much more responsibility while I've let you do as you please with your head in the clouds. Or more aptly your nose in books. All those adventures you have in your head—it's time to take a real one."

"But..." Jem knew any denial would be little more than a whine, so he kept quiet.

"When one of your hatchlings is ready to fly but afraid to leave the nest, what do you do?"

Jem didn't want to say it aloud. Still sitting on the bed, Santo oh so helpfully said, "I do believe you give them a nudge."

"I'd hardly call this a 'nudge'!" Jem retorted.

Mother took hold of his shoulders. "It's a shove. You're right. I should have eased you into your duties. But you insisted yourself today that you're a man. Time to act like one. You are a prince of Neuvella, and you must do your duty." She attempted a light tone as she stroked Jem's hair once more. "Cador seems just as blindsided as you, if it helps. His father swears he is not a cruel man, despite appearances. That he will make a fine husband. Perhaps this will bond the two of you."

He remembered the curl of Cador's lip and how he'd accused Jem of being merely a boy. No, Cador's disgust with him did not help matters whatsoever. Surely they wouldn't be expected to share Jem's chamber when they returned to Neuvella? He wanted to ask, but it would make it all too real. No, the castle had many wings, and certainly Cador could have a chamber to himself.

"My darling boy, you didn't ask for this adventure, but I know you'll find your way on this new path. You'll make me proud." She pressed a kiss to his forehead.

Throat thick, Jem wanted to clutch her close and forget the world, safe in her arms. Instead, he nodded and watched his parents retreat, his mother sweeping from the room and his father sparing him an encouraging smile.

He dropped down beside Santo on the side of the bed, suddenly exhausted like he'd been swimming for hours on a hot summer's morning.

Santo gave his shoulder a playful punch. "Think of the bright side. The barbarian is certainly a fine piece of flesh. Those muscles!" They grinned. "I'd be jealous if I didn't have a perfect husband already." Their fingers traced the fine gold chain that nestled in the hollow of their throat.

Along with their marriage brands, Santo had received a plain twisted necklace, their doting husband insisting anything else would detract from their natural beauty. At fourteen, Jem had thought it the most romantic thing he'd ever heard, and Santo and their love were still just as smitten with each other now.

"I don't want his muscles. I don't want anything to do with him." Jem crossed his arms tightly.

Santo scoffed. "As if you weren't ogling him all day. No one else might have noticed, but you can't fool me, brother. You've always given burly men the eye."

"That was only looking! A harmless imagining! Nothing more. I've never—" He broke off, humiliation rushing through him like a flame to tinder. At his age, most had dallied for several years before committing to a spouse.

Santo's eyebrows shot up. "You can't be serious. You've never... You're a..."

Squirming, Jem jumped up and began pacing. He muttered, "A virgin."

"But, but—*how*?"

Jem scowled. "Surely I don't need to explain to you the lack of certain activity."

"Sorry. No. I just thought... I know you were a little heartbroken by that soldier after that prank from Pasco and Locryn. But that was ages ago."

"I made a complete fool of myself, and I haven't been keen to repeat the experience."

"He was the fool for passing you up! I understand being hesitant to find a proper suitor, but there are so many options for dallying. No coopers or farmers? Groomsmen or stonemasons or—"

"None of them! No one." Jem was ready to climb out of his skin. Talking about it made it even worse.

"Huh." Santo shook their head. "You always watched the big men, so I assumed you'd seek them out to play once you were of age."

He scoffed. "No one wants me."

Santo pressed their lips together. "That's not true. But since that awful prank, when has anyone had a chance? You've kept yourself hidden away. You know, if you don't have the longing for a bedmate, there's nothing wrong with that."

"I know!" He exhaled noisily. "Must we speak of this?" When Santo only waited with an arched brow, Jem sighed. "It's not a lack of wanting. There's so much longing in my mind, in my... In me."

"And do you satisfy yourself?" Santo motioned crudely with their hand.

"Yes!" Jem wasn't about to go into detail. "But making it real with another person... Flesh and blood and not merely fantasy—it's too daunting." Too utterly terrifying.

"I understand."

Jem rolled his eyes. "You bedded half the kingdom before you fell for Arthek."

Santo grinned briefly. "True. But sincerely, I understand. It comes more easily to some, but when you meet the right person—"

"That beast is not the right person!"

"Well..." They grimaced. "I grant you it's not ideal. But I can give you some tips. First off, think of your mouth as—"

"Stop talking! Think of your mouth as something to shut immediately!" Jem was about to stick his fingers in his ears.

Santo held up their hands. "All right, all right. But if you change your mind, I'm here for you." They smiled sadly. "It'll be over soon. You'll wed him, we'll have the celebration, and in a day or two, we can go home. It's a political match—you'll be free to take as many lovers as you like. Or as few as you like. You'll have done your duty to the family. And I'm sure this Cador will find no shortage of enthusiastic lovers in Neuvella."

Perversely, a twist of jealousy tugged at Jem. Utter madness! He steadfastly ignored it.

Santo added, "Soon, you'll be home by your lake, re-reading *The High Tide of Morvoren* for the hundredth time."

Jem sighed warmly. Morvoren was a Southern girl born of land and took a muscled merman lover from the sea, escaping with him to far-off worlds of sea creatures. It had been his favorite book since he'd sneaked it from the library's adult section, and he looked to his dog-eared copy on the table beneath the stack of newer books he'd brought. He always kept Morvoren close at hand even though he could likely recite her adventures by heart.

"So you've really never..." Santo motioned vaguely with their hand. "Not even some light play?"

"Not so much as a kiss," Jem admitted, his cheeks flaring hot. "As I said, it's not lack of want. Merely lack of courage." He shook his head. "I think I shall like to be alone."

After a firm-yet-gentle hug, Santo left him in peace. A servant brought him a dinner tray later, but Jem couldn't touch a bite. He forced himself to swallow the sweet wine, curled under the blankets, and opened Morvoren's book to his favorite part.

He read of Morvoren's daring escape from pirates to her reunion with her lover on an empty isle where she rode his giant cock on the wet sand with the sea washing around their striving bodies.

As the night wore on, he read it again.

And again.

And, well, why not? Again.

Chapter Two

H E WAS TOO short, as usual.

The robe pooled around his shiny boots, and Jem felt like a silly child playing dress-up instead of a man on his wedding day. Scowling, he rolled up the sleeves of the traditional wedding robe a cleric had brought him that morning, neatly folded and smelling of lemons.

The white, lightweight material went over his head and draped down over his body, his arms poking through wide, overlong sleeves. It was designed to fall to a person's knees, and he wore his regular thin, tight breeches underneath. Cador would wear the same white robe, although his would surely be quite a bit larger. The robes had wide collars, and Jem's dipped down almost to his nipples.

The austere chamber had no looking glass, but any doubt about how ridiculous he may or may not have looked was put to rest as Locryn and Pasco burst through the door without pausing to knock, a bottle in hand. Jem cursed himself for not barricading it.

He nodded, jaw tight. "I look foolish. I'm well aware."

"Oh, don't pout!" Pasco grinned. "It does nothing to elevate your stature."

"Nothing would but lifts in your boots," Locryn added. He and Pasco were tall, with the same glossy dark curls as the whole family. Locryn winked at Jem and nudged his shoulder. "Cheer up, brother. You'll finally get your wish."

"My wish is to go home and be left alone," Jem muttered.

Putting the bottle on the little table in the corner, Pasco rolled his eyes. "That's not what you want."

"It is! I want to go home!"

Pasco's gaze narrowed shrewdly. "Come now. What you want is a burly man to sweep you up in his arms and fuck you 'til you can't walk straight."

Locryn chortled, agreeing with Pasco as always, and Jem huffed. Pasco was the eldest and bossiest and hadn't outgrown playing pranks even after marrying the daughter of a wealthy trader and becoming a father. They'd never been close, yet Pasco still seemed able to peer into Jem's soul and read him so very easily.

"I don't want it to be *him!*" Jem exclaimed before he could school himself. He hadn't confided in Pasco so much as his favorite flavor of summer iced treats since he was a child and didn't know better. Pasco could take even the most innocuous information and twist it into some prank.

Locryn laughed, but Pasco only sighed. "No, I don't suppose you do. He's no brave and handsome royal soldier, that's for certain."

That particular debacle was the last thing Jem wanted to contemplate. "Please, can you leave me be? I assure you I'll be humiliated enough today without you lending a hand."

Pasco scoffed. "We've no wish to see you humiliated, as much as you enjoy playing the victim."

Bristling, Jem clenched his fists. "Don't give me that. You made me think that soldier desired me—"

"Because I thought he did! And I knew you were far too timid to proposition him without encouragement." Pasco ran a hand through his curls before letting his arm drop. "You know the outcome wasn't what I intended. I thought the soldier had good taste and would accept your offer. I was trying to help."

Jem opened his mouth to retort, then closed it. For once, Pasco wasn't smirking. His brown eyes regarded Jem steadily with...sincerity? Still, he muttered, "I *know* no such thing."

Locryn watched Pasco with a furrowed brow. "Do you mean that winter feast when the Eastern queens visited? The one when—"

"*Yes*," Pasco snapped.

Locryn's confusion only seemed to grow. "But that was *ages* ago. You're still bothered by it?" He blinked at Jem incredulously. "Forget that fool of a soldier."

"Perhaps that's easy for you two, but I'm not—I don't—" This was why he'd spent his nights with his books instead of seeking a lover. He'd been safe. He'd been in control. He hadn't had to deal with the chaos of other people.

Pasco sighed. "I did try to convince Mother to call it off, but she won't. You've no choice, I'm afraid."

Jem hesitated. Again, Pasco seemed unnervingly genuine. "You did?"

"Yes, but she won't be budged. I'd actually thought you and Treeve of the West might be a good match. Alas." Pasco uncorked the wine and filled a goblet, passing it to Jem. "Here. This will calm your nerves."

Yes, Treeve was handsome and muscled in a much more reasonable manner, and though the West had long been their adversaries, he was far less terrifying a prospect as a husband. But it was apparently too late now.

Glumly, Jem sniffed the wine, ready to gulp it even if it was some trick. Santo came in, not bothering to knock either. Santo frowned at their brothers. "What are you two up to?"

"Celebrating our brother on his wedding day!" Pasco insisted with indignation so sincere Jem had to snort.

Jem said, "Like my birthday when you gave me cakes full of hwyja berries and I spent the day with the chamber pot? Or when you told me you'd found a nest of dillywig hatchlings in the caves and I searched for hours and was left in the dark when my torch burned out?"

"You conquered your fear of the caves, didn't you?" Pasco opened his arms wide. "You're welcome."

Santo sniffed the wine bottle. "You two drink first."

Pasco and Locryn did, insisting there was no trickery. Santo poured themselves a goblet and sipped it suspiciously, but Jem didn't risk it. The last thing he needed was to be violently ill at the altar in front of everyone.

"Why do you think they've come back recently?" Jem asked. "It's been lifetimes. I didn't even think there was anything in the Askorn Sea but ice and rock. Has anyone sailed to the North but the clerics?"

"Not that I know of," Pasco said. "The new bits of trade with Ergh goes through the clerics too. No one would risk that icy sea without the gods' permission. The clerics have always nattered on about making Onan whole again, but we've done just fine without Ergh if you ask me."

Locryn shrugged. "Perhaps they're lonely."

"They must want something," Santo said. "Aside from peace and unity."

"They want our baby brother, it seems." Pasco grinned, white teeth gleaming. "It's just like one of your fanciful stories, Jem. Married to a savage! Come on, it's exciting. Admit it."

"It's exciting when it happens on the page! Not when it's

real."

Pasco shrugged. "Well, that leather conceals nothing, and the barbarian's prick seems very real. So do try and enjoy it. You've stayed a virgin long enough. Take the plunge."

Santo frowned. "How did you know he's still a virgin?"

"How did you not?" Pasco threw up his hands.

Locryn unhelpfully added, "Even I knew that. Remember when—"

"Can we please stop discussing it?" Jem begged. He gulped the wine, throwing caution to the wind.

His mind whirled with images of his betrothed—muscles and stubble and yes, an impressive bulge in that tight leather. What would it feel like under his fingers? Like his own cock? Would it taste sweaty and…wild? Morvoren's merman tasted of salt and freedom, and she loved it when he fucked her mouth and spent down her throat.

Jem imagined himself on his knees. Naked, though the barbarian still wore boar skins and fur and those massive boots that came up to mid-shin, the leather and buckles rough compared to the smooth, supple material of Jem's thin boots.

He imagined the ache in his jaw as he submitted, taking the thick rod of flesh into his mouth. Letting the barbarian use him. Thick, rough fingers tugging his curls, holding him in place. Perhaps his hands would even be bound tightly behind him. He'd be helpless, at the mercy of the barbarian and his huge cock, barely able to breathe…

Jem coughed and turned to the window, glad of the voluminous robe. His imagination had always run wild, but the thrum of desire was quickly doused by an icy shiver of fear. His mind was his own kingdom. He was master there, but the barbarian he was being forced to wed was all too real and beyond Jem's control.

"To Jem on his wedding day." Santo held their goblet high. "May he find love and good fortune."

Pasco added, "Not to mention—"

"Even more love and good fortune!" Santo said loudly, glaring at Pasco.

Jem drank to that, praying to the gods he didn't believe in that his groom wouldn't be as beastly as he feared.

THROUGH THE MARBLE archway, the courtyard temple was awash in brilliant sunlight. Standing back in the shadows of the tunnel, Jem blinked and shielded his eyes. He could just make out the altar and hear the murmur of the waiting delegates.

The wedding herbs had always reminded him of sweet summer bread baking at dawn. But as the scent drifted down the tunnel, it was cloying. His parents and brothers were already seated in the courtyard while Santo hovered near Jem, talking nonsense and trying to cheer him up. They'd been waiting far too long.

"Maybe Cador was able to run," Jem whispered to Santo.

"Don't get your hopes up," they whispered back, glancing at the young cleric in her plain gray robe at the tunnel head who was kindly pretending not to listen.

Any mild buzz from the wine Jem had gulped had faded away into sickening dread. The lemon scent of his wedding robe mixed with the burning herbs. He thought he might retch. Behind them, someone cleared their throat. A servant had appeared, slightly out of breath.

"I beg your pardon. Your groom is—" He opened and closed

his mouth. "Unwell."

Jem frowned. "Oh." He had no idea of the protocol for such things, having never been forced into a political marriage with a barbarian stranger before. "Have you fetched the healer?"

"I don't think it'll do any good."

Jem frowned. "The bar—Cador is *that* ill?" Good gods, had he been poisoned? He'd certainly seemed in hearty shape the day before.

"It's not illness so much as...indulgence." The servant's face was scarlet.

Santo chuckled. "Ah. He's being dragged by the horse this morning? We've all been there, haven't we?"

"We most certainly have not." The cleric's eyebrow arched for a moment before her placid expression settled again.

Jem couldn't take it personally that Cador had been in his cups the night before, as inconvenient as it was. "Surely he's well enough to stand at the altar and repeat these ridiculous vows?"

A raucous shout echoed up the tunnel, followed by slurring laughter and too-loud, off-key singing. Jem went still with sudden understanding and fresh humiliation that chilled and burned all at once.

Cador wasn't bleary and headachy or vomiting—what they called being "dragged by the horse" the day after drinking too much. No, he was *still* in his cups.

Jem's groom was drunk.

Falling-down drunk, as Cador appeared in the tunnel with a shout of laughter and promptly sprawled onto the dusty stone with a thud Jem felt in his thin boots. Cador still wore the fur-trimmed leather and rough material of the day before.

It still clung to his incredible muscles.

Cador's sister appeared, and she gave him a swift, none-too-gentle kick to the side. She had quite a few muscles as well. "Up, you swine," she hissed, nodding to a few burly Northern men who followed and now hauled Cador to his feet. His boots were thick, black leather, but despite the sturdiness, Cador slipped and spun.

The sister eyed Jem the way she might the unwelcome runt of a litter of dogs. "My brother should be marrying a fellow hunter, so he's not especially pleased."

Santo stiffened beside Jem. "My brother is none too pleased either."

She sighed. "I'm sure he isn't. But here we all fucking are. It's a sarf in the shit house, but there's nothing to be done for it."

Jem startled at her crudeness. Also, he'd never considered the notion of a sarf, the slithering, limbless reptiles that could bite and kill, hiding in a toilet. He shuddered.

"I'm Delen," she said.

Santo made introductions, and the whole while Cador muttered and cursed, tugging against the unwavering grip of his comrades holding him up. An older male cleric appeared holding the neatly folded wedding robe for Cador and wearing an expression of furious disapproval rather than typical calm.

"Fuck this," Cador grumbled.

Jem certainly shared the frustration, but as Delen had noted, there was apparently nothing to be done for it. One of the Northerners had a horned tankard, and Delen forced her brother to drink from it. Whatever was inside must've tasted abhorrent considering how red Cador's face became, but he choked it down.

Then he vomited onto the dusty stone.

And vomited.

And vomited some more.

Jem, Santo, and the clerics scuttled to the mouth of the tunnel. The Northerners seemed alarmingly unfazed, and were actually laughing.

My first kiss is going to taste like puke.

Jem wanted to throw himself into Santo's arms and weep, but he kept his chin high. When Cador was through, the Northerners stripped off his dark shirt, revealing a broad chest dusted with dark blond hair. Curving tattoos were inked into his pale skin. There were ridges of muscle over his stomach, and a V of hair that disappeared beneath his belt.

Jem tore his eyes upward from the bulge outlined by the tight leather trousers. This beast of a man was to be his husband. Jem stared at the hairy chest and corded arms, the stuff of thrilling fantasies, and shivered with anticipation despite himself.

"His groom might break him in two!"

The laughing jest from yesterday echoed now, dread obliterating the flare of desire. Even if Jem only had to spend a single night with him, would Cador be cruel? This was why he'd stuck to fantasies instead of seeking out partners. The reality of coupling with such a man would surely be different than the escapades in his novels.

While Jem's robe hung long over his wrists, Cador's was comically short on his arms, even though it was much bigger. Cador grimaced down at himself in apparent disgust, then seemed to notice Jem for the first time. His gaze was clearer, the disgust remaining.

"You," Cador growled.

Santo puffed their chest, standing closer to Jem. "This isn't Jem's fault."

Cador muttered something, then asked—accused, really—

"What kind of name is 'Jem'?"

"Uh... I don't know?" Jem cleared his throat. "My mother said my eyes were like jewels of honey. No one calls me 'Jowan' much at all."

Cador grunted, and Delen said, "Let's get this over with."

A massive hand caught his elbow, and Cador tugged Jem out of the tunnel and under the marble arch into the packed temple. Jem dug in his heels instinctively and heard nervous titters from their audience.

Cador pressed his full lips into a thin line and yanked. As if he weighed nothing, Jem practically flew to the altar in the center of the courtyard, the too-long robe tangling around his boots. Good gods, this brute could overpower him using only a finger.

True fear snaked down Jem's spine. When he'd imagined a husband, he'd thought of a good and gentle man, a companion with whom to while away long, peaceful days by the lake. He'd never expected his secret passions of the flesh to come to fruition any more than he'd anticipated a muscled merman to whisk him away like Morvoren.

Now that he stood at the altar, his half-drawn sketches of an ideal husband clarified into stark lines. He wanted a husband who'd make him laugh. Who'd keep him warm on cool winter nights and share his love of reading and swimming and tending needy birds. A man who surely wouldn't fulfill his dark, dangerous fantasies, but who'd make love to him tenderly.

Instead, he was to give himself body and soul to this brute? Marriage was supposed to be an even exchange, yet standing at the altar with the barbarian towering over him, Jem felt like an untested boy. He'd insisted he was a man the day before to derision, and it surely was a joke.

Cador released Jem's arm, and Jem tensed his thighs so his knees didn't knock. His skin itched with the weight of hundreds of eyes. At home, most people tended to forget he was there. Now he stood on the dais before the high cleric, a pawn in a political bargain, his barbarian intended looming at this side.

He'd never felt quite so small.

Chapter Three

OF ALL THE feeble, pissant princes in Onan to make him marry, this one had to be the worst.

Cador laughed to himself, because what else could he do? His head still spun faintly, a dull throb of pain at the base of his skull growing stronger. He remembered too late he was actually at the altar, all eyes on him. He coughed to disguise the laugh, but fuck it.

He glanced around to find his brother and share a look. Maybe a grimace. Yet Bryok stared at the temple's stone floor with a face to match it, his thin mouth pressed into a thinner line, a twitch of the jagged scar on his cheek the only sign of life—a sign Cador knew betrayed a dangerously icy fury.

The irritation and unease simmering in Cador since the night before when Bryok hadn't joined in the drinking only boiled hotter. Cador didn't damn well like this either, but what was he to do? This marriage was vital to their plan. He would do his duty.

Although he'd expected to wed a *man*, not this pathetic little prince. Sitting on display in the temple the day before while the mainlanders gawked, he hadn't even noticed Jem at the end of the row where the Southern royals sat. That the mainlanders thought this...*nothing* of a boy worthy of wedding Cador was such an insult he hadn't needed to pretend his shock and outrage.

He looked to his groom with disgust. The Southern prince was tiny and weak. *Jem.* A foolish, useless name that suited him well. His eyes were pretty, Cador would grant him that. They were a rich honey, set off perfectly by his golden-brown skin. But what use was prettiness? None that Cador had ever known.

Clearly the mainlanders thought differently. Yes, the ancient temple to the gods was austere, the clerics clad in plain robes. But the delegates from the three mainland kingdoms wore so much frivolous color Cador wanted to shield his eyes from the glare.

He'd seen the rare bloom of yellow and pink daisies one spring, but that was nothing compared to the rich, bright shades he didn't even have names for. Never mind the soft, flowing fabrics that looked as if they wouldn't survive a ride on the gentlest mare over a meadow, let alone a hunt through the dense forests of Ergh.

Since childhood, he'd been told the mainlanders were greedy and idle. That Ergh and its people were far better off alone without Onan's false gods. Then everything had changed, and here he was with mainland earth and stone under his boots, marrying an unworthy prince.

The acid remains of emptying his stomach clung to his tongue. Delen could have at least brought a mint twig for him to chew. The pleasant diversion of being too drunk to think was gone, and now he wanted the cleric to get the fuck on with it.

The damn woman droned about unity and balance, about the four corners of Onan and pleasing the gods of earth, fire, wind, and water. As if it hadn't been clear enough the day before and they were all fools who didn't understand why this marriage was happening.

Of course, the true reason was known only to a small few.

It was necessary, Cador reminded himself. Kenver, his *tas* and surviving parent, Ergh's chieftain, had first returned to Onan in peace two years ago and had tried to find a solution. It did nag at Cador that Tas hadn't tried simple honesty in asking for what they needed, but it seemed honesty was in short supply when it came to politics.

It was evident Ebrenn's king despised the Neuvellan queen and that the feeling was very mutual. Yet they played pretend as the clerics made themselves out to be lambs instead of wolves. From what Cador could tell now that he was on the mainland himself for the first time, everyone in Onan was as treacherous as he'd always been warned.

The longing to be back on Ergh stole his breath like a punch. To be home in the forest with only the goats and chickens to bother him. Oh, to *hunt* again. He had his sword with him, but his spears were home.

So long, Ergh had been isolated in peace. Well, they'd fought amongst themselves from time to time, but not in Cador's memory. Wishing would not turn back the years. He would do his duty. Even if it meant he must marry this pampered prince.

Jem barely came to Cador's shoulder, and a gentle breeze could be the end of him. Cador cursed himself for not wedding one of his lovers when he'd had the chance. Jory had an easy smile and a love of sucking cock. Or there was Rewan, whose prick was almost—*almost*—bigger than Cador's own. Kensa was lethal with a spear and would have been a dependable wife. They'd always shared an affection for ale on a cold winter's night.

Anyone would have been better than this *Jem*.

"Now for the sacred, unbreakable bond," the cleric intoned.

Thank fuck. Since Jem was quivering to his left, Cador stuck out his left hand. The cleric slowly moved to take the hot iron from a ceremonial pot that sat over flaming coals. Cador couldn't make out the design of the brand that would have been chosen by Jem. Or in this case likely his parents.

The cleric shuffled back toward him, taking so long the iron would be ice by the time it met his flesh. Meanwhile, the sun beat down on the back of his neck, no clouds in sight. Sweat dripped down his spine, his hair damp with it. Cador missed the dependably gray skies of Ergh. Was it always so damn hot and sticky on the mainland? This was supposed to be spring.

Finally, the cleric took his wrist with her gnarled fingers that held surprising strength. With her other hand, she branded his palm. Cador didn't so much as flinch as the iron seared his flesh, keeping a bored expression on his face.

Fine, it hurt. It hurt so much that bile rose and a cry clawed at his throat. He would have retched if he'd been alone. Fortunately, his stomach was newly empty.

The cleric shuffled back for the other iron, this one cast in the traditional boar tusks. All hunters on Ergh bore a similar tattoo and used this symbol when they wed their mates. Tas's palm was marked with the tusks since he'd been wed to a great hunter.

With a familiar, distant twinge, Cador wished their second father was still with them. He'd been gored by a boar when Cador was only a boy, an honorable death that had left his husband, their tas, their only parent. Tas had become chieftain after Cador's grandmother had died. She'd been a mighty leader until the end, even as her body had stooped like the cleric who stood before him now.

The cleric waited as Jem reluctantly held out his right hand, palm up. He jolted and made a pitiful cry as his skin sizzled, but he didn't pull away. He stared down at the tusks, his hand trembling.

Cador examined his own palm, the design of curved edges difficult to make out with the swelling of his burned flesh. "What is it?" he asked.

In the sudden silence, thick and shocked, Cador glanced around. The cleric's wiry brows met, and everyone seemed to hold their breath. Apparently speaking during the ceremony was frowned upon here on the mainland.

Jem whispered, "A dillywig." Then added, "I like birds."

Of course you do. Now Cador would have delicate wings etched into his hand forever. He fought a rebellious urge to grab at the other iron and blot out the bird with mighty tusks but instead grunted and looked to the cleric to finally finish this.

After a few more minutes of sermonizing, Cador gripped Jem's right hand in his left, sealing their seared palms tight. Jem stood stiffly, barely breathing, clearly in agony. His hand was small in Cador's as Cador muttered, "May this seal never be broken and love be eternal under the eyes of the gods."

In Ergh, it was the chieftain who performed marriages, and Cador had always expected if he decided he enjoyed someone's company enough to marry, it would be his tas sealing the bond as chieftain. That it was a stooped old woman made it seem even more wrong. And to speak of *love*?

He knew most couples chose marriage. Somehow they actually believed love would last, even in Ergh, where practicality had ruled. *Love.* It wasn't real, only a figment of the lesser-minded. Fucking and hunting and feasting were real. That was all Cador needed.

Jem repeated the vow in a hoarse voice. It was done. The cleric stood before them again and raised her hands to the skies as polite applause filled the courtyard. All that was left was the usual kiss.

Fuck it. Instead of kissing his new husband, Cador announced, "Let's eat," and strode from the temple, towing Jem along in his wake. If he had his way, he'd never kiss this little prince. And he really liked getting his way.

GULPING FROM A fresh cup of sweet mead, Cador waited for the servant to leave him and Tas alone in the guest chamber. The northern wing of the Holy Place's guest housing was neat and clean and in good repair, as if it hadn't sat empty for lifetimes.

Tas leveled him with a glare. "Didn't you drink enough last night? Not to mention this morning."

Cador couldn't argue with that, cringing to be scolded like a child even when he deserved it. He was a grown man, but even now he didn't disobey Tas, lowering the ornate cup to the table. As much as he liked getting his way, he followed his father's orders. Not only his father—his chieftain.

"I know this isn't easy for you." Tas sighed, removing his headdress and prodding over his ear. "Damn tusks rub." He ran his hands through his thick blond hair, blunt nails scratching his scalp. For a moment, he closed his eyes and looked so very tired.

Guilt flared in Cador. "Let's sit." He pulled out a chair for himself from the small table, knowing that it was the only way to get Tas to rest.

Indeed, Tas nodded and took his own chair. He unclasped the furred cloak from around his neck and let it fall to the floor. He wore a formal tunic of boar skin and pushed up the sleeves over his freckled forearms. The lines on his face seemed to have grown deeper overnight, although Cador knew that wasn't so.

Cador slid the cup toward him. "You need this more than I do."

Tas chuckled and drank. "Perhaps. It's good to have a moment to ourselves, although we should return to the feast soon." He took another drink, then slumped in the chair. "I wish there was another way."

"Are you sure there isn't?" Although it was a little late now that Cador was married to the tiny prince.

"Time is running out. We came in peace. We followed the clerics' rules and tried to establish trade with the mainland. With Ebrenn. Subjected ourselves to more sermons on the gods than anyone should have to sit through. They preach harmony and pious devotion to their gods, but make no mistake, my son." Tas clenched his hand into a fist, his voice low. "It's control they're after. If we reveal our weakness, they will exploit it. Before we know it, they'll be building their damn temples on Ergh."

"Even if we told them the true reason for needing Ebrenn's resource?"

"They will use it to their advantage! Already some of our people turn back to the gods in despair. We've allowed the clerics to visit in the past because they were never a threat to our way of life. They brought us valuable news of the mainland, and their attempts to convince us to follow their teachings were like flicking away gnats. But if we allow the clerics to put down roots, they will poison Ergh day by day."

Yet doing nothing would lead to Ergh's demise just as surely. Slowly. Agonizingly. Cador was glad he hadn't had the rest of the mead as he tasted bile. He couldn't bear to think of the suffering, locking up that part of his mind and throwing away the key.

For now, he must do his part. As much as he hated this farce of a marriage. As much as he hated that it would all end in war. Ergh's need was great—its burden unbearable—but the price of war would not be cheap.

Cador ventured, "Perhaps it would be a sacrifice we can accept to have temples on Ergh. If the clerics could convince Ebrenn to trade…"

Tas shook his head. "Now that you're here on the mainland yourself, surely you see the disdain Ebrenn's king has for us? More than disdain. Hatred. Suspicion. Contempt. We've tried to approach him in friendship and establish fair trade. He's sneered in response. His stubborn arrogance will be his downfall."

Tas had been accused of stubborn arrogance himself from time to time, but Cador quashed that traitorous thought. He couldn't argue that he wanted to bring Ebrenn's haughty king down to size. But at what cost? "Surely if we give Ebrenn a better price on fish and boar—"

"They have their own fish. A long coastline and warm, teeming seas. They don't need our catch. Or our boar, at least not at what it's worth. Even if they did want it, they don't *need* it. There's a difference. They refuse to trade fairly, and whether it's stubbornness or hatred for us doesn't matter."

"But if we drop the cost—"

"We starve." Tas opened his weathered hands, palms up. "If we lower the price of boar, we must increase hunting. If we kill too many, the boar will disappear. You know how rare the blonek are now. We hunted too many for their pelts. If the boar die out, Ergh will follow. Our waters provide us enough fish for now. Our few crops suffice. It is a balance, and it has already been vitally disrupted."

The hair on the back of Cador's neck stood. "But…we have never wanted for food. What I mean is, we've never gone hungry."

"Not yet."

"Is there nothing else we can barter? We must keep the blonek pelts for ourselves, but what of our wool?"

"They have plenty of their own. Meanwhile, we must restore balance to Ergh."

Cador shifted on his stone chair uneasily. He tried for a joke. "If you keep talking of balance, I'll start to think the clerics have gotten under your skin after all."

Tas barked a laugh. "Throw me to the depths of the Askorn Sea before that happens, I beg. You see how they preach unity and make it sound pretty, but the clerics are not to be underestimated. It's their power they protect. They would make slaves of us to get us under their thumb. The mainland would benefit, of course, but the clerics do nothing without benefiting themselves."

Cador exhaled in disgust. Still, the worry nagged. "But if we go to war and lose—"

"We cannot lose." Tas thumped the table with his fist. "We've been patient. Our strategy must be one for long-term success. Yet how can we keep waiting at such a cost? If we admit our need to Ebrenn, the king will only tighten his grip. His prices will soar. And now, the Southern queen's quarrel with Ebrenn is ready to boil over. It's the perfect opportunity."

"Even if innocent people die in a war with Ebrenn? Even if—"

"The war is looming with or without us. With our help, it will be quick. The South will bring the East. Ebrenn will have no choice but to surrender. Then we will possess what we need. We have no quarrel with Ebrenn's people. We will be fair. We will be just."

"You make it sound so easy, but we've never actually been to war."

Tas's nostrils flared. "Nothing about this is easy. Ask your brother how easy these years have been!"

Shame sliced him, as red hot as the brand had been. "Forgive me."

Tas sighed, giving Cador's forearm a brief squeeze. "Of course, my son. And you're right, Ergh has been able to stay away from Onan for centuries. We've had no wars to wage." He sat straighter, his voice a growl. "But we are warriors. Make no mistake. We must fight for our children's future, even if that means spilling blood in the meantime. Ebrenn holds the key, and they will never give it freely."

It was Cador's turn to slump. "You truly think war is inevitable?"

"Even if I let the clerics build their temples on Ergh—let them spread their devotion to gods that don't exist—they will not be able to convince Ebrenn to help us. The clerics think too fucking highly of themselves. We've seen enough of the West and its king to know it's useless. We must act and join forces with the Southern queen. When I met with her upon our arrival and she suggested this union, I knew it was the moment we've waited for. Which brings us here to your wedding day."

"It does." Cador reached for the cup and drained the dregs.

"My son." Tas watched him seriously. "Do you regret it already?"

"Of course not." His branded palm ached, but he ignored it. "It's meaningless. I'd rather not be burdened with him until the time comes, but it's my duty." He'd feign displeasure tomorrow as if he didn't know the plan was to travel to Ergh with his new husband. It might help Prince Jowan trust him if he believed Cador was as pitifully ignorant as he was.

"He seems a meek sort. I'm sure you'll barely notice him. It's only several months until you're due to return for the Feast of the Blood Moon."

At least five, but who's counting.

Cador didn't voice the sulky thought. "And what do you think the clerics have in mind? It was surely they who initially proposed this union between Ergh and Neuvella."

"Oh, I'm sure they've cooked up something. But they've provided us an ideal opportunity to align with the queen. The ideal opportunity to exploit *her* weakness. We must act."

"You're sure the kidnapping won't be blamed on us?"

"I'm sure. Our spies will pose as Westerners and snatch him on your journey back to the Holy Place for the feast. You'll be duly outraged as you demand vengeance. In the meantime, I have the opportunity to grow closer with the queen now that our families are bonded. We'll declare war together."

"You're sure the queen will join us?"

"Absolutely. As I said, she's perched on the blade's edge. The spies I placed are certain. When she hears the West has kidnapped her favorite son to force her to redraw the border in Ebrenn's favor, it will be the excuse she's waited for. And Gwels will follow her—their bond is strong."

"But what if Ebrenn's king denies it?"

"Of course he'll deny it, but by that point, it'll be too late. When the queen receives her dearest child's hand severed in a box, she will act."

Cador remembered Jem's small hand gripped in his own,

their brands fresh and oozing. "I do pity him," he admitted, glad Bryok wasn't there to hear.

Tas's mouth pulled down. "Yes, he's an innocent in all this." Waving dismissively, he added, "He won't be harmed otherwise."

Having one's hand chopped off was a damn big exception, but the prince's fate had been determined. It wasn't Cador's doing. It was the cost of war. The cost of ensuring Ergh's future.

"You're sure Jowan's the favorite?" The queen's other children seemed far more useful than the daydreaming youngest.

"Quite. She'd never admit it, but what parent would?" He smiled wryly, and Cador's heart skipped.

Tas leaned forward and grasped Cador's uninjured hand. "You must know you've made your father and I proud beyond measure. You always have." His blue eyes so much like Cador's shone with tears. "If he were here with us, I know he'd say the same."

Lungs tight as his heart seemed to triple in size, Cador could only nod. He could almost imagine Father watching them from a place with the gods, even though he'd never believed such fantasies.

Yes, he'd do his duty and mind the little prince until the kidnapping. Father was gone, but he'd make Tas even prouder if it was the last thing he did.

CADOR BELCHED.

Beside him at the small table in the center of the dining hall, his husband—*husband!*—flinched. Cador suppressed a grin. It was childish, but he'd anticipated the reaction and took petty joy from it.

The feast that had started as a luncheon now dragged on past sunset. Jem had poked at his plates, barely eating from the endless courses and not even sipping from his wine. Cador had filled his stomach early, banishing the lingering effects of too much mead the night before. Not to mention that morning.

He had to admit he wasn't eager to be dragged by the horse again, and he'd have preferred water or ale to the sweet mead traditional at weddings. He drank sparingly—only five cups all day. It gave his head a tingle, but nothing more.

Around the four sides of the high-roofed hall at long tables, delegates ate and drank and enjoyed the feast far more than the grooms, though Ebrenn's representatives glowered aside from the king's pretty son, who seemed to have a special interest in Prince Jowan and kept looking his way. Perhaps they were friends.

The king's sour face had been constant no matter what he ate, for he surely knew this alliance of Neuvella and Ergh did not bode well for him. Cador felt no less sour himself. He scowled at Delen as she devoured another piece of fluffy cake with enthusiasm. He shouldn't begrudge her. Feasts at home were hearty, but he'd never seen such fancy, complicated food. Some tasted just as ornate and confusing.

There were so many colorful fruits and vegetables, including seemingly endless bowls of sevels, the purple skins glossy over sweet, crisp flesh with seeds at the heart. He wrestled the temptation to cram his pockets full.

At least the servants had brought out the sweet cakes, and the feast would be ending. Cador just wanted to finish the day, sleep well, and get on the road north to their waiting ship. He dreaded the return trip across the Askorn Sea but would withstand it.

He wondered how Prince Jowan of Neuvella would enjoy the voyage. He had a feeling Jem didn't know he would be sailing north from the mainland with them. Cador would feign surprise himself and make a show of his reluctance. Which again, wouldn't be entirely false. When he thought of being stuck with Jem until the kidnapping...

Cador choked down a groan. Months would feel like a lifetime. First, he had to make it through his wedding day. If the absurdity didn't do him in, the boredom would. He stared up at the arched, painted ceiling of the hall, the mural representing the four gods of Onan and their domains. It was the most colorful thing he'd seen at the Holy Place.

On Ergh, desperation was sparking a return to faith. Perhaps he'd see murals like this at home if the clerics had their way. Cador understood the misery and drive to believe in something. Anything but meaningless suffering.

But he would have no part of these false saviors. From what he'd experienced, if the gods truly did exist, they were spiteful vipers who punished the innocent at a whim. They could sink to the bottom of the Askorn Sea and rot.

He believed in what he could see and smell and taste and touch. He imagined mounting Massen's broad back and galloping until his stallion tired. He could almost feel Massen's powerful flanks between his thighs, the jolts of his hoofs on the earth rippling through Cador's body, the snorts of his breath, the bracing wind reddening Cador's cheeks as they practically flew. He longed for the dependable weight of his spear in his grasp and the spurt of hot blood as he felled a boar.

Cador flexed his branded left hand. It throbbed, the design still blurred by swelling. He'd tried to refuse the salve and bandage, but grudgingly admitted to himself the brand hurt like the god of fire was torturing him.

"Do you believe in the gods?"

Cador looked down from the mural at Jem beside him. Jem had tipped his head back and gazed up at the ceiling with those honey eyes. Honey was one of the rarest treats on Ergh, with only a handful of beekeepers and wildflowers blooming for so short a time. His eyelashes were dark and thick in contrast to the amber gold. Cador glanced back up at the mural and the painted scenes of destruction.

There was Dor of the earth with the power to cleave the land and crumble it to dust. It was Dor who legend said had severed Ergh from the mainland before Hwytha, the god of wind, blew it into the Northern abyss with help from Glaw, who ruled the water.

Fire was controlled by Tan, with myths of mighty blazes that reduced forests to smoldering ash. Tan had stayed clear of Ergh, and Cador wondered why they hadn't created a god of ice on Ergh in his absence.

Cador hesitated before answering, even though it was a simple denial. Did the mainlanders think the people of Ergh were godless heathens? Resentment stewed in his full stomach. "Of course I believe in the gods," he lied. "Don't you?"

For a moment, Jem's expression tightened, but then he murmured, "Of course. The gods are generous and wise."

Cador choked down the argument galloping through his mind, gulping more wine instead. No surprise the Neuvellan prince believed the gods so benevolent. What suffering had the South seen? None. Not compared to Ergh.

"What beasts do you hunt in your land?" he asked. Anything to make the minutes go by.

"Hunt?" Jem asked.

"Hunt. Kill. Do you use spears?"

Jem's fine brows drew close. "I don't hunt. Of course others do." He glanced at the remains of roasted meat on one of the feast tables.

Disgust curled Cador's lip. "Exactly how do you spend your days?"

"By the lake. I swim sometimes and care for orphaned birds in my aviary. I read in the evenings."

Cador stared, waiting for the jest to be revealed. *Read*? What wasteful luxury. Cador had learned the basics, enough to read contracts and the like, but had no use for books. As the seconds ticked by, it seemed there was no jest. "You are a prince. Do you do nothing for your people?"

Jem opened and closed his mouth. "I... Well, I collect pretty flowers for the elders in the local village."

Flowers? It was fitting that Jem, with his fanciful name and honey eyes, valued all that was meaningless. The elders would surely prefer gifts of grain or meat.

"Pretty things are a waste. Ugliness is far superior. Ugliness puts food in bellies. Ugly lovers fuck the best."

Jaw tight, Jem muttered, "Then I suppose I'm in luck."

Ha! Cador had to award him a point for that insult but kept his expression blank and drained his cup. He purposefully breathed in through his mouth and... There. Another belch. Jem grimaced, jerking his body to the left. He was trying to shift the stone chair, but it didn't budge.

Jem fiddled with the food on his plate instead of eating it. He nibbled at a crumbly cake's edges, then awkwardly dipped his gleaming gold spoon into a thick pudding with this left hand, letting the pale yellow treat plop back into the bowl untasted. He bit into a sevel with a crunch, taking only one mouthful before abandoning the fruit back to his plate. More time passed, and the sevel's red flesh began to dry and wither.

"Are you just going to waste that?" Cador barked.

Jem's eyes flew wide. "What?" He sounded genuinely perplexed.

"All that food. Is the mainland so rich you can leave this to go rotten?"

Jem looked at his plate as if seeing the meal for the first time. "Oh. I…"

Cador shoved back his chair to stand and stretch, done with the conversation. The chair's stone legs scraped back on the dais so loudly that it caught the attention of the entire hall. A shout rose up from his so-called friends from the North.

"Ah, time to bed your groom!" that traitorous prick Jory called, to rousing cheers from the Ergh delegates.

Cador would be fucking the spoiled little prince around about *never*, but he put on the expected show, nodding and grinning. The pious clerics looked aghast, which warmed Cador's black heart.

Most of the mainlanders appeared shocked—but with an undercurrent of delight tugging their lips into smiles as they watched and whispered. This was clearly the most exciting thing they'd seen at the Holy Place in some time.

Jem sat, his body rigid as the drunken delegates of Ergh made crude suggestions. Tas chuckled, but Bryok remained sullen, his scowl unchanging. Everyone else wanted a show.

A show they'd get.

Cador bent and hauled Jem over his shoulder, ignoring his yelp. He easily held the slim body with his right arm across Jem's thighs, Jem sprawled over his back, his fingers grasping at

Cador's waist over the white robe.

"Put me down!"

Ignoring him, Cador strode past the Southern delegates, noticing Jem's parents stone-faced along with the sibling who'd been with him before the ceremony. Cador almost paused to assure them he wouldn't fuck Jem if he was the last person in Onan, but of course the game had to be played. He swaggered on, waving to the hall with his other arm.

A cleric with a pinched expression and flat lips escorted them to the traditional wedding chamber, Jem squirming and muttering over Cador's shoulder. In Ergh, a wedding night would be spent anywhere from a hut to a cottage to a hole in the ground, but the mainlanders clearly enjoyed ceremony.

Thankfully, the cleric backed away at the chamber and left them without any further blessings or platitudes. Cador had had more than enough of unity and balance and all that horse shit.

Candlelight flickered over the tapestry-covered walls of the chamber, more stinking wedding spice burning in a dish at the foot of the four-poster bed. As the cleric closed the solid door with a thud, Jem landed a surprisingly sharp kick to Cador's knee.

With a curse, Cador dumped him onto the rug. Jem landed on his arse and stared up, nostrils flaring. Cador wanted to rub the bony cap of his knee to soothe the sting, but he'd be damned if he'd betray any weakness. Puffing out his chest, he loomed over Jem.

"Well, *husband*."

Jem pulled his knees to his chest, wrapping his arms around them, but didn't retreat. Spine ramrod straight, he stared up at Cador. He took a shuddering breath. "I know we are wed, but I don't—we aren't—" He mumbled a few other words Cador couldn't make out.

"What?" Cador demanded.

Jem flinched. Was the boy genuinely afraid?

"Speak," Cador ordered. There. He was being reasonable.

Head down, Jem barely whispered. "Please don't... I've never..."

"Never what?"

Jem exhaled a long breath and flapped his hands, motioning to the bed. Cador blinked. Was he talking about fucking? Did the boy think he was actually going to bed him? He laughed, and Jem hugged his knees so tightly he'd bruise himself.

Wait. Was he actually...

A *virgin?*

Sympathy flared. Cador didn't give a shit, but he still imagined being in the boy's flimsy boots. *If I was a useless layabout who'd somehow never even fucked...*

Cador frowned. "How old are you?" Alarm gripped him. Had they made him marry an *actual* boy?

"Twenty years," came the meek answer. Jem's gaze stayed on the fancy colored carpet.

Relief gave way to bafflement. "Then how the fuck are you a *virgin?*"

No answer.

Cador huffed as he stared down at the huddled, slim form. When he'd slung Jem over his shoulder, he'd been surprised at the lean muscles he'd felt, but now Jem looked tiny. A virgin at twenty? Unheard of in Ergh. Was this common with mainlanders? What was wrong with them? Were they all so...delicate?

"Do you prefer women?" Cador enjoyed fucking anyone who'd make sport of it with a hearty laugh and shared lust for release and pleasure. But he knew the desires of some were more specific.

Jem shook his head.

Then what was wrong with him? Had Cador been nervous the first time? Perhaps, but it was so long ago he barely remembered. Fucking, hunting, feasting—the three pursuits that made life joyful. Yet Jem cowered. He seemed truly fearful, and Cador's gut clenched uneasily.

All right, he'd joke and put Jem's mind at ease. The boy had no idea of the fate awaiting him on Ergh, but aside from his childish belching, Cador had no desire to make Jem suffer needlessly in the meantime. He'd much rather just ignore him, but they were stuck in the chamber together for the night. All that simpering would be tiresome.

Cador grinned. "Terrified of my massive cock?"

Jem's shoulders jerked, and he made no reply at all. No comeback. He'd made an excellent insult earlier, but that spark had apparently been smothered.

Cador tried again. "Think I'm going to throw you down and break your puny body in two?"

Why wasn't the boy laughing? An Erghian would have jested back—perhaps saying they'd chop off Cador's prick and throw the paltry meal to the boars, or that they'd had bigger slivers from a twig and wouldn't feel a thing.

"Think you'll be able to suck me without choking to death?"

Jem stared up with those honey eyes and whispered, "Please don't make me."

Oh, for the love of—why was the boy acting like Cador was a monster? "Your *virtue* is safe with me. Sleep well knowing I wouldn't touch you if my cock was on fire and you were…made of…water." He grimaced. Not his finest jest, but it had been a damn long day.

But Jem had no insult to give in return. Cador shook his head. *Mainlanders.* Humorless, the lot of them. If Jem wanted to weep and whimper all night, he could go ahead.

Cador marched past him to douse the candles and stinking herbs, tamping them out with his fingers and ignoring the flare of heat on his calluses. In the darkness, he yanked off his boots, trousers, and the damn marriage robe before flopping naked onto the too-soft bed.

He'd rather sleep on the rug, but the boy would probably begin shrieking if he approached in the dark. The bed was large, so if Jem wanted to take a corner of it, he could climb up. It wasn't Cador's concern.

Still, as he heard the soft little breaths from beyond the bed, more sympathy tugged at him. The boy hadn't asked for this any more than Cador had. And his role when the time came would be…unpleasant. But if he chose to spend the night cowering and feeling sorry for himself, that was up to him.

The question was barely a whisper, and Cador had to strain to hear as Jem asked, "But don't we have to…"

"Fuck? Who will know we didn't? Not a soul will hear it from me, and if you keep your pretty mouth shut, no one will be the wiser. We're both free to bed whoever we want. You can find a soft lover who will screw you with care and tender words. Unless you want to—"

Cador broke off. He was going to joke: *Unless you want to bend over to take a pounding and become a man.* But he didn't want to listen to any more whimpering. Instead, he said, "If anyone asks, we fucked." After a moment, he added, "And I was magnificent."

Resolutely, he shut his eyes. Now he would sleep and get this cursed night over with. He shifted to his side. The bed dipped too low and it was too damn quiet. If he was out on a hunt at home, the night would be full of sounds—horses snuffling, fellow hunters fucking. Or if he was in his cottage, the fire would be crackling, the wind howling beyond the stone and timber.

Here, it was silent but for his breath and the prince's. The muffled beats of his own heart filled his ears. Nothing was as it should be. He longed for the way life had been. The simplicity of it that he'd taken for granted. But all he could do was wait for sleep to capture him.

When he opened his eyes again, it would be dawn. He'd return to familiar gray skies and wild boars to hunt. He despised that he had to bring his weak new husband home, but at least he wouldn't have to put up with him for long.

Chapter Four

THE BEAST WAS naked.

Cador had been snoring off and on as the black hours ticked by interminably. Jem was wide awake, desperately relieved they'd simply pretend they'd lain together. He'd heard many terrifying stories of Ergh, and Cador certainly seemed capable of violence. Jem had waited in the darkness, jumping at every sound, his branded hand throbbing.

Meanwhile, Cador had annoyingly slept like a babe. In the weak light now diffusing through the high windows of the chamber, Jem peeked over the bed frame. The pale dawn illuminated Cador's sprawled body.

His naked body.

His naked body that, despite his cruel and crude demeanor, was Jem's secret, dark fantasies in the flesh. The completely naked flesh.

The sheets had twisted in the night, now tangled around Cador's powerful thighs. Jem's gaze roved helplessly. Cador's lips were parted, his stubbled chin more shadowed than the previous day. His nipples amid coarse hair were a dark red in the weak light, the ink of his tattoo shadowed.

Jem puzzled over the pair of curved lines that extended out and up from the center of his chest to his collarbones. Gritting his teeth, he eased the bandage from his hand and squinted at the brand he'd been too nervous to ask about.

The brand and tattoo were similar, and they were clearly tusks, surely that of the wild boar he'd once believed to be mythical. Massive boars were real, and the Erghians themselves existed—the proof of which was splayed right in front of Jem's eyes, close enough to touch.

Not that he ever would.

Cador's cock was, as promised, enticingly massive. Springing from a nest of curls, the ruddy shaft and meaty bollocks were impressive even at rest. Jem imagined sliding his tongue up that rod, tasting…what? Sweat and skin. *Man.*

If he stretched his jaw wide and sucked down as far as he could, how much would he be able to swallow? The thought of choking on it was both alarming and tantalizing.

"If you keep your pretty mouth shut…"

Jem was certain Cador hadn't meant anything by the word *pretty*—that if anything, it was an insult and not praise—yet it echoed in his mind. He ached to be called pretty by someone who meant it.

Whether or not his mouth was attractive, now he could only think of opening it to swallow that thick staff of flesh. What would Cador's seed taste of? Was a barbarian's different from a civilized Southerner's? Jem had experimentally tasted his own a few times. It had been salty and a little metallic.

Cador snorted and kicked, his rumble of a snore cutting off suddenly. Holding his breath, Jem dropped to a ball on the rug, which wasn't thick enough to truly soften the stone floor. He hadn't even bothered attempting sleep. He still wore the white wedding garment, but only for warmth as the night had cooled. His palm stung intensely now.

Curled on his side, he listened. Cador was still breathing evenly. Jem counted to a hundred, then rolled to his knees and peeked up again. He bit back a gasp.

The beast's cock was alive.

That most intimate flesh was filling, and Jem watched in awe as it rose to full mast. Cador's legs had spread even wider, and he murmured in his sleep, licking his lips.

Jem often woke hard and eager for release, and he kept luxurious, sweet-smelling oils by his bed so he could pleasure himself while he imagined being taken by a hairy, muscled man who made him scream in ecstasy. Just like Morvoren's bold merman in the worn pages of that beloved book, where it happened quite often and in shockingly creative ways.

Some mornings—in the dark of night as well—Jem oiled a candle and penetrated himself with it, imagining it was a hard cock belonging to a strong, broad man who might push him to his hands and knees ruthlessly or shove his ankles up around his ears, pinning him down helplessly while he was taken.

Jem eyed the barbarian's hard cock now, his mouth going dry at the forbidden sight. Between silky sheets in his own chamber with the door locked, it was only him and his imagination. He was safe with his books and his trusty candle, which he'd actually packed in his trunk for the journey, just in case.

The idea of taking Cador's very real cock was terrifying and thrilling at once. What would it be like to actually touch another so intimately? To have that rod of iron flesh inside him? To be filled with it. Not in control. At this beast's mercy...

Cador shifted and murmured again, grumbling something and kicking so suddenly that Jem stumbled back. His arse hit the rug with a too-loud thump before he curled into a ball again, heart in his throat.

Silence stretched out, no more mutters or snorts emanating from the bed. Cador was awake. Jem could sense it, as though

the air itself had become thicker with the force of his conscious-
ness. Cador yawned audibly, the sheets rustling, and Jem could
imagine the stretch of his strong limbs, the arch of his spine, his
hard prick—

Bare feet hit the floor, and Jem squeezed his eyes shut. Cador moved a few steps, and Jem sensed him looming.

"You're not sleeping," Cador stated.

Jem cracked open an eye, then bolted up to sitting. Cador
did indeed tower over him. Still naked. Cock still hard.

In fact, Cador lazily stroked himself, his callused fingers
teasing the hood of skin at the head. Jem stared, a slave to his
fascination. He was undeniably excited, his own manhood
swelling. Thank gods he still wore the long white robe that
pooled over his thighs.

Thick brows meeting, Cador looked down at himself, following Jem's avid gaze. He grunted and dropped his hand to his
side as if he hadn't even realized what he'd been doing. He
shrugged and ambled to the water basin, in no hurry whatsoever.

Now Jem's view was of Cador's rounded, firm backside,
which did nothing to cool the arousal that flushed him from
head to curling toes. He remained sitting on the rug with his
legs tucked beside him and his shame concealed by the wedding
robe.

Cador's flesh was pale all over his body, and Jem wondered
if the globes of his backside were smoother since there seemed
little hair there. He'd never been in such proximity to a naked
man who wasn't family, and that had been in childhood. How
would it feel to—

Stop! He's a beast! Please retain a shred of dignity.

Jem tore his eyes from Cador's body and pushed to standing, his feet cramped in his boots. The servants had apparently left him and Cador fresh clothes during the wedding feast, and he went about changing. It was a relief to get the boots off even for a few minutes. His feet were often bare by the lake.

His erection thankfully waned as he ignored Cador's nakedness. How bizarre to think that this rude, crass stranger was his *husband,* and would be forever more, barring an early death. Jem considered that, but couldn't wish death upon the man, no matter how cruel he was.

Jem buttoned a red silk shirt after quickly stripping off his breeches and pulling on a fresh pair that clung to his slim legs. It would be as Cador said—they'd take all the lovers they wanted, which would be expected. Not that it was spoken aloud, but Jem could name plenty of couples who lived separate lives for the most part. His parents were an exception.

If Ergh was to truly be part of Onan again, then he and Cador would reunite sporadically for ceremonies or peace summits or whatnot, remaining acquainted strangers as the years passed and they came up with a variety of excuses for their separation. It would be perfectly manageable, and Jem would have done his duty to his kingdom.

Then why did such sadness wash over him? Why did he yearn for so much more? He'd been perfectly content with the heroes of his books and the birds with broken wings who always left him to fly freely again.

Perhaps it really was time for him to be bold. There was no reason he shouldn't seek a lover of his own choosing, but the knowledge that connection would never be found with his husband grieved him in a way he hadn't expected.

Still, there was nothing to be done for it, was there? He and Cador dressed, with Cador donning his leather trousers, boots, and coarse tunic. They left the wedding chamber and followed a servant who told them breakfast waited in the great hall.

"Not hungry," Cador grumbled.

Jem asked the girl, "Is my family ready to leave for Neuvella?"

She cut him a glance. "I believe they'll be ready after breakfast." Judging by the tightness in her voice, there was something amiss.

Jem examined her as they neared the hall, the morning breeze wafting in through the open walkway. "Is there something else?"

She shook her head, walking faster. Jem's stomach clenched, and he glanced at Cador, hoping to share a worried look or some acknowledgment that there was clearly another unpleasant surprise awaiting. But Cador marched on with his gaze forward.

Most delegates were absent from the dining hall, likely still abed and being dragged by the horse after far too much mead. Jem was relieved to see Santo sitting beside their parents, Pasco and Locryn mercifully absent.

"Ah, the happy couple!" Jem's father announced, and the smattering of murmured conversations ceased. "You must be starving."

To Jem's horror, Cador boomed, "Yes, it was a strenuous night."

The high cleric who'd married them—Jem was *married*, and he still couldn't wrap his mind around it—appeared, a placid smile on her wrinkled face. Jem was struck by the urge to grab her robes and shake her, demanding that she unleash whatever else she had in store for them.

"You'll certainly both need warm food in your bellies before you begin the journey across the Askorn Sea," she said.

Jem swore he could actually feel his blood run as cold as the North was purported to be.

Both. Journey to Ergh.

Oh, gods. No. No! He couldn't go *there* of all places. He had to go home. He had to return to his hatchlings! To his chamber. To safety.

Cador sighed impatiently. "Yes, yes, fine. But—" He broke off, a heavy silence descending. Jem didn't look at him, but could practically hear Cador's jaw tightening. "Both?" he echoed, the question low and dangerous.

Jem was rooted to the spot, his heart racing and palms sweaty. Surely they couldn't force him to sail to *Ergh*. He hadn't even quite believed the cursed place existed! In the space of a day, he was married to a brutish stranger and now expected to sail north into the unknown? Alone?

As he watched the cleric and her horribly calm smile, he knew they could and very much would force him to go, because it was for the good of Onan to build peace and partnership with Ergh. It would please the gods and bring balance and all that rot. What Jem wanted didn't matter.

His muscles seized with the urge to run. If only he could go home, he'd forget his dark fantasies and find a good, gentle man to love him. He could pretend he wasn't wed to the barbarian towering beside him. He'd get his head out of his books and leave his birds—for a spell—and perform whichever duties to Neuvella his parents wanted. Anything! Anything but this.

Gods, he didn't want to go anywhere with these wild people who sneered at him and would take him farther away from home than he'd ever believed possible. They cared nothing for him—his new husband perhaps least of all.

What if I never come home?

Mounting terror clawed at him. He told himself there was no way to know his fate, but some primal instinct hissed that if he left now, only a treacherous world of stone and ice waited. A world that could be his doom.

Jem's gaze darted to the massive doors of the great hall, which were open to the morning birdsong and honeysuckle breeze. He couldn't run—it would be pointless. He would be hauled back to snickers and whispers, shame-faced and made even more small and pathetic than he was.

His parents and Cador's father joined them. Jem resented bitterly that this discussion was apparently to occur in front of anyone who happened to have roused themselves for breakfast. Surely it should have been done in private. But clearly it was not to be a *discussion* whatsoever.

Jem's mother smiled placidly. "We have invited Ergh's chieftain to be our honored guest in Neuvella. Jem, you shall visit Ergh in the meantime and enjoy the picturesque late spring and summer months in the North. Then we'll reunite here at the Feast of the Blood Moon. Won't that be wonderful?"

Jem wanted to shout a denial, grab her and beg for mercy, but what could he do but agree? Miserably, he nodded.

She added, "Just think—you'll be the first person from the mainland to journey to Ergh for lifetimes, aside from the clerics."

The head cleric beamed. "You have truly been honored by the gods."

If this is honor, who needs smiting?

"Tas, this was not what we discussed." Cador bit out the words like he'd eaten cherries picked too early, still hard and sour.

"No, but the clerics are wise. One night is simply not enough for grooms to be together before parting. And in fellowship, I shall be gifted with Neuvella's hospitality and visit Gwels."

"Yes, but—"

"These months will see the seeds of your bond with your prince grow tall and strong," the chieftain said. "Like a mighty sevel tree."

Cador said gruffly, "Then we shall feast before our fruitful journey." He marched toward the wedding table where they'd sat the night before.

Jem had no choice but to follow, although he didn't think he'd be able to choke down a single bite. Soon, he made his way along the table laden with meat, bread, rich pastries, and fruit, mindlessly adding items to his plate since that was what he was supposed to do at breakfast. Santo joined him, their face pinched.

"I'm sorry," Santo murmured.

Jem nodded, his throat too thick to speak.

"Perhaps it won't be so terrible." Santo leaned in to whisper, "How did last night go?"

Jem shook his head, keeping his eyes on the heaping platter of sausage. He speared one and dropped it forlornly on his plate.

Santo tucked one of Jem's curls behind his ear. "You didn't enjoy yourself?" Although they still whispered, their voice hardened. "If that beast hurt you—"

"No, nothing like that." Jem glanced about to make sure no one was in earshot. "He has no interest in fucking me. Not that I blame him."

"I do." Santo hissed, "He should be so lucky!"

"It was a relief." That was true. Mostly.

"I suppose so. But you are wed now. You've waited so long."

"No matter. We have no desire to bed each other."

Santo gave him a knowing look. "I think you should very much enjoy bedding him."

"Perhaps," he had to admit. "Who can say what will happen once we know each other a bit better. I'm in no rush for, for…that."

"Fair enough. It can be marvellous, you know. With the right person." Santo's eyes lit up as they spotted their husband enter the hall.

"Go on. Don't worry about me." Jem tried for a smile and went to join Cador, wishing he could even hope to one day feel such delight at the mere sight of his husband. Knowing that day would never come.

"Jem?"

He turned to find Prince Treeve giving a tentative smile, holding a plate of eggs and meat. "Oh. Yes?"

Treeve's smile was sympathetic. "Jem—may I call you that?" At Jem's nod, he added, "I wanted to give my congratulations." He paused, raising an eyebrow. "Or perhaps my condolences? Regardless, please know you have a friend in the West. I'd hoped to get to know you better during this summit, but…well."

Regret and longing filled Jem. To think he might have married this handsome, genteel prince. "Yes, well." He cleared his throat. "Thank you for your kind wishes."

Treeve frowned. "I do mean it, Jem. If we—" He shook his head. "Forgive me. I'm keeping you from your husband." After a short bow, he left Jem with the platters of fruits.

Though he wasn't hungry in the slightest, Jem took as long as he could choosing his breakfast foods, torturing himself with fanciful notions of what might have been.

Too soon, Jem was shepherded to the churned-up dirt outside the stable where no grass grew, wondering if he and Cador would be forced to ride in the same carriage for days. The Holy Place rested at the north end of the mainland. How far was it to the coast?

But wait… Where were the carriages? Jem gazed around and found none, which was most curious. There were only horses and carts with large wheels. Surely that didn't mean…

No. Surely not.

Cador had stalked off earlier after gobbling down a huge breakfast, and now he appeared. "This will be your horse." He held the mane of a massive animal with brown hair and white spots and hooves that looked bigger than Jem's head.

"My horse?" Jem repeated blankly.

"Get on. We've wasted enough daylight."

Jem couldn't have vaulted himself up onto the huge creature's back even if he wanted to. Which he did not. Not even a little.

Cador scowled. "Surely you've seen a horse before? There are horses in all corners of Onan, I believe."

"Yes, but… I can't *ride* one." He inched back as the animal snorted and shifted ominously.

Cador huffed. "What is this game? How did you get here if you didn't ride?"

"In a carriage." That way he could read, although he always felt vaguely sick to his stomach during carriage journeys. It was worth it.

More importantly, Jem had been terrified of riding horses since Pasco had tricked him as a boy into mounting a bad-tempered mare who threw him to the dirt and kicked him for good measure. Her hoof had struck the meat of his left buttock—a blessing since the damage hadn't been permanent. But he hadn't been able to sit for a week, much to the amusement of many, even Santo.

"A carriage," Cador repeated scornfully.

"Don't you have carriages?"

"Carriages would fall to pieces in a day. In the North, we ride."

"Some in the South ride! Many do." Jem replied defensively. "I simply don't care to."

"We're doing plenty of things we don't fucking care to, aren't we? You've never actually ridden a horse yourself when you weren't being pulled along in a gilded cage. Is that what you're saying?"

"Well, I wouldn't quite phrase it like that."

Cador's lips quirked into what might have been a smile before he scowled. "This is the horse you'll ride north to the shore. A few servants are coming along to return the animals once we're at sea."

"Then why can't I borrow a carriage?"

Cador ignored the question. "This will be your horse. Get the fuck up on her."

Jem backed away. "It's impossible."

Without another word, Cador strode forward, picked up Jem around the waist, and plonked him atop the horse's broad back. The animal whinnied and stamped, and Jem scrambled to clutch what he could of its mane, his branded palm flaring with pain so hot he felt sick. He prayed the horse wouldn't bolt and send him crashing to the ground, where he'd surely be trampled if the impact didn't kill him first.

"Oh gods!" Jem squeaked with terror, but he couldn't help it. The horse was sidestepping, and he was going to tumble to his doom before they even set foot—or hoof—outside the Holy Place.

"Sit up and control her!" Cador barked. "These aren't untamed beasts—they're the horses of gentle clerics."

Delen appeared, effortlessly wheeling around her mount. "It's his first time. You can't expect him to handle the animal right away."

"A virgin in all things that matter," Cador muttered.

Delen asked, "What was that?"

"Nothing!" Jem yelped, clinging to the horse's back and trying not to think about how shockingly far away the ground looked. He had no idea what he was doing, and he was about to fall, and the huge hooves would crush him, and—

He bit back a scream as he arced through the air. But Jem wasn't falling—Cador's strong hands gripped him, depositing him safely on the ground as his family approached with the chieftain. Jem pretended his heart wasn't beating out of his chest as Mother presented him with a plush cloak the color of ruby wine.

He clutched it around himself although the morning grew humid. He knew he should do his duty with pride instead of roiling resentment and fear, acid sharp at the back of his tongue and sweat stale under his arms.

As Cador spoke to his father, Jem's parents embraced him and promised to see him again at the autumn feast. Mother smelled like delicate lavender as she held him, but Jem found the scent cloying as he stood stiffly, arms at his side.

"Just think," she said. "This will be the first Feast of the Blood Moon with a whole Onan for centuries. You and Cador are symbols of this historic reunification. The gods will bless you."

"Will they shift Ergh back to the mainland so I don't have to go there?" Jem muttered.

His mother's embrace sharpened. She whispered, "Remember you represent all of Neuvella and the mainland. You represent me. I know you'll carry yourself with dignity and grace. I know you won't disappoint me."

Guilt surged. "I know, but..." He clung to her and whispered, "I'm afraid. How can you send me there?"

"Oh, my darling son." She held him tightly. "Just remember, they are like us in the ways that matter. It is time you fly free of the nest. You are braver than you know." Stepping back, she said more loudly, "And your new husband will guard you with his life."

In the silence, they all looked to Cador, who apparently took a few moments to remember she was talking about him. He said, "Uh, yes. Of course."

Somehow it wasn't reassuring.

Cador's father spoke in a gruff, commanding voice. "Your son will be an honored guest of Ergh. He shall be protected. In the name of the gods, I swear it."

Cador stood straighter, clearing his throat. "Yes. I will protect him." His dutiful words were rather lacking.

After a narrowed glare at Cador, Santo wrapped Jem in their arms tightly. The fact that they smelled of breakfast sausage would have made Jem chuckle on another day.

"You'll make sure the birds are cared for?" Jem asked. "Some only need to be fed and nursed until they are old enough to fly away into the forest. If a wing is broken or there's another injury—"

"I know. I'll be sure your flock are tended. Don't fret." Santo ruffled Jem's hair and whispered, "Think of it as an adventure. What would Morvoren do?"

Despite himself, Jem did laugh softly, the release threatening to become a desperate sob. He clung to his sibling's tall frame, burying his face against their shoulder. He wanted to beg for help, but it would only burden Santo and likely delight Pasco and Locryn, who'd appeared bleary-eyed to clap him on the back.

"Enjoy the ride!" Pasco grinned. "Well, if you can. You must feel a bit tender this morning." He waggled his thick eyebrows.

There were titters of muffled laughter that Jem studiously ignored, his jaw tight. He watched Cador and his father grasp forearms and hug fiercely. They nodded at each other, but apparently had said all they needed to already. Cador strapped a wicked-looking sword over his back in a sheath.

Then it was time. Whether he liked it or not, Jem was leaving. He eyed the horse, steeling himself to try again. He could do this. Even if it felt very much like he couldn't, he had to try.

But before he could, Cador plonked him onto another horse. Jem bit back a squeak. The pale horse between his thighs was even bigger than the other creature, the solid warmth of the ground even farther away.

This time, along with being seated properly, there was a solid mass of man at his back, a thick, strong arm around Jem's waist securing him. Cador had plucked up Jem like he weighed nothing and mounted behind him in a single leap. He controlled the horse effortlessly with nudges and clucks of his tongue, his powerful, leather-clad thighs bracketing Jem's.

Jem's backside was wedged between Cador's legs against his groin. He remembered the heft of Cador's prick, heat flooding his body despite everything. He waved to his family, barely breathing as the Holy Place disappeared behind them.

Instead of a gilded, plush-cushioned carriage, Jem's cage was Cador's body surrounding him. His nose filled with musky horse and man, his prick filling too. Mortified that he could feel such fear and arousal in concert, Jem was glad for his cloak.

The horses bore no saddles, only simple leather reins attached to the bridles. Jem supposed this was how the barbarians rode. Cador reached around with his long, strong arms, one still snug around Jem's middle and the other loosely holding the reins.

The procession of riders and pulled carts continued. The horse swayed side to side as it walked, and Jem squeezed it with his legs, grateful for Cador's bulk keeping him in place. He was now entering a new world, riding one foreign beast with another pressed against him.

He thought of sun-dappled leaves and the chirps of dillywigs with a pang of grief and longing that thickened his throat and caught his breath. Santo would be sure the birds would be safe, but what would become of Jem sailing to an unknown kingdom with a wild stranger as his mate?

Santo's question echoed: *What would Morvoren do?*

Brave adventurer that she was, she'd kick the horse's flanks and gallop north with a rallying cry like, *"Onward to the ends of Onan!"* Why, she'd likely—

Gasping, Jem jolted with a gut-churning thought. "My books! Where are my books?"

The horse snorted, and Cador grumbled, "What?" as he leaned forward, pressing close to stroke the horse's neck.

"My books!" Jem repeated. They'd been piled beside the bed in his guest chamber when he'd last seen them before the wedding.

"Dunno." Cador didn't sound like he cared the slightest bit. "With your things in one of the carts, I imagine."

Anger flared sharply. "I need to be sure. Let me down!"

Cador said simply, "No."

Jem could hardly breathe. How had he not realized until now? Yes, he'd been distracted by being forced into marriage with a barbarian banished by the gods, but where was Morvoren? The fear building since the moment he'd found all eyes on him at the summit exploded into panic that had Jem's heart about to explode. To endure this journey without his books was too much to bear.

He whipped around, elbowing Cador in the stomach without meaning to. But he didn't apologize. Instead, he spat, "You might not be able to read, but I need my books! Where are they?" He shoved at Cador's stone wall of a chest with all his might, the terror and frustration boiling over.

Thick, rough fingers yanked his hair, and Jem flailed as he was thrust headfirst over the side of the horse, his weight precariously leaning to the right, the animal snorting its discontent.

Jem yelped, scrabbling at Cador's boot, the world upside down. "Please!"

Wordlessly, Cador wrenched him back up and nudged the horse into a trot. Jem grabbed at anything, his desperate fingers landing on Cador's knees. His face was hot with blood, head spinning and spine jolting with the horse's movement. Laughter rang on the wind from other riders. Jem squirmed with discomfort and embarrassment. He'd lashed out like a petulant child and had been treated as such.

Delen neared and snapped, "Behave, Cador!" She wore a

sword on her back as well, although not all the Northerners did. She asked Jem, "Are you well?"

He wanted to tell her that he wasn't well in the slightest, but Jem nodded, grateful that she'd asked.

"Oh for fuck's sake, he's *fine*." Cador nudged the horse to go faster.

They rode for hours without a break. Jem was sore and stiff all the way to his toes and more than ready to relieve himself. The puffs of Cador's breath were warm on his ear as Jem turned to squint at the nearest cart. There was no sign of his trunk, but he prayed Santo had packed his books.

They would have if they'd been able—of that Jem was certain. Gods, would he really see Santo again? Or their parents? Mother had made it sound like no time at all until the Feast of the Blood Moon, but it seemed a lifetime.

Jem wouldn't particularly miss his brothers, but the thought of never seeing Santo again made his eyes burn. The last thing he needed to do was start weeping, so he bit his lip, breathing deeply and blinking upward.

The brilliant blue sky of the Holy Place had faded into a cloudy gray as they journeyed north to the shore. Jem's backside ached just as much as it had as a boy when the horse had kicked him. How much farther to the sea? And then how far to Ergh? He wanted to ask, but after his regrettable outburst, he held his tongue.

When they finally stopped for a break, Jem was both desperately relieved to get off the horse and fearful of how far away the ground appeared. He tentatively swung one aching leg over the horse's back so he was sitting to the side, perched awkwardly. The last thing he wanted to do was ask for help, but—

Jem crashed to the muddy ground thanks to a merciless

shove from Cador. He rolled onto his sore backside, blinking up at his hulking shadow of a husband high above.

For a hideous moment, Jem fought tears. Not merely tears, but wrenching sobs that clawed at his throat. No. He would not give this barbarian the satisfaction. He must be strong. He must represent Neuvella and the entire mainland.

Jem pushed to his feet, his legs feeling strangely bowed, every muscle stiff to the point of breaking. Head high, he glared at Cador as the beast hopped down from the stallion with a shocking amount of grace given he was a giant.

Cador asked, "Are you injured?"

"What do you care?"

He shrugged. "I don't."

Jaw tight, Jem glanced about at the open fields, trees huddled in the distance. "I need to relieve myself."

"Piss, you mean? Go ahead. We don't have all day, *little prince*." The last words dripped with disdain.

There were a few guffaws from those within earshot. Jem realized that the Erghians were relieving themselves right out in the open, some not even bothering to walk a few paces from the dirt track. Cocks hung out and others squatted.

Sputtering, Jem whirled around, trying to find somewhere safe to look. He'd urinated outside before, in the privacy of trees or in the lake during long morning swims. But not like this!

"You need me to hold it for you?"

Jem clenched his fists at Cador's mocking tone. Ignoring him, he strode—well, hobbled—a few paces and tugged at the laces of his breeches. He pulled out his prick just enough, feeling like dozens of eyes were now focused on him.

Yet when he finished and peeked around, the Erghians were going about their business, checking horses and carts, distributing parcels of food that had likely been packed by the clerics. Jem ate his bread, meat, and cheese gratefully since he'd been barely able to swallow a bite that morning.

The last thing he wanted to do was mount the stallion again. His whole body hurt, but he had no choice. He didn't protest as Cador lifted him astride the horse and swung up behind him.

Jem sat as straight as he could, aching muscles tensed against the temptation to rest back against Cador's bulk. How strange to think that they'd exchanged vows of duty and protection in the temple. This stranger was his *husband*.

Yet Jem had still never been kissed.

He scoffed at himself. He'd probably perish on this journey to the unknown, and kissing was the last thing he should be worried about. Still, loneliness hollowed him. Instead of a loving partner to keep him warm and safe, Jem had only a wall of muscle behind him, his husband as cold and forbidding as Ergh promised to be.

Chapter Five

"WAIT!" CADOR SHOUTED after his brother, but Bryok galloped across a rocky field and into the forest without hesitating. Curse him to the very depths of the Askorn Sea. Bryok was maddening, but worse was Cador's thirst for his approval. It was one thing when he was a boy. Why did he give a shit as a man what his brother thought?

Delen appeared next to him on her own mount. "You can't hunt with a second rider."

Against him, Jem squirmed and said something.

"What?" barked Cador.

Between his legs, Jem went rigid. Still barely loud enough, Jem murmured, "I'm sorry."

Cador grunted, keeping his gaze on the rutted road. He could feel Delen's eyes on him, her judgment prickly. Fine, it wasn't the boy's fault, but Cador should be going on the hunt with Bryok and the others.

He muttered, "If you could damn well ride a horse like everyone in Ergh…"

Jem's head was bent, revealing the downy hair at the back of his neck where it had been shorn. It was a Southern style apparently to have hair longer on top, yet close underneath. Likely because of the stinking heat down there. It was said they had no winter to speak of, and he felt sweaty just thinking about it.

Delen still rode beside them, and Cador narrowed his gaze at her. "Why aren't you hunting with Bryok and the others?"

She shrugged, but there was something there. Delen was never one to pass up a hunt, even if it was for byghan, the too-lean, long-legged creatures of the forest that in Ergh were only hunted in desperation. No hunter wasted time on byghans when there was boar to track. Byghan were easy to fell with spear or sword, but the dry and stringy meat caught in your teeth.

Cador eyed his sister, waiting. Finally, she said, "Bryok's being a piss-head. Let him hunt it out. If he doesn't, perhaps he'll fuck it out tonight."

Bryok's wife was home in Ergh, but surely after so many years together was accustomed to her husband's roving appetites. Yet another reason Cador sneered at marriage—the notion of being faithful to only one person was laughable.

He shrugged in response to Delen.

Does he blame me?

Cador refused to ask such pathetic, childish questions aloud. Bryok hadn't so much as glanced at him since the wedding, even though he knew the soft little Southern prince wasn't the mate Cador would ever choose. Bryok's scorn for the mainland was legendary, but he knew it was Tas's doing.

Only a handful of the two-dozen people who'd made this journey from Ergh had been trusted with the strategy. No one at home knew the truth. The fewer who knew, the better. Cador hadn't expected to marry a skittish virgin, but he'd wed a hundred Jems if it meant success.

The time was so close that Cador ached to stop with the lies and damn patience. To take up his spear and sword and do what he must for his people. But not yet. He must wait, and his burden for his people was to mind the little prince.

Cador looked to where Bryok and the handful of hunters disappeared into the forest. The track sliced through fields that didn't seem able to grow much but grass in the shadow of woodlands. The sun that had been impossibly high and bright at the Holy Place now neared the horizon, a faint glow behind clouds. They'd stop soon to make camp and choke down chewy byghan.

Cador would never admit it, but he'd be glad to rest. His freshly salved and bandaged palm hurt more than he liked, a dull ache throbbed in his temples, and he was damn tired of making sure Jem stayed upright. He was tired of Jem altogether. Why did he have to ride with Cador? Delen should have taken him if she was so concerned.

To insist you're a man without ever having ridden a horse! At least Jem would eventually serve a vital purpose whether he liked it or not—and surely he would not. Cador ignored the twinge of guilt. It was for the greater good.

As they neared a cart, Jem leaned closer to it, peering carefully. He'd done so all afternoon, and Cador knew he was searching for his belongings. His books. Books were a luxury. Books didn't put food in hungry bellies.

Which was why he'd dumped them out of Jem's trunk before they left the Holy Place. Hunters of Ergh traveled light, not with useless lodestones. Jem himself was enough of a burden.

Cador looked toward the forest, but there was no sign of Bryok and the others yet. Soon, Delen called for a halt to set up camp in a shallow valley with a stream running through it. Cador reined in the borrowed horse and nudged Jem.

"Off."

Jem sat rigidly, staring down at the ground. "Please don't push me."

Guilt flared again and Cador grumbled. He'd expected Jem to land on his feet earlier, forgetting just how flimsy and useless the little prince clearly was. Besides, if Jem snapped a bone, it would only slow them down.

Cador dismounted easily, his boots squelching in the damp earth. "Bring your other leg around to this side so you're on your belly across his back."

Stiffly, Jem bent his left leg and inched it up and over, his fingers digging into the horse's flanks as he turned onto his belly. With Jem's pert arse in his face, Cador grabbed him by the waist and plonked him on his feet in those fancy boots. "See how your feet were closer to the ground?"

"Yes," Jem murmured, taking a few shaky steps. He rubbed his arse, wincing.

Laughter rumbled from nearby, Jory leering. "You should have gone easy on him last night. Boy can hardly walk!"

Jem whipped his hand away, eyes wide.

"Don't recall Cador being big enough to notice," Kensa said, her wicked smile gleaming. Her light brown skin glistened with sweat at her forehead as she hauled rocks to form a circle. She was a hunter, but apparently she didn't want to spend time with Bryok either and had stayed behind.

"You've ridden so many pricks that any man would get lost for days in there," Cador called back to a roar of laughter.

"Pass the lad over after supper and I'll introduce him to a real cock," Jory said, grabbing his shaft through his leather breeches, his pale, freckled face flushed with good humor. He raised and trained horses and went about checking hooves now, first tying back his mess of shaggy orange hair.

Cador laughed along with the continuing jokes, everyone relaxing after the long day, rubbing down their mounts and starting on casks of ale. He patted the horse on the rump and sent him off to drink from the stream and chew on the thin grass there. Jem remained standing with his head down and arms wrapped around himself, the bright, silly colors of his shirt and cloak melded like a rainbow.

"You've got plenty of options for cock tonight," Cador said. "Or if you fancy a wet cunt after all, Kensa might oblige." He glanced to her. "Small tits, but they're about the right size for you."

Kensa jerked her fist at Cador rudely with a grin. Cador gave Jem a friendly nudge, and the boy stumbled back, sitting on the damp ground with a sharp inhalation, his face screwing up in pain.

Oh, for… The jests still weren't easing the boy's tension, and Cador bristled. Why was he so fragile and serious? He bent and lifted Jem back onto his feet, Jem making a squeaky little sound like a mouse. He stayed standing, at least.

Cador said, "If you want to piss or shit, use the trees there." He nodded at the tall, thin elms to the south. During brief stops it didn't matter, but when making camp for the night, they used the southern direction for their toilet. Tas always guffawed and said it was like shitting on the mainlanders' heads.

Jem nodded, but stood in place while Cador went to drink. He laughed with a few people, watching Jem from the corner of his eye. Jem inched toward the trees, stopping and starting again.

A fire blazed now, darkness settling in. Jem took a few steps, stopping short when someone else went to piss. He inched closer and closer, freezing whenever someone else approached. Cador couldn't imagine what the fuck the problem was until the copse was empty. Jem gazed around and bolted into the trees.

"He doesn't want to piss near someone else?" Kensa asked, following Cador's gaze with her forehead furrowed.

"Seems not." Cador shook his head. "He was fussy about it earlier too." In unison with Kensa, he muttered, "Mainlanders."

"So…fiddly," she added. "Can't imagine fucking him."

"Me either," Cador said, then realized what he'd revealed. He quickly added, "Shoving it in while he lay stiff as a board wasn't what I'd call 'fucking.'"

Kensa grimaced. "What was Kenver thinking? He could have made a bargain with the South without resorting to this. And bringing him home with us? Madness." She gave Cador a thump on the back. "If you need a real fuck, you know where to find me."

The hunters returned with byghans slung over their horses and shoulders, Bryok still ignoring Cador completely. Cador gulped ale and laughed heartily at someone's story about buggering a byghan rather than eating it because it was more use that way. The meat was dry and bland as usual, but it was hot, at least. Cador ripped off a chunk and held it out to Jem.

Jem sat in the shadows at Cador's shoulder, behind him and not quite part of the circle around the fire. A few peered at him with suspicion, others curiosity, while some ignored him entirely. None spoke to him.

Eyeing the meat as though it was a sarf that might strike and sink in its fangs, Jem reached for it after a moment. He took a nibble and glanced around. "Do Erghians always travel so…informally?"

Cador snorted. "Yes. Did you expect us to cart around fine plates and gold spoons?"

"Of course not," he replied too quickly.

Cador muttered under his breath about mainlanders and

turned back to the circle. Along with the clerics' bread and sweet cakes, the meat filled his belly. People moved in and out, eating and drinking and telling tales. Eventually, a few grunts and moans echoed from the sleeping furs laid out under the cloudy sky, the odd star twinkling through, the moon at quarter strength.

Jem asked, "Is someone ill?"

For a moment, Cador stared at him. Was he finally loosening up and attempting a jest? But, no, he seemed genuinely concerned as he squinted into the darkness beyond the fire's glow. Cador shared a chuckle with Delen nearby.

She said, "That's just Enyon fucking Senara. He sounds like a wounded byghan at the best of times."

Jem stared. "He's—they're—" As Senara's moan echoed, her pleasure clear, Jem opened and closed his mouth. He whispered, "They're doing it right there?"

Cador had to laugh, Delen shaking her head as she left to find her own lover. He lowered his voice. "You really are an innocent. Good thing I'm not going to fuck you. You're so squeamish you probably don't even know where everything goes. Is everyone where you're from this joyless?"

Jem pressed his lips together tightly, apparently offended. That only made Cador laugh harder. Jem hissed, "I know where it goes, and we enjoy coupling just as much! The difference being we do it in private and not out in the open with an audience like wild animals!"

"Oh, I'm wounded!" Cador clutched his chest. "Prince Jowan of Neuvella thinks us animals." He picked up a byghan leg still warm by the fire and gnawed it. With his mouth full, he muttered, "Better a beast in the dirt than a pathetic prince who's never wanted for a thing."

Jem fell silent, poking at the bandage over his palm.

When Cador pissed later, Jem trailed behind. Then, as Cador spread out his furs on a patch of ground not too rocky and only a bit muddy, Jem still shadowed him. Considering he thought Cador was such a beast, why didn't he go find a spot on his own?

"Where's your fur?" Cador asked. It occurred to him there hadn't been much at all in Jem's trunk but the books. Perhaps he should have let them be, but the horses had enough load to pull.

"I don't have any."

"Where did you sleep on the journey to the Holy Place?" Did they sleep in their fancy carriages as well?

"In beds. We stayed at inns along the way. There aren't any inns on Ergh?"

Cador wasn't sure exactly what he meant, but was damn sure Ergh had none. "No."

"Do you know where my things are? Which cart?"

"No idea." Cador yawned, turning on his side and shutting his eyes. "Find a place." A couple rutted nearby, a man moaning. The wind here didn't howl, but the whistle of it was familiar enough to lull Cador.

"But…" the soft voice whispered.

Sighing, Cador cracked one eye open to find Jem still standing there. "Go to sleep," he commanded.

"Where? With someone else?" Jem asked sharply.

"If you want. I don't give a shit."

"No." Jem's voice was low and urgent. "Please don't make me."

"What?" Cador frowned. "No one will make you."

After a few beats of silence when Cador thought he might

finally get to sleep, Jem whispered, "You won't pass me to your friend?"

"Huh?" He opened an eye. Jem stood in the darkness, his trembling outline visible. Cador squirmed uncomfortably. He should have remembered the boy had no damn sense of humor. "Jory was only jesting."

"Oh." Jem exhaled noisily. "Truly?"

"Truly. Although he's a good fuck if you change your mind. Clever tongue."

"I—what? No." Jem shook his head vigorously. "No."

"Your loss."

Jem stood there silently for so long that Cador closed his eyes and ignored him. Finally, Jem whispered, "How do you know? About Jory? I thought you were friends?"

Cador grumbled and opened his eyes. "Friends fuck sometimes."

"Oh! You're all very..." He glanced around the camp, the grunts and cries filling the night. "Uh, free."

"What a dour place Neuvella must be."

"You're the ones who act like animals. No wonder the gods banished you."

"Oh, you wound me deeply. Now go the fuck to sleep." Tugging one of his furs free, he tossed it at Jem. "Wherever." He motioned to the valley where their party was spread out, some sticking near the fire, others off on their own or in pairs. Or threesomes or foursomes. Distant guards stood watch.

There was plenty of space, but Jem didn't go huddle off on his own. Instead, he gingerly spread the fur an arm's length from Cador, wrapping himself in it. Fine. Now they could sleep. Cador shut his eyes, letting the faint buzz of ale and a day's ride do its work and push him under.

He was almost there some time later, but... What the fuck was that noise?

It was a clicking that didn't sound like any animal Cador knew. It was close and had to be coming from Jem. What was he doing? Tapping something? Was this some strange Southern sleep ritual?

"Stop that," Cador ordered.

The clicking was now accompanied by breathy little pants. "I...can't."

"What the fuck are you doing?" Cador pushed himself up to sitting, squinting in the darkness. Jem was curled into a ball. He was still shaking, and he flinched when Cador leaned close to get a better view.

Cador realized Jem's teeth were chattering. That he shivered with cold and not fright. Well, probably still *some* fright, but he was definitely cold, which seemed impossible. Cador exclaimed, "But the ground isn't even frosted! Let alone frozen. How are you cold?"

"It's...never...this cold...at home."

"You truly have no winter?"

Jem shook his head, the motion barely visible. "And I don't camp outside. Ever."

Cador didn't know how Jem could stand being so weak. But there was no way Cador could sleep with him carrying on, so he rolled to his side and yanked the fur from under him. He tossed it to Jem, the thick pelt hitting him with a soft *whoomp.*

"Thank you," Jem whispered.

Cador grunted. "Just shut up and sleep."

Even without his furs, it was good to sleep under the moon once more instead of in a feathery bed. Cador stretched out on his back, the sounds of fucking familiar, blending into a hum.

He was almost asleep when guilt nagged him again like a stubborn mule kicking.

He raised himself on his elbow to check on Jem, making sure he wasn't shaking or chattering anymore. If the prince died on the way to Ergh, it wouldn't help their cause, and Cador had vowed to protect him. Even if he'd been forced into it, he'd given his word. Yes, he'd break his word when the time came, but for now…

Jem slept curled under the furs. Starlight glowed just enough to see his parted lips, pretty face soft, honey eyes closed. There. Now Cador could slumber himself. His duty was done.

Yet he found himself awake for far too long until finally drifting into the dreamworld, where he ate juicy sevels and felled boars, his spear heavy and true in his grasp.

Chapter Six

T HE BEAST WAS gone.

As Jem groaned on the hard ground, his body aching in places he hadn't known possible, he blinked in the murky dawn light at the empty grass beside him. He bolted up to sitting, the furs sliding to his lap. Had Cador abandoned him? He wasn't sure whether to be hopeful or terrified.

But no, the others were still there, although Jem was the only one still abed—if one could call huddling under animal pelts on the hard ground "abed." The fire blazed, some of the Erghians sitting by it eating, a few milling around. Cador wasn't in sight, but the pale horse they'd ridden still grazed at the stream.

Shivering at the layer of dew covering him, Jem pulled one of the furs tight around his shoulders. He inhaled Cador's lingering scent, musky yet fresh, like moss on a stone. Or perhaps it was ice after all.

No one so much as glanced his way, although at least that meant Jem wasn't being mocked for the moment. He hoped Cador's father would be more welcomed in the South. He would be, of course—Jem's parents were nothing if not gracious hosts. Jem supposed he should be grateful he'd been fed and given furs. He'd huddled under them, sticking close to Cador in the darkness.

Cador had given his word, and surely Ergh's chieftain would expect Jem to be in one piece come the Feast of the Blood

Moon, and Cador would be punished if Jem was carried off by wild animals into the night, human or otherwise.

He prodded the bandaged burn on his palm, wincing. The bonds of marriage had never felt so very real and imprisoning even though he and Cador hadn't even…

The memory of the carnal sounds he'd heard flooded back with a hot rush, his morning erection swelling despite his mortification. People had actually been coupling—in one case, Jem was certain it was a thrupling—right there in the open! Even if it had been too dark to properly see, they could certainly be heard.

Not that Jem had tried to see.

But the grunts, groans, moans and cries, the suckling and slapping of flesh—it had painted vivid pictures in his mind's eye despite his best efforts to ignore it and sleep.

In all his dark fantasies of being mastered, he'd never actually imagined it occurring outside on the earth. Morvoren riding her merman lover's cock on a warm, sun-kissed beach was one thing. Here on the muddy ground, it seemed all the baser and shockingly real.

It shouldn't excite him. It was crude and animalistic, and perhaps this sort of activity was exactly why the gods banished Ergh in the first place. Jem rolled his eyes at himself and muttered, "Now I believe in the gods?"

But the mainland of Onan was a land of civility, despite any tension or disputes. A place of sleeping in beds with feather pillows and nibbling on sweet cakes served on gilded plates. Though this was merely Jem's experience in the castle, and he knew others weren't nearly as pampered. He'd taken it for granted since boyhood.

Now he was trapped alone with these brutes who hunted

their food and skinned them while the animals were still warm. And yes, some of the animals Jem had grown up eating were hunted, but he'd only ever encountered the meat cooked on his plate, usually with a fragrant cream sauce. He'd never understood his privilege in eating meat without being confronted with the reality of the killing.

Regret stewed in his belly now. He could scarcely believe that less than a week ago he'd lazed in his own feather bed, safe and warm, sunlight beaming through the ornate glass windows. With not an inkling of what was to come.

Gripping the fur around him, Jem missed his home with a pang so fierce it stole his breath. He was wed, and of all the men he'd imagined for a husband, not one would shove him off a horse.

He spotted Cador strolling out of a copse of trees to the north with his friend Jory. They spoke and made their way to the fire, and Jem waited for Cador to at least glance in his direction.

Yet it was as though Cador had forgotten him completely. Jory sat beside him at the fire, his flame-colored hair wild. He passed Cador a steaming mug, and they took turns sipping from it, broad shoulders brushing.

What had they been doing in the woods?

"It doesn't matter," Jem muttered. "I don't care. They're free to do whatever they like."

By the fire, Jory laughed about something. Jem cringed, remembering how Jory had offered to bed him. Was he mocking him now? Had he and Cador gone off to pleasure each other? He imagined them jesting about how awful it would be to bed someone small and inexperienced like Jem.

Jem needed to get up and do... Well, he didn't know what,

aside from relieve himself. But he needed to do something—anything—other than watch Cador and Jory. Yet he couldn't tear his eyes away, examining this Jory.

He was smaller than Cador, though few were larger. Bigger than Jem, although that wasn't difficult. Cador had said they'd lain together, and Jem couldn't help but imagine the two of them naked. Did they kiss each other? Did barbarians even kiss?

He'd heard wet sounds the night before but wasn't sure if that was mouths kissing, or mouths…elsewhere. He put Cador and Jory into different positions in his mind until he realized his morning erection had grown rock hard.

Shame heated his cheeks. Although he sat in plain view, he felt like an invisible spy forgotten in the grass, like a sarf slithering on its belly. He'd imagined copulation so many times and in so many ways even though he'd never had the courage to actually reach out and touch another.

Jory and Cador had, and he couldn't look away. What would it be like to touch Cador properly? How would that bare flesh feel beneath his fingers?

Jory leaned in and whispered something in Cador's ear, his lips close. Cador smiled, his eyes crinkling and laugh soft. For the first time Jem had witnessed, there was no derision or boasting. It was a true smile that dimpled his cheeks, and it made Cador beautiful, his face seeming bathed in sunlight even in the gray dawn. Jem felt strangely hollow as he watched.

As if feeling his gaze, Cador turned suddenly to meet Jem's eyes. His smile vanished like a puff of smoke, and guilt surged in Jem that he was the one who'd stolen Cador's momentary joy. Yet it wasn't his fault they'd been forced together. And why should he care about Cador's happiness and whether he smiled or scowled? Cador certainly didn't give a damn for Jem's contentment.

Jem shrugged out of the furs, jumping to his feet and kicking them aside. His legs seized, the muscles strained and aching after a day on horseback. To his horror, he got tangled in the furs and toppled back to the grass. Where he'd been ignored before, now the entire group watched him, laughter ringing through the valley.

Quite tempted to curl up again and pull the furs over his head, Jem forced himself to find his feet and walk calmly to the trees to relieve himself. Head high, he ignored the barbarians entirely.

Yet he could not ignore Cador so completely once they were astride the horse. Cador deposited Jem over the stallion's back, and Jem couldn't stop a shamefully plaintive little cry from escaping his lips.

Seating himself behind, Cador growled, "What now?"

"Nothing." Jem sat as straight as he could, away from the heat of Cador's body.

"Bullshit. Speak."

Frustration nipped at Jem as the horses walked back to the dirt road. What did Cador think it was? "It hurts," he gritted out, keeping his eyes forward. "I'm not accustomed to riding, remember?"

Silence. Then, "Still?"

Jem had to laugh, although there was no true humor in it. "Yes. Worse today." He grimaced at that unfortunate truth.

"Are you all so weak and breakable here?"

"Are you all so thick-skulled and—and—smelly on Ergh?" He cringed inwardly at his attempts at insults. His brother Pasco could surely come up with much better.

"Yes. We work hard on Ergh. Build strong bones. We're not

spoiled princes who can't even sit without complaining."

"Didn't it hurt when you first rode?"

More silence before Cador said, "I don't know. Can't re-member a time before I rode."

After an hour, Jem's back throbbed and his rear was so ten-der he wasn't sure he'd ever be able to sit again. He had no choice but to sag back against Cador, who didn't seem to notice.

How far away was the Askorn Sea? As far as Jem knew, the Holy Place sat like a crown atop the mainland, and surely the ocean was nearby. It was said no fish or creature could live in the inky, icy depths. How far north was Ergh?

These questions remained unspoken as the morning plod-ded on, Jem's body hurting with each step. Then a cry rose up from ahead, Cador's terrifying older brother shouting some-thing on the brisk wind.

Although the Erghians spoke the common language of Onan, they had their own words and phrases that Jem didn't understand. The tone was harsh and short, although that seemed the usual for Bryok.

Before Jem could ask if there was something amiss, Cador urged the horse into a faster pace. With each strike of hooves on the hard earth, pain slashed up Jem's spine from his backside. He hunched over, trying to relieve the pressure. He snatched at the flowing mane to keep his balance, his branded palm protesting.

An iron band locked around Jem's waist, Cador's arm keep-ing him safely in place on Massen's back, which was a relief. Jem was grateful, although it was likely more bother for Cador than it was worth if Jem plunged to the ground and he had to go back and fetch him.

Salt soon filled his nose as they thundered along the dirt

track. The ground had grown rockier, the trees sparser. The wind chilled his cheeks as they reached the rocky shore, a fine mist swirling. Jem forced himself upright, blinking at the fierce animal waiting.

The boar's lethal tusks curved upward, the wooden head adorning the ship intricately carved. The vessel was anchored with its port side to shore, rocking in the white-capped waves of the Askorn.

Jem had only seen small, white-sailed skiffs bobbing lazily on the sea at the south end of Neuvella. There, clear water reflecting the turquoise sky lapped at soft, white sand beaches. Here, the gray sea roiled furiously, waves crashing loudly on the shore.

"This sea shall swallow us whole!" Jem hadn't meant to speak aloud.

Cador barked out a laugh. "It just might." He hopped to the ground, then thumped Jem down on his feet on the hard, rocky sand. Jem forced a step on stiff legs. A group had apparently stayed behind with the ship, and they called out from the flat deck. A single mast towered midship, its brown sail thick and coarse.

Under iron skies, Jem clutched his muddy cloak around him and watched as they rowed cargo to the ship in smaller boats. He hadn't been able to spot his trunk, although he'd been too afraid to look through the carts lest he anger the others.

He tried to accept that he was likely separated from his books for the first time since he'd been able to read. The loss rivaled being parted from his family, although he assured himself it was understandable when it came to Pasco and Locryn.

The wind whipped colder than he'd ever felt, and Jem

clutched his too-thin cloak around him. Footsteps approached, and Delen asked, "Ready for the voyage?"

"No." Jem didn't see the sense in lying.

She laughed, her white teeth gleaming in contrast to her smooth, dark skin. "Can hardly blame you. Your clothes won't do. Didn't they pack anything more practical for you?"

"I don't know. I haven't seen my trunk." Hope flared. "Do you know where it is? Did they bring my things?"

"I'll find out."

"Really? Thank you!" Jem was filled with such gratitude he could have hugged her. "I was hoping my books were packed for me."

She gave him a quizzical look. "Books won't fend off the cold, Prince Jowan."

"No, but…" He wanted to say they'd warm his heart, but didn't.

"Suppose we could always burn the pages for heat if need be."

He gasped. "No! Please, I beg you." He gripped her arm.

"Calm yourself—it was a jest." She frowned. "Cador warned us you have no sense of humor." With a thump on his back that almost made him stumble, she added cheerfully, "We'll toughen you up. Ergh will do you good." With that, she strode off.

Jem squinted across the waves. He'd hoped to see the shadow of Ergh on the horizon, but there was nothing but an unbroken line of gray sky and dark, churning water.

Just how far away was Ergh? What if the ship sank? Jem hadn't expected to leave home—what if he never returned? As much as he'd craved adventure in the pages of his tales, leaving the mainland to sail into the frigid unknown was something else entirely.

Before long, Delen strode back toward him easily carrying his trunk. Elated, Jem dropped to his knees when she lowered it to the sand. He thanked her profusely and pushed up the heavy lid, the metal hinges creaking.

Acid flooded his gut, bile rising. Within the trunk sat only folded clothing in bright, useless silks. He dug through the pile desperately. His nightshirt and robe should have been a comfort, but without his books, anything else paled—even his special candle, which was still tucked into one of his shirts. The trunk was barely half-filled, and his books could have easily fit, but it seemed they'd been left behind after all.

"You'll need proper clothes," Delen said.

Jem's throat was clogged. If he spoke, he'd wail. Perhaps it truly was spoiled and silly to be so very heartsick over losing his books, but those worn, beloved pages had been his comfort for so long. Those words were his lifelong friends, his companions in a way that might seem mad to others. He would venture into the unknown completely alone.

"Don't worry," Delen said, frowning down at him. "I'll find you something."

Jem nodded and closed the trunk with a dull thud.

When it was his turn to board the forbidding ship, he followed Cador to the sea's frothing edge, gasping at the icy water that soaked his boots instantly. It was instinct rather than true thought that had him stumbling back to the safety of the rock-strewn sand. Cador turned and scowled impatiently.

"No!" Jem shook his head, backing away. "I don't want to go." He knew he sounded like a boy and not a man, but despair surged before plummeting deep and leaving a desperate void. He wanted his bed and his books and his poor birds at the lakeside. In the space of hardly more than a day, he didn't recognize his own life.

Cador marched through the shallows while some aboard the ship jeered and laughed. Cador grabbed hold of Jem roughly. "Don't make me throw you over my shoulder again."

"I want to go home." Jem blinked away the pathetic tears burning his eyes.

The hard lines of Cador's face softened. "We do what we must. We do our duty. I didn't want to leave my home either."

"At least you weren't alone."

Cador opened his mouth, but couldn't seem to argue with that. Instead, he muttered something that was lost in the wind and picked up Jem around the waist, depositing him into the launch. Cador rowed with a few others, the snarling boar's head looming closer until it blotted out the sky, ready to spirit away Jem to a world well and truly abandoned by the gods.

Chapter Seven

CADOR REFUSED. HE wouldn't allow it. This weakness was not permitted.

Standing at the ship's rail, he fought it with his whole being—clenching his muscles, breathing deep into his lungs and blowing out slowly, willing himself to remain strong. Commanding himself to resist. He'd resisted already for hours. He would prevail.

He would not vomit.

Yet as the ship rolled side to side in the merciless sea, his stomach lurched ominously. The waves weren't even remarkably high—he'd witnessed far more treacherous conditions from Ergh's solid ground—yet the motion was unrelenting. Cador glanced around the deck in the darkening evening. No one else appeared affected, which made it all the worse. Not even Jem, which made it fucking shameful.

Jem huddled at the stern, Delen's fur-lined cloak dwarfing him, pooled around his feet. He'd been there since they left the mainland, gazing back the way they'd come, staring into the white-tipped waves that grew blacker by the minute as the rising moon battled clouds.

How would Cador feel if he'd been forced to stay on the mainland alone, with only the odd, fancy people there? Tas was there, but he was a brave leader. He'd chosen to remain alone rather than ask any of his people to stay away from Ergh longer than necessary. He was the strongest man Cador knew.

There was no denying it—Cador would feel lonely. Unmoored and adrift. But this hadn't been his choice. None of it was. Why should he be responsible for shoring up Jem's spirits? Especially when the boy was so thin-skinned. It wasn't his problem. Cador hadn't meant a word of the vows he'd made in the name of the gods before the head cleric.

Mocking him, his left palm itched. He clenched his fist. The constant sting of the brand was fading, the salve and bandage doing its work. Once it was all over, he'd cover the bird's wings with tusks. He'd blacken his whole palm to erase it if that's what it took.

He'd keep Jem safe from harm until the time was right for the next step, but there was no reason he should want to comfort him or coax a smile from that pretty mouth. He shouldn't give a damn for Jem's happiness. And he wouldn't. That wasn't part of this game.

Cador bit back a groan. Now he just had to concentrate on surviving the voyage home without being violently ill. His mouth watered, his head too light. Perhaps he'd find a quiet corner and curl up. The others were gulping ale and making merry, and he wanted no part of it.

A groan escaped this time as Bryok stalked toward the ship's side where Cador sucked in the salt air. Of all the times for his brother to deign to speak to him again, it had to be now? He forced a deep breath through his nose, gripping the wooden railing and willing his head to stop fucking spinning.

Bryok clapped him hard on the back, and Cador clenched his teeth. "Enjoying the voyage?" Bryok asked, looking down at him as if he didn't know the answer.

When Cador was a boy, he'd dreamed of one day growing

taller than his brother, and although he towered over many, he'd never caught up with Bryok. Always seeking and never quite measuring up.

Cador muttered, "Piss off."

Bryok frowned with false concern. "Something amiss, brother?"

"Not a fucking thing."

"No, not a thing." Bryok sneered, and any amusement for Cador's affliction vanished. "We should be on the mainland taking what we need instead of begging for scraps."

Perhaps Bryok was right. Instead of playing these games of peace and politics and secretly planning for war, should they give up the pretence? "Tas says—"

"'*Tas says,*'" Bryok mimicked in a high pitch. "Fuck what he says."

A spray of seawater stung Cador's wide eyes. He'd often known Bryok to be impatient and surly, but he'd never heard such dagger-sharp resentment. Such *hatred*.

He schooled his face, keeping his tone calm as he might when Massen was in a foul mood from too many days stuck in the stable after a long blizzard. "I'm as frustrated as you are."

"Horse shit. You're too soft. Always have been. You're only too happy to play nursemaid to that pathetic little prince."

Jaw tight, Cador dug his blunt nails into the wet wood of the railing. "I'm performing my role as Tas commanded. Nothing more."

Bryok grumbled something that was lost in a gust of wind.

"Surely you know this isn't my doing?" He cursed his pleading tone. Why did he care what Bryok thought?

As a boy, of course Cador had wanted to please his parents, but Father and Tas weren't men who were overly harsh with their children. Pleasing them hadn't been hard—though Bryok had battled with them even as a child. Cador and Delen had followed the rules.

Bryok kept his beady gaze distant, his voice flat. "What I know is that Tas cares far too fucking much about what is right and just. I will slaughter everyone in Ebrenn if that's what it takes."

Cador jerked as if his brother had struck him. "The people are innocent. It is their king who must be conquered. Aligning with Neuvella and Gwels promises a quick surrender. If we can achieve our goal with little or even no bloodshed—"

"I don't fucking care how it's done," Bryok snarled. "I have waited too long already."

"But we're greatly outnumbered," Cador hissed, glancing around. Delen knew the truth, but none of the others journeying home did.

And Jem certainly did not, although what could he do even if Cador confessed the whole plan to him? He was powerless. It was why he wasn't bound and caged in the ship's hold—there was no point when he was helpless to stop them. Jem was their prisoner whether he knew it or not.

"Outnumbered by who? Those weak mainlanders? We are mighty hunters. Warriors!"

"Yet we have never been to war!"

"Because we had no cause. No enemy. Now we do. We must take what they have so plentifully in Ebrenn. What they selfishly hoard. We must be the ones with control." He thumped the railing in emphasis.

"And we *will*! But Tas is right. If you tell the enemy what it is you need, they cling to it with all their might. This way, they won't even know why we truly fight."

"We would defeat them now even with their numbers. You saw those mainlanders with their silks and jewels and sweet cakes sculpted into fucking butterflies." He glared toward Jem at the rear of the ship, far enough to be out of earshot, although Bryok wouldn't care. "You see him shivering there like a wet kitten. Your *husband*."

"Not by choice," Cador gritted out.

"We always have a choice, brother. He's yours."

Cador followed Bryok's gaze to Jem's back in Delen's too-big cloak. *My husband.* Even in name only, but it was undeniable. Resentment surged like the swell of seawater that lifted the bow of the ship and churned his stomach anew. No amount of pretending would make it go away.

Bryok muttered, "Tas has chosen to be 'patient.' To be fucking weak. Father would never stand for it."

It was true that their father had been a man of swift action. If he was still alive, would they have simply invaded Ebrenn without forming an alliance with the rest of Onan and be done with it? Cador didn't know.

He sighed. "I know it's harder for you to wait." He tried not to think of his nieces and nephews most of the time, but now he had to, especially Hedrok. "I know—"

"You know fuck-all!" Bryok roared. "When you have children, you will know. Until then, you can keep on doing Tas's bidding, and Creeda and I suffer. Our children suffer. Not just ours. More and more of Ergh's children the longer we wait."

Cador had never been close with Creeda, Bryok's wife, but he wished he could ease her pain and the pain of all suffering parents. If Tas believed patience and forming bonds with the Neuvellans was the way forward, Cador had to trust he was right. Tas had such faith in him, and Cador would not disappoint him now.

Bryok sneered toward Jem. "Bet he fucks like a wet kitten too." His razor glare turned to Cador. "Did you lower yourself so far as to stick your prick in him?"

"No!" He exhaled a sound of disgust. "I'd rather fuck a boar." Since Bryok knew the plot, there was no need to deceive him and pretend the marriage was real. Cador was pathetically relieved he could honestly deny it. Relieved the truth would please his brother, despite trying not to care.

Bryok spat over the railing into the churning sea. "That's something, at least."

As they stood in uneasy silence, Cador found himself glancing over at Jem and wondering what the boy *would* fuck like if he ever got up the nerve to spread his legs.

It would surely be as Cador told Kensa—like screwing a plank of wood, except the wood wouldn't cower. But what would it be like if Jem actually embraced desire and passion and the joy of fucking? What kind of sounds would he make as he took Cador's cock inside his small, lean body? As he surrendered? He would surely be deliciously tight…

"You deserve better."

Cador couldn't stop the sweet flare of gratitude at Bryok's words and the brief clasp of his hand on Cador's shoulder. He despised how much he treasured those gifts from his brother— the rare, muttered kindnesses or compliments. He hated how he yearned for more, like a dog begging for scraps.

It was the thought of food that did it. Without warning, he heaved over the side. Bryok's laughter echoed in his ears along with blood rushing as Cador hung his head, the rail hard against his ribs.

Bryok's mocking continued, others joining in. Most of them

hadn't spent much time on ships, so why did Cador seem to be the only one afflicted by this shame? For minutes, he spit and heaved again and again even though his stomach had surely emptied completely.

When he finally straightened, his mouth tasting like the foulest concoction, he tried to laugh along. Bryok had abandoned him there in his shame. The others eventually went back to their groups over the deck, many playing a game of dice in the shelter of the great mast. Delen shook her head at him with both mocking and sympathy.

Cador caught sight of Jem slowly approaching. "What?" he growled, forcing himself to let go of the rail.

Jem stopped short. "I only wanted to see if you're well."

"Do I fucking look well?"

"No."

Jem's simple honesty took Cador by surprise. He cringed at the thought of his appearance, wiping his mouth on his boarskin sleeve. He was a hunter of Ergh. Bryok was right—he was a warrior! He would not be defeated by a weak belly. "I'm fine."

"It's only..." Jem took a step closer. His dark curls were damp from sea spray that shone in the light of the thin moon. "I know a trick. We go sailing down at the seaside every summer."

"How wonderful for you."

"Although that sea is typically gentle, the swells can get large and the tides powerful. I learned that if you apply pressure to the right spots, it eases your stomach."

Cador scoffed. "Sounds like mainland nonsense. Is there a prayer to go along with it? Does the god of earth ground the swirling? Or Glaw calm the sea?"

"No. The healer said it's to do with the currents in the body. Also, if you close your eyes, the sickness will be worse. Keep watching the water and the horizon."

"I am! I don't need your help."

"All right." Jem turned.

"Although if I were to humor you, what is this trick?" Cador had tasted enough acrid bile already, and they had weeks to go aboard the ship.

"Hold out your wrist."

Watching Jem carefully, he extended his right arm. Was this a trick of another kind? There was no way Jem could overpower him, but perhaps he had something else in mind. "I warn you, if you try to fool me or…"

Jem took hold of Cador's wrist, his fingers light and gaze steady. "I only want to help."

"Why?" Cador glowered down at him.

Jem glanced over to Bryok and the others. "They don't seem willing to try."

And why should they? Why should I have help? It's my own weakness. I'd mock me too.

Carefully, as if he handled the hoof of a boar who wasn't quite dead yet, Jem turned Cador's un-branded palm to the heavens. Bending his head, he pressed three of his fingers to the softer skin of Cador's inner wrist, his thumb firm on the other side. He continued pressing and did nothing else.

"Well?" Cador demanded. "What is this trick?"

"Pressure here helps alleviate the sickness." Although his hands were cold, the steady force warmed the skin where Jem touched. "In some, one side is more effective than the other. For most people, it's the right."

Cador scoffed. "This is it? This is nothing!"

"Just wait."

"For fuck's sake." He tugged his wrist—but Jem held on with

unexpected strength. Cador was so surprised he let him.

"Be patient."

And that was the order of the day, wasn't it? If Cador had to trust Tas and wait, perhaps he could spare a bit more patience for Jem. Especially since his empty stomach clenched ominously as the waves grew higher. Especially if it could actually work. Cador did as Jem said and kept his eyes on the shadowy horizon.

Jem followed his gaze. "Don't you find it…"

After a few moments of silence, Cador couldn't resist asking, "What?" There was no reason he should give a shit what Jem was thinking, yet curiosity tugged.

"There's so *much* of it." Jem stared out at the silver-capped waves. "I never imagined the world could be this vast." He sounded both awed and afraid. "When I sailed in the Southern Sea, the water was so clear in the sunlight that I could see schools of fish zigzagging. We only went out for the day and never lost sight of the land. Here, it's…endless." He shuddered. "How do you know the way to Ergh?"

"I don't, but Meraud will guide us true. She knows the Askorn Sea like the back of her hand."

"How? If Ergh has remained solitary all these years, where would she have gone?"

"She grew up fishing and now captains this ship around the island to make trade. The land is impassable in parts, so we use ships for goods. But I'd rarely been on one before we came to the mainland."

Jem pressed steadily with his fingers, a little smile lifting his lush lips. "I imagine you prefer solid ground."

"Yes," Cador admitted since he'd obviously betrayed this weakness. If Jem's trick worked, at least it would make the days to come more bearable.

"Wait, did you say there is fishing in Ergh? I thought the Askorn Sea was too forbidding to hold any life."

Cador had to laugh at that. "What nonsense. Of course there are fish in these waters." He couldn't resist adding, "All sorts of creatures lurk beneath the surface."

Jem's eyes widened, and he stared down at the heaving waves. "I can imagine." Then light seemed to dance in his eyes in the pale moonlight. "Has anyone ever spotted a merman?"

"What? Of course not." More mainland nonsense. Their heads were all full of clouds. Still, Cador found his lips twitching at Jem's fanciful expression.

"Hmm. Suppose not. Watch the horizon," Jem reminded him as icy wind whipped. "Seems Glaw is determined to torment us. Hwytha of the wind too. Earth and fire must be napping."

Cador didn't try to keep the scorn from his voice. "Do you imagine them in the heavens, peering down as we would watch ants scurry? Flicking us and playing their games?"

"Honestly? No."

"No?" After witnessing the piousness of the clerics and obedient delegates, it wasn't the answer Cador expected. Certainly not from timid little Jem. "But I thought all mainlanders believe."

"Most, I imagine. It's the way we're taught. That when we die, we ascend to the heavens to be one with the gods, to become part of the very wind and water and earth, sparks for an eternal flame. It's a nice idea."

"Yet you rebel?"

Jem shrugged. "I suppose, although I don't..." His brow furrowed. "I've actually never told anyone I don't believe. Not even Santo, my favorite sibling."

It was an odd sensation to be the one receiving the confession. Jem's fingers pressed against Cador's wrist, warm and firm. Cador almost tore away from his grasp, suddenly wanting more distance between them.

Yet he found himself asking, "When did you stop believing?"

"I'm not sure. Years ago now." The wind gusted, and he leaned closer, gripping Cador's wrist.

If Cador bent over him, he could feel the damp softness of those soft, glossy curls against his cheek. He had no interest in that, but they stood close enough.

Jem said, "I think the seas roil because of the tides and the wind, and in dry summers, the earth is parched and fires are easily sparked. It's simply the way of the world. Sometimes the way of the world is puzzling, but it's nothing to do with fanciful gods and their whims." He glanced up and flashed a smile. "Heresy, I know."

That spirited grin sent a bolt through Cador, reminding him of Jem's solitary jest at their wedding feast. Seemed the boy wasn't entirely timid after all. "I'd say it's reason. A relief to hear that at least one mainlander resists the teachings of the clerics."

"And in Ergh?"

"Most think it's garbage, although some believe. Especially now."

Jem frowned. "Why now?"

Cador cursed himself for his stupid mouth. Why was he even wasting his time speaking with a spoiled prince who could never understand a thing about Ergh or true hardship?

He shook his wrist free as the ship heaved—sending Jem off balance, arms wheeling as he struck the railing. The motion of the sea lifted him off his feet as the ship rocked, dipping to that side, saltwater spraying up.

Grabbing for him, Cador got a handful of Delen's cloak. He grasped for flesh and bone with his other hand, finding Jem's shoulder and steadying him.

"Tossing him overboard already?" Jory appeared, reaching for Jem and helping secure him.

Cador laughed. "Not yet. Maybe tomorrow."

Jem yanked free with a violent jerk of surprising might. He was most definitely not laughing, staring daggers at Jory.

Cador huffed. "It was a jest." This was why he shouldn't waste his time with Jem. He stalked away, determined to join the dice game, tugging Jory along.

Yet his stride faltered, and he spun around. "Sleep below," Cador ordered Jem. "Use my furs." It was too cold for him on deck, that was certain. "You're no use to us dead," he grumbled, walking away before Jem could reply.

After laughing along with more jabs from his friends at his sea-weak stomach—Cador didn't want to turn into a sulky mainlander who couldn't take a jest—he sat on a crate and took his turn at dice, gulping down ale that at least coated his throat and tongue with a pleasant flavor and wouldn't taste so bad if it came up. Although he was feeling better.

Beneath his cloak as the night grew late and bitter in the north wind, he pressed his fingers to the inside of his wrist and kept his gaze glued to the horizon.

Chapter Eight

J EM HAD BEEN right all along—Ergh didn't exist.

It couldn't, not when day after endless day passed with the ship sailing on and on and on. When he'd woken below after the first long night rocking on the waves and ventured up, he'd found not a speck on the horizon in any direction. It was an unbearably lonely sight, and he'd been gripped with a strange despair.

He'd known it would take longer than a single night to reach Ergh, yet beholding all that nothingness in the milky gray light of a new day had shaken him in a way he hadn't expected and could barely explain—although no one had asked. It made him feel unbearably small and lost, yearning for his family. Even Pasco and Locryn, for at least they were familiar.

That morning, Cador had been laughing with Jory about something across the deck, and Jem could imagine how they'd mock him if he confessed his fear and loneliness. Why should they care? Cador was his husband in name only. The tusks seared into Jem's flesh were meaningless. He'd retreated back into the hold, where he didn't have to see how very far from home he was.

He'd stayed huddled in the hold since, as near the stove's warmth as he could get without the cook glaring at him. When he went above to relieve himself through a hole at the stern—which he only did when absolutely necessary—he was typically ignored. Although at times, Cador's gaze made his skin prickle.

His fear that he'd perish and never return home lingered, its stubborn teeth sharp. Even if Cador didn't hurl him into the endless depths of the Askorn Sea, Ergh would surely be a place of danger. A wild land of wilder people who would likely sneer at Jem too. And who was to say Cador wouldn't be rid of him if the opportunity arose?

Though he knew Jory had indeed only been jesting about Cador tossing him overboard, and there were signs of goodness in his husband—small kindnesses such as giving Jem his furs. The flash of dimples when Jem had declared himself a heretic.

He'd also given his vow to keep Jem safe. Not only during their wedding—which neither of them had meant a word of—but on the morning of their departure. Cador had promised Jem's mother he'd protect him, although he hadn't sounded particularly enthused by the prospect. Jem could only hope he was a man of his word nonetheless.

He'd been both relieved to be left alone in the hold and resentful that Cador didn't ask what was amiss. Over the past few days or so—it was hard to keep track—Cador had begun appearing in the hold. Each day, he loomed over Jem and asked the same question:

"Are you going to laze about down here all day?"

The sight of the unbroken horizon was still too terrifying, so Jem would nod in reply, and Cador would grunt and stalk away.

Today, he hadn't come. Jem had slipped up to the main deck before dawn to relieve himself in the darkness before retreating to his corner, the cook boiling bitter tea when he returned. Listening to the ship's creaks and groans, footsteps noisy above the wind's hiss, Jem had waited for Cador to come and ask his question.

Was he ill? Perhaps he was merely occupied with some task. Or perhaps he'd tired of asking his pointless question. Jem told himself that, whatever the reason, it was of no concern to him whether or not Cador checked on him.

He sipped the horrible tea from a chipped mug while the cook stirred a thin broth across the way. Jem had offered to help with the food, although he admittedly hadn't done so much as boil a pot of water in his entire life. The cook had practically growled at him to get away.

If Cador *was* ill, surely someone would tell him? Not that Jem could do anything about it. He could heal birds, but knew nothing about people. And why would they tell him? If anyone, it would be Jory kneeling at Cador's side to comfort him. Perhaps wipe his sweaty brow if he had a fever. And why shouldn't it be Jory? They were lovers, after all.

His stomach sour, Jem gulped down the rest of the tea. As if conjured by his musings, thudding footsteps approached the open doorway to this area of the hold. When Cador filled the passage with his broad shoulders, frowning down at Jem curled in the corner, unexpected relief flowed. Clearly he was not ill or injured or washed overboard.

Jem waited for the question, wondering for the first time if he should give a different answer. The endless sea was no less real for being hidden from view. Perhaps it was time to stop feeling sorry for himself and face his fate.

"Are you ill?" Cador demanded.

Jem blinked in surprise at the different question. Aloud, he only said, "No."

"Then what the fuck's the matter? You've barely been outside."

Jem shrugged, not wanting to voice the reason, shame prickling him. He shouldn't have given in to his fear, yet now he was stubbornly stuck.

"You act as though you're imprisoned down here. You're not!"

Unsure why Cador sounded so angry and defensive, Jem shrugged again.

Nostrils flaring, Cador crossed his meaty arms. "Do I need to beat it out of you?"

Some mad impulse had Jem shrugging a third time. Perhaps he wanted to see if Cador really would. One way or another, he'd have a better measure of his husband. *Husband.* It was absurd! Yet here they were.

Cador's jaw clenched, a muscle twitching in his cheek. His beard had grown, and Jem oddly wondered what it would feel like against his own stubbornly smooth face.

"It's not good to be shut away down here. You need air."

"We speak and breathe right now. Clearly there's air."

"*Fresh* air. If you're not sick already, you'll make yourself weak. Weaker."

Jem risked another shrug.

Cador dropped his arms to his sides, exasperation joining his annoyance. "For fuck's sake, what is wrong with you? Stop being like..." He motioned roughly at Jem. "*This.*"

So it seemed the threat to beat him was indeed an empty one. Despite reminding himself not to lower his guard, Jem couldn't stop the little bloom of warmth in his chest. "It's fine. You don't need to worry."

"I'm not!" He ran a hand over his shorn head.

"Why do some of you wear your hair short and others long?"

Cador blinked. "What?"

"There seems to be meaning to it."

"Oh. Yes." He ran his hand over his head again. "Only hunters crop our hair."

"Why?"

Cador seemed stumped by the question. "Tradition. And don't change the subject. Tell me what's wrong with you."

"Why?" Jem found himself wanting to test Cador's patience. See how far he could push and prod. How Cador would respond. Likely unwise with a ruthless hunter who'd threatened to beat him, but Jem couldn't resist knowing more about this man.

"I swear, if you ask that again…" Cador glowered down at him. Yet there was no weight to the threat, not really. "You can't be this lazy and useless. Tell me what's wrong so I can fix it."

There. That was a confession. Oh, how Jem understood the urge to *fix*. The answering need in him to help—to soothe Cador's agitation—rose up, and the truth tumbled out.

"I hate seeing nothing but the sea. It's frightening to be so removed from home. From any land at all. Down here, I don't have to see it. I can pretend I'm not so very far away."

Cador stared, seemingly surprised. Whether by the words themselves or that Jem had uttered them at all, he wasn't sure. Cador opened and closed his mouth, the silence following Jem's admission stretching out.

Finally, he said, "Then you're in luck."

"Am I?" Jem asked dubiously.

At that, Cador smiled suddenly, dimpling his grizzled cheek and making Jem's belly somersault. "Might be a strong word, 'luck.' But Ergh is in sight."

Jem's spine straightened. "Truly?"

"Yes. Come. See for yourself." After a moment's hesitation,

he extended his hand.

Jem's breath caught. Part of him wanted to remain huddled under the furs, safe within four creaking walls, yearning for his books. Alone with his daydreams of Morvoren and her adventures where all ended well without fail. But how long could daydreams sustain him? He was weary of his own self-pity.

A new excitement cartwheeled through him as he reached up and took Cador's callused right hand. The clasp was only for the space of a heartbeat—Cador hauling him to his feet as if Jem weighed nothing at all, his hand big and warm and enclosing Jem's completely in a powerful grasp. The brand twinged, but it was mostly healed now. Cador let go, marching to the stairs and leaving Jem to follow if he chose.

Jem took a deep breath and followed, ready for his first glimpse of Ergh. Perhaps it would be beautiful after all. Perhaps it would be a land of remote tranquility and—

Rock.

Jagged stone looming from the bitter iron sea. The sky hung heavy with clouds, looking as though they met the merciless cliffs, forming an impenetrable wall of gray. Jem had returned Delen's cloak to her ages ago and left Cador's furs below. He wished he had them now as the wind pummeled him. Strange clouds appeared in front of his face, and he jerked back, briefly clutching Cador's muscled arm for balance.

"What's that?" Jem swatted at the clouds.

Cador chuckled. "Your breath. You can see it in the air when it's cold."

Sure enough, the mist escaped his own mouth and nose. Jem tentatively moved his hand through the white air again, yet felt nothing, the clouds disappearing after a few seconds.

"You've really never been anywhere cold." Cador sounded

mystified.

"No. Well, this is certainly cold." Jem stared at the gray island, trying to find a hint of beauty or a reminder of home. His body had gone so rigid that he thought he might shatter. With stiff fingers, he pulled his red cloak tighter around him.

A wave of new loneliness washed over him, even stronger than it had been when he was huddled alone below. This distant land might as well have been the moon in the sky. He saw not a bit of color or comfort. Ergh was barren. He yearned for verdant grasses and honeysuckle breezes, his aviary by the lake where he was safe and in control. Where everything was as familiar as the worn pages of his favorite books.

Jem realized he had to speak lest he be unbearably rude. Not that Cador cared what Jem thought, but still. "It's...impressive. I've never seen such cliffs before."

That was true, at least. Jem had once visited Ebrenn's mountains, snow-capped high above, soaring above evergreen forests and crisp, clear rivers that cut through fields of wildflowers in spring. It had been warm enough that he hadn't even needed his lightest cloak.

Cador said, "The Cliffs of Glaw are a natural defense. Any invaders would be spotted by the watch before having to sail farther around."

"Yes," Jem agreed, peering up at the sheer rock faces. The cliffs jutted out in a series of impossibly narrow peninsulas. There was no shore below, the rock faces disappearing into the roiling white water.

"They're like the fingers of a hand."

"Oh, yes." Jem could see it now, five massive peninsulas with the sea between them, darkness in the depths.

"Anyone who tries to scale these cliffs will be crushed in

Ergh's fist."

"Seems likely," Jem agreed. He squinted at the nearest rock face. "What's that blob there? Not too far from the top."

Cador followed Jem's gaze. "Likely a dred nest. They're huge birds. They feed on fish and nest on cliff faces where their young are safer from predators. The rock face looks smooth from a distance, but there are some deep, narrow gouges. The dreds build out their nests with thick branches of pine needles, keeping their young safe behind them in the rock's crevices."

Jem listened avidly, wishing he could get a closer look. Signs of life! Birds he'd never heard of! A small bloom of excitement fought to unfurl. "Ah. There aren't many large birds in Neuvella. Why don't the dreds nest high in the trees? Surely that would be safer than perching on the side of a cliff?"

Cador frowned. "I don't know. Never thought about it. They eat fish, so I suppose they like staying close to their food. The nests are damn impressive. Built to withstand the fierce Askorn wind. When I was a boy, my brother once lowered me down on a rope. I could sit right in the nest and it bore my weight. I was a child, but not a particularly small one."

"That is impressive. And if they use branches for their nests, there must be trees on Ergh?" Jem asked hopefully.

"Of course. You think we live on nothing but rock and dirt?"

"No!" Jem opened and closed his mouth. "Well, these cliffs give a rather…foreboding first impression."

Cador looked up at them, the cliffs towering higher and higher. He grunted, which Jem thought meant he agreed.

The rest of the ship's passengers went about their business, ignoring Jem near the bow. Delen did come to ask if he wanted her cloak again, but it didn't seem right. He could stand being cold. He had to toughen up. Cador didn't offer his.

White flakes soon swirled in the air. Hard pinpricks pelted his face as the wind gusted, and Jem realized it was snow, of course. He held out his palm, watching pale flakes sit on his skin before melting. Morvoren had once journeyed to a northern land, where she'd frolicked in soft pillows of fresh snow after defeating a dragon king. Her merman lover swam under the ice and surprised her, whisking her off to make love before a roaring fire. She'd never mentioned her ears feeling so cold in the wind that they burned.

"What do you think of snow?" Cador asked.

"It's terribly unpleasant." Jem held out his hand for more flakes. "Yet beautiful as well. I've glimpsed it before only from a distance, atop the mountains in Ebrenn."

After a few beats of silence, Cador asked, "What do you make of them?"

"The mountains? Don't you have any here on Ergh?"

"Yes, in the north. I meant the people."

"Oh! The Ebrennians?" Jem considered it. "The people themselves are fine, I suppose. Their king is a miserable sort. Usually fighting with my mother about something. They've been threatening battle against her lately, but I'm sure the clerics will smooth it over. I've met some at official events, but I can't say I actually know anyone from Ebrenn. But I keep to myself except when my parents force me to be a prince."

"Have you always shirked your duty?"

Jem cringed. He did sound spoiled, didn't he? "It's just that I'm not very good at it. Diplomacy. Politics. I'd much rather be tending my birds or reading."

"We'd all rather be doing something else."

"What would you be doing if you could?"

"Hunting," he answered without hesitation. "Riding Massen

deep in the forest."

"Massen?"

"My stallion." There was fondness in his tone.

The ship rocked, the mast creaking in the gusty wind. From the corner of his eye, Jem spotted Cador gripping his own wrist, pressing the spots Jem had shown him.

Pleasure flushed him warmly, an odd feeling of accomplishment at the small aid he'd given. Still, it was no match for the wicked wind, colder than Jem had imagined possible. He hugged himself, his cloak far too thin. Soon, his teeth chattered.

Cador scowled. "Why are you doing that? Put up your hood. Where are your gloves?"

"I don't have any."

"For fuck's sake," he grumbled. "Why didn't your people pack what was necessary?"

Jem thought of his books with a pang of longing. "Isn't it supposed to be spring?"

"Soon. It comes later to the North." He yanked at Jem's hands, grasping them between his own and rubbing. "We'll arrive at Rusk in an hour. Don't want you to lose fingers in the meantime. Tas wouldn't approve, and you'll be even more useless."

Jem couldn't tamp down the sparks of pleasure from Cador's rough ministrations. He tried not to think about the fact that it was the most he'd ever been touched by another man he wasn't related to. Which was silly—they were standing on a ship with people milling around. This wasn't *that* kind of touch.

His mind very helpfully conjured memories of the night in the valley, the Erghians bedding each other noisily out in the open with no shame. He scoffed at himself. This was far from coupling, even if Cador's hands sent spirals of heat not only through Jem's chilled fingers but all the way to the tips of his cold toes, traveling through his groin.

Gods, Cador was so big and broad, towering over Jem, standing as close as they had at the altar. He had full lips, and Jem peeked up at them through his lashes. What would they feel like on Jem's mouth? How would they taste? What of Cador's tongue? Jem had dreamed of kissing a man like him—of being swept up in his burly arms, his mouth plundered, breathing in little gasps, tasting hungrily…

What was wrong with him? He didn't even like this brute! Although… Cador was being kind now, warming Jem's hands. But *was* he being kind? There was no reason whatsoever Jem should want to kiss him.

No reason to want to see a true, dimpled smile from him again. Jem must rein in his curiosity and remember he was on his own. He tugged his hands free and stumbled back. "Thank you! I'll be fine!"

Cador shrugged and walked away, and Jem kept his hands balled in his cloak pockets as the voyage continued around the west of Ergh, the cliffs giving way to more rock that was slightly less terrifyingly sheer. The snow tapered off, although the wind remained icy.

The land eventually sloped closer to the level of the sea, these cliffs topped with mud and what had to be dead yellow grass that would hopefully turn green soon.

Huts and cottages appeared, a village revealing its edges. The island curved, providing a natural harbor, the ship angling toward the shore of black rocks. There was no beach to speak off, just inky black stones.

Perhaps they were stopping briefly in the village before continuing on their way to Rusk, which Delen had told him was the capital. She'd said there were villages scattered all over the island, but the chieftain had always lived in Rusk.

Cador returned to order, "Get my furs from below."

"Are we stopping here?"

Cador frowned. "Of course. We're here."

"We're where?" Jem glanced up at the stone huts.

"Rusk."

"But..." Jem stood on tiptoes, craning his neck. "Where's the castle?"

"Castle?" Jory repeated, appearing at Cador's side. He laughed and shouted to the ship, "Prince Jowan wonders where the castle is!"

Jem shrank into his cloak as more laughter roared. He muttered, "I just assumed..."

Jory grinned. "This isn't the mainland. No castles on Ergh. That's not how we live." He slapped Jem's shoulder. "But if you make Cador love you, perhaps he'll build you one. He's a fine builder when he sets his mind to it."

Jem shrugged away Jory's hand with a violent twitch as Cador said, "Piss off!" without real heat. He and Jory left, laughing together.

If you make Cador love you.

Was such a thing even possible? Jem scoffed. Even if so, it was the last thing he wanted. When he returned home—the thought of Neuvella's verdant warmth filling him with an awful yearning—he'd find a good, reasonable man for a lover. Someone with whom he could share comfortable affection. Companionship. Thrilling adventures and wild passion with a muscled man could stay on the pages of Jem's books.

Another ache of longing racked him so forcefully he had to close his eyes and grip the rail. If only he had the familiar comfort of his favorite tales with him in Ergh, the time would pass so much more quickly. There was nothing to be done for it but soldier on. Jem had to focus on representing his people with dignity.

He stared up at the cliffs of Rusk, people gathering atop. He couldn't see them well at a distance. Soon he trudged behind Cador up the path cut into rock, a zigzagging trail too steep to ride. His legs burned, and he could certainly see why there were no carriages on Ergh if the land was all this harsh.

Jem felt the needles of the Erghians' curious attention. He could handle curious—it was the hostile looks boring into him that had him tripping over his own feet. He stumbled, and Cador hauled him up, his stride not faltering. Jem would have thanked him, but he couldn't spare the breath. His heart pounded and sweat gathered on his lower back despite the chill.

The people of Rusk wore the same kind of clothing—leather skins, furs, rough material. Some women wore thick skirts, others trousers. There wasn't a color in evidence brighter than a child's dark green hat, and Jem was like a beacon in his red cloak. He felt foolish and small, and gods, so very cold as snow fell anew.

People hugged roughly and spoke low, the villagers all seeming quite serious. There were hardly any smiles, and Jem wondered why it wasn't a more joyous reunion with the traveling party.

The boy with the green hat seemed too old to be carried, yet a stone-faced woman held him before passing him to Bryok. Jem presumed she was his wife. Her skin was a light copper, her hair dark and knotted tightly.

She approached, and instead of calling to Cador or greeting him with a smile or wave, she stepped in his path. Although thin—her granite face bordering on gaunt—there was some-thing bullish about her. A good match for Bryok, Jem presumed.

"Creeda," Cador said, his smile not coming close to dim-pling his cheeks. "Are you well?"

For several moments, she merely stared up at him. Ignoring his question, she said, "Come to the house for a feast. Hedrok misses you. All the children do."

Cador's gaze flicked to the too-old boy Bryok carried. He waved to the child with a grin that still wasn't true. To Creeda, he said, "Soon. I'm not free to feast." He looked to Jem at his shoulder with a rueful twist of his expression. Not quite a sneer, but certainly not a smile. "Let me greet him now."

Cador went to Bryok and the boy, presumably Hedrok, giving him a long embrace and speaking to him with what looked to Jem like false cheer. Curious, Jem moved to join them, but Creeda blocked his way.

Her eyes were narrowed with suspicion. Did the people of Ergh hate mainlanders they'd never met on principle? Had the clerics made such a bad impression? Well… That was certainly possible. Not Onan's greatest ambassadors unless the Erghians enjoyed being lectured and bored silly.

Creeda stalked away to her husband while Cador continued to speak with her son. Delen approached her and they hugged tightly. Jem hung back, letting Cador have his privacy. When he returned, Jem opened his mouth to ask what was wrong with the boy, but instead found himself scurrying to catch Cador's long strides.

The buildings in Rusk were constructed of rough stone and timber, the main part of the village clustered in the distance. Certainly no castles in evidence, with the largest building long and low, and none of the houses more than a single level. No rolling fields of flowers stretched to the horizon, nor was there any evidence of the lush, green vegetation of Neuvella.

In the leaden sky, large birds of prey cawed in greedy cries instead of trilling songs that hung on the breeze. Jem had never worked with the taloned eagles of the mainland since they were only common in the West. These birds of Ergh looked impossibly huge, more like flying beasts than the fluttering creatures Jem knew.

People stared outright at him now, hissing to each other, the news of the marriage clearly spreading through Rusk. Jem's cheeks burned, but he forced himself to keep his head high, his gaze on Cador's broad back as he trailed behind him. There was no presentation of him to the townsfolk. No introduction to any of the people who greeted Cador as he made his way.

Evergreens like in Ebrenn grew deep and forbidding beyond the village, unlike any sun-dappled forest Jem had seen before. As much as he loved trees, he wasn't eager to venture near. Naturally, toward the forest was precisely where Cador marched, Jem scurrying to keep up, the pressure of hundreds of eyes boring into him.

He breathed a sigh of relief when they neared a stable, apparently leaving the main area of Rusk and its people behind. A young man with long dark hair tied back led a truly massive stallion outside, its midnight coat gleaming.

The man stared curiously at Jem, giving him a tentative smile after handing over the reins to Cador. But he said nothing before disappearing inside. No introduction. Jem supposed Ergh had never had the opportunity to welcome a visitor before aside from the clerics, and the clerics would be tiresome guests.

The horse whinnied, butting Cador with its head as Cador

laughed—a new, gentle sound unlike the laughter he'd shared with Jory and the others. Cador nuzzled the horse, caressing its flowing mane and murmuring to it.

The animal had clearly missed him, rubbing against Cador and nickering. If it had been able, Jem imagined the horse would stand on its back legs and envelope Cador in a hug. And Jem had no doubt this fierce barbarian would have hugged it back.

As Cador scratched the horse's ears, Jem caught some of the low words.

"I missed you too. My special boy."

There was no reason for the words to send a forbidden thrill shooting down Jem's spine. He wasn't a boy—he was a man! He didn't want to be anyone's boy, least of all Cador's. And he didn't care to be special to Cador either. Not at all.

There was no reason to be suddenly, deeply, profoundly jealous of a horse.

No reason to wonder what it would be like to have Cador whisper those words in his ear, lips close…

"Are you ready?"

Jem realized Cador was addressing him. His prick had swelled shamefully, luckily hidden beneath his cloak. What was the matter with him? The man was reuniting with his horse, and Jem was somehow aroused by innocent words.

He blurted an honest answer. "No."

Cador laughed—another quiet rumble, not one of the loud roars he made when he was in his cups. "I suppose I can't blame you." He turned away, and Jem had no choice but to follow.

Although they could have ridden Massen, Cador walked him, perhaps eager to feel solid ground beneath his boots after the constant rocking of the ship. Jem's backside was grateful.

Massen carried Cador's furs and a few sacks on its broad back.

At the edge of the forest, Jem realized they were quite alone now. He stopped, glancing behind. Snow dusted the muddy ground, and smoke trailed lazily into the gray sky from Rusk's chimneys. Peering into the murky forest, Jem couldn't even spot a path. Alarmingly, Cador and Massen almost disappeared with only a few strides into the trees.

"Wait! Where are we going?" Jem wasn't sure which he feared more—being left alone in the village or vanishing into the forest with Cador. The wind had died down, at least.

Cador turned, his face in shadow. "Home." He frowned. "To my home, I mean. My cottage."

"In there?"

"Clearly. Now come. The light will soon fade."

Standing on the edge of impenetrable shadows on the frozen island of Ergh, Jem truly understood how fortunate he'd been his whole life long. Until that day at the Holy Place when he'd discovered he'd been betrothed. When had it been? A week? Two weeks ago? He wasn't even sure. It felt like forever.

Until then, he'd been able to do exactly as he pleased. He'd lived in comfort and safety with wealth and his mother's protection and indulgence. The last thing he wanted to do now was follow his barbarian husband into the impossibly dense forest as darkness threatened.

Yet Jem straightened his shoulders and did just that, sending a silent prayer to Morvoren—she was far more of a god to him than those of earth, wind, water, and fire. May she guide his steps and give him courage.

Cador led the way, and Jem realized once they were in the forest that there was a path cut through the trees, wide enough for Massen. Here there was barely any snow on the ground, instead it hung on the boughs above. A fresh, almost minty smell filled Jem's nose, the needles of the trees surprisingly soft underfoot.

The desperate chirping was at once wonderfully familiar and alarming. Cador strode right past it, but Jem stopped, peering into the gloom to locate the nest. He called to Cador, "Wait, please!" before leaving the path and following the sharp cries.

There! Jem raced between trees and fell to his knees by the fallen nest, which was a bramble of twigs and needles. The hatchlings were abandoned in their broken eggs, these shells colored a dark, rusty orange-red that looked like dried blood.

The dillywigs and sparrows back home had pale blue and speckled brown shells. These hatchlings cried, their eyes not even open, no feathers yet on their gray bodies. Their mouths gaped wide.

"Shh, it's all right." Jem wished he could cradle them, but it was too soon. Twigs snapped as Cador approached. Jem asked him, "What birds are these?"

He loomed over them, his brow creased. "Askells."

"Askells," Jem repeated, rolling the word over his tongue. "We don't have askells on the mainland."

"You'll see plenty here." Then Cador raised his foot.

At the last second, Jem realized his intent and launched forward from his crouch. "No!" He grabbed onto Cador's thigh, knocking him off balance enough to halt the motion of stomping on the nest. He wrapped his arms around Cador's leg, which felt rather like warm iron. "Don't kill them!"

"What? Why? Get off me!" Cador seized Jem under the arms and yanked him to his feet. "They can't survive. Better to end it quickly."

"They *can* survive! I can help them! I've done it before with other birds."

Cador glanced down at the askells, frowning. "Impossible when they're hatched too early."

"I can do it. At least I can try."

"But…" He seemed genuinely confused. "They suffer. You'd prolong that rather than be merciful?"

"I will ease their suffering and help them live." Jem unclasped his cloak and knelt on the scattered needles. He folded it, gently placing the nest inside. "At least I can try."

"It's a waste of time."

Jem ignored Cador, carefully lifting his precious cargo. "We must hurry. They need food quickly."

Cador shook his head, but didn't argue as he stomped back to the path, Jem rushing after him. When they reached Massen, Cador unceremoniously lifted Jem onto the stallion's back, then wrapped him in the furs with quick, harsh movements. Jem enveloped the nest, keeping it protected in his cloak and under the furs.

"Thank you."

"Don't fall off!" Cador barked. He muttered, "I must be fucking mad," as he mounted. He secured one strong arm around Jem's waist, holding him safe.

Ignoring the twinge in his backside from being on horseback again, Jem hid his smile, murmuring to the birds as Cador urged Massen into a gallop, deeper into this strange new world.

Chapter Nine

ALL MEEKNESS VANISHED, Jem barged right into the cottage. Who did he think he was? Although Cador had to admit he preferred the show of spirit and purpose over Jem's sad huddle in the ship's belly during that endless fucking voyage.

It had gnawed at him, although even Delen had said he should leave Jem be. But Jem hadn't been a prisoner yet, and it'd been maddening that he'd acted like one. It had scraped at Cador like rusty nails, his guilt festering.

Besides, what if Jem had taken ill and died because he couldn't be bothered to get fresh air? Cador couldn't have that. They needed him alive. At least until the time came. But even then... If everyone cooperated, there would be no need for Jem to *die*.

Pushing all of that aside and locking it away, Cador strode after Jem now, torn between going to the goats bleating at the fence of their pen and finding out what Jem was going to do with those suffering birds. Curiosity won.

On the stone hearth by the wide fireplace, Jem crouched, holding a log from the stack. He placed it on the iron grate, then gazed around the hearth. "How do you light it?"

"You've never sparked your own fire, little prince?" He should have guessed.

"It's not usually cold enough for a fire. Only once in a while, and yes, a servant lit them for me." The bundled nest sat at

Jem's side, and he peered in seriously, a faint screeching coming from within. Eyes on the birds, he asked, "Can you please light a fire for me? It feels just as cold in here as outside."

Cador gritted his teeth. Of course it fucking did—he'd been gone for weeks. It wasn't some failing on his part or Ergh's. Who did this spoiled brat think he was to criticize? This was Cador's home, and Jem would end up sleeping in the stable if he didn't watch it.

The birds cried pitifully.

Muttering under his breath, Cador stomped to the fireplace. "Move!" he ordered, bending to build the fire. He set the logs, added kindling from a box tucked against the chimney's base, then grabbed his flint stone, childishly satisfied when Jem gasped at the shower of sparks and scurried out of the way, cradling the nest.

Kneeling, Cador blew steadily on the tinder, flames soon licking at the logs stacked in just the right way for a fire to burn steadily for hours once it took hold. He couldn't remember not knowing how to build a fire. Not knowing how to ride or fuck or even create warmth—what a strange existence Jem had. He likely couldn't cook either. What *was* he capable of? Did he really know how to nurse the birds?

"Thank you," Jem said.

Cador grunted, teasing and prodding the kindling. "Why do you care about these doomed creatures?"

"Because no one else will."

Cador thought of the rocking ship, Jem pressing on his wrist, easing his suffering when others only mocked it.

"Are there worms in the earth?" Jem asked.

"Worms? Yes." What the fuck did worms have to do with anything?

"Can you fetch me some, please?"

Jem bent over the nest on the hearth at Cador's side, fussing and murmuring. Fetch him some worms? Since when did Cador take orders? He surely didn't from this little prince.

Yet the trembling askells cried, and Cador soon found himself outside the cottage, eyeing the mud. He hadn't dug up worms since he was a boy. He clawed at the thawing ground until he had a writhing fistful.

By the flickering fire, Jem knelt with the nest. Cador stalked over and dropped the worms on the hearth. He stood back, waiting to see how Jem would get these birds to eat worms twice their size when they hadn't even opened their eyes and were clearly doomed. Cador should have done the merciful thing when he'd had the chance. He should have—

He had to choke down a startled shout when Jem plucked a wriggling worm from the stone floor, wiped dirt from it, and popped it straight into his mouth.

"What the fuck!" Cador gawked as Jem chewed patiently, then spat the mushed remains of the worm into his palm. He pinched a small portion between his fingers and dropped it into the gaping beaks of the birds one after the other.

Gaze glued to the shaking, crying babies, Jem merely said, "They must eat. If these askells are anything like dillywigs on the mainland, this is the way."

"You just ate a live worm." He'd have thought this prim boy would shy away from touching a dirty, wriggling worm, let alone putting it in his mouth. But to save the birds, it was apparently needed, and Jem had done it efficiently and calmly, focused solely on the welfare of the orphaned creatures.

He thought again of the patient press of Jem's fingers against his wrist on the ship. That trick had somehow worked to calm

Cador's heaving stomach. Perhaps the worms would work miracles too.

"I masticated a live worm into a pulp. I didn't swallow it." Jem gave him a curious look. "I wouldn't have thought you squeamish."

"I'm not!" Although as Jem calmly popped another wriggling worm into his mouth, Cador had to admit he was more comfortable with blood and guts than *that*.

He strode off to see to Massen and greet the other animals before Jem could ask him to help with the worm-chewing. Massen grazed lazily. A fresh chorus of bleats from the goats made Cador smile, the chickens squawking excitedly.

Cador opened the gate to the large pen that took up most of his clearing. The goats butted him, the chickens racing in circles. He petted the goats and laughed as Massen neared. "Getting jealous?" Cador asked.

His closest neighbor, who was still some distance away, had cared for the animals in Cador's absence. They all looked well, but Cador stayed, scratching and petting the goats and clucking to the chickens.

After a time, his skin prickled with the sensation of being watched. He looked back to find Jem in the cottage doorway, his arms crossed over his thin blue shirt. When he said nothing, Cador asked, "Do you need more worms?"

Jem shook his head.

"Then what?"

"Oh, I just…" He seemed to struggle for words. "I was going to ask you for some water."

The youngest goat nudged Cador's hand, and Cador absently scratched its ears. "Then don't just stand there."

But Jem didn't move, instead nodding at the animals. "They

like you."

He scoffed. "They like the food I give them." He looked down at the ugly goats. They baaed contentedly, sticking near to him. Because he killed boars to eat didn't mean he had to be cruel to other animals. The chickens laid eggs that filled his belly, and the goats' milk quenched his thirst. Why should these beasts not be happy?

He felt oddly as if he'd been caught out. Bryok had often sneered that he was too soft to be a hunter. But he loved the thrill of it and was grateful to the boars that were Ergh's lifeblood. Although now they knew the boars weren't enough…

"I've no experience with farm animals. They seem friendly."

"They are. As long as you know how to handle them. Goats will happily bite if you surprise them."

Jem nodded, and after a few moments of peering curiously at the animals asked, "Would you show me?"

He couldn't see the harm in it. "All right."

"Thank you." Jem shivered, rubbing his arms through the thin shirt.

Cador grumbled. "You'll need warmer clothes. Those Southern fabrics are useless here except during the height of summer. They'll deliver your trunk in the morning, but I'm sure that won't do any good."

Jem shrugged glumly. "My books are gone. There's not much else in there."

An uncomfortable twist of shame squeezed Cador's insides. Jem was still mourning the loss of his books? That trunk was far too heavy! Why should Cador feel guilty for putting the good of the horses and the traveling party ahead of a spoiled prince used to getting his way? He shouldn't.

But perhaps someone had collected the books and brought

them to Neuvella? Jem might have them again one day.

If he survives.

That nagging thought stalked Cador's mind. There was no reason for Jem to die. Tas said he'd be returned safely. Eventually. Minus his hand.

Cador shifted restlessly. It'd been easier to doom the Neuvellan prince to kidnapping and maiming when he'd been a faceless stranger who only existed to play his unwitting role in sparking war.

"How will I pay for new clothes?" Jem frowned. "I have no coin."

"How do you get things in Neuvella?"

Jem shifted, his gaze on his boots. "Ask for them."

"Naturally." Cador shook his head, reaching for the familiar resentment for mainlanders he'd been taught all of his days. "Well, don't worry. We share and trade here. I'll take care of it."

Jem looked up from under his thick lashes, quietly saying, "Thank you." His eyes really were striking.

"I'm stuck with you, so I can't have you freezing. Your teeth chattering will drive me mad. Get back inside!" He forced the reminders through his head.

Lazy little prince! Useless! He doesn't matter! Only Ergh matters.

After settling Massen in the small stable beyond the chicken coop, Cador went about his chores, welcoming the distraction. He'd built his cottage from stone and the trees he'd felled to create the circular clearing. Bryok hadn't understood why Cador didn't want a bigger house in Rusk, in a place of honor as befitting a child of the chieftain.

Both Bryok and Delen had built homes with multiple rooms, but Cador was satisfied with his one-room cottage for now. It was far enough from others for peace, but close enough not to be lonely. If he did marry one day and have children, he'd build on and carve out more of his clearing.

Standing at the well's pump filling his bucket, Cador faltered, splashing icy liquid over his hands. He *was* married. Which he knew—of course he did. He had a foolish bird burned into his palm, didn't he? He'd never cared to marry and knew love was a fool's game. So why should he care now? Why should an odd hollowness haunt him?

There was something about having Ergh under his boots, the mint of evergreen needles filling his nose, smoke curling into the darkening sky from the chimney he'd built. Here in his clearing, on his little corner of the land, he didn't have to represent Tas or worry about what Bryok thought, or do anything except be.

Yet now Jem was here in Cador's sanctuary. With his ridiculous name and stupidly pretty face. His dark curls that looked so wonderfully soft. He was real. He was inside Cador's cottage, by his fire, trying to save doomed little lumps of bird with quiet determination.

Cador was not returning to life as he'd always known it. Would he ever reclaim it, or was it gone forever? Would war be the answer? What if they were asking the wrong questions?

The wind rustled thick boughs, and Cador drew his cloak tighter. He felt scraped raw for no good reason. Jem's fate shouldn't be of any consequence. One prince didn't matter compared to Ergh's children. Ergh's very future.

Thoughts of his poor nephew, Hedrok, invaded his mind instead. Cador inhaled sharply against the surge of nausea. He couldn't fix Hedrok no matter how hard he'd tried, and now it hurt too deeply to even think of him, let alone see him.

Cador knew he was the worst kind of coward, but he tamped down the guilt yet again and locked it away. Marrying Jem was what Cador could do for his nephew. What became of Jem when the war was over was of no consequence.

Sloshing more water out of the bucket, he marched back to the cottage. Enough foolishness. Inside, Jem still sat on the hearth, watching his bundle. He barely spared Cador a glance.

Cador decided to ignore him, yet a minute later demanded, "Well?"

Jem looked up. "They ate. If they live to morning, they should survive."

Cador was oddly relieved. It made no sense—the askells didn't provide him food or bear him around Ergh as Massen did. There was no reason to waste time nursing them. He'd have ended their suffering quickly with one blow, but now they were here in his cottage, which hadn't had this many occupants in...ever.

Standing, Jem stretched his arms over his head. His lithe body arched, breeches clinging to his tight arse. Cador poured the bucket into a pitcher on the battered table near the fire, cursing as he spilled it.

"So, this is your home?" Jem asked. "It's cozy."

Cador's hackles rose as he sopped up the water with a rag. He imagined the windowless cottage through Jem's eyes: a large wood-framed bed with a proper hard mattress, fireplace, table and chairs, pantry, chests holding his clothing and a pile of furs. It was plain, but he had no need for fanciness.

"We all can't live in a castle, your highness. Don't want to."

"No, of course not." After a silence, Jem noted, "There are few decorations. No tapestries in Ergh?"

"Not many." Cador wanted to point out the pinecones scattered on the mantel. What was that if not decoration?

Jem tentatively neared the spears lining the rough stone by the timber door as if they might leap off the wall and impale him. Cador had left his sword sheathed there. Bearing their swords on the mainland had been strategic, but he far preferred his spears.

"I suppose this is your art," Jem said, examining the various spears.

Cador had to laugh, the emotion unwelcome yet undeniable. "Suppose so."

Jem seemed about to say something else, but then his spine snapped straight, his gaze darting around. "There's only one bed."

Fuck.

It was true. Cador's bed wasn't feathery like the ones at the Holy Place, but it was a long and wide pallet, giving him room to sprawl. It was plenty of room for two—although Cador had rarely welcomed anyone there for long. Jem looked as though he'd rather sleep with a sarf.

Cador shrugged. "I only need one." At Jem's troubled gaze, he rolled his eyes. "Don't worry. I wouldn't fuck you if you were the last person on Ergh. I'd bugger a boar first."

Jem smiled thinly, crossing his arms. "How reassuring. I'll sleep on the hearth regardless. I need to keep watch over the hatchlings."

"Suit yourself." Maybe they should imprison Jem after all. Cador would be tripping over him for months.

He irritably went about the rest of his chores before serving up smoked boar meat from the pantry with dried berries and ale. Tomorrow he'd hunt and replenish his pantry in Rusk. Jem thanked him for the food and picked at it, watching over the birds. They'd quieted, and Cador wasn't sure if that was a good sign or bad. He didn't allow himself to ask.

Jem's gaze still darted to Cador and the bed every so often. Was it only nerves? He tried to imagine being a virgin at twenty years. He would have been desperate for a fuck. To plunge into someone else's body, or be taken himself. Desperate for the sweat and grunting and release.

He examined the curve of Jem's bent head, curls tumbling over his forehead where he knelt by the nest. Cador could imagine palming his head, tangling his fingers in that glossy hair as he eased him forward to his hands and knees…

What kind of cries could he earn from Jem as he pushed into the tight sheath of his body? Would Jem be bold when he had Cador's cock inside him? Would he merely whimper and be taken, or would he beg for more? Not that it was of any real interest.

As Jem reached for his cup of water, his breeches stretched over the swell of his arse. "Do you wish to bathe?" Cador found himself asking. It wasn't because he wanted to see Jem naked. He was merely being welcoming.

That got Jem's attention. "May I?" He glanced around. "Where?" He gave a little half laugh and grimace. "I confess that I'm accustomed to servants heating the water and filling my tub."

"I'm sure you are." Cador had to admit that didn't sound terrible. He went to the corner beyond the hearth where a small wooden tub sat and dragged it closer to the fire. Hauling in the buckets of water to heat over the flames didn't take long, and soon the tub was half full and Cador was unwrapping a square of soap.

Jem took the offered soap hesitantly, his gaze flicking back to the tub. "It's…smaller than I've seen? How do you…?"

Small? How did they bathe on the mainland? Why would a tub be bigger? Puzzled, Cador stripped off his clothes and stepped into the hot water, which rose around his shins. He bent to scoop the water over his body with a cloth, squeezing the deliciously hot liquid over his head and shoulders and soaping his skin.

"You see?" he asked Jem. Did the boy need to be taught everything?

Jem made an odd little squeak. When Cador looked to him, Jem nodded so hard his head might fly off his neck. Frowning, Cador asked, "What's the matter with you?"

"Nothing!" Jem seemed to be looking everywhere but at Cador.

"There's another cloth in the chest over there." Cador finished scrubbing and rinsing, then stepped out. Still naked, he dripped water all over the floor, but it would dry. He held out the soap to Jem.

With shaky fingers, Jem plucked the soap from Cador's hand and then stood rooted to the spot, staring at the tub.

"Was the method not clear?" Did Jem expect him to fetch fresh water and go through the whole process again? That was madness.

"No, it was clear. Very clear. I just…" Jem screwed up his face. "Can you please look away?"

"From what?"

He sighed in a rush. "From me! Taking off my clothes!"

"Why?" Cador motioned to himself. "I'm not wearing any."

"I noticed!" Jem shook his head. "Not that I was looking or *trying* to notice."

Cador had to laugh. "Why are you tied into knots about

something this ordinary?" He made a show of turning his back. "There you go. I won't look."

"Thank you," Jem mumbled.

True to his word, Cador didn't so much as peek. He had no interest in the slim form of a spoiled prince who couldn't even ride a horse. He stood waiting although he should have gone about any remaining chores. His damp skin dried, gooseflesh rippling over his body despite the fire's warmth behind him.

With his back to the hearth, he could hear the splash of water and imagine Jem soaping, the gray suds pale on his brown skin as he bent and lathered his limbs. Water surely trickled down his chest. Did it catch on his nipples? How much hair grew there? If Jem rubbed the cloth over his skin, would his nipples peak?

A minute ticked by. Then another. Cador stood rooted to the spot, listening. He imagined the drag of the soapy material over Jem's prick and behind to his arse. Over those round, perfect cheeks. Between them...

Water shushed and a log cracked in the fireplace. If Cador turned, Jem would be in reach. If he...

"I'm finished," Jem whispered. "Thank you."

Cador shook himself, turning to find Jem dressed again in his silky shirt that fell to mid-thigh. Standing before the fire's blaze, his body was outlined in the light fabric. His hair was damp, the curls sticking out, and Cador was struck by the mad urge to step close and smooth them down.

"Why are you wearing that?" he asked too loudly.

Jem frowned. "What?"

"You sleep in that garment?"

"Oh." Jem glanced down at the silky material, his body still outlined clearly by the fire. "Not usually, but it's quite similar to my nightshirts." He squirmed, tugging at the hem. "Not as long, but it will have to do. Well… Goodnight."

Cador grunted and turned away. Even their nightclothes were impractical. It would give no warmth. Why not just sleep naked? Speaking of which, it was time to enjoy his own bed after so long away.

He stretched out under his furs. In the dead of winter, he had to wear layers to keep warm, but though spring was late, it was warm enough for him. He'd always loved sleeping naked and free.

Glancing over to the fire, Cador caught Jem's stare before the boy whipped his head toward the flames. Although he sat on the hearth, he still crossed his arms tightly. He was so delicate he'd likely freeze even an arm's length from the blaze. The last thing Cador needed was to be kept awake by chattering teeth.

Besides, the stone hearth was not a comfortable place to sleep the night. Grumbling, he threw back his coverings. Jem watched with wide eyes as Cador crossed to him and spread out two of the thick furs from his bed on the hearth.

"From the blonek in the north," Cador said, needing to fill the silence. He crouched, stroking his palm over the soft, light brown fur. "The animals are rare now, so these pelts are special. Should be plush enough for your tastes."

Jem's eyes were locked on the orange flames. "Uh-huh! Thank you!"

Cador stood, scratching his chest. "Are you well?"

Jem nodded, not looking away from the fire, his knees to his chest and arms locked around them. Cador shrugged and grabbed one of the pillows from his bed. They were stuffed with straw instead of feathers but would be better than the stone hearth. He liked two, but placed one on the furs by the fire.

"You're free to sleep in the bed. As I said, your virtue is quite safe with me."

"Thank you," Jem replied stiffly. "I'll sleep here."

Cador certainly wasn't going to beg him to take up half of his bed—not that he would, being so slim. Jem would surely fit right in the curve of his arm or curled back against his chest...

Shaking his head, Cador climbed back under his remaining fur. He closed his eyes and willed himself to think only of the morning's hunt and not beyond, pretending he was alone, and his life was as it had always been.

Chapter Ten

"**W**ELL?"

Leaning over the nest in the faint light of the fire's embers, Jem jerked up. He hadn't realized Cador was awake, and he braced to find him unashamedly naked again. Fortunately—or not, depending on one's perspective—Cador was still nestled under the furs on the bed. He blinked sleepily at Jem, just visible in the shadows.

"Three have died. I put them in the fire. But one lives. I'll feed her again soon."

"Her? How can you be sure?"

"I can't, but it feels right. I'll know for certain when she's ready to leave the nest and her mature feathers grow in. That's assuming askells are like dillywigs. Time will tell. I shall call her Derwa in the meantime." In the books, Derwa was Morvoren's closest friend, a sturdy and dependable girl.

"If you insist."

"When is the sun up?" Without windows, he had no idea of the time. It felt quite early in the dawn, still hushed, the forest birds beyond the cottage's walls silent. Or perhaps the stone was so thick their song was muffled.

"Not for a couple of hours, but the hunt begins early. Our days are shorter here." Cador threw back his furs, and there he was in all his considerable glory, inked tusks on his broad chest, his half-hard prick jutting out proudly.

Who needed birdsong or a rooster's crow to signal morning when you had *that*? Jem resolutely kept his gaze on the nest. Soon Derwa would be squawking for breakfast, he hoped. He winced as he stretched the crick in his neck. He should be used to sleeping on the floor after the voyage, but he had to admit he missed his bed.

Thoughts of his chamber and books and soft sheets threatened an eruption of the unwanted longing he'd forced deep inside, so he busied himself with chewing worms.

The morning passed by quickly enough, watery dawn light not getting all that brighter. Thick clouds obscured the sky beyond the tall trees, where Cador had disappeared to hunt, grinning to have his spear in his grasp once more. Jem explored the clearing, petting the friendly goats and not daring to venture any farther than the outhouse.

Cador returned empty-handed, yet it didn't seem to dampen his spirits. Jem's trunk was delivered, and after feeding his hatchling midday, he poked through his meager belongings. When he pulled out the candle he used to pleasure himself, he threw it back inside as though it was lit and dripping burning wax onto his fingers. He closed the lid with a thunk.

The journey to Rusk to acquire warmer clothing didn't take long. It was less painful to ride, so that was something. Sitting between Cador's powerful thighs, keeping his spine rigid, Jem tried to ignore the open stares and suspicious murmurs as they entered the village. His red cloak was now a makeshift nest, and he wrapped a rough wool blanket he'd borrowed more tightly around his shoulders.

The air smelled of smoked meat and horse dung. Then, as the wind changed, fresh bread. Jem was no expert, but the villages he'd visited on Onan's mainland had seemed...

He struggled to marshal his thoughts. It wasn't that they were prettier—although they were, with bright flowers in ceramic pots lining the cobbled streets. In Rusk, the streets were dirt, and Jem couldn't imagine flowers. Perhaps in summer, the place would come to life.

He realized the other fundamental difference was that the people—when they weren't glaring up at him or staring and whispering about him—kept their heads down, going about their business without cheery greetings to each other. Where were the gossiping old men that would gather to sip tea at the temple that was a tribute to the gods?

Ah! Jem gazed around at the huddle of huts and mishmash of streets. That was the biggest difference—Rusk had not been built to fan out from the central temple.

In the village near the castle where Jem lived, the temple was similar to most on the mainland—a large, open, four-sided stone square. A statue of Dor, Tan, Glaw, and Hwytha in the center was carved on a mighty pedestal, as though the gods surveyed the villagers from the heavens. The local clerics preached from the base of the statue.

Steps surrounded the raised temple on all sides, as well as a village square that was the heart of the community. Children played there on the grass, old men made themselves comfortable on the steps with their tea and shared rumors, and villagers passed through as they went about their days, chatting and laughing. There seemed to be no such tribute and village heart in Rusk.

The squat stone house where they stopped bore no sign. The seamstress was an older woman who poked and prodded him, *tsking* under her breath while Cador leaned against the door frame, watching impassively.

"Are they all this small?" she asked Cador, as if Jem wasn't there even though she was measuring the length of his arm, her bushy gray hair tickling his cheek as she bent near.

"No," Cador answered.

She grunted. "Maybe he didn't grow right."

"I certainly did!" Jem cringed at his outburst. He should have learned to ignore it from years of Pasco's and Locryn's teasing. If Santo was there, they'd sling an arm around Jem's shoulders and tell him a silly joke to make him smile.

He pressed his lips together, the pang of longing fierce, escaping its box despite his best efforts. Was his family back home in Neuvella now? He supposed they must be, likely ages ago while he was still on the ship to Ergh.

Do they miss me?

At least he hadn't voiced the plaintive words aloud. The seamstress was measuring his legs now, and Cador announced he was leaving, adding something else Jem didn't hear. Jem said, "Pardon?" but Cador was gone. The seamstress stripped him down to his small clothes. At least Cador wasn't watching anymore.

No sooner had the thought flickered through his mind than Jem was imagining stripping down while Cador watched. Safely alone in his chamber back home, he'd indulged certain fantasies, such as a burly woodsman having his wicked way with him. Sometimes, Jem imagined the intruder would bind him, making him helpless and unable to do anything but surrender…

Or the man would watch while he brought himself release. What would it be like to have Cador's icy blue gaze on his bare skin while he—

This isn't the place!

Fortunately, the seamstress had her head in a trunk of fabrics. Jem quickly filled his mind with worries of the hatchling and how she fared in the cottage. If Cador *had* still been watching the fitting, Jem would probably be sporting a humiliating erection.

Soon, the seamstress beckoned a team of workers from another room and they all went to work. Her helpers stole glances at Jem that varied from suspicious to wary to curious. The seamstress's gnarled fingers flew as she worked with a wicked-looking needle.

"You're lucky I have a pair of boots that will fit you," she muttered. "They were made for a child. Should do you fine since you're so puny."

The workers tittered at this, silenced immediately by her glare.

Jem forced back a retort, instead smiling. "Thank you. But won't the child need them?"

Needles froze in mid-stich, and the air grew instantly heavy. Jem had clearly offended them or raised a delicate question. Gods, had something happened to the poor child? He was about to stammer an apology when the seamstress spoke, going back to her work.

She simply said, "No."

Jem waited in silence as they made remarkably quick work of the new garments. Before too long, he was clad in dark shades of leather and spun wool, a fur-lined cloak over his shoulders and the thick-soled boots that came to mid-shin heavy on his feet. The seamstress promised him a delivery of tunics, trousers, hat, gloves, and scarves of differing weights.

"Er, thank you. But it's spring, isn't it? Surely it will soon be too warm for all that?"

Her teeth flashed wide in a wrinkled face, the ensuing laughter sending dread sinking through him as she just laughed and laughed, sharing smiles with her staff. Jem tried to smile too, likely failing miserably. She shooed him out as more customers squeezed into the small house.

Clutching his bundle of old clothes, the blanket, and his thin boots on top, Jem shrank back against the seamstress's cottage, trying to ignore the stares of passersby. Where had Cador said he was going? Couldn't he have simply waited? Now Jem was meant to stand there and be gawked at until he returned?

Irritation simmered to a low boil. He thought not. Head high, Jem strode down the dirt lane, his heart thumping. It wasn't as if Rusk was large enough to lose himself in.

Yet he soon realized the town was deceptive in size. Although the buildings weren't tall or grand, they stretched into the distance in a mess of directions.

He pulled up the hood of his new cloak, trying to blend in. At home, villagers would greet him by his title, the old women at the bakery grinning at the flowers he brought them, gifting him with delicate cakes that left sugary syrup on his fingers to lick clean on his stroll back to the castle.

Jem's new boots sank into a fresh pile of dung, and he cursed Cador anew, hurrying through the maze of Rusk. He jolted in surprise when he turned a corner to find that there was a tribute to the gods after all.

This statue clearly depicted the four gods and their elements, although it wasn't nearly as high as those on the mainland, and it wasn't in a temple surrounded by steps and a village center.

This tribute stood at a seemingly random spot where a house would have been. In fact, the charred remnants of floorboards poked up from the dirt. Likely one of the timber huts, since there was no stone in evidence.

The tribute was also much newer than those on the mainland. The gray stone had a richer shade to it, not faded and worn over many years. Although it wasn't as tall and grand, it had been carved with skill, each god easily recognizable. Hwytha had been Jem's favorite as a boy, their cheeks ballooned, blowing the wind in the direction dictated by their whims.

The dirt surrounding the tribute was laden with dead branches. The gnarled, twisted wood had clearly been piled there purposely. There were no trees in sight, and so many branches couldn't have fallen naturally in one spot. It was strange, since these branches were certainly not from the evergreens that filled the forest.

Jem wasn't sure why the display sent a shiver of dread down his spine, but he drew his cloak around him tighter and hurried away. Above the scent of dung, he detected the smell of horses and a faint whiff of hay and followed it.

Sure enough, he finally reached the main stable at the edge of the village by a rolling pasture churned with mud and brown, ugly grass. Horses grazed on hay bales or trotted about. The vast stable doors stood open. With a fortifying breath, Jem rolled his shoulders and marched inside. He was going to learn to ride. He was going to—

Jem skidded to a stop, hay crunching on the hard-packed dirt floor. He almost dropped his bundle, one of his old boots hitting the ground. Jory gave him an affable smile and wave.

Ugh.

"You look like a proper Erghian now!" Jory nodded approvingly.

Struck by the urge to yank off the new clothes and go back to his silks—even though he'd surely freeze—he barely managed a paper-thin smile in return as he plucked up his dropped boot.

Jory looked beyond at the door. "Where's Cador?"

"I don't know." Jem was unaccountably annoyed. Hadn't Jory spent enough time with Cador on the voyage? Always laughing together.

"Just wondering why you're here." Jory gave him another easy smile.

"Aren't I permitted to be here?"

Jory's ginger brows drew close. "Of course."

Although Jem was very tempted to turn around and leave, he admitted, "I'd like to learn how to ride." He grudgingly added, "Please."

"Ah! I'd be happy to teach you!"

Jem couldn't imagine why. So Jory could gain even more favor with Cador? Not that Cador would care if he learned to ride. "Er... I'm sure you're far too busy." He cursed himself. He should have known Jory would work at the stable.

Jory waved a dismissive hand. "I could make time."

"I can teach you," a voice said from beyond a stall. A slim-hipped young man about Jem's age stepped out. He was the one who'd brought Massen to Cador after they'd arrived.

He had narrow eyes, a thin, straight nose, and a complexion of wheat, his hairless forearms corded with muscle, sleeves rolled to his elbows. His long hair was glossy and dark like Jem's, tied back at the nape of his neck.

"Are you sure?" Jory asked him. "I do have to ride out to Casek's farm across the valley to check in on his mare. She'll give birth soon."

"It's no problem," the man said. To Jem, he added, "I'm Austol."

"Hello. Thank you. Are you certain it's no bother?"

"It would be my honor. You're Cador's new husband. A Neuvellan prince, I hear. I'll teach you."

Jem wasn't sure if he was being mocked or not. Austol seemed sincere, so he repeated, "Thank you."

"I'll leave you in capable hands!" Jory clapped Jem's shoulder, almost knocking him over. When Jory had left, whistling as he went, Jem cleared his throat. "Are you sure I'm not being a bother?"

"I'm sure." Austol chuckled. "You don't seem keen on Jory, so I thought I'd rescue you." He tilted his head. "Why is that? Most people are drawn to him like flies to shit. Not that he's shit—he's a good man. A bit talkative, but there are worse crimes."

"Oh, er…" Jem had to admit—reluctantly—that Jory had been nothing but friendly to him even when others glowered. "I'm sure you're right. I just don't want to be a nuisance."

"You're not. I hear it's different on the mainland, but on Ergh, you must ride."

Jem could only imagine all the gossip that had been flowing since the travelers returned. He wanted to ask what they'd said about him, but managed to retain a shred of dignity. That was, until he tried to mount a horse.

"With confidence," Austol repeated.

They were mercifully still inside the stable, so at least Jem's humiliation wasn't being witnessed by anyone passing by. He grasped the mare's chestnut-colored mane. Called Nessa, she was plump and a great deal smaller than Massen, patiently waiting for Jem to swing up onto her back—which still seemed awfully high from the ground.

Jem had shed his fur-lined cloak and rolled up the sleeves of his rough-fibered tunic. His new leather trousers felt stiff, and he wasn't sure he'd be able to swing his leg over Nessa's back. Gripping her mane, careful not to tug harshly, he bent his knees and made a half-hearted jump.

"You have to mean it," Austol said. He leaned against a post, filing an obedient horse's hoof. Jem was taking so long to mount that he'd gone back to work.

"Are there truly no saddles or stirrups on Ergh?"

"Truly." Austol shrugged. "When we're children, we mount from standing on a rock or fence until we're tall enough to do it properly."

"Then why aren't I using a fence?" Jem glanced about the stalls. "I could climb up there."

"Because you're not a child."

Oh. Right. Jem had insisted so loudly he was a man. Now was his chance to prove it. He held Nessa's mane, rocked his weight back, and threw himself upward. Nessa sidestepped and he yelped, his left foot almost atop her. He hopped on his right, desperately trying to avoid landing flat on his face.

Austol laughed, but it wasn't cruel. "That's it. More power."

"I don't want to hurt her."

"You won't." Austol left his task and came to give Nessa a pat. "She can take a rider, I promise."

Jem had been trying for ages. He sighed. "I'm hopeless."

He came so close, but Jem couldn't quite hook his leg over the mare. Clenching his stomach, he fought the inevitable for a breathless moment, then tumbled back down. He landed with an *oomph*, Austol's arms coming around him as he broke Jem's fall and toppled back himself. Facing the barn's roof of cobwebbed timber beams, they laughed.

Austol's chest rumbled under Jem's back, and Jem was about to roll off and offer his hand to pull him up when Cador stormed into the barn. Upside down, he appeared even bigger than usual.

"What the fuck are you doing?" Cador thundered.

Jem scrambled off Austol and shot to his feet. Why was Cador so angry? He opened and closed his mouth, baffled. Cador strode to Jem's side and seemed to be looking him over for injuries.

Austol unhurriedly pushed himself up, brushing dirt from his trousers. "He's learning to mount." After a beat, he added, "The mare."

Cador huffed, nearing Nessa and scratching her neck. "I didn't know where you were," he said to her, although presumably it was directed at Jem. "You shouldn't go wandering. You're so delicate you'll get yourself into trouble."

Jem clenched his jaw. "I'm perfectly fine on my own. I was just about to hop onto Nessa and learn to ride. So move. Please."

Taking a deep breath, he launched himself, gripping Nessa's mane. He came heartbreakingly—humiliatingly—close before stumbling back. This time, Cador caught him easily, and Jem batted away his hands.

"This is only your first lesson," Austol said kindly. "Come again tomorrow and we'll keep working."

Cador scowled. "Surely you have better things to do."

"No," Austol said simply. "I'm here every day. Surely you want your husband to be able to ride?"

Cador glared at Austol. "If he chooses."

"I…" Jem didn't know what to think. Perhaps he was foolish to believe he could learn. The ache for the familiar safety of home flared so powerfully it almost brought him to his knees. He shook his head. "I don't know. I need to get back to my bird." Austol gave him a quizzical look, and Jem was about to explain when a horrible cry rose up in the distance—a child's wail.

Austol tensed. "My sister needs me. Come back any time, Jem." He gave a fleeting smile. "It would be fun." He broke into a run out of the barn as the plaintive keening continued.

Jem followed to the doorway, calling, "Thank you!" He watched as Austol hopped the fence around a small plot of land nearby with a stone cottage and chickens clucking around the yard. The girl's cries came from inside.

He asked Cador, "Should we help? We could fetch the healer or—"

"It's none of your business. Come." Cador strode to where Massen grazed. He mounted with an aggravating amount of grace considering his bulk.

Then he wheeled Massen toward Jem, reached down, and plucked Jem up and astride Massen with one arm as if Jem weighed no more than a basket of cut flowers. Even more vexing than Cador's grace was that it gave Jem a thrill to be handled with such confidence and strength.

He'd barely remembered his bundle, and he clutched it, twisting his fingers in his soft shirt. The wailing had ceased, although the quiet now from the neat little cottage felt strangely ominous. Jem had never heard cries like that.

"Are you sure we shouldn't try to help?" He whispered the question although they were alone. Didn't Cador care? How could a man murmur endearments to a horse yet ignore a child's suffering?

Cador said nothing, urging Massen back into the forest's dark embrace.

Chapter Eleven

"WHY IS THIS mainland prince living with you?"

Idly patting Massen's neck, Cador glanced up at Ruan's question. Ruan toyed with his spear. He had brown skin and a ready smile, his hair shorn close to his head as befitting a hunter, light gray showing. Wrinkles spread around his brown eyes, but he was as fierce and mighty as he'd been since Cador was a boy.

Peering through the rain-damp pine needles, Cador still saw no sign of their quarry. Holding his spear against his thigh, the point toward the ground, he considered the question.

"I don't know," he murmured honestly, matching Ruan's quiet tone.

Cador realized it actually hadn't occurred to him that Jem didn't *have* to live at the cottage. Even if Jem made a run for it, he wouldn't get far on Ergh. Tracking him would be laughably easy. He was trapped with no need of bars on his prison. Surely there was a place for him to live in Rusk until the time came.

He could have his own house where he wouldn't insist on passing long nights on the floor since apparently the thought of sharing Cador's bed merely to sleep was beneath him. Jem had now slept three nights on the hearth and tried to hide his winces in the morning.

Yet the idea of Jem living alone left Cador uneasy. He wouldn't know anyone in Rusk. He had no friends or family in

Ergh. His growing hatchling could only provide so much company, although he seemed content nursing her.

Still, it wasn't as though they said much to each other. Perhaps Jem would be glad to live on his own. Maybe he'd be relieved. It should be a relief for them both. The people of Rusk would certainly not blame Cador for not wanting to be burdened with a useless husband with whom he shared nothing.

Although, if Cador thought about it, he supposed they both had an interest in animals. He'd answered Jem's many questions about chickens and shown him how to milk the goats. Jem was a surprisingly good student given he was used to servants catering to his every whim. Surprising too was that Cador found himself enjoying the lessons. Looking forward to them, even.

He'd found more little subjects to teach as the days passed, showing how the well operated and the method for fixing the fence around the animals' enclosure. Jem gave him shy little smiles whenever Cador praised him and had answered Cador's occasional questions about the birds on the mainland, and the special place Jem had built for them that he called an aviary. Well, the place servants or craftspeople had built on his behalf.

"You only wed him for the good of Ergh," Ruan said after a long silence.

Cador looked at him sharply, although Ruan's gaze was still on the trees beside them. Had Ruan learned the plan? Did he know Jem would be kidnapped? If it was known to more than absolutely necessary, the more dangerous it became. It was best to pretend he and Jem were true husbands. At least that they'd fucked. He tried to find the right words for the lie when Ruan spoke again.

"It's not as if you fell in love at first sight with *him*. Clearly this is politics. No need to put on a show for us. We all know this is not a true marriage. That should be of the heart. The soul. When I married my Gerren, it made me whole."

Cador had always scoffed at such romantic notions, although he knew Ruan and Gerren were very happy living in their cottage in Rusk's eastern valley. "Prince Jowan certainly doesn't make me whole. But he is my burden. No one else's."

"Is it true he can't even ride?"

"Aye."

Ruan made a sound of disgust. "How lazy life must be there."

Cador grimaced in agreement, fighting the odd impulse to defend Jem even though he'd said the same many times. Branches rustled—the only hint of her approach—as Delen appeared in their little clearing on her mount.

"I heard Austol tried to teach him," she said.

For fuck's sake. Cador could imagine the gossip slithering through Rusk. He wasn't sure why he felt so annoyed, but forced a shrug. "A lost cause."

"At least Jem's trying," Delen said mildly.

"Shouldn't be taking Austol away from his responsibilities," Cador muttered.

She gave him a long look. "I imagine Austol is eager for a distraction."

Yes. That was fair enough. The three of them shared a heavy silence. Guilt pricked at Cador, the echo of young cries in his mind.

Delen said, "Hedrok asks for you. You should visit soon."

The guilt swelled into a torrent. "Yes," Cador agreed miserably, thinking of his nephew, who would soon be bedridden. "I will. Tomorrow." Or perhaps the next day. It wasn't that Cador didn't want to see him, it was that...

You're afraid. Admit it!

Talk mercifully returned to the hunt as they moved out to another spot, and Cador banished the thoughts of Hedrok and the dark cloud shadowing Ergh. He scratched Massen's neck, mind wandering when it should have been sharp like the end of his spear.

Would Jem want his own cottage? If he did, why hadn't he asked? It wouldn't be any skin off Cador's nose. It would be cause for celebration! Still… Might be wise to keep an eye on him. Make sure he didn't unknowingly disrupt the plan.

Besides, Jem would be safer with Cador. The villagers would be curious, and he could imagine them competing to bed Jem if they knew Cador had no interest. Not because they desired a puny mainlander, but for the sport. Perhaps that was Austol's purpose, although it seemed unlike him.

It shouldn't bother Cador one way or the other, yet when he thought of Austol and Jem in a tangle of limbs on the barn floor or sharing a smile, he wanted to smash his fist into Austol's smooth face. Such nonsense since he'd ever only had friendly respect for the man.

The forest was still, and he urged Massen through a thick stand of trees, needles scraping Cador's cheeks. Above, askells chirped and called to each other. It had been a surprise even one of the birds Jem had rescued survived.

Cador still wasn't sure he shouldn't have just put them all out of their misery with the mercy of his boot, but Jem had such confidence he could heal the tiny survivor. Cador watched sometimes in the night, the fire's glow orange on Jem's face as he tended the hatchling, waking at its faintest cry.

There was discipline in that kindness. Cador could admit that a lazy man would never have rescued the hatchlings in the first place. Jem was not lazy. He remembered the steady press of fingers on his wrist aboard the ship and thought if he was truly ill or injured, he could do worse than returning home to Jem's care. Of course, the boy would be gone soon enough, so it wasn't even worth thinking on.

Yet now the thought of what came after the war nagged. Once they were victorious—he couldn't allow himself to ponder what would happen if they somehow lost—Jem could be returned to his castle in Neuvella and his easy life.

He remembered the press of fingers on his wrist once more. It would be Jem's right hand removed to send to his mother since that was the one branded with Ergh's tusks. It seemed unfortunately to be the one he favored. But surely he'd be able to adapt.

Not that he'd have a choice.

Acid churned Cador's stomach. He had to admit it was easier to agree to the plan when it'd been merely words and not deeds. And once the war was done, Jem would still be his husband. How often would they see each other? He supposed not very.

The thought made him strangely uneasy instead of relieved, and Cador's traitorous mind returned to Jem time and again when he should have been focused on the hunt. Instead, he mused that Jem was equally intent with the goats and chickens as he was with the hatchling, as if listening to them—as though he could understand their language of bleats and clucks.

But when Cador returned daily from hunting with Massen, Jem kept a wide berth. He really should learn to ride. His fear of horses would do him no favors on Ergh.

Jem would surely enjoy horses once he knew their sweet loyalty and overcame his fright. Massen would love him if Jem only gave him the chance. Cador was duty bound to teach him, wasn't he? Especially since there was no need to trouble Austol. No need at all. In fact—

The unmistakable thunder of boar hooves came from a distance. Cador's heart boomed and all other thoughts finally fled. The chase was on.

Later, after Ruan had skinned that day's kill and it was taken into Rusk for distribution, Cador headed Massen toward home. Massen had galloped without hesitation or complaint for hours, so Cador let him meander along the path, eventually joining up with the trail from his cottage that led to Rusk.

They entered the clearing to find Jem at the edge of the trees on the other side, his body tense. The new leather trousers hugged his arse as he bent forward a bit, staring into the forest. Frowning, Cador hopped down from Massen, approaching Jem silently lest he scare away whatever Jem was looking at. Perhaps a byghan.

When he stood an arm's length away, Cador whispered, "What is it?"

Whirling, Jem yelped, jumping right off the ground. He and Cador stared at each other for a stunned moment—then burst out laughing. It was a sudden release of pressure Cador hadn't even known was needed.

It felt damn good to laugh. More than that, it felt good to laugh with Jem. He realized that since that flash of Jem's heretical, spirited grin on the ship, he'd wanted to see it again. There had been little smiles, but not this joyous expression.

"You scared me!" Jem pressed a hand to his chest. His teeth gleamed in his wide smile, his honey eyes crinkling.

Cador had to smile in return. "Not my intention. I thought you'd hear me coming."

"You'd think so. You're so big, and…" Jem's eyes flicked down over Cador's body. "What I mean is, you—I would have thought you'd make more noise." Clearing his throat, he motioned to the forest. "I heard some birds, but I can't spot them."

"Just go closer."

Jem glanced between Cador and the trees. "It's so dark in there. Even in daylight. Granted, it's cloudy again, but…" He peered into the gloom.

Cador laughed and opened his mouth to ask why Jem was so skittish, but bit off his words. He'd grown up in these woods, but he looked into the shadows now, putting himself in Jem's boots. Perhaps this forest *would* seem dark and daunting.

Instead of his jest, he said, "There's no danger."

Jem shot him a skeptical glance. "I'm not sure our definition of 'danger' is the same."

"Perhaps not." He chuckled. "Let's say there's *little* danger. Provided you stay well clear of the boars and don't lose your way and—all right, there's *some* danger."

"That is precisely why I'll stay on this side."

Cador almost said that Jem shouldn't worry—that he'd protect him. That he had nothing to fear in the forest's depths or anywhere else if Cador was with him. Yet that was a lie, and that growing, vexing shame held his tongue.

Jem squinted up into the trees from the safety of the clearing, moving around the circle as Cador rubbed down Massen. Cador asked, "Shall I teach you to ride? I'm sure I'll do a better job than Austol."

After giving him a quizzical look, Jem shook his head. "Massen is far too big. I'd rather go back to Nessa if I can." He turned to peer into the trees once more.

Clearly his fear of the forest was why Jem had ventured no farther and hadn't returned to Rusk for more lessons. Cador opened his mouth to offer to take him, but snapped it shut as he thought of Austol and Jem sprawled together on the barn floor.

Not that he gave a shit. But if Jem wanted inferior lessons from Austol, he could walk into Rusk himself. Cador was far too busy. Jem could do as he pleased.

Soon enough, Jem won't be able to do as he pleases at all. For how long? Until the end of the war? What if it drags on? What if it all goes horribly wrong?

Boxing up that growing concern and slamming down the lid, Cador went inside and stripped off his tunic. A strange little noise reached his ears, and he stilled, glancing around the room. Nothing moved in the flickering firelight.

Squeak!

Ah, of course it was coming from the nest. He shouldn't touch the delicate bird. Jem would be furious if he hurt it. More than that, he'd be heartbroken. No, Cador should just let it be.

Yet he tiptoed closer, his mud-caked boots squelching. When he peered into the bundle of Jem's red cloak, now with the addition of twigs and moss, Cador exclaimed aloud. The bird was already bigger, its gray blob of a body sprouting a few feeble yellow feathers. It trembled and squeaked again. Was it hungry? Thirsty? Ill? In pain? If Cador picked it up, he'd surely crush it without meaning to.

Squeak!

The sparse feathers shook as the tiny creature whimpered. Its eyes were closed. What had Jem named it? That's right— Derwa. Ridiculous name for a bird that wouldn't even survive. Beak agape, she cried for food.

Well, if he didn't feed her, she'd never shut up, would she?

Jem had dug up fresh worms, so Cador plucked one from a box and wiped away any clinging dirt. The worm wriggled, and he forced aside his hesitation. If Jem could eat them, so could he. He'd never get any peace otherwise.

Holding his breath, he shoved the worm into his mouth and chewed. *Don't swallow! Don't swallow!* The squirming sensation in his mouth almost had him gagging, and he spat the crushed worm into his palm with a loud curse. He only tasted dirt and sludgy flesh, but it was disgusting.

Why did he even care if the hatchling went hungry? If Jem was so keen on saving her, he shouldn't be neglectful—although to be fair, he'd spent countless hours tending her. Another cry filled the air, and Cador sighed. He'd already chewed the worm, so he might as well feed it to her.

His fingers were huge in comparison to the mouth of the hatchling, but he managed to drop the mush into that ravenous maw. "That's it," he murmured.

It was only the current of chilled air on his bare torso that alerted Cador he was no longer alone. Now it was his turn to be surprised, feeling oddly embarrassed as he turned to find Jem in the doorway watching him. Cador jumped to his feet as if he'd been caught smothering the creature rather than feeding her.

"She was making too much noise."

"It's what they do, really." Jem smiled softly. "I fed her not an hour ago, but she'll beg for it all day. She'll be ready to perch soon enough if askells are like dillywigs. It's remarkable how quickly they go from trembling lumps to scruffy feathers to being ready to fly. I'm not sure how to keep her safe without an aviary though."

"What is that exactly?" Cador pulled on a clean tunic and removed his boots.

"A large outdoor room, I suppose you could say. Big enough for the birds to take little flights as they gather strength, but secure enough to keep them protected from predators. I can walk ten paces in mine back home."

"Hmm. What is it made of?"

"Iron and wood." He chuckled. "Like a little prison, I suppose. But it's for their safety." Jem turned that pretty smile on Cador. "Thank you for feeding Derwa."

"It was nothing," he said, then quickly added, "It was only so she'd shut up." He needed to rinse the worm from his mouth and strode to the pantry, a nook built into the cottage wall.

He poured ale into his tankard and gulped before setting about baking flatbread from the hardy grain farmed on Ergh. He often traded boar for goats' butter that he couldn't be bothered churning himself, but he couldn't traipse into Rusk daily for his food.

The bread was easy to make, and Cador enjoyed kneading the dark flour with an egg and butter into dough. From the corner of his eye, he could see that Jem's attention had wandered from the nest.

In fact, his gaze was trained on Cador's hands as Cador kneaded the dough on the battered tabletop, his sleeves rolled to his elbows. The marriage brand on his left hand had healed, the small bird's wings spreading from the base of his thumb in a diagonal flight across his palm.

"Haven't you seen someone make bread before?" Cador asked.

Jem whipped his head down to the nest. His voice was thin. "No, actually. Especially not a mighty hunter."

Cador shrugged and kept kneading. After a long day of pursuit and being on guard, he enjoyed the simple movements of forming the bread, spreading his fingers and working the cubes of butter until it was even. When he was satisfied, he rolled the dough into a ball.

He kept the baking stones on the side of the hearth, and Jem scurried out of the way as he approached. Cador didn't know what had spooked him—he thought they were growing accustomed to each other. What the fuck was the problem now?

Suddenly vexed, he barked, "What is it?"

"Nothing!" Jem fidgeted, cradling the nest and avoiding Cador's gaze.

Cador positioned the stones and stoked the fire, tossing on more logs and jabbing at the smoldering ashes with an iron rod. He wasn't sure why he was so on edge. But they had to live together for months, and he wasn't going to tiptoe around his own home.

Perhaps he should offer to find a place for him in Rusk after all. It would be easier for both of them. If Jem was lonely, that was his problem—Cador wasn't his damn nursemaid. He didn't have to worry about him not knowing how to ride or sleeping on the hearth when there was a perfectly good bed not ten steps away. Yet no words reached his stubborn tongue.

Soon, the scent of baking bread filled the cottage, and Jem tentatively said, "That smells incredible."

It shouldn't have pleased Cador so much, but he couldn't hide a smile before shrugging. "It's nothing. Everyone in Ergh can make this bread."

"Would you... Will you show me how?"

Cador hid his surprise with another shrug. "If you want." He could easily eat a loaf on his own, so making more wouldn't go to waste.

He used the same wooden bowl, measuring out the flour by

rote and adding salt. "Roll up your sleeves," he told Jem. Jem did as he was told, exposing his lean forearms, dark hair scattered over his brown skin.

Again, Jem was a good student, creating a well in the flour and adding the egg, cubing the butter with a knife, then kneading it all together.

Jem asked, "Is this right?" after Cador had fallen into silence, watching Jem's hands work the dough. The branded tusks on his right palm curved up toward the base of his fingers. They disappeared into the dough and then reappeared.

"Don't be afraid to be rough with it." Cador stepped close behind, reaching around him to guide his hands. He spread Jem's fingers, working his own between them, pushing the butter evenly through the dough.

Jem nodded, his curls bouncing. Cador was struck by the mad urge to dip his head and rub his cheek against that glossy hair. Jem's slim hands felt soft compared to Cador's calluses and scars, yet were surprisingly strong.

Although he was far too small, there was something pleasing about the way he tucked against Cador's body. In fact, Jem seemed just the right height to bend over the table, his feet flat on the floor so he could relax his torso over the wood.

He could turn his head and rest his cheek on the worn pine, pliable as he let Cador open him with fingers and tongue. He'd be comfortable as he gave himself, as Cador offered him hard thrusts and sweet pleasure, the stoked fire building as he tangled his fingers in Jem's hair and buried himself in that lithe body, coaxing cries from his sweet mouth—

Cador jerked back, dropping Jem's hands before Jem felt the prod of his suddenly swelling prick. "You see?" he managed, his mouth dry.

Jem only nodded, his head lowered to his task. Cador's heart drummed. Showing him how to knead bread and milk goats was one thing. It was madness to think about teaching him how good fucking could be. He'd never sought innocents. What use did he have of virgins? He liked lovers who were his equals. Who knew what they were about and didn't need coddling.

He wasn't cruel with his partners, but he'd never had the urge to...what? Soothe them? Guide them? What was this foreign *tenderness* that rose up in him and felt at home? Felt as though it had been missing and was found. Fired his blood and inflamed his cock. Was it some mainland spell that had been cast on him?

Cador believed in magic even less than the gods. Clearly he needed to seek out release. It had been too long, and his physical need was addling his brain. Yet before he backed away, he found himself brushing a spray of flour from Jem's forearm, needing to touch. A stubborn pale dusting remained, and he brushed again, his fingers curling around the lean muscle.

The bird chirped loudly in the silence, and Cador stumbled away completely from Jem, almost tripping on the door to his small root cellar. The first scent of burning filled his nose, and he rushed to the fire to flip the bread. Clearly he needed to hunt down Kensa or Jory or *anyone* for a good rut. He was going fucking mad.

He salvaged the bread, cursing himself for letting it singe. Glancing back at the table, he found he was being watched. Jem swallowed thickly and dropped his eyes to the bowl. Good thing they'd have another loaf soon.

CADOR WHISTLED AS he entered his clearing the next day, looking forward to sharing his portion of the kill with Jem. Yet his song died on his lips as Jem did not appear in the doorway. He wasn't in the clearing either. No smoke rose from the chimney, the stillness complete aside from the goats' excited bleats and the chickens flapping around as usual.

Cador realized it had only taken a week to grow accustomed to Jem greeting him when he returned. It wasn't unpleasant to see Jem's shy smile, to have him listen eagerly to Cador's recounting of the hunt as though it was a story in one of his books.

On cue, there was that now-familiar stab of guilt—for the books, the plan, the secrets—but there was no time for it today. Today, Jem was gone. Cador called to him, but there was no answer. The cottage door remained shut. He left Massen to graze, unease simmering in his gut.

Inside, the cottage sat empty, though not lifeless. Derwa squawked in her nest—now resting inside an old crate big enough for her to hop around in. It was set a safe distance from the embers of the fire, which were practically nothing but cold ash.

Where the fuck was he?

Had he finally ventured beyond the clearing? Perhaps he'd screwed up his courage and returned to the main stable for more lessons with Austol. Cador scowled. And so what if he had? He was free to do whatever he pleased. They both were.

Cador was acting like a damn fool. He shook his head and went back out to fetch the meat and set about preparing it. He should be glad of the time alone in his own home without his unwelcome guest. He was! He made himself whistle another tune.

Yet... What if Jem got lost? It would be easy to do for someone unfamiliar with the forest or Ergh's terrain. Cador tensed as he imagined how frightened Jem would be alone in the shadows.

What if he was injured? Or someone had hurt him? What if he was *taken*?

Standing at the table, he whirled around to examine the cottage. There were no signs of disturbance. Nothing out of place. Jem's furs were folded neatly on the hearth. When Cador peered over the nest, Derwa cried up at him with a gaping mouth. Always hoping for food, although he knew Jem wouldn't have left her hungry.

Unless it wasn't his choice.

Cador had to admit the jest in worrying that Jem had been kidnapped when that would be his fate. But that would have purpose! It would be worthy. If someone had snatched him now for some other reason, it could put the entire plan in jeopardy. He couldn't allow that. He couldn't allow just anyone to come along and take Jem.

His teeth were gritted and fists clenched, and he forced a breath. Why was he imagining the worst? Perhaps Jem had taken the trail to Rusk. There was only one—it should have been easy to follow.

But what if he *did* get lost? Useless mainlander that he was, he surely would. He was so delicate he might drop dead at the slightest chill. Or he might encounter a boar. He'd be helpless without Cador. Just like the hatchling he cared for.

She chirped noisily, and Cador wished the damn thing could speak. Jem had been loath to leave Derwa the past days. Why would he go now? And where?

"Doesn't fucking matter!" he muttered. He poured a tankard

of ale from the heavy cask in the pantry and gulped half. He would enjoy this time alone and that was that. Derwa chirped again, and he stomped to the fire to stoke it. The little creature didn't deserve to get cold, even if she grew feathers already.

He threw logs into the large mouth of the fireplace with too much force, then had to stamp out sparks on the hearth with his boot. Jem wasn't a child. He'd be fine on his own.

Yet Cador couldn't sit still. Food was tasteless. Even ale didn't go down well. He kept checking the clearing, unable to nap as he usually would after rising early for a long hunt.

Where the fuck was Jem?

With a curse, Cador tucked two knives into his boots, strapped his sword over his back, and grabbed one of his spears. Outside, he whistled for Massen, spurring his faithful stallion into a relentless gallop.

Chapter Twelve

"EVERYTHING'S FINE! I'M perfectly safe."

Somehow, the sound of Jem's own voice in the forest's sinister hush only made the hair on the back of his neck stand even taller. But was it truly sinister?

A carpet of pine needles and dirt muffled his boots. He dodged patches of mud where the night's rain had soaked through the dense foliage. Yet here and there, wildlife scurried and birds called.

It wasn't the steady hum he was accustomed to in Neuvella, where the year-round warmth seemed to encourage insects and animals that were far noisier, but hidden life surrounded him. The forest was only sinister if he made it so.

Although he wished it wasn't quite so *dark*.

It was another cloudy, dreary day, but even if the sun had shone brilliantly in a cobalt sky, the light would struggle to penetrate the towering evergreens. Jem shivered, drawing his cloak closer around him as he walked on.

It had taken days of peering into the trees, skirting the perimeter of Cador's clearing and building his nerve. He'd made sure Derwa was well fed and pulled on his stiff new boots. It was time to properly break them in since he couldn't simply hide away in the cottage. He would take up kind Austol on his offer of lessons. Why shouldn't he?

An owl hooted, and Jem's heart leapt to his throat. Forcing a chuckle, he continued, reminding himself the only true danger in the forest—according to Cador—was the boars. Jem did not imagine those hulking beasts moved quietly, although Cador could.

He smiled, remembering how they'd laughed the other day. How Cador had patiently shown him the technique for kneading bread, his huge hands holding Jem's in the bowl.

"Don't be afraid to be rough with it."

Jem groaned softly to himself. It was becoming more and more inconvenient, this effect Cador had on him. How Jem had burned to push back against that big body. How he'd wanted to drop to his knees and beg for cock.

Lust soared through him as he followed the twisting path. Of course he'd never do that. He cringed to think of how Cador would laugh and mock him. Cador's lovers were fierce, or at least tall and broad like Jory. He grumbled, trying to banish the instant imaginings of Cador's callused fingers threading through Jory's fiery hair, using his mouth roughly and spending down his throat...

For a mad moment, Jem was tempted to steal deeper into the forest, just beyond sight of the path, so he could release his aching prick from his new trousers and rid himself of this persistent arousal.

He schooled his desire and kept going, although his mind drifted back to forbidden fantasies again and again. So distracted was he that Jem didn't hear the approaching rider until the trotting horse—a massive dark stallion like Massen—was in sight carrying Cador's brother. A dead boar was slung over its hindquarters, guts hanging out. Blood dripped from Bryok's spear.

Instead of pulling on the reins, Bryok seemed to spur on his mount, and Jem had to dive out of the way, his cry stuck in his throat as he slammed into the ground, needles scraping his palms. Bryok wheeled around on the narrow path as if to take another try at trampling Jem under thundering hooves.

There was no time to do anything but throw up his hands in front of his face and make a pitiful whimper. He was going to die in the dirt, broken and bloody, and the boars would eat the pieces and—

The horse's hooves skidded as it yanked back to a stop, rearing up on its back legs before slamming back down, so close to Jem the ground shook. He couldn't tell whether the horse had balked or Bryok had reined it in.

Bryok towered over him atop his mighty steed, and amid the clammy press of terror, Jem was struck by the memory that he'd once stared up from the ground at Cador in much the same way after being shoved from the pale horse. Gods, that seemed long ago. Now he knew much more of his husband.

Cador hummed to his goats and spoke to his stallion as though it understood. He gave Jem his furs so he wouldn't be cold. He snored and belched but also made little sighs when he woke and stretched sleepily. He grumbled and complained about Derwa, but fed her patiently when he thought they were alone.

Cowering on the earth in the forest's depths, Jem realized Cador didn't frighten him at all anymore. Perhaps if he spent more time with Bryok, he'd discover him just as real and…safe.

Safe.

That was Cador. Staring up at Bryok's scarred, sneering face, his fear grew like vines wrapping his limbs. This man was not safe at all. Jem shouldn't have come into the woods alone! Bryok's eyes were flinty with something Jem feared was true hate. Not indifference or frustration, but an insidious venom that kept Jem frozen in place as though it flowed through his veins.

"Cador is close behind." If only his words could summon Cador, his voice so hoarse the lie barely escaped.

Now a smile—no less terrifying—cut across Bryok's face. "Do you think he'll save you? Do you think he'll let his weakness win over the will of our people?" Bryok's laugh struck like a blow. "Your fate is sealed, Prince Jowan."

With a spray of mud, Bryok galloped into the shadows, disappearing as though he'd only been conjured by Jem's imagination. Yet his face was splattered, and he wiped the mud with his cloak before pushing to his feet, knees shaking.

The temptation to race back to the cottage vibrated through Jem's limbs. Why had he thought he was brave enough to walk this path alone? Around him, the life of the forest went on as though it hadn't been disturbed at all. The wind rustled pine needles, askells sang, and a distant hawk screeched.

The noise that didn't belong was the hammering of Jem's heart and the rush of blood in his ears as he stood torn by indecision. He could escape back to Cador's cottage and pray to false gods that he would return soon from the hunt. Then they would be safe together amid the scent of fresh bread and crackling kindling. Or...

Jem forced himself to look the other way, where the path wound between two mighty firs that all but blocked out the gray sky. He didn't know how much farther it was to Rusk. Was it even the correct path? He thought he'd followed it faithfully, but how could he be sure? It would surely be best to retreat.

Yet hadn't he retreated time and time again? Secreted himself away at the aviary or in his chamber, licking his wounds, too spooked to reach out for what he wanted. Too timid to take chances.

Taking a mighty breath, Jem stepped in the direction of Rusk. He wanted to learn to ride. He would not retreat. He would not allow Bryok's theatrics to frighten him. Austol had offered his assistance, and Jem would take it.

He would learn to ride. Even if he fell a hundred times and made an utter fool of himself, he would not retreat. He only had to take another step, and another and another and another until he was there. His fate was his own.

What would Morvoren do?

With a smile, he shouted to the trees, "To Rusk or die trying!"

JEM HAD TO admit it was a relief he didn't perish on the way to Rusk. He emerged from the forest intact, hurrying straight to the stable. There were some villagers around as he passed, and he couldn't quite tell if their stares were curious, suspicious, or murderous.

He didn't dillydally for clarification.

Austol seemed pleased to see him. He brought Nessa into the stable and told Jem to acquaint himself with her before he bustled off to finish some task or other. Jem stared up at the beast in the stable's murky half-light. The beast stared back, broad and unwavering. Neither of them blinked.

Then the mare chuffed, her tail switching. Reaching up, Jem offered Nessa his hand to sniff. She dropped her snout and gave his palm a wet, rough lick. That was good, wasn't it? He wished he'd paid more attention to horses growing up and worked through his fear of them.

He'd spent hours on horseback with Cador, but that was different. He had to learn to ride by himself and take the reins. Now that he was on Ergh, the idea of a carriage in this foreign land of rutted paths and rocky terrain was absurd. He couldn't just stay around the cottage for months on end. Perhaps if he'd had his books, but he did not.

He tentatively patted Nessa's head, pushing away the ache of loss and worry. His books would be fine! Even if he never saw those precise volumes again, they could be replaced. Although the thought *hurt*, and he imagined those worn pages that opened easily to his favorite scenes.

Nessa leaned into his touch, and Jem imagined she could sense his distress. He'd been foolish to avoid horses for all these years. It was time to conquer his fear. There were only so many chores to do around the cottage, and if Jem lazed around day in and day out, how would Cador respect him?

When Jem had quickly mastered milking the goats, the approval in Cador's nod and fleeting smile were like drinking sweet, heady wine. Their marriage was false, but they were to be companions for the time being. The two of them out in the forest, alone for miles…

Nessa butted her head against Jem's hand, and he laughed as he scratched behind her ears. "Apologies, my lady," he murmured. "I shan't neglect you."

"She'll have you petting her all day if you let her," Austol said, approaching with a fond smile for Nessa. "Won't you, girl?" He asked Jem, "Are you ready to try again?"

"I won't be taking you away from your work?" Jem tried to focus on excitement and not fear. He could do this. He truly *wanted* to do this.

"Horses are my work. I can still do my tasks while teaching you. So come on. You remember what I showed you?"

Jem had Austol go through it again. The technique mainly required momentum and confidence. He struggled for both.

"You won't hurt her, I promise." Austol watched from where he swept out a stall.

Breathing the musty air deeply, Jem removed his cloak, sweat gathering at the nape of his neck. His new leather trousers were still tight, and he wondered if he'd have better luck in his soft breeches. No matter—he would keep trying.

Before he did, he gulped from a flask of water that Austol had kindly offered. At home, Jem brought a flask crafted of thick green glass to his aviary, but on Ergh they were made of boar tusks, which he supposed was far more practical. The stopper was rough iron instead of fine metal topped with a jewel. "Why are you helping me?" he asked bluntly before he could think better of it.

Austol shrugged. "Why shouldn't I?"

"Bryok would surely say because I'm mainland scum and not worth your effort."

Austol curled his lip. "Bryok can go jump from the Cliffs of Glaw." As soon as the words were out in the dank air, he looked to the door as though ensuring they remained alone. "What I mean is... Bryok doesn't speak for all of Ergh. Has he threatened you?"

"Oh, uh..." Jem knew he should be cautious. Bryok was Cador's brother and the chieftain's eldest child who would rule one day. "He hasn't been particularly welcoming."

Austol smirked. "Indeed. I can imagine what he's said to you."

"Is he always so angry?"

"Yes." Austol sighed, lowering his gaze and busying himself with a pail of feed. "He's not without reason for his anger. He's suffered. But he's not alone in that, as much as he acts it."

Jem thought of the terrible screaming he'd heard from the nearby cottage on his previous visit. What was wrong with Austol's sister? He attempted to compose a probing question that wouldn't be unforgivably rude or upsetting, but quickly abandoned the idea. If Austol wished to share more, he would.

Instead, Jem asked, "Why are you being kind to me?"

"Why shouldn't I?" Austol replied with an awkward laugh.

"It's just that no one else seems eager to speak with me. They stare quite a bit, though."

Austol grimaced. "Sorry about that. You're the first main-lander we've seen aside from the clerics, and there's not much interesting about them. They only want to talk about the gods and repentance and Ergh regaining favor. But you're a prince—and you're Cador's new husband. A good deal more intriguing."

Jem laughed. "I hate to disappoint, but I'm of no interest whatsoever. My siblings would have far more tales to tell. Unless you want me to recount fictional stories from my favorite books."

Austol chuckled. "Did you bring any with you? I've read the same books aloud too many times to count."

For his sister? Jem still didn't ask, although the idea of books nearby had excitement bubbling. "Sadly I couldn't bring any. Are there many books here? Cador has none in his cottage."

"Mostly tales brought by the clerics, so cautionary tales about angering the gods. With Ergh of course as the example of the horrible fate awaiting."

"You know, I never really believed Ergh actually existed. Yet here I am."

Austol gave him a sad little smile. "Apparently we all should have learned our lesson about the danger of falling out of favor with the gods. I can't imagine what you did to deserve being banished here."

Jem laughed hesitantly. "I'm sure there are many wonderful things about Ergh."

"Once. But now…" Austol shook his head and put on a too-bright smile. "All right, enough delaying. Try again."

Although Jem's curiosity only grew, he was grateful for the change in subject before he asked something impertinent and alienated his only new friend. Leaning back, he launched into the hop-skip, gripping Nessa's mane and tightening his stomach, willing himself up and over her back. He almost crashed back down, but this time, clenching and grunting, he swung over her.

"There you are!" Austol applauded.

Jem could only laugh in delight and rub Nessa's neck. "I did it. I actually did it!"

Austol neared with a grin. "I told you. Now you can take her into the fields."

"Can't I enjoy this first?"

Laughing, Austol patted Jem's knee, but before he could answer, Cador blasted into the barn with—ugh!—Jory on his heels like a loyal dog.

"There, you see?" Jory said.

"Where the fuck have you been?" Cador demanded. He halted in a skid of hay under his boots, glowering up at Jem as though he'd yank him off Nessa's back and throw him over his shoulder.

Ignoring the highly inappropriate pulse of excitement that tightened his bollocks, Jem clenched his jaw. "Clearly I've been here. Learning to ride."

Cador narrowed his fury on Austol, who stroked Nessa's side, tilted his head, and asked calmly, "Is there a problem?"

Jory laughed. "He was w—"

"Fucking tell me before you wander away," Cador bellowed, cutting off Jory. "You can't go wherever you please, little prince."

"Why not?" Jem shouted back. "Am I to be prisoner here on Ergh after all? Will you bind me to the bed and keep me captive?" And curse it, his own words had lust racing, heat flushing his face and blood thundering south.

"No," Cador gritted out. "Of course you're free to do whatever you choose." He glared at Austol.

"You just said—" Jem shook his head. "Never mind." The euphoria he'd felt in accomplishing his goal soured. As much as he hated it, he wanted Cador proud to see him seated on Nessa's back. He wanted dimples in Cador's stubbled cheeks. He wanted to be told he wasn't delicate or useless.

"You left Derwa," Cador accused.

"She's fine now to be alone for an afternoon." He wasn't sure if he was more outraged or hurt that Cador would think him neglectful.

Without another word, Cador stormed out, Jory quick on his heels. Jem burned with resentment, acid bubbling in his stomach. He had half a mind to spur Nessa after them, though he'd likely tumble off in a most humiliating fashion. No, Cador was free to go sulk. Jory was probably eager to soothe him.

And now all sorts of images flooded Jem's mind, and he bit back a shout of frustration. He could imagine Jory eagerly dropping to his knees. Releasing Cador's swelling cock, nuzzling his bollocks, sucking him right down as far as he could…

"Damn it all," he muttered.

"Cador's being a prick," Austol said. "Ignore him. You've done very well."

Jem was ashamed at how eager he was for the praise. "Thank you." Why couldn't Cador have at least said that much? He'd only just met Austol, but he'd been patient and understanding. Too bad Jem hadn't been forced to wed him instead of Cador.

The thought struck like a lightning bolt. Hadn't Cador said they were both free to take lovers? If Cador was going to be off gallivanting with Jory or anyone who struck his fancy, why shouldn't Jem?

There was no reason. Their marriage was in name only, foisted upon them. Cador had declared that he'd never want to touch him in a million years, so why should Jem be lonely and pining?

His heart thumped. He was going to take charge. Austol seemed to like him. There was no reason they couldn't be friends who pleasured each other. This was what many people did, wasn't it?

Filled with purpose, he asked, "Will you help me down?"

Austol smiled. "Sure you don't want to try a ride first?"

"I'm sure." He was going to do this. For years, he'd hesitated and hid away, letting one soldier's rejection defeat him. Perhaps he'd secretly hoped Cador would see him in a new light, but he was kidding himself. He could likely get down from Nessa's back without assistance, but he waited for Austol to reach up his hand.

Standing again on the hay-strewn floor, Jem clutched at Austol's tunic and leaned in, determined to finally—finally!—have his first kiss. To the depths of the Askorn Sea with Cador.

Yet Austol took Jem's shoulders firmly, keeping him at

arm's length. "Whoa, whoa."

He should have known better. Humiliation crashed down over him. Of course Austol would reject him. Jem simply wasn't desirable. He was laughable, though Austol at least wasn't mocking him. Instead he was gazing down with obvious pity, which was perhaps even worse.

"Jem, I'm sorry if I gave you the wrong impression. Let me make tea and we can—"

"I don't need tea! I need to finally kiss someone! I need to not be a pathetic virgin anymore!" His voice threatened to crack, shame growing with each word that tumbled out helplessly.

Austol's thin brows shot high. "You and Cador haven't lain together?"

He could have bitten off his tongue. *Stupid!* "Well, you see, it's that—" He shook his head. "I shouldn't have said that."

"It's all right." Austol glanced about, keeping his voice low. "It'll be our secret." He guided Jem to sit on a bale of hay, perching on another close by, but not close enough to touch.

Jem stared at his dirt-caked boots, wishing he could disappear. Gods, why had he done that? *Why?* Hadn't he learned with the soldier? He was a glutton for punishment.

Austol said, "I'm happy to be your friend, but I can't be more than that. I don't favor men. I'm planning on marrying Hedra, one of our healers, if—if I can."

"Oh. Yes, I understand. Of course." Unable to meet Austol's gaze, Jem nodded miserably. After his brief burst of bravery, he felt utterly deflated. Was he truly so off-putting? He acknowledged that he'd only made advances to two men in his life, but to be rejected again *hurt*. Gods, he'd burst into tears if he wasn't careful.

No. He had to retain some dignity this time, or at least composure. He cleared his throat. "I'm sorry. I shouldn't have done that. I've been timid for too long, and now…" He glanced at the door where Cador and Jory had walked out together. "I'm so frustrated. Confused."

"And you're a *virgin*?" Austol whispered in the same tone he might have asked if Jem was a merman.

He nodded miserably. "It's apparently unheard of here."

"Oh, there are some who aren't interested in fucking. But you seem keen. The way you and Cador stare, I thought you were having each other every spare moment."

Jem gaped at him. "The way we… I admit I'm keen, as you put it. But Cador doesn't want me." The very idea was madness. Cador could surely have anyone he desired—he'd never want *Jem*.

Austol did the strangest thing—he burst out laughing. "Of course he does!"

Baffled, Jem tried to find the jest. It *had* to be a jest, but Austol looked utterly sincere. Perhaps this was more Erghian humor that Jem didn't understand. "Cador doesn't want me," he repeated.

Austol was still laughing. "Then why is he jealous of any man who gets within reach of you?"

"Jealous? Cador?" This *had* to be a jest.

"You know how you feel when he's with Jory? That's jealousy, my friend. And he feels the same way."

"But…" Jem couldn't believe it. "I'm not jealous of Jory!" he insisted.

Austol rolled his eyes. "You say I'm the only one here who's been kind to you, but hasn't Jory tried? And haven't you resisted for no good reason?"

He squirmed. "When you put it like that…"

"Trust me, Jory is no threat." His smile faded. "But you and Cador haven't fucked?"

Jem shook his head. "He said he'd rather bed a boar."

Austol winced. "Then he's a piss-head, not to mention a liar. He wants you. And why wouldn't he? You're smart and determined and beautiful."

"I'm not. I'm far too small. I'm—"

"Whatever litany of faults you're about to repeat, please don't. Don't tear yourself down. Trust me. Cador wants you. Even if he acts like a prick sometimes."

"But…" Was it possible?

"Is it true he was drunk at your wedding?"

"Oh, don't remind me. I thought him the foulest of barbarians. Such a beast. Yet…"

Austol smiled slyly. "Yet there's some appeal in…beastliness, is there not?"

Face hot, Jem confessed in a whisper, "I am drawn to him. To the notion of being…taken by him. I can imagine…much."

"I bet you can." He grinned. "There's no shame in it. Even if he's a prick, he's built for fantasies."

The urge to defend Cador rose up unexpectedly. "He's not always like that. He's been surprisingly kind in many ways. At first, I thought him horrible, but not anymore. He can be crude and…" How much should Jem say? Could he truly trust Austol?

"Is 'arrogant' the word you're searching for?"

He had to smile. "That fits the bill. Yet there's another side to him." Austol's amused smirk stung. "There *is*."

"I agree. Despite clearly acting like a childish arse sometimes, Cador is a good man. A worthy man. He's nothing like his brother. Cador or Delen would be far better leaders when the time comes." Austol shook his head. "But that's a matter for the gods. As for Cador saying he'd rather bed a boar, he's full of it. His foolish ego and stubborn pride are getting in the way, no doubt. I know desire when I see it."

Jem's heart leapt despite his denial. "It's not possible."

A smile tugged at Austol's lips. "You should give him something to really be jealous of. That'll teach him."

"What? How?" Blood rushed in Jem's ears. Was Austol right? Did Cador truly desire him? It wasn't merely fanciful daydreams on Jem's part? Daydreams he'd ruthlessly attempted to quell.

"Oh, it'll be easy. It would be *fun*. I haven't had fun in…too long." Austol smiled quickly, but Jem saw the weary sadness in his eyes.

"Some fun would be welcome," he said tentatively. "But I won't do anything deceitful or hurtful."

"No, nothing like that. Come back tomorrow for another lesson. That alone should do it."

Jem scoffed. "I doubt it."

"Right. Just like it wouldn't bother you at all if Cador spent the day with Jory tomorrow."

"I see your point," he muttered. "Although I'm not convinced you're right. Cador wanting *me*? It's as far-fetched as my favorite tales." Jem was no Morvoren.

Austol shrugged. "Come for riding lessons regardless. No harm in it." He looked to the barn door as a few children ran in, breathless and rosy-cheeked.

A girl with dark braids asked, "Can we visit with Eseld and read her a story?"

Austol sighed. "I'm sorry. Not today."

The two girls whined their disappointment in matching

tones while the boy's shoulders hunched. All their bright-eyed enthusiasm had vanished, and Jem's heart hurt for them. Eseld had to be Austol's sister, and he wondered again what was amiss.

He asked, "Would you like me to tell you a story instead?"

Their heads swiveled to where Jem still sat on the bale of hay. Eyes wide, they shared a glance. Jem could practically read their thoughts and almost said, "*Yes, it's me, the mysterious Southern prince. No, I won't bite.*"

Instead, he shrugged. "If you like, that is. I know many stories that should be new to you." He lowered his voice conspiratorially. "None of them written by the clerics."

The children shared another glance, then smiles bloomed over their faces. The braided girl said, "Yes, please."

So Jem stayed on the bale, and the children sat by his feet in their practical leather trousers and tunics. Austol made tea for everyone, offering ginger cookies as Jem recounted Morvoren's first grand adventure—minus the detailed sex she enjoyed with her huge-cocked merman lover.

Austol listened as he half-heartedly worked, laughing along with the children at all the right parts. It was lovely to make them laugh, and Jem felt satisfied in a way he couldn't quite explain. He happily agreed to tell more stories the next day. After the slap of Austol's rejection—even if he understood the reason—it felt wonderful to be wanted.

Later, as he followed the trail back to Cador's cottage, his mind spun with the question of Cador's desire or lack thereof. He ran through a cycle of disbelief followed by cautious hope, then thrilling anticipation before returning to disbelief.

Could Cador truly desire him? Austol had been so certain. Of course Jem barely knew Austol. Perhaps the man was often mistaken.

Perhaps not.

Darkness was still an hour off, but the shadows grew deep as he walked the path of dirt and rocks and roots, all dusted with pine needles. Jem couldn't raise his hopes. He knew the bitter disappointment that would follow. To be rejected a third time would devastate him. This was why he'd buried himself in the safety of books—Morvoren never let him down.

Around a bend, a horse whinnied. Jem jerked to a halt, his throat going dry. Did Bryok lie in wait? Surely not. He would charge forward and trample Jem if he chose, not sneak around. Still, Jem tiptoed onward, heart thumping as he peeked around the trees.

He exhaled in a rush. Cador sat atop Massen, worn leather stretching over his thighs and across his shoulders.

Safe.

They stared at each other, Jem hardly able to breathe.

Cador cleared his throat. "The path is deceiving here. See? It looks like it could go right or left. It's left."

"Oh." Jem tore his gaze from Cador and examined the path before him. He hadn't noticed the first time they'd galloped past, and going into Rusk there was no reason to glance back. "Yes. It is deceiving." It truly did appear to be a fork in the route. He would have surely stopped in his tracks and agonized over which way to go.

"If you get lost, I'll have to waste hours finding you," Cador grumbled. "If the Neuvellan prince dies on my watch, my father will be furious."

Jem nodded and found he wanted to smile. He wanted to *grin.* Cador had waited for him so Jem wouldn't get lost. Cador had worried for him earlier. Could Austol be right? The sting of rejection gave way to a warm flicker of hope even as Jem reminded himself not to get carried away.

"Now you know. Go to the left." With that, Cador spurred Massen and disappeared down the path without offering Jem a ride.

But he didn't mind the walk at all. The cottage wasn't far, and his steps were lighter.

Chapter Thirteen

J EM WAS NOT skilled in the art of inspiring jealousy.

His confidence waxed and waned. At the moment, he was sure there was no chance Cador favored him and that letting himself believe it was possible was a fool's game. The best he could hope for was companionable friendship until the harvest and their return to the mainland that felt so very far away.

Oh, how he missed Santo and his parents. He even missed Pasco and Locryn, gods help him. Sitting by the hearth, Jem laughed to himself, imagining the gods he didn't believe in granting some sort of mercy. Perhaps the god of water would carry him home on a massive wave.

His chuckle died as the cottage door opened with a gust of frigid air, the weather still not resembling what Jem knew of spring even a little. At least it wasn't snowing again. Cador clomped inside, grunting a greeting to Jem before fetching a tankard of ale and gulping from it, mud and slush tracked across the stone floor.

Nostrils flaring, Jem pressed his lips together. Would it kill the man to take off his boots by the door? Jem managed it without difficulty. He said nothing, though. The past week, he and Cador had spoken little, a new, nameless uneasiness between them.

Jem had gone for his lessons each day, staying until late afternoon to tell stories to an ever-growing group of children.

They gathered at his feet and gazed up at him with avid faces that were sometimes smeared with dirt.

Several parents had lurked, creeping closer by the day to hear the stories. One woman now sat right down with the children, and she gave Jem encouraging smiles.

Austol had told everyone to bring their own cups for tea since he didn't have enough to go around. The next day, two women began bringing the crunchy, slightly bitter ginger cookies Ergh seemed to favor.

But Cador hadn't appeared in the barn again and had said nothing about Jem's hours there. He hadn't asked how Jem had gotten on with his lessons and certainly hadn't expressed any jealousy. Austol had to be mistaken.

Derwa fussed, and Jem crawled to the crate. On his hands and knees, he peeked in and murmured some nonsense words of comfort as she blinked up at him, her eyes open fully now. It had taken longer than he expected, but her development mimicked the dillywigs' closely enough.

He topped up the water dish in the corner of the crate from the pitcher he kept nearby and registered the strangely weighty silence in the cottage. Still on his hands and knees, Jem looked up to find Cador watching him from the middle of the room, callused hands frozen at the neck of his fur-topped cloak, as if he'd been about to remove it.

"What?" Jem asked.

Shaking himself, Cador spun away, wrenching off the cloak. "Nothing," he muttered.

Jem's belly flip-flopped. Hmm. That look on Cador's face... Austol had said he knew desire when he saw it. Was that what it looked like? Did Cador want Jem on his hands and knees?

And *that* was an enticing prospect that had Jem's cock swelling. He shuffled back to his furs. He'd taken to wearing his soft, clingy breeches and silk shirts inside the cottage, saving the leather and rough tunics for outdoors. His breeches hid nothing, so he snuggled back under the furs and opened his book.

"What's that?" Cador asked after a time. He sat at the table, drinking more ale. A candle flickered by him, casting light in that corner of the cottage.

"A book."

Cador's tone was flinty. "Yes, I see that."

"I wasn't sure if you were familiar with them given there's not one to be found here."

"I have better things to do than laze about reading. If we didn't hunt, our people would starve."

It was a fair point. Jem said nothing.

Cador muttered under his breath. Then, sharply, he asked, "Where did you get it?"

"Austol. He has wonderful books." In truth, they were either dry-as-dust morality tales about the gods or children's stories on the same subject, but Austol had lent him a few of the clerics' books and assured him Cador likely wouldn't approve.

"Does he," Cador ground out before gulping more ale.

Jem kept his tone chipper. "He does! And he showed me how to control a horse today. I'm quite comfortable sitting atop Nessa now, so we rode her together. He taught me how to apply pressure the right way with my legs. He sat right against me. With his thighs pressing mine, I could really feel it." Jem parroted the words Austol had told him to say.

Cador shoved back his chair so violently it toppled with a crash on the stone, making Jem jump. Standing, his chest rising and falling rapidly, Cador opened and closed his mouth. Finally, he gritted out, "Good. Soon you won't need lessons."

With that, he stalked out of the cottage, the door thudding shut in his wake. Jem grinned. Perhaps Austol was onto something after all.

HOW MANY TIMES would Jem have to clean the floor in a single week?

He'd come in shivering from his riding lesson, the wind bitter despite all the promises that true spring would arrive any moment. Once again, Cador had tracked in mud. On some days, he returned home for a midday meal before hunting again, and his boot marks told the tale. The mess didn't seem to bother him a whit, but Jem couldn't relax until it was clean.

Grumbling, Jem filled buckets from the well and put them on the smoldering fire to warm. He mopped the floor, which at least kept him warm until he was ready to strip off, fill the tub, bank the fire, and settle in to soak.

He didn't mind having to curl up in the too-small tub, closing his eyes and listening to the fresh kindling crackle in the fireplace. Derwa chirped contentedly. She'd need a proper aviary shortly, or else she'd have to learn to fly outside and take her chances.

Too soon, the water cooled, and Jem snuggled into his robe, wishing it was thicker. Grunting, he shoved the tub back toward its corner. If he was to be mopping the floors constantly, Cador and his muscles could empty the tub.

Said muscles played on Jem's mind as he settled on the toasty furs before the fireplace. He idly toyed with his damp nipples. It had been an age since he'd been able to pleasure himself. He'd worked his body harder than ever before with all the riding, his muscles sore and stronger. He needed release, and with Cador out on the hunt...

Why not?

Smiling to himself, Jem practically skipped over to his trunk to fetch his candle and vial of scented oil. He removed the stopper, inhaling the gentle rose perfume, a clean smell with only a hint of perfect sweetness. It was one of the luxuries Neuvella had perfected.

He thought of his mother's tension over Ebrenn's rising oil prices that would impact Neuvella's industry of scented oils and perfumes. He really had taken for granted all the wonderful little comforts of home. After tipping a drop onto his fingertips and rubbing them together, he inhaled the delicate fragrance and vowed to appreciate such gifts more.

On his back in front of the fire with the furs soft beneath him, Jem opened his robe, slipping his arms out so he was unencumbered. He left the candle and oil beside him for now, first merely running his water-wrinkled fingers over his body, the fire's warmth delicious on his bare skin.

What would Cador think if he discovered him like this?

Jem moaned softly, spreading his thighs. He oiled his hands and reached down to fondle his stiffening cock and heavy bollocks. Caressing the sensitive skin leading to his hole, he pressed and explored, stroking his shaft slowly with his other hand. His eyes drifted shut.

He imagined he was back in the safety of his chamber at home, the door securely bolted. Touching himself, he relived his favorite fantasies of displaying himself for a burly soldier or woodsman or one of the marauding pirates from Morvoren's adventures. Imagined a fierce man hard for him, watching as

Jem worked his body, as he fucked himself with the candle, stretching his arse wonderfully.

Mmm. He reached blindly for the candle—and an icy gust of air spread gooseflesh over him. His eyes flew open to find Cador filling the doorway, his lips parted, snow whirling in around him. His gaze lowered to Jem's splayed thighs and hard prick in his grasp.

For endless moments, they were both frozen in place, Jem holding his breath. Cador snapped his jaw shut. A muscle in his cheek twitched, and he seemed to be waging a war within himself.

Finally, Cador twisted his mouth into a smirk. "Don't let me interrupt." His voice was hoarse.

Jem snatched back his hand and rolled onto his knees, yanking a fur over his lap. "You—you're supposed to—"

With a shrug that looked anything but careless, Cador kicked the door shut with a thud. "It's snowing now, and the wind is up. No visibility. We'll hunt tomorrow." He hung his fur cloak. "You must have to pleasure yourself often since no one else will."

"I—I—that's none of your concern! So what if I do?" Jem's face burned. Gods, it was humiliating to be caught so very exposed.

"So nothing. As I said, don't let me interrupt." Cador's gaze dropped to the candle on the furs. His dark brows shot up. "Well, well. I wouldn't expect such play from someone of your...delicacy."

Jem's whole body clenched, his heart pounding with an angry surge of defiance. He lifted his chin. "I'm not delicate."

"It seems not." Still in his damn boots, Cador sauntered over to the table as Jem sat back on his heels, his cock throbbing under his fur, the fire hot at his back.

Jem's breath was harsh and quick and too loud in the stillness. "I am not delicate!" He bunched his hands in the fur. He'd have torn it apart if it wasn't so sturdy. "I breach myself often."

"Do you?" Cador sounded bored, although his body was a wall of tension, his fingers twitching anxiously. He had the manner of a man playing a role.

What was this game? Jem wanted to shout. He wanted to *scream.* Instead, he lifted his chin. "I do." He forced away the embarrassment, filled with the need to somehow prove Cador wrong.

If this was a game, Jem wanted to win. He would prove just how strong he was. How bold. How brave.

Cador seemed to ignore him now, but no—he was contemplating the candle that sat atop the table. He worked it free of its iron holder, where extra wax pooled around the base. He turned it over in his hands, examining it, running his rough fingertips up and down the length. Jem's bollocks tingled, lust tugging deep in his belly.

"And you've 'breached' yourself with a candle like this one? With that very candle next to you?"

Heart in his throat, Jem nodded.

"You mean you fuck yourself with it?"

Jem couldn't stop a sharp inhale at the crude language, a bolt of desire tightening his groin, his cock leaking under the fur. He nodded again.

Cador laughed. "Are you too timid to say it?"

"No!" He gritted his teeth. "I fuck myself with it." A thrill shivered through him. "I do. I fuck myself. I shove the candle deep inside. I was about to before you barged in."

"As I said, don't let me stop you, little prince." Cador carefully replaced the candle onto the table. Was that a tremor in his hands?

Part of Jem wanted to cover himself and run to safety. Wanted to hide and bolt the door. Yet where would he go? Into the storm? And why should he run? Cador thought him so meek, and Jem had reached his limit.

What would Morvoren do?

Gripping one end of the fur, he yanked it aside. Now his entire naked body, specifically his dripping cock, was exposed. Terrified and exhilarated, he grabbed his faithful candle, fighting the urge to cover himself. He wasn't delicate. He wasn't!

"I'll show you."

He'd meant it as a battle cry. Yet his own low, hungry words uncorked a deep reserve of urgent desire that stole his breath. Here was his fantasy made real—*showing* himself to another man. Naked and aching for release. Displaying himself, letting another watch him at his most vulnerable. Submitting although he was the one wielding the candle, the one touching himself.

There was something incredibly arousing about being watched. He felt powerful, yet eager to present himself on his hands and knees for another man. For *Cador*. This was truly happening, and there was no running away now. He'd explode with need. He'd die.

Cador stood watching, thick eyebrows high as if he couldn't believe what he was seeing. His chest rose and fell rapidly. His blue eyes were dark. Hungry.

I'll show you.

Any lingering shame was no match for the raging river of rebellious courage pulsing through Jem's veins. Excitement and lust and desire too long dampened had Jem oiling the candle and reaching back for his hole. Normally, he took his time opening himself with his fingers. Now, he'd combust if he waited.

He groaned, working the hard cylinder of wax into his body. The edges at the bottom were rounded from use, and he bore down on the familiar intrusion. He closed his eyes, twisting the oiled candle slowly, leaning on his left hand on the furs, his hips tilted.

He squeezed around the wax, gasping as it pressed that secret spot inside. If he opened his eyes and he was wrong—if Cador was unmoved—it would shatter him.

The groan was so low that Jem almost missed it.

Almost.

In a wonderful rush of relief, he knew Cador was aroused. Aroused by *him*. Cador did want him. Vibrating with sweet, hot anticipation, he opened his eyes to meet an icy blue gaze undeniably dark with lust. Cador licked his lips, rubbing the heel of his hand over the enormous bulge in his leather trousers.

"What does it feel like?" Cador asked, his voice a growl.

Apparently they were done with pretending. They were doing this. No more smirking. No more games.

"Full," he answered. Spreading his knees on the furs, he sat back on his heels, exposing his whole body. One hand behind steadied the candle inside him, while the other roamed his torso, fingers circling his nipples. His cock was ruddy and hard, another drop of fluid hanging from the tip. But Jem didn't touch it yet.

Over the years, he'd become adept at fucking himself on the candle, flexing his thighs to raise himself up and down, the wax hard yet warm and slick. The fullness as he squeezed around it was heaven. His eyes drifted shut on a moan, but he opened them again, watching Cador watch him.

Cador's gaze followed Jem's hand down to his groin, to his fingers tangling in the nest of dark hair at the base of his prick. He reached farther to cup and roll his bollocks, little cries and sighs of pleasure escaping his parted lips. Cador was silent, his chest heaving, his hard cock stretching leather.

Jem swiped at the fluid at the tip of his shaft, easing down the skin. He lifted his finger to his mouth to taste it.

"*Fuck*," Cador groaned hoarsely, fumbling with his trousers to free himself. His thick, proud erection made Jem's mouth water.

Perhaps Jem should crawl forward and beg to suck that beautiful cock. Beg to choke on it. Beg to be fucked with it, pounded hard until he was shaking, split open and filled with cum...

He cried out, twisting the candle inside him, fucking himself and desperately stroking his prick all at once, his own musk on his tongue. His eyes were locked with Cador's. His skin was on fire. He was finally being watched, and Cador *did* desire him. His cock was full for *Jem*.

He gasped as Cador jerked himself roughly, his tree trunk legs spread for support, hand flying over his swollen shaft. Oh, to have that iron rod of flesh inside, throbbing and alive—

"Gods!" Jem shouted, coming over his hand, splashing the furs. His release burned through him so powerfully he saw stars, squeezing his eyes shut as he shook, clamping around the candle.

Cador made a strangled sound, and Jem looked up to watch him come, milky seed spurting from the purpled head of his cock. Cador's gaze was glued to Jem's as he stroked and stroked his shaft until he flinched. Panting, Jem eased the candle from his grasping body, his fingers clumsy.

Thick white drops splattered the stone floor between them. Cador stared down at his spend with mouth agape, his softening prick hanging out, fist still gripping it. He panted, and Jem fought for breath as well, remaining on his hands and knees.

He'd made Cador come.

Even if he hadn't actually touched him, watching Jem breach—*fuck*—himself had made Cador hard. Had made him stroke himself and find a shouted release, the evidence of which was stark, right in front of Jem's eyes.

Cador *wanted* him.

Before he knew what he was doing, Jem crawled forward and dipped his head, licking up the briny seed, desperate to taste it. He lapped with greedy little noises, shocked by his own animal behavior but unable to stop.

His bollocks pulsed, and he groaned and tugged his shaft, spilling a few more drops, his fevered flesh painfully sensitive now. He licked desperately. He ached for Cador's spend. Wanted it inside his mouth, his arse—wanted to be covered in it. Claimed.

A loud groan rumbled. Then Jem was flying up to his feet— the tips of his toes barely brushing the floor. Cador lifted him, full lips parted and lust-dark eyes searching Jem's face. His hands were warm, gripping Jem's ribs.

They stared at each other, their harsh exhalations mingling. Jem wanted to yank Cador's head down for a kiss. They must kiss on Ergh. He still didn't know for certain, but it was time to find out.

Before he could, Cador set him down and backed away, stalking to the door and out into the swirling snow, not stopping for his cloak. The door thudded in his wake. Jem stared at the wood, trembling in the lingering blast of freezing air, suddenly feeling incredibly exposed—not only because he was naked.

He snatched his robe from the hearth, the slicked candle resting on the furs so innocently. Cheeks flaming, he tried to understand what he'd just done. What *they'd* done. Cador had stormed out without a word, and his sudden absence left a hollow void.

The candle was like an accusing finger, and he quickly washed it and bundled it away in his trunk with the oil. He bent to pull on breeches, and his backside twinged. He'd been deliciously rough on himself, and even now, a thrill throbbed deep within.

Had he truly *done* that?

It didn't seem real. He'd pleasured himself in front of another man. He'd put on the filthiest show he'd ever imagined even in his fevered fantasies. Cador's musk lingered heavy on Jem's tongue, forbidden and intoxicating.

Gods, he'd *licked it off the floor.*

He squirmed in shocked embarrassment, pacing restlessly. At least he'd mopped earlier? Jem laughed out loud, a hysterical note rising. Yes, good thing he'd mopped before getting down on his hands and knees and crawling before Cador, lapping up his spend like... He didn't even know what! It should have been utterly demeaning, yet...

He laughed again, slapping a hand over his mouth. No matter what Cador thought about it, Jem found he couldn't regret it. Instead of lessened, he felt richer. Joyous, even. Nourished, like he fit into his own skin more snugly.

He couldn't control how Cador reacted in the aftermath, and surely the man was shocked given he'd fled into the storm without his outerwear. Perhaps he was disgusted, although Jem fervently hoped not. He'd finally—*finally*—acted out one of his secret fantasies, and Jem felt *brave*.

This hunger had lurked too long deep within. And now?

He was ravenous.

Chapter Fourteen

S NOW BLIND, CADOR forced himself to stop after a dozen steps. He welcomed the wind's icy bite on his hot face, his breath coming in soft pants. He welcomed it less on his exposed prick and quickly tucked himself back into his trousers, the rough material sending sparks over his half-mast.

Though he'd just spilled, his cock had life yet. When he'd walked in and found Jem naked and unashamed—*wanton*—lust had seized him with sudden violence, a tusk impaling a hunter who'd let down his guard for a fatal moment.

It had taken every bit of control he could muster to feign disinterest. He cursed. He'd been a fool to goad Jem even a bit. For when Jem had defiantly fucked himself with that candle, Cador had barely resisted the urge to bend him over the table or toss him to the bed or claim him right on the floor.

He'd fill him to the hilt—slam into his lithe, perfect body and take him until they both came even harder. Until Jem screamed his name and Cador's cum was dripping out of him, pale and stark on his beautiful brown skin.

Cador had fucked dozens of people in his time, but he'd never... No one had ever... He shuddered, the image seared into his mind—Jem crawling toward him, bending his glossy head of curls, lapping up Cador's seed desperately.

Not to mention the sight of Jem penetrating himself with the candle, fucking his arse mercilessly, his curved prick slender and deliciously hard. How Jem had eagerly stroked himself, his fine hands forceful, grunts and moans loud and shameless.

This was a *virgin*?

Finding the well in the swirl of white, he leaned heavily on the freezing stone ledge, considering the question. Perhaps Jem wasn't an innocent and had only said that to gain Cador's sympathy on their wedding night? Perhaps he was practiced after all.

No.

Honesty had shone from Jem from the moment they'd met, just as brightly as those honey eyes. From the moment he'd leapt to his feet at the Holy Place and protested he was a man. He was no deceiver.

Why shouldn't Jem pleasure himself? Squeeze his nipples into hard nubs, fuck himself and seek release, sweat slicking his bare skin, long eyelashes fluttering, prick straining…

As much as Cador wanted to take him roughly until they both screamed, he also burned to see Jem's face when he pushed home, filling him to the breaking point and giving him the cock he craved. He wanted to kiss those smooth cheeks, that luscious mouth. He burned to show Jem how good it could be.

Damn it all, he hungered to hold Jem close. To make him smile—*grin*—hear him laugh, watch him tend his hatchling, listen to him speak about the most mundane things. He hungered to know Jem in a way he'd never wanted to know another. Never wanted to protect another.

It made no damn sense.

He groaned remembering the innocent and eager way Jem had licked up Cador's seed, the naked need as he'd lifted his head, creamy spend at the corner of his mouth. They'd both just come, but it had felt like barely the beginning. Far from completion—the beginning of something much more powerful than mere fucking. He'd hungered to kiss and taste himself on Jem's tongue.

So Cador had run, and the tremors within now had nothing to do with the cold. There was only so long he could hide outside. Snow whipped more thickly now, and his fingers were numb. He rubbed his hands, gaze caught by the marriage brand, the small bird's wings in flight. He curled his fingers into fists, hiding it.

There was nothing to fear. It was his own home! He'd march back in and go about his business like any other day. He didn't know what to say to Jem, so he'd say nothing at all. Why should he? He'd given a challenge, Jem had risen—quite impressively—to the task, and they'd enjoyed fleeting pleasure. There was no need for anything to change. They would continue on as they had, marking time until—

"Damn it all!" His shout was swallowed whole by the wind. He couldn't bear to think of what the future would bring. In the meantime, he would *not* fuck Jem. He would regain his senses and slake his lust with someone else as soon as he could. Jem could do the same.

Why shouldn't he? Cador had never known Austol to fuck men, but that didn't mean he didn't or couldn't. He was free to. Jem was free to. It was the perfect solution. Austol could fuck Jem and Cador would be left in peace. Well, until they went to war.

Except the thought of Austol claiming Jem made his blood boil. Made his fingers grasp blindly for his spear. Deep within, a gnawing greed consumed him.

Mine.

Frustration and fury mounting, he stormed back to the cottage. He couldn't abide this. He would tell Jem another place would be found for him in Rusk tomorrow. He'd regain his senses once he was alone again. Jem could do whatever the fuck he wanted, and Cador would go back to his simple life.

He went the wrong way in the blinding snow, reaching the stable. He couldn't see them, but the goats bleated from their covered pen, the chickens safe in their protected coop.

Cursing, Cador yanked open the barn door, snow swirling around his boots before he pushed it shut against the wind. He wasn't ready to return to the cottage after all. Massen snorted as if mocking him. There was true danger in getting swallowed by the white maelstrom, but Cador knew this land. His home.

Yes. *His* home. He had nothing to fear. He and Jem had done...*that*, and it would never happen again. Cador would master this weakness. He had no choice.

For there was nothing he could do about Tas's plan and Jem's part, and if he was to bear the knowledge of what was to come, he must keep Jem at a distance. He couldn't allow this ripening temptation to take root.

He'd vowed to follow Tas's orders. More than that, Tas trusted him completely. He'd been so proud of Cador's loyalty and strength. How could Cador defy Tas now? He'd never rebelled like Bryok. How could he disappoint his only parent when there was so much at stake?

Breath clouding the air, he paced. Not only disappoint—that was far too weak a word for it. It would be a betrayal. A betrayal of Tas and their people. Cador and Jem and whatever madness had briefly consumed them paled in importance. He had to put Ergh first. It was his duty above all else.

Even my husband?

"But he's not!" Cador shouted, the protest loud in the muffled silence of the barn and swallowed by the wind's howl beyond. None of it was real. It never had been and never could be. He couldn't let himself care about this mainland prince. He couldn't fuck him. Couldn't let himself worry about Jem's fate. Though...

There truly was no reason Jem had to suffer for the plan to work. There was no doubt his severed hand would have a powerful impact on his mother, but surely it wasn't necessary. The kidnappers could send a curly lock of his hair. Jem could write a plea, and his mother would know his script. There were plenty of ways to make it believable.

Cador paced on, arms crossed as his mind spun. Tas would be with the queen, and she was already prepared to declare war. If she hesitated, Tas would convince her. And Jem could be safe. He could be part of it! They could stage the kidnapping with Jem as a willing participant.

He rubbed his hands, his confidence growing with each step. Tas would not be disappointed or betrayed as long as the outcome was the same. He'd understand. Perhaps even be impressed with Cador's initiative. Surely the better way was to involve Jem, who they'd underestimated. Now Cador knew better. Yes, when the time was right, he would confess to Jem and they could formulate a new plan.

His chest tightened as he imagined the horror on Jem's face when he learned the truth. It would not be an easy discussion, to say the very least. He swallowed hard over a surge of nausea.

Not easy at all.

Yet there was no rush! Why trouble Jem with it now? They had months still. Cador had time to work on the solution and find the right words. He'd make sure no one would hurt Jem. Then he wouldn't feel guilty and ashamed, like he was choking on lies.

"But I still won't fuck him," Cador told Massen. "That would be a terrible idea." He fetched a carrot from a box of treats and fed it to him, imagining Massen was nodding in agreement because he was losing his damn mind. "It's settled," he said.

Striding again with head high despite the sharp daggers of icy snow pelting his face, he reached the cottage and shoved inside. With a little exhale of relief, he kicked the door shut.

"Where did you go?" Jem had dressed, and he jumped up from where he poked the fire. "The storm is so much worse! I thought—" He shook his head, hands twitching in agitation.

There was no reason for Jem to have been, what? *Worried* about him? There was even less reason for it to please Cador with a traitorous rush of warmth. Forget the danger of the storm—here was more peril. He didn't need anyone to fret he was lost in a storm or ease his sickness at sea or greet him after a hunt with a sweet smile and eagerness to speak and listen.

He'd never needed this. He refused to need it now.

Cador managed to sound calm. Cold. "None of your concern. I'm not bothered by the storm." He tried to think of a false task he could have needed to complete outside. But why was he explaining himself? This was his house! Jem wasn't his *real* husband! There was no need for worry or explanations.

He'd made himself far too fucking soft. He stomped to the pantry to fill a tankard of ale, almost dropping it with his clumsy, thawing fingers as he gulped. He had to regain control. He felt like an untested boy riding his stallion for the first time, when Massen had raced across the rocky fields, not heeding any of Cador's panicked commands.

"Must you wear your boots inside?"

Swallowing his mouthful of ale, he turned blankly to Jem, his agitation giving way to puzzlement. "What?"

Jem's jaw clenched, his hands in fists now. "I said, *must you wear your boots inside?*"

It was the last thing he'd expected. Cador looked down at his snow-clumped boots, puddles growing beneath them, then back up at Jem. "Clearly."

Jem's nostrils flared. "Why don't you take off your boots by the door instead of tracking mud and snow all over the floor?"

"It dries eventually." He shrugged.

"Not before I tread in it!"

"You should be more careful."

"*Me?*" Jem's voice rose. "It's—" He sputtered. "Uncivilized!"

Cador mock gasped. "Is it? You know how much I hate to be *uncivilized*. So fucking sorry for getting the floor dirty."

His words hung in the air, and Jem's gaze dropped to the stone he'd licked clean. And damn it all, Cador had to look too, his prick swelling in an instant. Control slipped from his grasp with every heartbeat.

He forced another gulp of ale down his throat before stalking to the door. This time, he grabbed his cloak and gloves before stepping into the cold. Cador hesitated on the threshold.

If Jem worried about him, it was of no consequence, yet he muttered, "I'm tending to Massen," and left, bracing in the bitter wind.

An hour later, he paced the barn, Massen snorting at him in annoyance. He'd rubbed down Massen's coat and fed him more treats, and now the horse clearly wanted to be left the fuck alone. Cador couldn't blame him, but he continued pacing and muttering to himself, going over ideas for alternate plans.

He reached the door and spun back. It wasn't a big space.

There were three stalls for horses, Massen of course in the biggest and the others empty. The other corners were used for storage of various equipment, and Cador could cross the square barn in no time. Although currently he had to skirt the new object taking up half the creaky timber floor.

He should just throw out the damn thing. Take his ax to it and recover what he could for firewood. Which wouldn't be much, since most of it was a crisscross of thin iron. The blacksmith had done a fine job making it delicate but sturdy. Barely tall enough for Cador to stand in, so there was plenty of room for Jem and Derwa.

He sighed. There was no getting away from it—he had to face Jem again. And why should Cador be timid? Jem was the one who'd displayed himself so wantonly. Who'd been so desperate for cum he'd licked it from the floor.

Damn, it fired Cador's blood. It was no use denying it. Jem's display of fucking himself, his submission that was both innocent and deliciously filthy, aroused Cador like never before. Thoughts of how he would take Jem if he was given the chance rioted through his mind.

There were so many options—fucking his pretty mouth, spreading him open and licking into his arse, filling him with fingers and cock, binding him and making him beg for it. After the way he'd crawled and lapped up seed, Cador had a feeling Jem might enjoy being restrained...

He swore. He was hard again, aching and hot, and it took more pacing and forcing his thoughts on the most mundane tasks until it subsided. He eyed the aviary. Once the snow was finally done for the season, it should make a good home for Derwa until she could fly away.

Hmm. Perhaps it would make for a neutral topic and he and

Jem could move forward. Return to normal—or whatever passed for it now—and pretend the rest had never happened.

The snow had stopped and the wind was calmer now, so Cador returned to the cottage and announced, "I have something to show you."

It seemed Jem had been pacing too and now stood frozen in the middle of the room. He said nothing, and Cador returned to the barn, tugging off his gloves for something to do. Either Jem would follow or he wouldn't. Sure enough, Jem appeared before long in his new boots and cloak. He poked his head inside tentatively, then gasped.

Face alight and cursedly beautiful, he rushed to the aviary. "Oh!"

Cador couldn't deny the pleasure spreading through his chest to see Jem's joy. To have had a hand in it. He forced a shrug. "The blacksmith made it."

Jem ran his fingers down the twisted iron bars set into a wooden base. The metal was thin and delicate, but unbreakable. "It's wonderful."

"I'm sure it's smaller than you're used to."

"It's still wonderful." He turned his rich eyes on Cador, and it felt like sunlight breaking through gray skies. "Thank you."

Their eyes were locked through the aviary's spindles. Cador felt rooted to the spot, caught in that brilliant sunshine of Jem's gaze and the joyful gleam of his smile. As the smile faded, they stared at each other. The cool, dank air of the barn seemed to crackle and spark, alive with possibility.

"Do you kiss here?" Jem blurted. His eyes went wide, and Cador imagined he was about to clap his hand over his mouth to block any more words from escaping.

His heart sped. "In the barn?"

"No, I mean—never mind!" Jem studied his boots, his slender fingers gripping the aviary's spindles.

"You mean do we kiss here on Ergh?" Cador had to chuckle. Did the mainlanders imagine them only rutting like savage beasts? Not that he didn't enjoy that, but kissing fulfilled a special hunger. Cador's eyes dropped, and Jem's tongue darted out to nervously lick his red-pink lips.

After a shaky exhalation, Jem raised his head. "I've never been kissed."

Cador couldn't breathe. For an endless moment, he and Jem stared at each other. In the wake of the whispered confession, Cador's resolve crumbled, his surrender complete.

It was only a few strides around the aviary, and he had Jem's smooth face in his hands before either of them could protest. He dipped his head and captured Jem's mouth, swallowing his gasp and tasting a trace of ginger.

Cador kissed him hard, then slow and soft. He inched back just enough for Jem to part his lips on a sigh before sweeping his tongue inside. Jem startled, going rigid, his cry muffled by Cador claiming him with patient strokes of his tongue.

Melting into the kiss, Jem swayed closer, moaning. Cador still cupped his face, circling his cheekbones with his thumbs in the same steady rhythm of his tongue.

It was like drinking the sweetest summer mead, and Cador was sure his thirst would never be slaked. Jem's whimpers and moans were stirring music, his fingers grasping at Cador's waist, so trusting as he opened himself, his tongue clumsy but guileless. He was eager and honest and unlike anyone Cador had ever kissed before.

As Cador eased back and straightened, he slid his hands to Jem's shoulders. He should have let go, yet of course he didn't.

Now that he'd allowed himself to touch, the tide was too powerful.

He tried to keep his voice light although his throat tightened with foreign emotion he couldn't control. "Yes. We kiss here."

Eyes closed, Jem's little breaths ghosted over Cador's face. His long, thick lashes fluttered as he met his gaze. "That was…" He ran his fingertips over his spit-shiny lips. "Is kissing always like this?"

Cador bit back a groan. Jem's innocence was a spark to dry tinder eager to burn. He hungered for more, unable to deny it as he claimed Jem's mouth, his tongue demanding, Jem answering the call. Panting and clutching each other, they licked and tasted, Jem on tiptoes as though he wanted to climb Cador.

Cador couldn't think about what would happen. The future would come, and they would face it. But not yet. Not for months. He couldn't deny Jem nor himself this pleasure, especially if peace was fleeting. Tomorrow held no promises. There was only now.

"I want you in my bed," Cador growled. Ready to beg.

Throat working, Jem nodded, his eyes earnest. "Please. I need—" He nodded again. "Will you show me how?"

Cador couldn't imagine there was a man in all the world who could resist that plea. He scooped Jem into his arms and strode into the snow-still night, the only sound his boots crunching and their quick breaths clouding between them.

Jem's slim, firm body fit perfectly in his arms, Jem's fingers scratching at the short brush of hair at the base of Cador's skull and sending shivers over his scalp.

Oh, yes. Cador would show him.

Chapter Fifteen

I T WAS ACTUALLY happening.

Heart soaring, Jem clung to Cador's neck, pressed against spectacular muscles as he was carried off. He'd dreamed of this scenario countless times, but the reality was even better. Because these weren't just *any* spectacular muscles. Not a nameless fantasy man.

This was Cador, and Jem was safe.

Cador, who was maddening and crude but also tender. Jem thrummed with nerves and elation, afraid to finally walk through this door—although he didn't need to walk at all since he was being carried.

He trusted Cador wouldn't hurt him. He'd have never imagined such trust when standing at that altar in the temple, Cador an intimidating stranger, a barbarian from the unknown North.

As Cador swept him into the cottage, barely hesitating to kick the door shut behind as he marched to the bed, that day at the altar seemed a hundred years ago. Jem's life on Onan's mainland was so distant it could have been imaginary—a fever dream he barely recalled.

There was only Cador lowering him to the bed and wrestling with Jem's clothes, tugging off his boots and almost tearing everything else in his haste to make Jem naked. Jem reached for a fur to cover himself, but stopped. Breathing deeply, he vowed again to be bold.

Cador stood at the foot of the bed, eyes glued to him. Jem's cock ached, curling up toward his belly. Slowly, breath shallow, he spread his thighs. He loved to watch Cador shudder, knowing it was for him—improbable but somehow true.

Cador tore his cloak over his head, then his tunic. He bent to yank at his boots, then held them up after discarding the dagger he kept sheathed inside. One eyebrow raised, he made a show of returning to the door and placing the dirty boots on the floor beside it.

A jubilant laugh bubbled up in Jem. He could fall in love with this man. Gods, he already was, wasn't he? Falling, falling, falling.

There was no time to question it because Cador was back and naked now, crawling onto the bed between Jem's legs, covering him with blissful weight and kisses. Jem rutted up against him, barely able to move.

"Please!" he begged.

The fire flickered, in need of stoking. In the long shadows and orange-red ripples of light, the cottage seemed private and new, a cocoon where nothing else existed but the burn of Cador's beard against Jem's face as they kissed.

There was nothing but the rasp of it as Cador moved down Jem's body, sucking his nipples and teasing his ticklish skin, encouraging the sighs and moans that poured from him helplessly.

There was enough light to see Cador move lower. To see him push Jem's legs wider and higher, bending his big body to his task. Jem fisted his fingers in the furs cushioning him, expecting Cador to engulf his cock with his mouth. Finally ready to experience it.

Yet Cador dipped lower still. With his spear-rough hands,

he spread Jem's arse cheeks wide. Jem's breath caught. He squirmed, not knowing for certain what was to come. Would Cador—was he going to—would he actually—

The wet pressure of Cador's tongue against the entrance to Jem's body had him crying out. Derwa chirped distantly from the hearth, but Jem couldn't have stopped if her life depended on it. Gods, if his own life depended on it! He was powerless to a pleasure stronger than he'd known possible.

The intimacy of it was so intense he could barely stand it. Even in Morvoren's most scandalous pages, mouths were never used quite like *this*. The wet, rough texture of Cador's tongue set Jem's most delicate, hidden part alight. Cador was licking over the entrance to his body, and for some reason it seemed more shocking than sucking a prick.

The shameless stroke of Cador's tongue and hot gust of his breath, the scrape of his beard on tender flesh—it felt like something an animal might do. It felt wild. Forbidden. *Perfect.*

Jem's lips parted on a soul-deep moan, and he reached blindly for Cador's head, fingers gripping the short hair. "Gods," he whimpered.

The warmth of Cador's chuckle rippled over Jem's skin. "No gods here. Only beasts." As if to prove his point, he licked right *inside* Jem, using the power of his tongue to open him fully.

"Oh!" His hips bucked. He was spread wide, knees to his chest, never so exposed for another person save perhaps for earlier that night when he'd pleasured himself with the candle before Cador's eyes.

Cador very well might devour him like this, his broad shoulders pressing close and face buried in Jem's arse, hands keeping Jem spread and a willing prisoner to the tyranny of tongue and lips and scraping beard.

Jem's barbarian would devour him whole. What a glorious way to go.

Dripping, Jem's cock flushed hard and purple as sparks of pleasure danced over his whole body. He wanted to touch himself, but he couldn't bear to let go of Cador's skull for fear he might stop the exquisite torture.

Breathy cries escaped Jem's lips, and he thrashed his head side to side on the pillow. A finger stretched the rim of his hole. It wasn't unlike the candlestick he'd played with, and he welcomed it greedily, bearing down.

Cador groaned against him, his mouth still at Jem's entrance. His voice was clear enough as he muttered, "That's it. Take it the way you'll take my cock. That's my good boy. Every bit of it."

Jem squeezed around his finger, wanting it to be true, wanting to be able to take the whole of Cador's prick despite his doubts on the mechanics of it. He wanted to be good. Wanted to be wild in the way he'd only dared dream.

Cador crooked his finger just so, finding that spot with the perfect angle. Shuddering, Jem cried out. "Yes. More!"

His finger was deep inside, pressing and rubbing and making Jem shake. Cador kissed his inner thighs, looking up at him. "You're certain?"

Jem could only huff, half laughing. "Do I seem anything but certain?"

Cador grinned, but eased out his finger. "Say it."

"I'm certain." His voice was hoarse, throat dry with anticipation.

"You want my cock?" Cador sat back on his heels and stroked himself slowly. Gods, he truly was enormous, the head shiny, his veined shaft long and thick, jutting out proudly.

"Yes. I want your cock. No one else's."

With a growl and a shockingly swift movement given his size, Cador covered him once more, kissing him deeply, the musky taste on his tongue from Jem's own body. Jem groaned into the kiss eagerly. He wanted everything.

Cador heaved himself away and crossed to his trunk, dumping clothes and several more sheathed knives onto the stone floor without a glance. He returned with a dark vial of oil and poured it over his hand before slicking himself and opening Jem's arse with his fingers.

The oil was deep inside Jem, and Cador's prick gleamed with it. He waited for Cador to shove him onto his hands and knees and mount him. It would hurt, but he could withstand it. He craved the invasion.

He wanted Cador to seek his own pleasure, to take him hard and fast and flood him with seed. Jem ached to be claimed and filled, to wonder no longer. He needed to *know*. After years of imagining and fantasizing, he was ready, no matter the cost.

He nodded at Cador and said it aloud, needing to hear the words for himself. "I'm ready." Desperate to touch, he ran his hands over Cador's chest, hair tickling his palms as he traced the curve of the ink tusks.

Yet Cador didn't haul him over roughly to enter him. Instead, he cupped Jem's face in his hands, fingers slick with oil, and kissed him softly. Deeply. His tongue made long, slow sweeps until Jem could only whimper. Knees pressed higher to his chest, he was pinned deliciously.

Then he felt the prod of Cador's cock at his arse. Was he…would they…like *this*? He'd expected to be mounted like an animal, and he gasped, breaking their kiss as the head pushed at his hole. He blinked up at Cador, who smoothed a hand over

Jem's hip.

Face-to-face it was almost too much. Cador's lust-dark gaze pinned him just as much as his body. Part of Jem wanted to close his eyes and hide, yet he couldn't. Cador's blunt fingertips circled his hole, positioning his cock and helping it breach Jem.

For he was definitely being breached now, the stretch so intense he held his breath, his arse burning. Any moment now, Cador would plunge inside. Jem braced, squeezing his eyes shut now. Yet there were only tiny advances, Cador taking an eternity to enter him.

"That's it. Slowly." Cador's breath puffed over Jem's lips before pressing a kiss there. "Look at me."

Jem's lungs expanded painfully as he opened his eyes, the swell of emotion too much to bear. For Cador was treating him like a baby bird cradled in the nest of his palms, safe and warm. Peering down at him with patience and kindness, brushing back his curls with a gentle touch.

Yes, the pain of Cador's cock stretching him to the breaking point was undeniable, his shaft far bigger than fingers or a candle. Yet Cador claimed him with such care, bestowing feathery kisses to Jem's forehead. He cupped Jem's cheek with his palm, and Jem could feel the whisper of the healed brand, the dillywig wings spread wide.

As when Cador had licked his very core, the intimacy of this joining was so intense Jem could barely stand it—their breath becoming one as their bodies did, the blue of Cador's eyes so close Jem feared he might drown in those depths, the weight of him perfect. He pulled at Cador's broad shoulders.

Cador's smile crinkled the corners of his eyes. "You want more of me?"

"Yes!" Jem didn't hesitate. Couldn't.

"Do you like my cock inside you?"

"Oh, yes." Despite Cador's weight, Jem was able to roll his hips. He squeezed with his arse. "I want more."

Cador groaned. "Careful. I won't be able to control myself."

Jem squeezed around him again. "Don't care. I need it. Need to know." He rocked and clenched, the burn now stoking an inner fire that inflamed his blood and engorged his cock. "I can take you." He squeezed hard. "Go on. Hurt me."

He knew as he spoke the words that Cador wouldn't truly do him harm. Trapped by his muscular body, touched by hands that could snap his neck like a twig, Jem knew with every thump of his heart that Cador would keep him safe.

Cador groaned, gripping Jem's face and kissing him hard. "Little prince," he murmured.

Jem's heart soared with an askell's wings. For the first time, that didn't sound like an insult. He cried out at the searing thrust of Cador's shaft, the thick flesh like iron as it impaled him.

And gods, it *did* hurt. Head back and neck arched, Jem squeezed his eyes shut. He took shallow gasps through his mouth, fighting the tears that threatened to leak.

His hole was stretched more widely than he'd thought possible. He was so full of Cador that he would surely be cleaved in two. Where Cador had devoured him before, now he would shatter him.

Yet Jem did not shatter nor break. He was bent practically in half, the bristle of Cador's wiry hair at the base of his prick scratching the sensitive skin around his hole. His seized lungs expanded, and he sucked in air gratefully, eyes burning. Cador was seated in him fully, the entire length and girth of his prick inside.

Jem dug his fingers into Cador's thick arms, feeling the tension in his corded muscles as Cador held himself still. Lips ghosted over Jem's face, pressing into the corners of his eyes, kissing gently as he murmured something Jem couldn't make out. When Cador captured his mouth, Jem tasted the salt of his own tears.

He gasped into Cador's kiss, the burning pain in his arse easing. He squeezed his inner muscles cautiously. In response, Cador pushed a hand between them and grasped Jem's shaft. It had gone soft, but it was the work of only a few slick strokes to unleash a river of fiery blood flooding south.

Against all odds, pleasure coursed through Jem's veins like a surging tide from his bollocks. With his arse stretched, his body deliciously full, and now Cador's surprisingly nimble fingers teasing his cock, Jem forgot any lingering pain. He asked, "How?" Then he cringed and waited for Cador to scorn his ridiculous question.

But Cador didn't laugh at him. He only pressed a sweet kiss to his lips. "You're made for my cock. You're going to come with me inside you," he whispered. "Even though it hurts."

He moved, only little nudges at first, still buried to the hilt inside Jem's body. Jem whimpered, but Cador nuzzled and kissed him, his patient tongue opening Jem's mouth the way his cock unfurled his body. Movements grew in tiny increments until he retreated almost all the way, only the head of his prick inside Jem.

Jem clenched at him, his own cock straining between their bodies, Cador's clever hand still teasing it. Cador captured his gaze and asked, "Do you want me to fuck you?"

"What else have you been doing?" Jem blurted.

Cador laughed, a rumble from his chest and cheeks dimpling. He looked younger when he laughed like this with true happiness, not the short, caustic barks of derision or grudging snorts. He looked *beautiful*, and Jem had to kiss him, pulling down Cador's face to taste his joy.

When they gasped for breath, Jem begged, "Fuck me. Please."

Cador wasted no time thrusting deeply. They cried out in unison, groans and grunts filling the air with a song of soul-deep pleasure. It still hurt, but that was nothing now to the bliss building in Jem's bollocks, soaring through his bent body, in every bead of sweat slicking his skin.

Cador was flushed and sweaty as he fucked Jem powerfully—although not too hard, clearly still reining himself in, unwilling to cause Jem any true pain. Jem's chest tightened, his heart too big, and he wanted to kiss Cador forever.

Yet all he could do now was be fucked, jerking with Cador's thrusts, hands scrabbling at slick muscles, keening cries escaping open lips. It was better than he'd ever imagined. It consumed him body and soul, and he burned for even more. He needed to come. He needed Cador's seed filling him.

Cador seemed to know, and where his hand had only been loosely fisting Jem's shaft, now he stroked with renewed purpose. "Come for me, my little prince. Fly." He reached down with his other hand and pressed on the sensitive skin behind Jem's balls. The pressure of Cador's shaft inside and his clever hands had Jem's bollocks tightening before they erupted.

The world was soaring and endless as Jem came, crying Cador's name, his spine arched and mouth open. Helpless, he shook and shuddered. As the pressure subsided into trembling aftershocks, Cador thrust with renewed vigor, filling Jem with his seed, his shout of pleasure echoing off the timber roof.

Pinned with Cador's shaft still inside him, Jem wrapped his shaking legs around Cador's waist. He'd finally done it. He'd lived his fantasies—although there were so many more he was already eager to explore. And if this was all a dream, he'd blissfully sleep forever.

Chapter Sixteen

THERE.

Cador had slaked his stubborn desire and claimed Jem's virginity. He'd spent himself fully and eased out of his husband's deliciously tight body. Now he should roll away and order Jem to sleep on the hearth. Make it clear this would never happen again. That would be the smart thing to do.

Cador sighed. He'd never been renowned as a great thinker.

He brought Jem with him as he rolled to his back, tucking him under his arm and pulling the furs over them. Jem rested his cheek on Cador's chest, and Cador smoothed his hand over his curls and played with the sweat-damp ends at the nape of his neck.

He was a damn fool, and he cursed himself violently even as he caressed Jem's body, resting a hand possessively over his hip. Knowing he was the first man inside him satisfied a deep, primal instinct.

There was more, though. That Jem, who'd cowered on their wedding night, now trusted him enough to be bold and display himself, to give himself so eagerly without coy games—it filled a hollow place in Cador he hadn't even known was there. Suffused him with tenderness he'd never experienced. Tenderness he didn't fucking want.

Tenderness that would destroy him if he wasn't careful.

Jem had been caressing Cador's belly with his fingertips, and he stopped, raising his head. "What is it?"

Cador had tensed without realizing it, his body rigid with the terrible knowledge of Jem's fate and his part in it. But he would change that fate. He would earn the trust Jem had given so innocently. He would find a way, no matter the cost.

After a painful breath, he released the tension and focused on now. Now, they were safe. Jem was in his bed and no one had to know. In this moment, the future didn't exist.

"Nothing," Cador lied. He ran his hand over Jem's arse. "Are you sore?"

Jem's gaze flitted away, and he dropped his head, chuckling awkwardly. "I'm fine."

Cador lifted Jem's chin with a finger. "*Now* you decide to be bashful?"

This drew a laugh, a full smile creasing Jem's face. "Apparently."

Making Jem smile gave Cador a dangerous contentment and feeling of peace. It would become an addiction if he wasn't careful. But he was powerless to deny himself the luxury.

He gently slipped his fingers into the crease of Jem's arse. Jem tensed, and Cador murmured, "It's all right." He could feel the wetness of his own seed and tried to ignore the pulse of satisfaction. "You're not damaged?"

"I don't think so. It's a miracle, really." Jem shot him one of those special grins, and his heart skipped. Propping himself on Cador's chest with an elbow, Jem eyed his prick.

Lazily, he traced Cador's soft shaft where it curled to the left. The touch was curious rather than inciting, wonderfully innocent. He teased the coarse hair at the base of Cador's shaft and around his groin. It was intoxicating to be studied so intently, to be the subject of Jem's quiet scrutiny.

Cador found himself spreading his legs, allowing Jem to investigate his spent bollocks—although eventually the lazy pleasure of the touch would spark into a fire once more. But before long, Jem snuggled back into Cador's side, fitting under his arm.

They slept, and when Derwa woke them before dawn with hungry chirping, Cador ordered himself the strength to let this have been one night together and nothing more.

Yet he was weak. He kept Jem in his arms, nuzzling him with kisses until Jem squirmed free, laughing and complaining at how cold the floor was as he answered Derwa's cries.

Naked, Cador built the fire and wrapped a fur over Jem's shoulders. They watched Derwa hop around the crate, her yellow feathers full now. Soon enough, they'd turn gray and she would fly.

But not today.

"Do you want to ride?" Cador asked.

Jem's eyes dropped to Cador's prick, then flicked to the bed. His tongue darted out to lick his lips. Cador had to laugh and brush back a stray curl from Jem's forehead.

"I meant Massen. We should go easy on your arse."

Ducking his head with a shy smile, Jem said, "Riding horseback isn't much easier."

"True."

"Don't you have to hunt? Or does the snow stop you?"

Cador went to the door. "If snow got in the way of hunting, we'd have starved to death long ago on Ergh." Brisk air peaked his nipples as he peered outside. "And it's melting already—it'll be gone by midday. I don't feel much like hunting, though. Unless you want to try your hand at it."

"*Me*? I couldn't. I can barely trot on Nessa. Austol still has much to teach me."

If that smug prick went near Jem again… "I'll teach you." He decreed it in the tone his grandmother had used when she would brook no arguments.

Instead of indignance or confusion or argument, Jem laughed. He grinned wickedly, which woke up Cador's cock. Cador was about to demand what was so funny when Jem said, "He was right. You *are* jealous."

"What? Jealous? Of Austol?" Cador scoffed and strode to the table, splashing water from a pitcher into a cup. "Don't be stupid. I don't care what Austol does. Besides, he favors women."

"I know. He told me when I tried to kiss him."

The metal cup hit the table with a clatter, water spreading over the battered wood. Cador coughed and choked down his mouthful. "When the fuck did you kiss him? You said you'd never!"

"I didn't kiss him." Jem was trying not to laugh. "I only leaned forward with the intent and he turned me down flat. You'd said we were both free to be with anyone we want." His smile faded. "But you're the one I want. I desired you from the moment I saw you across the temple."

Shame that he hadn't even noticed Jem on the other side of that same temple slashed at Cador, mixing with the absurd jealousy and frustration. Yet control was like smoke he grasped at uselessly, the wisps slipping through his fingers.

"Austol said—"

Growling, Cador plucked Jem off his feet and kissed him, invading his mouth with deep strokes of his tongue until they both moaned. He tumbled Jem to the fur still spread by the hearth. They rutted together, Jem's smaller cock just as hard and hungry. Cador took their shafts in his hand and worked them desperately, not pausing for the oil.

They spilled from the rough friction in no time, and Cador didn't even feel ashamed at the speed, knowing he'd be hard again soon enough. Knowing he had so much more to be ashamed for.

Jem ran his hands over Cador's chest and shoulders. He murmured, "It's true."

For a mad, panicked moment, Cador thought Jem had heard his thoughts. "What?"

Jem grinned. "What Austol said. That it would be easy to make you jealous."

The relief was asinine. If Jem could know his thoughts, he would have run long ago. If Cador was a better man, he would tell Jem to run now instead of kissing him once more.

SCREWING UP HIS face and apparently his courage, Jem took a little run at Massen and tried to mount. He came closer than Cador expected, but Massen was twice the size of Nessa the gentle mare. Cador caught Jem's arse and boosted him the rest of the way before he tumbled to the slushy ground.

They laughed, and Cador mounted behind him. He scratched behind Massen's ears, leaning into Jem. How perfectly Jem fit before him, snug between his thighs. He could easily press a kiss to the top of his head, so he did.

It was as though he'd drunk far too much ale or mead, intoxicated by Jem's mere presence. Dipping his head to nuzzle his cheek, Cador inhaled his sweet, earthy scent. Jem sighed contentedly, running his hands over Cador's thighs.

"Or shall we return inside?" Jem murmured.

He chuckled and gave Jem's ear a kiss, reaching down to rub Jem's prick through his leather trousers. "First, we ride."

Jem thrust against Cador's hand. "You tease me cruelly."

"Aye." He rubbed the growing hardness. "I plan to torment you most of the day."

With that, Cador took the reins and clucked his tongue, only needing to give Massen a nudge with his heels before they were off into the forest. In stark contrast to their tense slog north on the mainland, Jem seemed much more comfortable riding. He had much to learn, but the stiff, constant strain was gone.

The memory of shoving him to the ground from the pale horse they'd ridden to the shore on the mainland struck him like a blow. Cador tightened his arm around Jem's waist. He'd been so careless with him.

How strange to feel such peace and ease between them. Although it could not last, he again locked away those truths. Today, he rode with Jem safe against him. Today was not tomorrow. Today, he directed Massen on a trail north, away from Rusk.

The forest gave way to snow-patched fields where sevels had once grown and now only hardy vines snaked over the twisted trees' ruins. Massen knew his way over the haunted tracts, and soon the sea's salty kiss carried on the brisk wind.

Though the sky was gray as usual, the day did warm, the snow melting and ground soft with the promise of spring. They galloped atop the cliffs, which offered a sweeping view of endless white-capped waves and the black rock beach that extended along Ergh's western shore.

Jem gasped, jolting so hard that Cador tightened his arm around him. A dred had soared up into view, massive wings spread as the wind carried it. The bird seemed to make no effort, harnessing the air as effortlessly as the little askells despite its size.

"A dred?" Jem shouted into the sharp wind as they galloped.

"Yes." Cador reined in Massen so they could watch the bird—the *beast*—circle prey below the depths.

They meandered the cliff at Massen's pace, letting him stop to graze the new sprouts of grass. Jem's hand rested above Cador's knee, and he drew idle circles with his thumb as they watched the dred. Without warning, the bird dove with shocking speed.

Jem cried out, clutching Cador's knee. "Oh!" he breathed as the dred's mighty wings flapped, water splashing in the gray sea as its talons emerged gripping a massive fish. It disappeared from view, surely returning to its nest on the cliff's side below them.

Cador felt Jem's shiver and wasn't sure if it was fear or excitement. Both, he thought.

"It goes on forever," Jem said, his head turned to the sea.

"Mmm," Cador agreed.

"Has anyone ever tried to find how far it goes?"

"There are tales of it, usually ending in the gods forcing ships back to Ergh or sinking them into the depths."

"Naturally," Jem said. After a silence, he added, "It terrified me when we sailed here from Onan. I've seen Onan's Southern Sea and it too had an endless horizon. But it didn't fill me with such...emptiness. Perhaps because it was warm, or because I wasn't alone."

Cador's throat went tight. "And now? Does the Askorn Sea terrify you?"

"A little." He laughed softly, his thumb still stroking Cador's knee. "I try to think of how fearless Morvoren would be and let her guide me."

"Is she a friend from Neuvella?"

Jem laughed again. "Yes, but she lives in the pages of my tales. She charges into one adventure after another with her muscled merman lover."

The guilt over the books knifed through him. Cador wasn't sure he'd heard correctly. "What kind of lover?"

"A merman. From the sea."

He had to laugh. "Does he have a tail like a fish?"

"When he's in the water. On land, he has legs like ours."

"Hmm. I wonder what kind of cock a merman has."

"Oh, it's huge. In the water and on land."

"This is mentioned in the book?"

"Yes. Morvoren describes it in great detail."

"Do you jest?"

Jem shifted to look behind with a smirk. "Not at all. Morvoren is a woman of…lusty appetites."

He laughed in surprise. "And this is all written down?"

"Are you scandalized? Does Ergh truly only have books written by the clerics?"

"As far as I know, but I've never been one for reading. Perhaps I'd be keener if I could read about this Morvoren." He didn't add that he could if he hadn't dumped the books from Jem's trunk. How terribly petty he'd been.

"I could tell you the story of Morvoren."

"Would that please you?"

"It would. I miss her so much. I've been telling the children all of her stories. They come to the stable when their lessons are over."

Cador sputtered. "You've been telling the children stories of a merman's giant cock?"

Jem laughed. "Of course not. I've recounted a carefully edited version for them with no more than a dramatic kiss, which made some of the children squirm but their mothers swoon."

"Mothers?"

"A few have joined the story time. Other parents too. It's lovely to be given smiles instead of suspicious stares."

Cador's chest ached to think of how alone Jem must have felt on Ergh and how little he'd done to ease that.

Jem added, "Perhaps the word will spread that the Neuvellan prince isn't so terrible after all."

He smoothed back Jem's hair and kissed his forehead, unable to find the right words.

With a little smile, Jem asked, "Shall I tell you, then?"

Massen ambled along, the wind easing pleasantly so that Cador's ears didn't burn. He listened happily as Jem recited Morvoren's adventures and how she'd come to have a merman lover with a giant cock.

"Was she innocent when they met?"

"Yes." Jem had faced forward again, and he glanced back now through thick lashes. "Her merman was gentle with her at first."

"Mmm." He idly stroked Jem's stomach, his hand slipping beneath his cloak. The tunic bunched under his fingers.

"Then she begged him to take her hard."

"Did he?"

Biting his lip, Jem nodded. He looked forward again, a tremor rippling through his stomach under Cador's palm. "They were on a beach—soft, white sand and warm water flowing around them as the tide came in."

Cador glanced down at the black rocks below. "I can hardly

imagine such a place."

"It's wonderful. You can walk right into the water without a flinch. It's clear as glass and the richest blue."

The Holy Place's heat and explosion of green and flowers had been foreign enough. This kind of sea would be breathtaking. "And did Morvoren beg her merman to fuck her on this beach?"

"She did." Jem hesitated. "On her hands and knees, she begged him to take her."

Cador dropped his hand to cup and squeeze Jem's prick, the leather straining. "You're already hard. I bet she was wet for her lover before he even touched her."

"Yes," Jem breathed, pushing back against Cador and rolling his hips up. "He filled her with his cock, and they rutted like animals in the shallows."

"Right there in the open?" He thought of Jem's shock that first night of their journey when others had fucked under the stars. Pulling up Jem's cloak to his chest, he quickly freed his prick and exposed him to the gray midday. "Where anyone could come along and see?"

Jem moaned, his fingers digging into Cador's thighs, his own legs spread over Massen's broad back. His cock was flushed and full despite the cold air. Cador spit into his palm and worked him patiently.

"Did the merman fill her with his seed?"

"Yes." Jem whined, leaning back even more for leverage. "Faster. Please."

Cador did as he asked, increasing the speed and grip of his strokes. Fluid leaked from the straining head. He put it to his task, spreading it with his thumb. "And you pleasured yourself like this while you read about Morvoren taking cock?"

"So many nights. Mornings. Afternoons."

Laughing, Cador bit his earlobe. "I bet you did. And you fucked yourself with that candle and dreamed of a lover like her merman."

"Yes. But also like you."

His own cock had swelled in his trousers, and now Cador groaned. "Me?"

"Big and tall. Strong. Hairy. Twice my size. Overpowering."

Fuck. Cador had only intended to bring off Jem, but now he battled the urge to bury himself in Jem's tight arse. He thrust, leather between them, and Jem ground down.

Jerking Jem's shaft even faster, Cador gritted out, "If I'd thought to bring oil, I'd have you on your knees so fast. I'd plunge inside you and fuck you until you screamed. Fill you with my seed and lick it from your arse and feed it to you with my kiss."

Jem did cry out then, spurting creamy seed into Cador's hand, head back against his shoulder and mouth open. Massen had stopped as they'd begun thrusting together, and Cador didn't hesitate, yanking his cloak over his head and tossing it to the ground. He tore and tugged at his own trousers and Jem's, pushing him forward enough so that he could angle his cock between the cheeks of Jem's round little arse.

They'd probably tumble off if he tried to actually penetrate him on horseback, and without oil it would be too painful given Jem had been a virgin not a day before. Cador wouldn't risk hurting him no matter how much Jem urged him on. This was close enough—Jem braced on Cador's arm around his middle, tipping forward as Cador fucked along the tight crease of his arse.

He came quickly, spending on Jem's bare skin and the hem

of his tunic. Gasping against the nape of his neck, Cador leaned them back. Massen snorted impatiently, and Jem giggled in Cador's arms, his shoulders shaking.

"He deserves extra treats," Jem said.

"He does. I wonder—" Cador's musing died on his tongue as the hoof beats echoed close. Too close. Had he mistaken their approach for the drum of his heart?

Jem had gone rigid, and now he scrambled to right his trousers and cloak. "Who is it?"

Normally, Cador wouldn't give a damn if someone caught him at play. There was no shame in it. But it was different with Jem. He didn't have time to examine why—he only wanted to cover Jem quickly and tell whoever it was to fuck off.

But Jem was so frantic he lost his balance, and Cador couldn't untangle his hands from the fastening on his trousers fast enough to catch him. With a cry and muffled thud, Jem hit the ground. A burst of panic seized Cador. Jem was a few arms' breadths from the cliff's edge, but it was still too close.

Of course it was Bryok who appeared atop a gentle rise, and Cador froze in his brother's glare as if he'd been turned to rock.

"Where the fuck have you been?" Bryok reined in his mount. Blood splattered his cheeks. His glare lowered.

Cador followed it to Jem on the ground. Heart thumping, Cador moved to at least reach down his hand, though it would be far too high for Jem to take. Jem jumped to his feet, his gaze finding Bryok's before skittering away, his head lowering.

He didn't seem hurt, at least. Cador wanted to leap down and run his hands over Jem to ensure he was unbroken, yet he remained frozen in place.

Coward.

Another rider had approached, and now Delen watched the

three of them from her horse. Calmly, she said, "We wondered if all was well. It's not like you to miss a fine day for hunting. Ruan spotted you at a distance riding this way."

Cador searched for an excuse. His mind was blank.

"I asked to visit the sea," Jem said. He stood straight-backed, his cloak in place, the hem muddy.

"Ah." Delen tilted her head and smiled. "You didn't seem keen on it during the voyage. Well, it's a fine day for it." Her gaze dropped to the ground.

Cador's discarded cloak was abandoned on the muddy, yellow grass. *Fuck.* Cador wouldn't let himself look down at his tunic or trousers—which felt too low on his hips, as though he hadn't been able to fasten them properly in time.

"Prince Jowan, let me show you the Rocks of Lowenn," Delen said, dismounting. "It's an interesting tale." She plucked Cador's cloak from the mud and tossed it to him before striding off. Jem followed without a glance at Cador. Delen's loyal horse wandered nearby to nose at the ground.

They were barely out of earshot when Bryok growled, "Don't tell me you're fucking that mainland scum. I wouldn't let my dog mount him."

Icy fury slashed through Cador as he battled the urge to smash his fist into his brother's scarred face. His silence was a confession, and Bryok's sneer gave way to true shock. True disgust.

"Don't tell me you have? That you…enjoy it!" Bryok spat. "It's bad enough you've allowed Tas and his plan to bring you so low by marrying that pathetic prince in the first place." He grimaced. "It could barely even be good sport to split that prim little shit in half with your cock."

Cador's mind filled with sounds and images—Jem's cries of

pleasure, his hole stretched around Cador's prick, pushing Jem's knees to his shoulders and thrusting into that impossibly tight heat. Kissing him and never wanting to stop.

It had been far more than good sport.

Jaw clenched, he barely held himself back from launching off Massen and slamming Bryok to the mud.

"But you must be playing with me," Bryok said. He laughed, but it was oddly nervous. Uncertain. "No way you're actually fucking *him*."

What would Bryok say if Cador told him the truth? That he was bedding Jem with joy and the only way anyone was chopping off Jem's hand was over Cador's mangled, rotting corpse.

Bryok hated Tas's strategy, but only because he was out of patience and wanted to charge to the mainland and declare war no matter the consequences. Not because he cared a thing for Jem's wellbeing or that of all the innocents that would be lost in an impulsive war. Cador would only alter Tas's plan, not throw it to the mud and trample it. Too many lives were at stake.

Still, the lie was ash on his tongue. "Of course I'm not."

Bryok clapped him on the back. "You had me worried there, brother. I should have known not to doubt you."

All you do is doubt me.

For as long as he could remember, his brother's praise had left Cador lighthearted, that rare approval gratifying and exhilarating, an addiction leaving him craving more no matter how many times he ordered himself to stop.

Now, there was only remorse and a terrible, hollow shame, even if the lie would keep Jem safe. If Bryok knew the plan was changing, there was no telling what he might do.

"Creeda secreted away some honey and has made her winter

berry cakes," Bryok said. "Hedrok's favorite. Yours too. Why don't you come for a roast tonight? It's been too long." Bryok glanced at Jem in the distance where he stood listening as Delen spoke and pointed to sea. "Come alone. I'll ask Jory as well. Kensa, Ruan and Gerren. Our sister, of course. She and Creeda spend more time together than ever. And there'll be plenty of ale."

Shame upon shame churned his gut. It had been far too long since he'd set foot in his brother's home. Cador had only spent fleeting minutes with Hedrok when they'd arrived back from the mainland. He'd told himself it was because he was stuck with Jem and had no wish to burden Bryok's wife and children with having to be in the presence of a spoiled prince for even a minute. Such lies.

Even more untruths came. "Can't trust him alone for long." Cador drew his lips into a sneer in Jem's direction, knowing he was out of earshot. It was best for the moment to pretend he cared nothing for Jem. He'd barely even had time to accept that he *did* care. "Why do you think I'm with him today? Useless little fuck almost burned down my cottage last night. Never learned to spark a fire. Tried it too close to furs."

Bryok snorted in disgust. "Typical. Fine. Come see Hedrok another time." It was an order—one Cador knew he should obey. He owed poor Hedrok that much.

"Soon." It was cowardly, but he just wanted to lock himself away with Jem and shut out the world. Forget about death and kidnapping and war and not have to think about anything but making Jem smile. Kissing him and fucking him and feasting on Jem before they faced what was coming.

Confronting his brother's disapproval—or fury—was too much when he could make his escape with his lover. His *husband.* He could hardly wrap his mind around it. Was it too much to ask to savor each other? To have a few days of peace while they found their way? It was so new. Cador couldn't bear to have Bryok tarnish it.

Jem and Delen returned, and Jem kept his gaze low as Cador pulled him astride Massen and they all turned south. When he and Jem were alone in the forest's dark embrace, they still rode in silence, Jem sitting stiffly as though they were back on the mainland. As though touching Cador was the last thing he wanted.

Cador could hardly blame him after he'd left Jem splayed on the ground. He bent his face to nuzzle Jem's neck, wrapping him in his arms as he pressed little kisses to jaw and neck and cheek and the shell of his ear.

His heart skipped, relief undeniable as Jem relented, slumping back against him and turning his face for a deep kiss. Jem should have told Cador to plummet to the depths of the sea. He should have at the very least demanded the apology he was owed.

"I'm sorry," Cador murmured against his lips.

Jem sighed into the kiss, safe in Cador's arms as they left the world behind.

Chapter Seventeen

A S THE DULL echo of Massen's steps reached the barn, Jem's pulse raced. Crouching, he arranged twigs and pine needles and scrub from the underbrush into a pleasing aviary floor. Derwa watched from her perch on the side of the crate, which Jem had tucked in the aviary's corner. Gray feathers mingled with yellow, and her chirp was merry, not a constant cry of hunger.

Jem should have been angry with Cador. Sitting in the mud when Bryok and Delen appeared, he'd felt foolish and cast aside. Cador had ignored him, and given what they'd just shared, it was a blow.

He should still be angry now, but his hurt had been defeated by Cador's simple apology and tender, remorseful kisses. Jem couldn't seem to regret it. After all, they *were* wed. Would it be so unthinkable that they find happiness together? Comfort and laughter and desire? Even love, although Jem knew he shouldn't dream of that. But surely Bryok wouldn't object to his brother's contentment.

Nor was Jem sorry he'd spent another night in Cador's bed. He definitely could not regret having Cador's prick buried inside him again. Although his fantasies had been rougher, his heart swelled at Cador's continued restraint. His arse was undeniably sore, and he had to be patient. The problem with patience was the niggling fear that this chance for discovery wouldn't last.

Cador hadn't entered the barn yet, although he could hear Massen's chuffs in the clearing. Jem had been flushed and half-hard all day. He *throbbed* with it. He'd always taken pleasure in, well, pleasuring himself. Now he itched to touch himself almost constantly, although he didn't, the urge to *be* touched even stronger.

He waited for Cador's return like an animal in heat, pacing and impatient. Perhaps this should have shamed him, but he found it absolutely delicious, eager for Cador's touch, for his cock. And especially those kisses.

As Cador finally appeared, Jem turned a smile to him. His stomach clenched at Cador's stricken expression. Standing in the aviary, Jem asked, "What's wrong?"

Cador shook his head, his voice hoarse. "Nothing. It's— you're—" He cleared his throat. "You're inside."

Jem motioned at the twisted iron bars surrounding him. "There's plenty of room for me. Certainly for Derwa."

Cador's blond hair had grown just enough that it looked a richer gold in the torchlight. Jem's fingers itched to touch as Cador asked, "How is she?"

Jem smiled. "Come see for yourself."

It was warm enough that Cador hadn't needed his fur-lined cloak. He stripped off his outer leather shirt and hung it on a hook on the barn wall. He was left in a leather vest with no sleeves that clung to his torso. He tugged at the laces on the vest, opening them enough to scratch at his sternum, his blunt nails rasping through his chest hair and over the tusks of his tattoo.

Closing the barred door behind him, Cador kneeled in the aviary, offering his extended finger to Derwa. She eagerly hopped onto this new perch, and he brushed her growing feathers with the fingers of his other hand, his touch careful and light. He dwarfed her dramatically.

"Hello, little one," he murmured. She chirped happily, and Cador beamed at her. When she wobbled, he instantly cupped his free hand under her. "Careful." He slowly returned her to the safety of the padded crate, smiling as she hopped and flapped.

Jem watched, affection melding with a roar of desire.

Still kneeling, Cador glanced up at him and jolted. "What?"

"Come here." Jem had meant it as a command, but it had come out breathless.

Cador's gaze roamed up and down Jem's body, a teasing smile tugging on his lips. "Is there something you need?"

He groaned. "*Yes.*"

"What might that be?" Cador tilted his head with a bland expression of mild curiosity.

As impatient as Jem was, he had to laugh. He never would have thought Cador would make him laugh so much. "You *know*. It's been all day!"

Cador's lips twitched, but he kept a calm expression. "All this time an innocent, and now insatiable."

"Yes. Get up here."

Trying to hide a smile and failing, Cador stood, his head inches from the aviary's roof. "What will you do with me now that I'm your prisoner?"

Jem could hold back no longer. With a grunt, Cador caught him in his arms, his surprised laugh cut off by Jem's tongue in his mouth. Jem's feet didn't touch the floor as he clung to Cador's broad shoulders and kissed him noisily, panting and moaning.

Cador kissed him back with an answering hum, tasting

faintly of the ale he carried in his tusk flask. When they broke apart, he lowered Jem to his feet and nuzzled his hair, inhaling deeply. Jem rubbed his cheek against Cador's chest, reveling in the scratch of hair on his skin.

Mine.

He unlaced the tight vest down to Cador's ribs so he could get his hands in, scraping with his nails, marking him. The scent that made him think of moss on stone filled his senses, and he kissed and licked, catching a nipple in his teeth. Jem was fully hard, and he rubbed himself on Cador's hip, not caring how wanton he seemed. *Loving* it.

Cador chuckled warmly. "What do you need, my little prince?"

"Isn't it obvious? I wasn't trying to be subtle."

Chest rumbling with laughter, Cador kissed him, sweeping his tongue lazily through Jem's mouth before pulling back. He whispered against Jem's lips, "Tell me what you want."

He brimmed so full with desire that Jem hardly knew where to start. He wanted *everything*. But, yes, there was one fantasy that had recurred through the day. Taking a deep breath, Jem rubbed his hand over the bulge of Cador's hard prick through his snug trousers.

"Mmm." Cador pushed his hips forward. He traced a finger down Jem's cheek. "You want my cock?"

"Yes," Jem breathed, rubbing harder. "In my mouth. Can I?"

"Can you?" Cador echoed.

Jem hesitated. "Er... *May* I?"

A laugh boomed from Cador's chest, his cheeks dimpling. "I'm not worried about your fucking grammar."

Head spinning with joy, Jem asked, "Then what...?"

"*May* you what?"

Jem swallowed hard, his throat gone dry. Knowing that Cador wanted him to say it aloud in greater detail made his own prick strain in his britches. "May I suck your cock?"

"Oh yes, you can suck me morning, noon, and night." He groaned. "Go on, get that pretty mouth on me."

Dropping to his knees on the twigs and pine needles, Jem asked, "Like this?" He burned to know what Cador wanted. It was a thrill to give him what he desired, like a perfect circle of need and response.

"Mmm." He caressed Jem's head, threading his fingers into the curls that he seemed to enjoy touching.

Jem opened his mouth—then clamped it shut as a burst of chirps filled the small aviary. They both looked at Derwa perched on the crate, barely more than an arm's length away. Jem playfully hissed, "Shh!" at her and tugged at Cador's trousers.

But Cador batted away his hands. "She's watching!"

"She's a bird." Truthfully, he'd rather not have her there, but Cador's prick was inches away, and Jem's mouth watered.

"Yes, an innocent little creature! It's not right."

Jem's chest warmed with laughter. "So the barbarian hunter is suddenly shy?"

In response, Cador hauled Jem to his feet, out of the aviary, and over his shoulder before Jem could do more than squeak. Cador strode to the cottage, Massen barely glancing at them as they passed.

Inside, Cador ordered, "Take your clothes off. Let me see you."

Jem almost tore his tunic getting it over his head. When he was naked, the stone floor chilly under his bare feet, Cador lifted him. Jem wrapped his legs around his waist. Before the fire,

Cador lowered him to the hearth. Jem's knees were cushioned by the soft pile of furs, and the glowing embers warmed his bare skin.

He stared up at Cador towering over him, still clothed. A thrill rippled through him, and he licked his lips, not even minding that Cador still wore his muddy boots. Tentatively, he spread his hands over tree-trunk thighs and leather trousers worn and soft.

"You want it like this? On your knees for me?" Cador asked in a rumbling whisper. He traced a fingertip over Jem's lips. His prick had swelled, and Jem eyed the straining bulge hungrily.

Nodding, Jem unlaced the rest of Cador's vest so he could rub his face against the trail of hair leading south. He freed Cador's thick shaft from his trousers, peeling down the leather so he could cup his heavy bollocks, coarse hair tickling his palms. Faced with it so closely, it all seemed quite *large*.

Cador's chuckle was low and intimate. "Suck me. Go on. You can do it."

And he could. He'd imagined it countless times since he was a lad, and now he was finally doing it. Although he was the one on his knees, he felt empowered and strong. *Free*. He could do this, and by gods, he would.

He began with fleeting kisses and licks, breathing in Cador's musk greedily. Cador stroked his head and murmured encouragement as Jem explored and experimented. "That's it," he said with a moan. "I like that."

When Jem was ready, he opened his mouth and sucked on the head of Cador's cock, tasting drops of early seed. Cador groaned heartily, tightening his fingers in Jem's hair. "Suck harder."

Jem did, easing down the foreskin and bobbing his head. His

lips stretched around Cador's thick shaft, his jaw wide. He sucked until he choked, coughing and dribbling spit. Cador pulled out, caressing his cheek and rubbing the tip of his cock on Jem's lips.

"Slowly," Cador murmured. "Good boy."

Jem cried out softly at that, his prick pulsing, close to coming without even touching himself. He sucked Cador again desperately, gripping his leather-clad hips, nostrils flaring. His jaw ached. He could hardly breathe. He loved it.

"*Fuck*," Cador growled, tightening his fingers in Jem's hair. "You were born for this."

Jem moaned around his shaft, straining, every muscle tensed, seeking Cador's release and his own, their fates intertwined. The tug of his hair seemed connected to his bollocks. As he sucked with all his might, the cottage filled with wet sounds of pleasure.

Cador throbbed in his mouth, gripping Jem's head as he came with a mighty groan. Jem swallowed and sputtered. Cador pulled free and finished himself off, splattering Jem's mouth and face.

"Born for this," he repeated, chest heaving, the leather vest hanging open. Using his thumb, Cador swiped at his seed and fed it to Jem. Jem licked, eager for every drop, salty and wonderfully male.

Jem was about to explode, his bollocks almost painfully tight. Before he could reach down to finish himself and find sweet relief, Cador dropped to his knees, toppling Jem back onto the furs. He opened Jem's legs and pressed his knees wide.

Cador took him to the root, sucking fiercely. It was mere seconds before Jem emptied down his throat, Cador swallowing, his wide hands hot on Jem's inner thighs. Jem cried out until he was whimpering, his body going slack.

Panting, Cador released him with a slow, wet slurp. He lowered Jem's knees but kept them spread, fitting between them and pressing him heavily into the furs with pleasing weight, his leather clothing providing ripples of friction.

Kissing lazily before the smoldering fire, their seed mingled on their tongues, Jem thought he might never want to leave Ergh after all.

"AUSTOL!" JEM CALLED as he burst into the stable on Rusk's outskirts.

It had been days of play with Cador, and Jem could still hardly believe it was real. Could barely stop grinning. Although he didn't know Austol well, he was eager to confide in him. He yearned for Santo, but his sibling was across the sea. Austol had seemed kind and patient, and Jem hoped he didn't impose upon him too much.

"Prince Jowan! Greetings." With a wave and smile, Jory appeared, wild ginger hair tucked behind his ears.

Ugh.

Jem struggled to keep the grimace from his face. His distaste for Jory was unfair—the man had been nothing but friendly. Austol was right that it was jealousy, and now that Jem and Cador were lovers, there was no need for it.

What if Cador likes him better? He said Jory used his mouth expertly—how do I compare? Will Cador tire of me and go back to Jory? He's bigger and stronger and they're a better match. What if—

Physically shaking his head, Jem silenced the nagging voice

of worry. Well, he muffled it, at least. "Er, hello."

"Have you come to continue your stories? The children have clamored for more. Some of their parents too. They've missed you."

"Oh!" It hadn't actually occurred to him that he might be missed. "I'll be happy to read for them later. I mean, not *read*, but talk for them. Tell them stories." He was pleased and flustered all at once. He glanced about. "Is Austol here?"

Jory's smile sagged. "Not today. Did you need something?"

"Is he unwell?"

Jory's freckled cheeks creased in an attempted smile. "Nothing to worry about." His gaze skittered to the wide, open doors of the stable. Jem thought of Austol's cottage nearby. He hadn't heard any tortured cries, but…

"Is it his sister?"

Now Jory was decidedly uncomfortable even as he denied it. "No, no. Nothing for you to worry about, as I said."

Jem nodded, although he was uneasy, remembering her cries of agony. "Do their parents live in that cottage too?"

"No. They died some years ago. A fishing accident."

"Oh. I'm very sorry." Heat flushed his cheeks. He was being unforgivably nosy. "Is Nessa here? I was hoping to ride her."

Jory's smile brightened his freckled face. "She's in the pasture. She could use some exercise." He grabbed her bridle and reins and Jem followed. "How is Cador?"

Jem stiffened. "Fine." Why was Jory asking?

"I've barely seen him. You're getting on well?"

"I suppose." Jem watched Jory from the corner of his eye. The man loped along easily. Perhaps he was genuinely curious or merely being polite. If he was jealous of Jem, he hid it well.

"He's a good man. I hope he'll be a good husband, but then I never thought I'd see him with the brand."

Jem cautiously asked, "Why not?" Was this some game?

Jory whistled to Nessa across the yellowed, muddy grass, but she remained chewing lazily. He rolled his eyes at her. "When he was in his cups, he always insisted he'd never wed. That he'd never love someone enough."

"Maybe he just didn't love *you* enough." The words escaped before Jem could clamp his jaw shut.

Jory's ginger brows met as he turned to Jem. After a moment, he erupted into laughter. "Me? I should hope not. We wouldn't fit as husbands. No, no." He laughed anew. "He's far too grumpy. You've nothing to fear from me, Prince Jowan."

"Fear?" Jem sputtered. "I don't—of course not—I only—" His boot squelched in fresh dung and he grimaced.

Jory still smiled, but his gaze was shrewd. "Cador and I have fucked over the years, but nothing more. Only friendship between us. In fact, I've never seen him turned inside out for anyone. Until you."

Jem forgot about the shit under his feet. "Me?" he repeated, heart skipping. *Inside out?*

"I admit I would never have predicted it. But I know my friend. He doesn't make himself sick with worry often. I thought he'd wring poor Austol's neck with his bare hands. He huffed and puffed and shouted because he feared for you. Because he wants you all to himself."

Heat flooded Jem's face all the way to his ears, images of the ways Cador had taken him cartwheeling through his mind. He dropped his head, but of course Jory was—regrettably—no fool.

"Ahhhh! The two of you have made good use of your time hidden away in the forest. Such a cock on him! He's an excellent fuck. I'm sure you are too."

Squirming, Jem scoffed. How was he having this conversation? *Out loud*? They were so *open* on Ergh!

"You are small, yes, but there is iron in your spine. I see it. Cador wouldn't want you if there wasn't." He whistled again. "Come here, you damn lazy beast!" He trotted out to Nessa.

As Jem waited, he chewed over Jory's words, grinning to himself one moment and fretting the next. Iron in his spine? He'd never thought of himself that way, and he doubted others had. Did Cador? The way Jem had submitted to him—begged for his cock and worshiped it at his feet, given his body to be fucked and controlled—surely there could be no iron will in that?

Yet… Hadn't Jem felt powerful and wanted? Hadn't confidence flowed through him even as he'd lapped Cador's seed from the floor? Confidence in his own desire. The power in choosing to finally surrender his body. The strength in choosing to trust. Perhaps his iron was constructed of slim twists like the aviary's bars, but it was just as unbreakable.

He rode Nessa around the muddy pasture, Jory having disappeared back into the stable. Jem was content for Nessa to amble, nudging her into a trot from time to time, relishing the twinge in his arse. His mind wandered, gnawing on Jory's words. Thoughts of Cador made him giddy.

When he realized Nessa had wandered near Austol's cottage behind the stable, Jem couldn't resist. He looped her reins over a worn post on the short fence and peered at the cottage. A thin trail of smoke curled into the bleak sky, and all was quiet. He was around the back, where there was a curious structure.

Was it a work of art? Indeed it seemed to be a small statue that rose as tall as Jem. Instead of carved from stone, it was molded from some kind of clay. Taking a step closer, Jem squinted at the four heads. It was Hwytha's telltale bulging cheeks that revealed it was a crude tribute to the gods.

He hadn't realized Austol was so religious, but Jem remembered vaguely that Cador had said there'd been a revival of faith on Ergh. He took another step nearer to get a better look at the curl of fire atop Tan's head. Wood snapped under his boot.

Looking down, Jem realized the same twisted twigs and branches that surrounded the tribute in the village carpeted the ground here too. A chill shivered down his spine, although he wasn't sure why. The gnarled wood reminded him of clawed hands grasping. He scurried back out of reach, then tried to laugh off his childishness.

Uneasy, he circled around to the front of the cottage where chickens clucked in their pen. He'd just pop in for a minute and ensure Austol was all right and fetch him anything he might need.

Surely Austol would be keen to hear that he'd been correct—it had been wonderfully easy to make Cador jealous. Yes, and he'd get Austol's opinion on what Jory had said.

Still, Jem found himself creeping toward the battered timber door. The air was heavy and still save for the odd cluck from the chickens. A single window was curtained. Instinct warned him to leave, but he ignored it. His imagination was getting the best of him—he'd read too many books of adventure and intrigue.

Perhaps Austol was napping. Why shouldn't he enjoy a day off? His sister was likely out playing with her friends, racing around Rusk and causing mischief as children did. As they should! Jem would knock and say hello.

Yet before he could, a *thud* sounded, the anguished cry on its heels not a little girl's. *Austol!* Jem shoved open the door, Austol's name dying on his lips as he squinted into the too-dark cottage. By the light of embers in the fire, he could see only shadows.

Then the girl screamed.

Jem couldn't say if her cry was borne of pain or fright or both. He stood on the threshold, blinking down at the child on the floor, Austol behind trying to heave her up. He could barely make out Austol's face, but the anger in his voice was unmistakable.

"Get out!"

But he could help! He would help fix whatever this was. In the gray beam of light from the door, Jem strode forward and crouched by the girl's bare feet. He reached out to take them so he and Austol could lift her thin body together, but his hands froze in midair.

As his eyes adjusted, he was aware of a strange sort of rash that covered the child's feet and legs, stopping above her knees. Her plain nightshirt was rucked up to mid-thigh, and Jem could see that the horrible marks were redder and fresher at the top as opposed to the old rash over her feet that looked brown and dry.

More than that, he could see that her legs were wasted. While she was thin generally, her lower legs were husks, and Jem was afraid to touch them. He crouched motionless, shame and fear battling.

"Get. Out." Austol's teeth were gritted, his face flushed. Behind his sister with his arms around her, he heaved. She screamed.

And Jem despised himself for hesitating even a moment. He took her lower legs under her knees, the limbs feeling boneless, her skin unnaturally parched. He lifted and Austol did too even as she screamed anew. They shifted her to the nearby narrow bed shoved against a wall beside the hearth.

Austol murmured comfort, tucking furs around her tightly and kissing her forehead. Jem flushed with shame as he realized that it was only once her wasted legs were covered that he could focus on her face.

She had the same long black hair as Austol, although it hung lank and stuck to the sides of her clammy face. Her eyes were narrow and nose small, wheat skin paler than her brother's. Her face was contorted in agony. Jem couldn't tell how old she was. Eight? Ten? Twelve?

"What the fuck are you doing here?"

Jem tore his gaze from the shivering girl, retreating a step in the face of Austol's snarl. "I'm sorry. I wanted to see you. I didn't think…" He held up his hands and repeated, "I didn't think. Forgive me."

Austol squeezed his eyes shut and rubbed his drawn face. He was sweaty and his tunic was stained. "Fine. Eseld needs to rest."

Jem knew he must leave, yet his feet were rooted to the worn floor. "What's wrong with her?"

Austol dropped his hands to his sides, brown eyes blazing. "Go, Jem. It's none of your concern."

"I only want—"

"Go!" Austol shouted so loudly Jem jumped. "How many times must I ask you?" Grief spasmed over his face. "Please."

Jem whispered, "I'm sorry," and backed away. But Eseld's eyes followed him, and he faltered under her vacant stare. He'd never seen such an affliction, but of course what hardship had he ever witnessed aside from hatchlings who didn't survive?

"I'm sorry," he repeated, turning as a small, stocky woman barreled inside.

Her skin was pale and golden hair knotted atop her head. She jerked to a stop. "You." Her tone was accusatory, yet her light eyes inspected Jem with apparent curiosity. Oddly, she wore a gray robe similar to those the clerics wore.

"He's leaving," Austol gritted out.

The woman, who was about their age, seemed transfixed by Jem, muttering, "Prince Jowan. A son of Onan. Favored by the gods."

"Er…" Jem gave her a little bow. "It's an honor to meet you. I'm sorry, I don't know your name."

"Hedra," she answered, her avid gaze roaming over him.

Jem squirmed, backing toward the door. He felt rather like a horse being inspected for purchase. This was the woman who would be Austol's betrothed—hadn't Austol said she was a healer? Perhaps they wore robes on Ergh.

"Again, I apologize," Jem said, backing right into another person in the doorway and finding Cador had arrived too.

Cador stood transfixed, staring at Eseld's shivering frame. Horror was written plainly on his handsome face, but there was also a terrible grief that had Jem reaching for him.

Cador backed away from Jem's touch, shaking his head. Jem followed, gently closing the cottage door behind them. His heart sank as he spotted Jory by the stable speaking with Bryok of all people.

Jem was embarrassed and confused, smarting from Austol's anger, worried for Eseld, and unnerved by Hedra. The last person he wanted to deal with was Bryok, but fortunately the two men disappeared into the distance.

"What are you doing here?" he asked Cador. He grabbed at Nessa's reins and led her back to the stable.

"What am *I* doing here? Massen needs a new shoe. What the fuck were you doing in Austol's cottage?"

For a mad moment, Jem thought Cador might be jealous

again, and his traitorous heart swelled. But no, this wasn't jealousy. "I only wanted to say hello." He cringed at his high-pitched defensiveness and sighed. "I heard a noise and thought Austol needed help. And he did! Although he asked me to leave and I should have respected his wishes."

Cador sighed as well. "Of course you wanted to help. It's not your fault."

There seemed to be more Cador wanted to say, but he didn't. The apprentice was busy with Massen in one of the far stalls, so Jem rubbed down Nessa himself while Cador paced in a brooding silence.

Finally, Jem quietly asked, "What's wrong with his sister? Eseld."

That horror and grief returned, creasing Cador's face. Cador was silent so long that Jem was afraid to breathe lest he break the spell.

Tell me. Please.

Jem whispered, "I want to help."

"I know. But she's not one of your hatchlings."

"Why won't you tell me what's going on?"

Cador winced, rubbing his face. "If only I knew where to begin." He gazed up at the high timber beams of the ceiling, as if the gods he didn't believe in had written some answer there.

"You can tell me." Jem waited, wanting to grab him and shake whatever this truth was free—or simply hold him and offer comfort. He pet Nessa instead.

Cador blew out a long breath before meeting Jem's gaze. "I will. Can you give me a bit more time? I have so many thoughts." He grimaced as he motioned to his head.

After the tension of what happened in the cottage and now Cador's miserable expression, Jem tried to lighten the heavy air.

"I imagine they have space to rattle around."

For a moment, Cador only blinked. Then a laugh punched out of him, his cheeks dimpling. "So you can jest after all."

Jem let himself laugh too, the relief sweet. "Who's jesting?"

With a chuckle, Cador brushed a hand over Jem's hair before his gaze grew serious again. "I will tell you everything. Soon. I swear it."

Jem nodded. "I'll be patient." Honestly, as much as he wanted to know, he'd had enough strain and worry for the day. "I'm about ready for bed. It's too early, though."

"Well…" Cador leaned in, his lips brushing Jem's ear. "It's too early for sleep. What else could we do in bed to pass the time?"

Desire skated over Jem's skin, his belly tightening. "Suppose we might think of something." He stole his hands under Cador's shirt, flattening his palms on—

"Jem!"

The girl's joyous cry echoed through the stable as she and a dozen children stormed inside. Jem and Cador leapt back from each other as if they'd burst into flames.

"Yes!" Jem said. "Er, I'm here. Uh-huh."

"Are you going to tell us more of the story?" Sowena asked, her dark braids swaying.

"Of course." He glanced to Cador. "I suppose we aren't in such a rush after all?"

Cador smiled at the children already gathering in a semicircle around the bale of hay that had become Jem's perch for story time. "I suppose not."

So Jem told them more of Morvoren's adventures, even more parents arriving to listen in as well. Cador stayed back, leaning a shoulder against Nessa's stall and scratching her ears.

But he followed the tale just as intently as the children did, and Jem felt the pleasing weight of his gaze on him like a caress.

Later, Cador boosted him onto Massen. Staring up at him, he took Jem's hand, tracing the branded tusks with his finger. Then he lifted Jem's palm to his lips for a tender kiss before mounting behind him and spurring Massen toward the forest.

He'd known already he was falling in love with Cador, but now Jem soared.

Chapter Eighteen

H E HAD TO tell Jem.

Not only the truth about the disease, but all of it. The whole tale from top to bottom, as much as Cador dreaded it. He'd been the worst kind of fool to take Jem into his bed. To allow himself that glorious indulgence. He should regret it, yet he couldn't.

While Jem fussed over Derwa in the barn the next morning, Cador paced the cottage, stone cold under his feet. Muttering, he threw another log onto the fire, welcoming the kiss of sparks on his bare toes.

Seeing Eseld's agony was unbearable. A stark reminder of what was at stake. Cador hadn't allowed himself to think of his nephew and the disease claiming him by inches like a bog of thick quicksand. Other children had had their legs amputated to halt the disease's progression. It had failed.

It seemed nothing could stop the suffering, and he was a coward to look away. It was beyond shameful how he'd avoided Hedrok since returning from the mainland. Shameful that he couldn't face the horror of it. Shameful that he'd married an innocent man knowing he was merely a pawn.

Of course Jem was so much more. When Tas first announced his plan, it hadn't occurred to Cador to ask the prince's fate. He hadn't even known Jem's name until that day at the Holy Place, laughing at this defiant little prince jumping to his feet to insist he was a man. It seemed an eternity ago.

He paced to the wall of spears and ran his fingers over the deadly wood. The weapons were like old friends in his grasp. Yet was he a warrior? He was a hunter, but he'd never been to battle. None of them had. What did they know of war?

Still, they must find a way forward without giving in to the clerics' demands. Tas was right that they sought control, for wasn't that what they all wanted in their own ways? Ergh must retain its independence. If they allowed temples and permanent enclaves of clerics, what was next? Would they be "tamed" and molded into the mainland's idea of civility?

He thought of carriages and silks and indulgent sweet cakes shaped like butterflies and shuddered. Perhaps those were meaningless things not worth a second thought, but he could envision a future where bit by bit, Ergh became unrecognizable.

Yet what of Ebrenn and its people? How would it be changed if Ergh and Neuvella and Gwels joined forces to conquer it? Ergh only wanted control of the sevel fields, but what would that control look like? There were so many questions Cador had buried, letting Tas lead, being an obedient son as always. Priding himself on Tas's trust and favor.

If only the sevels would grow on Ergh again, but they'd tried for years. Ebrenn was now the only place they flourished. And now the healers were certain it was the sevels that held the key to preventing this vicious, merciless disease. Eseld's heartrending screams echoed in his mind, and he desperately wanted to muffle them.

But he'd been doing that far too long. Avoiding his nephew as if not seeing him waste away could make it untrue. Blocking it out like a child sticking his fingers in his ears. Like a fucking coward.

Oh, how he longed for life to be simple again. To go back to the way things were before the terrible sickness and playing politics and planning war.

Yet he'd never have met Jem. Living his simple life in his little cottage, he'd never have even set foot on the mainland. Never have spared so much as a fleeting thought for distant royalty and a Neuvellan prince who loved books and birds.

He didn't know what was right anymore. All he knew was he had to confess to Jem, but if he simply blurted it all out before he had a solid plan of his own, he was sure to say the wrong things.

Cador couldn't tell Jem, *By the way, there's a plot to have you kidnapped and chop off your hand to spark a war. I'll die before I let anyone hurt you, but I'm not quite sure what we'll do instead. Nothing to worry about!*

He had to be certain. He had to be confident. If he was to be a warrior, he must act like one. Jem would need assurance. Cador could vow to keep him safe, but wouldn't those words be hollow without some meat behind them?

He had ideas, but he needed to mold them. Make them stone. He paced to the fire and back to the spears and it came to him. He'd seek his sister's counsel. Of course! Delen knew how Tas thought. They could hatch a new strategy that would protect Jem and still provide the children's salvation.

It was handling Bryok that would be the problem. Bryok would do anything for his son. For his infant girl who might any day show the first terrible signs of the disease stealing Hedrok from them. Cador couldn't blame his brother for that. Still, there had to be another way. A better way.

Delen was close to Creeda. They could work together to make Bryok understand Jem wasn't the enemy. If they could get

Bryok on their side and make him see Jem could help them, that was to the benefit of all.

For Jem would surely sympathize with their plight. He was good and kind and would do all in his power to help. And perhaps he could wield more power than they'd imagined. Cador had certainly underestimated him, as had Tas. Jem could be far more valuable than as a pawn.

Cador paced so quickly he was almost running the length of the cottage like a caged animal. There had to be another way, and he would find it. Delen was on the hunt today, and since Cador had begged off, he'd speak with her tomorrow. He'd tossed and turned all night, but later he could sleep well and be at full strength in the morning.

There. It was settled.

The energy that had tumbled through him madly subsided the way it did in the aftermath of a good fuck. He was drained, but satisfied. He and Jem could relax now. Enjoy one more day together before they faced it all. Surely not too much to ask for. A day of peace and coupling would be too rare soon enough.

They lunched on smoked boar and roasted turnips, and Cador was feeling quite satisfied with himself when Jem said wistfully, "If only I had my books."

Cador groaned inwardly. Of all the subjects to raise. He tried to wave it away like a pesky fly. "You know the stories by heart anyway. You tell them so well."

Jem smiled. "Thank you." He sipped his ale as they sat at the table. "I still treasure the pages. I wish I knew they were in safe hands."

Guilt flared like thorny vines encircling Cador. Here was one more to add to his list of betrayals. He was powerless to right this wrong. All he could do was stew in his dishonor for acting so childishly. So cruelly.

Jem didn't seem to notice his agitation. "Santo and my parents would have been sure to pack them. Even my brothers wouldn't have been so vindictive to make me go to Ergh without them. Perhaps—"

"It was me!" The shame erupted with his words, blood heating Cador's face. As Jem stared, eyes wide, he confessed in a helpless rush. "I saw servants struggling to load your trunk. It was too heavy." He exhaled sharply in disgust at his own attempt to pardon his treachery. No more.

Clearing his throat, he admitted the rest. "I felt burdened with you. I knew you were blameless, yet I punished you. I removed the books from your trunk. It was...*petty.*" He spat the word as though it tasted of sour milk. "I have no excuse. I'm sorry." For that and so much more.

For endless heartbeats, Jem only stared at him, blinking the hint of tears from his honey eyes. Cador ached to turn back time and erase his own stupidity, to rescue Jem from this pain. "I'm sorry," he said again. "What can I do?"

Jem didn't answer. Instead, he croaked, "What did you do with my books?"

"I..." Hadn't he already told him? Must he say it again? Cador hated himself as he repeated, "I removed the books from the trunk."

"Yes, but where did you put them?" Jem's voice grew louder, his hands shaking. "Where?"

Cador couldn't recall ever feeling so low and disgraceful as he admitted, "I left them on the ground."

Jem sucked in a sharp breath. "You left my books in the dirt? Like nothing but...trash?"

He nodded miserably, for what else could he do? "Beat me

black and blue. I deserve it." If Jem only knew how very much he deserved it. Perhaps he should confess it all now and be done with it, but he'd surely make everything worse piling hurt upon hurt, especially if he blundered through it without a calm, rational strategy.

Jem shook his head, his anger deflating. "I don't want to beat you."

"But you should! I acted no better than a sarf slithering on its belly."

"It won't magically make my books appear." Shoulders hunched, he kept his eyes down.

This shocked, disappointed hurt was even worse than anger and disbelief. "No, you should punish me!" *You must.*

Jem only turned away from him, and Cador wanted to beg. He slumped as Jem bundled into his cloak and left, likely escaping to the barn and his hatchling whose only betrayal would be to one day fly free.

"Jem!"

The gray sky grew darker as the afternoon went on. When Cador discovered Derwa hopping alone in the aviary, his heart had sunk. But surely Jem hadn't returned to Austol's cottage? Had he gone alone into Rusk? No. Cador was sure he wouldn't. Though he'd become popular with some of the children and their parents, he was still an outsider.

His trail had been easy enough to find once Cador searched. He'd been oddly proud that Jem had ventured into the trees. Now his stomach was knotted thinking of the dangers facing Jem within, and he gripped his spear so hard he wouldn't have been surprised to leave finger marks in the ancient wood.

This spear was shorter than those he used on horseback. He typically wore it slung over his back unless he had his sword, but he was too on edge, every muffled sound of the forest tightening the iron band around his lungs. He wanted his spear ready in his grasp.

"Jem!"

Was he hiding? Hurt? The shadows grew longer. Deeper. Cador knew these woods like his own cottage, yet he stumbled, pine needles scratching his face and muffling his steps. His heart drummed too loud in his ears in the silence—then even louder when a crow cawed from the branches above.

Cador had never felt lonely in these woods, yet he did now, jumping at shadows, worry gnawing. He understood Jem couldn't even look at him after what he'd done, but he needed to know he was safe.

As he searched, his mind returned to Jem telling the stories from his beloved books. How avidly the children and parents had listened, no traces of suspicion toward Jem remaining. Cador had thought it best for everyone to keep Jem apart from Rusk. He hadn't barred him from lessons with Austol—as tempted as he'd been to ease his own jealousy—but nor had he encouraged his people to know Jem.

He'd thought the mainlanders so different. They all had. Yet as much as he wanted to maintain Ergh's independence from the clerics, he could now envision a future of sharing and fellowship with the people of Onan. A future with Jem accepted and welcomed on Ergh.

Yet first they were to wage war, and Cador dreaded it more than ever.

"Jem!" He stopped to listen. Nothing.

No trace of snow remained, the ground muddy and thawed. The white flowers that burst up to carpet the forest at the first hint of true spring poked their heads through, eager for just a few hours of sunlight to bloom. Byghan calves would stand on spindly legs, and Cador would hunt in only his vest, soaking in the warmth before winter returned too swiftly.

For the moment, he was glad of his cloak and tunic although sweat clung to his skin. Shivering, he felt raw. Flayed. Perhaps it was for the best—let Jem hate him for this and all his treachery. Let them share no more forbidden pleasure.

Cador didn't deserve him. He'd always been so damn sure of everything. That the gods were false and the mainlanders the enemy and that he'd never fall in love.

Gripping his spear, he shoved aside a bough of sharp needles. *Love.* What madness! Surely he could not *love* so quickly. Bryok would scoff and say he should abandon Jem to the boars and the approaching night. Once, Cador might have laughed along with him as though it was a jest.

"Jem!" He screamed it now, his throat dry.

He slid to a halt, every muscle tensed as he listened. There had been something. A noise that didn't fit. A voice. A response. He strained, blood rushing in his ears.

There!

He rushed toward the call of his name—diving into the bitter embrace of a tree just in time, a hairy, snorting boar thundering toward him. Snorting, the boar skidded as Cador struggled in the mud, his boots slipping as he crashed to his arse.

Distractions were fatal, and Cador had let his churning thoughts take over. He reached for the spear on his back—no, he'd been holding it. *Where, where, where?*

Fingers grasping, his heart was going to tear through his throat as he scrabbled in the underbrush, reaching blindly, the boar's hooves deafening as it returned to defend its territory.

He yanked his dagger from his boot, a last resort. There was only a flash—bulging eyes, mighty tusks, teeth bared in a ferocious grimace—and Cador knew this was the end even as he slashed with his dagger.

He heard his last shout of defiance as if from a great distance, as though he was deep under the icy waves of the Askorn Sea. Another cry ripped through the forest, and Cador blinked at the boar, trying to understand why its tusks hadn't impaled him. His clean blade was still clutched in his hand.

Inches from his boot, the boar shook and snarled, a spear driven through its thick body. As it gave its final death rattles, Cador followed the spear upward to the hunter who wielded it.

Blood was flecked across Jem's sweet face. Lips parted, he gasped, eyes wild as he stared at the felled boar. He gripped Cador's spear so tightly his knuckles looked about to burst through the skin.

Cador dropped the knife and pushed to his feet. It would have been more honorable a death than he deserved, but he'd never been so grateful to still be breathing. The boar was barrel-thick and all muscle, and Jem had felled it.

"You saved me," Cador marveled.

Chest heaving, Jem stared down at the stilled boar. With a loud straining grunt, he yanked the spear free. Blood oozed from the fatal wound. Jem looked to the spear as though he didn't understand how it had gotten into his hands. He dropped it to the red-soaked earth.

"My little prince will be a hunter yet."

Almost flying, his cloak fanning around him, Jem leapt forward and shoved his palms against Cador's chest. Even fueled by resentment and the energy of a kill, his strength was no match for Cador's bulk. But Cador welcomed the aggression. It was either that or Jem might burst into tears, and he didn't think he could bear it.

Jem's harsh breaths filled the stillness. He looked from Cador to the boar and back again, his empty fingers twitching. "I—" His fine brows met. "You—" He bit out a frustrated groan.

Cador understood this mess of anger over the books, fear of the snarling boar, and the kill's undeniable rush. Again, Jem shoved at his chest with both hands. Cador barely budged and could have easily remained on his feet, but he guessed what Jem craved in that moment.

He willingly—eagerly—dropped to his back on the muddy, bloody soil, Jem straddling him and thrusting his hard cock against Cador's swelling shaft through their leather trousers. Jem shoved his tongue into his mouth, kissing him with a desperate moan.

He knew this frenzy well, and although he hadn't speared the boar himself, he joined in Jem's desperate drive. Taking Jem's face in his hands, he licked the warm spray of the beast's blood and fed it to Jem in a deep, sweeping kiss.

Gasping, Jem tugged at their fastenings, freeing their stiff cocks. Cador would have lifted his legs for Jem to fuck him, but Jem desperately stripped his lower half bare and impaled himself on Cador's prick, crying out.

It had to be painful. Indeed, Jem gritted his teeth as he took Cador fully. Cador tried to soothe with gentle caresses, but Jem impatiently slapped his hands away and tore off his shirt so he rode him naked.

What a sight.

Lean thighs flexing, mouth open and back arched, eyes screwed shut, Jem dug his fingers into Cador's chest as he fucked himself. His stiff prick was flushed purple, his nipples red and peaked.

Yet he couldn't seem to find the release he so clearly hungered for. He grunted and whined and didn't ease up despite the roughness without oil. Cador worried he might actually hurt himself, though he was taking his shaft like a warrior.

Cador would be ready to shoot his seed any minute, but there was something not right for Jem. As he rode Cador's cock, despairing confusion creased his face.

Gripping Jem's waist, he lifted him and shoved him into the mud, rolling atop before Jem could even protest. But he didn't protest—indeed, he moaned gratefully as Cador crushed him down and captured his wrists. Even with the fire of a fresh kill blazing through his veins, Jem craved being taken.

Cador surged with odd pride that he had been right about what Jem needed; it twined with pleasure at the trust in him. He took his face in hand and kissed him deeply. Cador had already been hard, but now his prick was absolute iron. How had he ever thought Jem beneath his notice? Beneath his touch?

"So eager for my mighty cock, hmm?" he taunted playfully, sitting up, keeping Jem's wrists pressed to the earth on either side of his head. At Jem's nod, Cador clucked his tongue in pretend disapproval. "Look at you. Naked in the muck." He sat back farther, letting go of Jem's wrists and straddling his knees. Jem didn't move aside from the heaving of his chest. His shaft strained and leaked.

Cador was still dressed aside from his throbbing prick standing proud from his open trousers. He unfastened his cloak from around his neck and let it drop behind. Keeping his tunic on, he let his gaze rake down Jem's bare body.

Jem's cock twitched, and he made pleading little sounds in his throat. Cador drew a finger down Jem's shaking chest. Never had he been so torn between merciless fucking or smoothing his hands over warm flesh with his lips following a tender path, slowly tasting until they both quivered with the need to join and spill their seed together.

"Cador?"

He shook off his reverie, realizing he was rubbing his prick with his other hand. "I want to do everything to you." *With you.* "You'd let me, wouldn't you?" He circled Jem's nipples with his fingertip.

"Yes," Jem breathed.

"You'll let me do anything." It wasn't even a question.

Yet he answered. "Yes."

The trust in that simple word—uttered while he waited in such a vulnerable position—made Cador's heart clench. That he was the first man Jem had allowed to touch him made it all the sweeter.

First and only.

It was more than a passing thought—it was a vow, swift and ruthless like the charging boar aiming its tusks for the soft, secret part of Cador's soul. The idea of another man putting his grubby hands on Jem, entering him and spilling seed in his core, sparked fury that rose up from deep within, like when he hunted and another challenged him for the prize.

The need for Jem to trust him burned blisteringly hot. He knew he didn't deserve that trust, but he ached for it all the same. He vowed to earn it.

"Please. I need you."

It was barely a whisper, but Cador jolted as though it had

been a shout. He had failed in so much, but this? He could give Jem exactly what he needed.

"Fuck me," Jem pleaded, and it fired Cador's blood to hear him speak crudely.

"Oh, I will." The urge to plunge right inside that waiting heat was hard to resist, but he suspected there was more he could give Jem first. "Naked in the muck and begging for my cock. Right here where anyone could come along and spy upon us." He made a show of glancing around. "Perhaps they watch already."

In truth, he saw not a flicker of movement but for the pine boughs in the spring breeze, and he wouldn't allow a soul to see Jem like this. So beautiful and free.

Mine.

Jem moaned at the fantasy. He enjoyed the thought of being watched, as Cador had guessed he would. After all, he'd enjoyed making a show of himself with that candle.

"You stayed innocent so long, but really you're a whore."

Jem gasped, his hips bucking. He lifted his hands from the mud to grasp at Cador's tunic.

Oh, yes, he liked that. Cador grinned at the piece of treasure he'd unearthed. "You love being fucked, don't you? Love bending over for whatever you can get." He held Jem's wrists together once more, pressing his arms back over his head in the mud. With his free hand, he stole low and fucked him with his middle finger, crooking and rubbing and finding the special place inside. "You could come just like this."

"Yes," Jem confessed eagerly.

"So hungry for cock," Cador murmured. "The men of Rusk would line up. Should I ask for volunteers?"

Sucking in a sharp breath, Jem's honey eyes went wide with

what looked to be genuine fear. He tugged against the grip on his wrists. "No! Only you."

He'd clearly gone too far, but fresh lust pulsed through Cador to hear those words, accompanied by a strange lightness in his chest as he let go of Jem's wrists and leaned over to kiss his cheeks and stroke his flanks. "Shh. It's all right. I'd never do that."

"Promise?"

"Promise." He nuzzled Jem's sweat-damp curls. "You're mine. All mine." He captured his mouth in a wild kiss and scraped Jem's face with his beard, their tongues meeting as they moaned.

Spittle strung between them as Cador ripped away and commanded, "Roll over for me like a good whore."

With an ecstatic cry, Jem wriggled over onto his hands and knees. Cador spit onto his prick, trying to slick it as best he could.

"Please," Jem moaned. "I can take you."

"You can," Cador agreed. With his hand firm on Jem's hip, he brutally thrust to the root.

Jem practically screamed his pleasure, and Cador was close to doing the same. He grabbed Jem's muddy curls and yanked his head back with an iron grip. He fucked him without mercy, mud and boar's blood splattering them both. Grunting, they rutted like animals. Jem squeezed his arse around Cador's thrusting cock, the punishing strokes tearing cries of ecstasy from them both.

He thought of Jem the young virgin pleasuring himself, locked away alone with his secret fantasies. "Is this how you imagined it with your candle?"

"Yes," Jem answered. "But…"

"What?" Cador demanded, pulling his hair. Whatever it was, he would give it. He'd do anything Jem wanted. Everything. Although Jem was the one being fucked, Cador felt as though *he* was at Jem's mercy.

He craved giving him what he needed. Wanted to see a smile crease his dear cheeks. The need to make Jem happy had him so desperate he could hardly draw breath.

"I imagined much, but—" He cried out as Cador pulled back and plunged deep again. "This is so much better."

Pride and joy rushed through Cador, bollocks tightening. Jem was small, but he took cock so perfectly. "My brave little prince." The words tumbled out as he thrust harder. He was going to spill, but he needed Jem to release first.

He reached down and stroked Jem's rigid prick. "Are you ready to spill for me like a good little slut?" Again, he pulled almost free before slamming back in.

Head back and mouth open, Jem cried out, milky splotches painting the mud. His prick jerked in Cador's grasp as he clamped down with his arse. It only took a few thrusts until Cador spilled himself in that tight, perfect heat.

Tunic clinging to his sweat-damp skin, he eased himself free, delighting at the evidence of his seed dripping from Jem's quivering hole. Ever so gently, he rubbed his thumb around the swollen ring of muscle.

Jem shivered, still splayed open on his knees and utterly spent in the mud, leaning on his elbows now. Even though Cador had just released, he wished he could grow hard again immediately so he could spill all over Jem's bare body. He was almost unbearably beautiful, and Cador would cover him in his seed until nary a drop remained...

The snap of a twig jolted Jem violently, and he whipped his

head around, spinning on his knees to face Cador, covered in mud. "Is someone truly there?"

Cador drew him into his arms, urging him to curl onto his lap, holding close. He grabbed for his abandoned cloak and wrapped it around Jem protectively.

"Shh. No one's there. It's only a byghan." In truth, he wasn't certain, and he peered intently into the trees around them. He caressed Jem's muddy hair. He could spot no one, so perhaps it truly had been a byghan or another woodland creature. "I won't let anyone see you." Wouldn't let anyone harm a curl on his head.

Jem's fingers tangled in the hair on Cador's chest above the loose laces of his tunic. "Thank you."

The trusting words made the sweet new sensation deep in Cador grow thicker like a juneberry bush in the fleeting summer warmth. Had Jem put a spell on him? Was this some mainland sorcery of the gods? Cador was lost. Consumed.

Guilty.

"Jem. I have done wrong."

Against Cador's throat, Jem nodded. "I'm still angry. But it's done. The books are gone."

"I was wrong about many things." He held Jem tighter.

"I believe you're sorry."

"I am. There's so much…" He swallowed hard. "There's much I would change. Much I *will* change. I swear it. I—" His throat was painfully thick.

"Cador?" Jem's slim fingers caressed his chest, stealing under his tunic.

"Truly, I am sorry for your books. And there is more you must know. More I must tell you. First, I will speak to my sister. I swear I'll tell you everything soon. I swear I will protect you."

Jem's fingers stilled, and he was silent in Cador's arms. He remained curled on Cador's lap, nestled in his arms, but clearly he was chewing over this information.

"Will you trust me?" Cador begged. "Though you have no reason to." Even less than he knew.

Jem sat up, his honey eyes serious. "If I didn't trust you, we'd be strangers still."

Cador had to kiss him, stroking their tongues together, tasting the metallic hint of blood, lips raw and swollen. Their breath one.

Eyes searching, Jem took Cador's face in his hands. "What's wrong with the children?"

"I'll tell you everything. Soon."

After an eternal silence, Jem nodded.

Glancing around as though a spell had lifted, Jem laughed softly. "It'll be dark soon. I'm naked." He shivered, drawing the cloak closer around him. "I killed a boar." He stared at the carcass. "Me! I did that." He ran a hand over Cador's head. "Will I have to cut my hair now?"

"No!" Cador didn't even stop to think, practically growling his answer. He buried his fingers in Jem's mud-caked curls. Reluctantly, he added, "Of course it's your choice. You've earned the honor. You're a hunter."

Jem wrinkled his nose. "I prefer healing over hunting. I was only jesting, though I feel you've grown fond of my hair, no?" He raised an eyebrow. "Now who's the one with no sense of humor?"

Cador laughed, tightening his arms around him. "Point taken." He glanced meaningfully at the forgotten spear, blood staining it.

"Very funny." Jem's smile faded as he gazed at the boar. "I

barely managed to dodge it. Then you were there and..." He shuddered. "It would have killed you. I had no choice."

"It's the way of the world. You should feel no guilt."

"I know." He still couldn't look away from the dead creature.

Cador gently turned Jem's face to him. "I owe you my life, Prince Jowan. What payment can I give?"

"Hmm." Jem tapped his chin, back to jesting. "What shall I demand?"

"I am at your mercy."

"I suppose you'll have to fuck me forever."

He sought Jem's mouth and kissed him thoroughly, swallowing his little gasps and smiles. That word echoed in Cador's mind—in his very soul—like the sweetest summer song.

Forever.

Chapter Nineteen

TO BE HONEST, Jem was glad Cador had come on foot. This way, he didn't have to ride Massen home on his tender arse.

Home.

The thought made him smile even as he warned himself against this giddy rush of affection for Cador. This same man had tossed Jem's beloved books into the dirt like they were worthless.

Yet that had been before, and it seemed very long ago. Today, Cador had searched for Jem in the forest because he was worried, calling his name with hoarse shouts of concern.

Cador pleasured him as roughly as Jem wanted, then cradled him after like he was precious. He was hiding some dark secret from Jem at his own admission, but Jem had grown to trust him. Grown to love him with his whole heart.

Still filthy, he knelt with Derwa in the aviary while Cador rode back in the descending night to field-dress and fetch the boar. Jem's kill. He was disgusted by it, yet victorious at the same time. Apparently he was a man of multitudes himself.

Derwa hopped around, chirping excitedly. Jem stroked her thickening feathers with the back of his finger. She flapped her wings and rose a few inches. Jem gasped in delight. Sitting back on his heels, he watched her try again. She flapped madly, and there—Derwa flew from one side of the aviary to the other.

When Cador returned, he shoved the boar into a cold cellar under the barn's floor. Then he turned to Jem still kneeling in the aviary and trying not to grin. Brow creasing, Cador asked, "What?"

"Look!" Jem whispered, as though he might shatter the spell that had Derwa flying around the confined area, stopping to perch on the side of the crate and chirp. Her gray feathers rippled, and he could imagine her pride.

Sucking in a breath, Cador dropped to his knees outside the aviary. He and Jem were only separated by the thin metal bars as they watched Derwa test her wings. Jem hadn't realized he'd wrapped a hand around one of the thin spindles until Cador covered his fingers with his own.

"Will she fly away now?"

A pang of regret tugged at Jem. "Yes. At least, I imagine it's the same with askells."

Eyes on Derwa's fledgling flights, Cador stroked Jem's fingers idly. "You did it. You healed her. I admit I hadn't thought it possible."

"Just takes patience." He eased his hand from Cador's and got to his feet.

Cador stood and peered at him seriously. "It takes more than that. You're a healer."

Jem shrugged off the praise, although it pleased him. With a deep breath, he opened the aviary's door, the iron creaking. He joined Cador and they watched as Derwa flew a few more short bursts from side to side in her enclosure.

Then, she flew out the aviary door, wavered, and flapped powerfully before sailing right out of the barn into the twilight.

Jem's chest tightened, and he pressed his lips together tightly. Beside him, Cador simply breathed, "Oh," and took Jem's hand, threading their fingers together.

After clearing his too-thick throat, Jem asked, "May we leave the barn door open in case she wishes to return tonight?"

"Of course. Do you think she will?"

"Likely not. Once they fly, my work is done."

"I'll miss her." Cador laughed ruefully. "Foolish, I know."

"That's never foolish. I miss them all, but it's worth it."

"And you never see them again?"

Jem sighed. "Not dillywigs, at least. It's likely the same with askells."

Cador lifted Jem's hand and pressed a kiss to his knuckles—then grimaced. "You're filthy."

They burst out laughing, the bittersweet pressure in Jem's chest releasing. It struck him that Cador could make him laugh when he needed to most. A memory of their wedding night returned—Cador's boasts about his massive cock—and he laughed now belatedly.

Cador went about hauling water from the well. Inside, he heated the water and filled the small tub for Jem. He was plenty dirty himself, but he stepped back and waited while Jem bathed. He watched, though, waiting naked. The fire crackled in the hearth nearby, the water sloshing as Jem sponged himself clean, standing in the tub with Cador's gaze heavy on him.

Although Jem wasn't trying to arouse him and Cador's prick was soft, it was still intimate. They were in their own world, safe and together, and nothing else mattered. For tonight, at least. The hush in the cottage felt secret. Special. Only for them.

He grimaced when he climbed out of the tub and onto the fur that still covered the hearth although he shared Cador's bed now. "You'll have to get fresh water this time."

"Nonsense." Cador stepped into the bath and lathered the

dull soap.

"You really are a barbarian."

Baring his teeth, Cador growled, and they laughed. Jem sank to the fur, droplets drying on his damp skin and holding out his hands to the fire's warmth. He couldn't hide a wince as he got settled.

Of course Cador noticed. "Was it too rough?"

"No," he insisted, and he wasn't fibbing. It had been everything he'd wanted and more that he hadn't even known he'd needed. But, oh, he'd needed it. "I told you to make it hard."

"Yes, but with no oil…" Cador splashed out of the tub and nodded at Jem's lower body. "Let me see."

This again! Jem's face burned as bright as the fire. "I'm fine, I assure you."

Cador raised an eyebrow. "Will you always be so shy after we fuck?"

Always. The word sent a flock of dillywigs flapping in Jem's belly. Cador's neck flushed pink down to the ink tusks on his hairy chest, as though he'd also realized the implication.

Forever. Always. These words they surely let fall from their lips all too easily. What was this secret Cador kept? What was wrong with the children? Why couldn't he simply tell Jem now? Why did he have to speak to Delen first? Why—

"Show me."

The swift change in Cador's tone to a command made Jem's breath catch and his spent cock twitch, his nagging questions fleeing. A quick smile lifted Cador's full lips, dimples flashing in his cheeks.

His tone brooked no arguments. "I said show me your hole."

A moan escaped Jem's lips despite himself, a fresh spiral of desire twisting through him. On his back, he lifted his knees, spreading himself open to Cador's sharp gaze. Cador dropped to his knees, inspecting his sore arse. He examined the swollen flesh with the gentlest of touches, bent to the task.

Jem wanted him so badly it made his fingers twitch and heart race and eyes sting with tears. It also made his prick fill instantly.

Cador's warm breath tickled his bollocks. He pressed his face into Jem's spread arse, kissing his hole. Jem shook, gasping at the sensation on his over-sensitive skin—at the wonderful closeness. Cador lifted his head, noticing Jem's straining cock.

"Already?" he teased. "So young."

He had to laugh. "Yes." His smile faded. "And a whore." The word tasted forbidden and thrilling, the stuff of his darkest fantasies.

Cador seemed to read his mind. "Mmm." His gaze lingered on Jem's cock. "Can you come again for me? I bet you can."

His heart drummed. "Yes."

Cador took hold of his knees and pushed. "Spread your legs for me."

Jem honestly wasn't sure he could take another fucking right then, but he obeyed, a thrill shooting down his spine. Mercifully, Cador went to work with his mouth, lapping at his bollocks.

Arching his spine, Jem groaned. He was splayed with Cador between his thighs, pleasuring him with enthusiasm even though they'd spent violently in the forest not long ago. He was helpless once again in the most perfect way.

Jem arched up into Cador's mouth, the desperate need to come again searing through his veins. He whimpered and strained, twisting the fur beneath him in his fists. His flesh was too sensitive, but there was no denying he was rigid again. He had to come. He'd die otherwise.

He moaned as Cador sucked his shaft, orange firelight playing on his face and beard. Jem wanted it to stop—but also *never* wanted it to stop. It wasn't long before he came, a wail escaping his lips as he shook. It was almost too much.

Almost.

Cador swallowed his seed—surely there was none left—and released him with a wet smack. Then he leaned close for a slow, salty kiss. A dirty, thrilling kiss. Soon, Jem slept tucked against Cador's body, dreaming of blue skies and Derwa flying free.

NAKED AND TOASTY warm under a mountain of furs on Cador's bed the next morning, Jem yawned and felt like the spoiled prince Cador had once assumed him to be.

Cador had woken obscenely early in the darkness, stoking the fire and baking fresh bread, the scent of which still permeated the cottage deliciously. He'd gathered eggs for Jem's breakfast and kissed his forehead. Told him to go back to sleep while he hunted, and Jem had.

It was all rather glorious.

Yes, there was the whole matter of whatever Cador was keeping from him, but he'd promised to reveal all today. Jem forced away the knot of worry and reminded himself he'd decided to be patient. He wasn't going to spoil a beautiful morning.

He stretched his arms over his head, arching his back. His arse twinged, his prick half-hard. It was all he could do to resist pleasuring himself with memories of kneeling naked in the forest, his fingers sinking in the muck, Cador's bruising grip perfect as he took him.

Jem stroked himself lightly. Or perhaps he'd imagine what Cador would do tonight. He had so many fantasies...

As long as everything would be all right. What was wrong with the children? What did Cador have to confess? What—

"No. I will enjoy this morning." He threw back the furs and leapt up, yelping at the chill compared to the cozy bed, even with the fire smoldering. He dressed quickly, another question lurking in the back of his mind needing an answer.

Jem held his breath as he tiptoed into the barn, letting his eyes adjust to the gloom. The aviary door stood open as he'd left it, and sure enough, Derwa was nowhere to be seen. His eyes filled even as he smiled.

He couldn't let himself hope askells would return—and he shouldn't hope for it—so he allowed himself the tears. Then he wiped his cheeks and indulged in some time with the goats and chickens in the enclosure outside before he ate the breakfast Cador had left him.

It wasn't too long until he headed toward Rusk, drizzle falling from the same gray sky he'd seen for weeks and weeks. But Jem hummed defiantly. He wouldn't let Ergh's miserable weather bother him. If he could forgive Cador for the books, a little rain was nothing.

And he could. Although it hurt his heart to think of Morvoren and the others abandoned in the dirt, he believed Cador wouldn't do that now. His belly was full of the fresh bread his husband had baked for him, and he would focus on that—and the flowers peeping through the damp soil.

Making sure not to venture too far from the path, Jem investigated the hardy little buds. The towering trees blocked the worst of the increasing drizzle, and Jem crouched on a bed of pine needles to get a closer look. The air was moist and loamy, rich with spring.

Ergh had been so gray and cold, but now Jem realized how fortunate he was to be here. To experience a true spring, new life bursting from its winter prison. He bent low and inhaled deeply, but of course the tiny, furled flowers had no scent yet.

A bird sang—an askell?—and he imagined it was Derwa. He'd never know if she survived her first night in the wild, but there was no harm in believing she fluttered above him now.

A voice suddenly echoing through the trees had Jem almost landing on his face in the dirt. Cador's voice. Springing up, Jem followed the distant sound before hesitating. Cador was hunting. Would Jem stumble into a dangerous situation? He should have brought one of Cador's many spears, although they were so big he'd have to drag it.

He could hardly believe he'd actually speared a boar himself. Amazing the strength abject terror could inspire. He shuddered as he remembered the sensation of the spear plowing through flesh and scraping bone, Cador open-mouthed in the mud. The relief that had swept Cador visibly and the gratitude in his blue eyes. The softening.

The love?

Standing in the shelter of giant pine boughs, a warm glow in Jem's chest had him smiling. He should leave Cador to the hunt and retreat to the path. Go to Rusk and offer Austol another apology. Offer him any help he could possibly give.

But Cador's voice rang out again on a gust of breeze—raised in…what? Anger? It didn't sound like triumph, although Jem couldn't yet make out the words. He was moving toward the sound before he even realized it, drawn helplessly.

Even as some instinct whispered to make his steps light.

Hidden in the shadows, he crept closer. Closer still. He spotted snatches of movement—leather-clad muscles. He tiptoed, bunching his cloak in one hand so it didn't get caught on the sharp needles as he slipped into a pine's embrace.

With no fur-topped cloaks today, Cador and Delen faced each other in a small clearing. Their arms were bare beyond leather vests, and Jem saw that Delen had another tattoo around her forearm, the ink making a tight swirling pattern in her dark brown skin. They stood holding spears dug into the soft ground, their horses nosing the underbrush.

"Then why have you been kind to him?" Cador accused.

Delen motioned with her free hand. "Why should I be cruel? He isn't to blame. It would serve nothing."

"Yet you'll stand by and let it happen?"

"You would defy Tas? Forget that he's our parent—he is our *chieftain*. He hasn't made his plan lightly. We need this war and now is the time."

"But he's innocent in all of this."

Jem could barely breathe. Only a fool would believe they could be discussing anyone but him. And what was this talk of war?

"He is," Delen agreed. "But what of the children? More and more are afflicted as time goes on. Are they not innocent? How do you weigh innocent lives against each other? We have a duty to Ergh. To Hedrok."

Cador's face creased with grief. "But Jem…"

His name from Cador's lips was a boot to the stomach, crushing the sliver of hope that they discussed another after all.

"I warned Tas you were too tender-hearted." Delen sounded truly saddened.

"Me?" Cador scoffed.

"Of course. For all your bluster, you're not the hardened

warrior you'd like to be. For all your insistence that marriage is for sentimental fools, it didn't take long for Prince Jowan to get under your skin. For that brand to mean something."

Cador looked at his left palm before curling his fingers into a fist. "Why do you insist on calling him that? Jem—"

"*Prince Jowan* must play his role. None of this has been decided lightly." Delen shook her head. "Honestly, when I saw him, I thought it would be all right after all. He's hardly your typical lover."

"That has nothing to do with this!"

She raised an eyebrow. "Doesn't it? Jory says it's obvious you're fucking him at the very least. We've never known you to be possessive, brother."

Jem swung from a helpless burst of joy that Cador might care for him more than any others back to the mounting dread. What was this plan? What was his role? It didn't sound as though he'd like it. Not a bit.

Part of him wanted to run and remain ignorant, but of course he stayed motionless, hidden in the tree. Needles poked through his cloak and tickled his cheeks. He gripped the rough trunk, waiting.

"I'm supposed to sit back and let him be taken? Let these kidnappers spirit him away?"

An icy fist squeezed Jem's heart. He couldn't breathe.

"You had no qualms before," Delen said.

"I didn't know him then!"

"Focus that tender heart on your nephew! On Austol's sister, on Meraud's son in his grave, on Jory's cousin in hers. How many more shall I name?"

As Delen rattled off a seemingly endless list, Jem's mind spun. Kidnapped. He was to be kidnapped. Of all the secrets

Cador could have hidden from him, of all the lies he could have told, Jem hadn't once imagined anything so horrific.

Heart galloping, he was suddenly very aware of how alone he was. His people were across the sea, and though he'd realized the Erghians weren't so very different after all, who could he trust if his husband was part of this plot?

He choked down a sob, a terrible grief welling deep within. For all his initial misgivings, he *had* trusted his husband. He truly had, but if Cador could hide this from him... He squeezed his eyes shut against the flood of tears, his fingers digging into the tree's bark.

Kidnapped.

Where was he to be taken? By whom? Why? When? He felt like he had on the shore of the Askorn Sea, staring into an endless, fearsome unknown. Alone. But worse now—*betrayed.* Sorrow and hurt swelled, blotting out everything like the fortress of clouds that kept Ergh in perpetual gloom.

He thought of his mother, and a pang of longing for her and Father and Santo and his brothers buckled his knees. He clung to the tree. Would he ever see them again? Would he ever go home?

Cador said, "We may need this war, but no one is harming a hair on his head. Let alone severing his hand and delivering it to his mother."

Darkness took Jem like sudden midnight. He choked down a surge of nausea, his breakfast threatening to come back up as the joy was snuffed by anguish. He couldn't breathe. Blood rushed in his ears and he stumbled back, his body taking flight of its own accord, unwilling to hear another word—unable to withstand the heartbreak.

Of course they heard the rustle of boughs and spun toward

him, spears in hand. *Run!* Yet his feet were stone as he met Cador's gaze, horror in those wide blue eyes.

"You were going to cut off my hand?" Jem didn't recognize his own voice, the words scraped from his throat barely a whisper.

Then he *was* running, unable to bear the answer. Cador had lied to him from the moment they met. He was to be kidnapped? His hand chopped off? Then what? Imprisoned? Tortured?

And Cador *knew*?

It had to be a phantom pain, but Jem's branded palm throbbed as he ducked below branches, tearing his cloak free and running like he never had before. Because Cador and Delen chased—of course they did.

They called his name, pleading, but Jem ignored them, wind rushing as he ran, ran, ran. His size worked to his advantage for once, and he evaded them by ducking between thick stands of pine although they knew the forest so well.

It rained heavily now, a wall of gray that broke through the thick boughs and branches that clawed Jem's cheeks. At some point, they had to have given up the chase, because they would have caught him eventually. His smallness was no match for their skill in the long run. Though he'd been the one running away, Jem couldn't stop a fresh burst of pain at wondering why Cador had given up so easily.

Somehow—perhaps the gods felt he deserved a bit of luck— Jem found Rusk and skirted the trees toward the stable. His soaked tunic and leather trousers clung to him, his toes squelching in his boots. It was surely almost midday, but the rainstorm made it dark, thunder clapping and making him jump.

The stable was the only place he knew to go. Surely Austol would shelter him, at least for the moment. At least until he could figure out what to do. Where to go.

He'd begun to feel comfortable on Ergh. Welcomed. Did the children and their parents who'd gathered for his stories know he was to be taken and wounded so grievously? He prayed not, but questioned everything he thought he'd known.

"Prince Jowan!"

Jem instantly scowled as Jory jogged toward him. Jory was soaked by the rain himself and out of breath, his ginger hair dark and plastered to his head.

"You must come with me. Cador—"

"Cador can sink to the bottom of the Askorn Sea!" Jem backed away, his boots slipping in the mud. He furiously wiped rain from his eyes.

Jory held up his hands, having to shout to be heard over the deluge. "Please. There's…" He shook his head. "There's so much you don't know."

"I know all I need to." He stumbled back. "Stay away from me!" Had Jory known all along? Had he and Cador been fucking and plotting? Had they been laughing about how gullible Jem was?

A small voice reminded him that Cador seemed regretful, and there was no reason to think he and Jory had been together, but the roar of jealousy and resentment paired with suspicion. Jory wasn't his friend. He'd assured Jem there was nothing to fear from him. Why would he say that?

"Jem." Austol's voice rang out as he strode toward them, and Jem moved to him eagerly.

"Please, you must come with me!" Jory said. "We must find Cador."

Austol eyed Jory warily. "He doesn't want to go with you."

"I know, but he must." Jory pleaded with his hands. "I think you're in danger."

"I know I am! Cador is a liar. I was a fool." The weight of Austol's arm squeezing around Jem's shoulders was a warm relief. Something solid to lean on.

Austol spoke calmly to Jory. "He's clearly upset. He doesn't want to go with you or see Cador right now. Come on, Jem. We can talk. Find out what this is all about." He whistled, and one of the horses trotted over from the pasture, its hooves spraying up mud and rainwater.

But Jory shook his head. "I can't let you leave."

Jem's stomach flip-flopped uneasily. He thought of Jory and Bryok together yesterday by the stable. What was this? Was Jory his kidnapper? He could well imagine Bryok being involved.

Austol huffed out a sound of surprise. "What? Are we prisoners, Jory? This is madness." He squeezed Jem reassuringly. "We're going to talk."

The horse who joined them wore no bridle, but stood obediently, a third point on the triangle of their standoff.

Jory repeated, "I can't let you go." There were no traces of his usual good humor, and his jaw set in a stubborn edge.

The hair rose on the back of Jem's neck. Jory meant it—he wouldn't let them leave. He was a big man—certainly bigger than Jem or Austol. Jory reached for the horse, and Austol suddenly shoved him into the mud, yelling at Jem to mount as he and Jory wrestled.

Grabbing the horse's mane, Jem sprang up—and made it!— his heart drumming. A moment later, Austol was behind him and they were off, Jory's shouts lost in the howling rain.

They galloped along the outskirts of Rusk before Austol

guided the horse across soaked fields. The deluge finally eased. Jem blinked at the unfamiliar landscape. Had they gone south? He thought so, but couldn't be sure.

It didn't matter—at least he was away from Jory and Cador and Delen. He needed time to think. He dismounted gratefully at the edge of a thick copse of trees on the swell of a hill and sank to his knees in the mud.

"Thank you," he croaked to Austol. "I just need some time. I…" He was in need of much more than time, but he couldn't begin to put it into words.

"I understand," Austol said. He petted the horse's neck and looked down sadly at Jem. "I know it's easy for me to say, but try not to be frightened."

He had to laugh dully. "Rather a lost cause. There's so much I didn't know."

"Me too." Austol sighed.

The dark clouds had departed, the sky brightening by the minute, a mass of white rather than gray for a change. Jem was so thirsty. He wanted to spill out the whole awful story to Austol and get his advice, but he was too heartsick.

Instead, he pushed to his feet and said, "I'm so sorry your sister is ill. What's causing it? Can I help?"

Austol leaned into the horse, stroking its neck rhythmically. He closed his eyes. "It's taken years to discover the cause. To find a solution." He swallowed hard, his throat working as he met Jem's gaze steadily. "Thank you. You're a good man. If it's any comfort, I think Cador really has fallen in love with you. I can see why."

It shouldn't have been a comfort—Jem shouldn't have allowed it for even a moment—but it was, and he did. He opened his mouth to respond but was suddenly blinded. He blinked, holding up his hand to block the staggeringly bright light.

It took him longer than it should have to realize it was the sun. The sun! Not only had the rain stopped, but now the sun was peeking from behind the clouds that had remained impenetrable for so long. Perhaps he'd even see blue sky.

In that moment, Jem thought he would weep for joy at feeling the sun's warmth on his face for the first time since the Holy Place. It overwhelmed with its simple beauty, and he closed his eyes, hands loose at his sides.

He was able to smile as he murmured, "Maybe it's a sign from the gods."

The words had barely left his chapped lips when hands were upon him, rough and merciless. Jem jerked open his eyes in time to see the world made black by the dark sack that encased his head and muffled his screams as he was dragged away.

Chapter Twenty

I T FELT LIKE hours Jem was slung over a stallion's back on his belly. He braced for dear life, his stomach bruised from the merciless jolting. A rider sat behind him and suddenly reined in the horse at the sound of a distant shout.

Jem crashed to the wet ground. He'd been given a hard shove, and at least his captors hadn't bothered to bind his hands so he could break his fall at the last moment.

His fingers were numb with cold and shock as he struggled with the knot on the sack over his head. The rough material touched his mouth with every ragged inhalation, and he tore at the binding.

The rest of him was freezing—the sun had apparently only made a brief appearance before a return of the relentless rain— but his face was hot with his muffled breath and the rush of blood from hanging over the horse.

Nostrils flaring, his mouth open as he gasped, Jem yanked at the sack. He tried to tear the fabric with his fingers, giving up on the knot in the twine that secured it around his neck. He kicked uselessly, a high whine escaping.

Off! Get it off!

He was suffocating, and no one seemed to care. There were low voices nearby, and he almost cried for help. Forcing a slow inhalation and exhalation, he stopped himself. He wouldn't give them the satisfaction.

In the mud, he curled into a ball and counted his breaths, reminding himself that the twine was just loose enough and the fabric porous enough that he *could* breathe. He'd have been long dead otherwise.

Sinking into the mud that had likely saved him broken bones, Jem breathed and listened. He balled his icy fingers into fists and rubbed them against his filthy tunic for a shred of warmth. Now that he was calmer, he noticed the air was briny. Above the rain, the voices moved closer.

"They should fucking be here by now." This bark was undoubtedly Bryok's. No surprise, but Jem still shuddered.

A woman said, "Be patient, my dear." Hmm. Given the affection in her words, Bryok's wife? Jem searched his memory for her name. Creeda.

He listened as a few others spoke of a ship. Was someone sailing to meet them? These kidnappers? Were they from the mainland? With the great distance, plans would have to be made long in advance and wouldn't be flexible.

Had the kidnapping always been scheduled for today? Was that why Cador had sought Delen's help? Because time was running out and he'd had second thoughts at the last minute?

Jem pressed his palms together, threading his fingers. The thought of losing one of his hands was unbearable. Which would it be? He only needed a moment to answer as the question entered his mind.

With his thumb, he traced the tusks branded into his right palm. He hadn't married Cador with any illusions of love. They were strangers forced together. But to think Cador had known Jem was to be hurt so grievously, even if now he'd sworn to Delen that he wouldn't allow it... And for what? A war? Involving Jem's mother? He couldn't make sense of it.

He waited to hear Cador's voice. Dreading it, knowing his heart would crumble to dust. Yet if Cador was amongst the group, he was silent. Jem imagined Cador's gaze on him—his pitiful collapse in the mud, curled helplessly. Would he just stand there and watch?

Had there only been a single dawn since Cador and Jem had rutted in mud like this? They'd undoubtedly given each other pleasure—Cador hadn't faked filling Jem with his seed. He'd cradled him after, his lips gentle. There had been true affection between them.

Hadn't there?

Jem didn't want to delude himself, but he clung to a stubborn thread of hope with numb fingers.

After a time, he set those fingers to work again on the twine. Controlling his panic now, he picked and tugged with small movements while Bryok and the others complained about a late ship. They seemed to pay him no mind at all. They underestimated him.

Jem would use that mistake. He'd only have one chance.

"And where the fuck is Hedra?" Bryok shouted. "We can't preserve it without her skills."

Again, Creeda tried to soothe him. "She will come. She has prepared for the ceremony for weeks."

Jem's fingers stilled on the impossibly knotted twine. Did they mean Austol's Hedra? Ceremony? Preserve it? Preserve *what*? His hand? The cold lump of dread in his gut grew heavier, and he willed his fingers not to tremble as he dug a blunt nail under the knotted twine. He had to escape.

Panic flapped its wings, and he bit his tongue to stop from crying out. His legs twitched. He tasted blood. But again, Jem forced slow breaths, and he worked on the damn knot while

Bryok ranted about unreliable conspirators.

Finally! Jem wanted to weep with joy as he wedged his nail in deep enough and patiently pulled at the knot. His throat felt bruised from the twine digging in around his neck, and it took all his control to ease the knot free and keep the rough fabric in place instead of tearing it off his head.

His hot breath was cloying in the sweaty sack, and he yearned to gulp fresh air. Instead, he slowly, slowly worked the material up over his nose. For a few moments, he inhaled gratefully and waited, still curled in the mud. No one raised the alarm.

Holding his breath, he eased the sack above his eyes.

The day was fading now, so it had been hours. Only gray light remained. Bryok and the others—five in total, including a woman who was indeed Creeda—loomed tall, but they were some distance away. Certainly close enough to see him if they looked down, but it would take perhaps five of Bryok's long strides to reach him.

That Cador was not among them released at least one knot of tension from Jem's spine. What of Austol? Had they hurt him? Although it was pointless, Jem said a quick, silent prayer to the gods or whatever forces might be listening. It was the only thing he could do, and it felt better than nothing at all.

Though the rain had finally ceased completely, the briny air was damp. Jem realized the shaking of the muddy ground wasn't his panicked heartbeat but approaching hooves. Was this Hedra? Whoever it was and whatever they might do, he couldn't wait to find out.

A horse nosed the ground near him, and as the approaching hoof beats grew to thunder, Jem sprang up, ignoring the wobble of his knees and stiffness in his bruised body.

The pale horse was tall, but Jem didn't hesitate, taking a running jump and tangling his fingers in its mane. It snorted and sidestepped as he heaved across its back.

A shout rose. "Grab him!"

With all his might, Jem spurred the horse with his heels, not looking behind as they leapt forward. A violent yank on his boot almost toppled him, but he kicked hard and was released, the figure crashing to the ground.

There were more shouts over the rush of wind and his heart. Still, Jem didn't look back. Bent low over the horse's back, fingers clutching its mane, he held on and kicked with his heels. "Faster!" he shouted.

He had no idea where they were aside from near the ocean. His captors pursued, so the only direction was onward over a ridge. Then he rode along a cliff, the Askorn Sea churning to his right.

Yet he also rode straight toward more cliffs and the sea.

It was only at the last moment, the horse rearing up on its hind legs in the failing gray light that Jem realized where they were. He tumbled, hitting the wet ground on his back with a mighty *whomp*, the air rushing from his lungs.

As the horse whinnied and retreated, Jem heaved to his belly and found himself at the land's edge. The others were too close, and he crawled, sinking his battered hands into the mud. He kept crawling, then pushed to his feet and ran.

Jem ran onto one of the narrow fingers of the Cliffs of Glaw.

The spit of land was only wide enough for three horses flanked. It felt like no room at all with a deadly drop to both sides. The tip narrowed even more before him. He stumbled to a stop, remembering staring up at these fingers of Ergh's fist, the southern-most edges of the land.

Hadn't Cador mentioned a watch here on the coast? Jem saw no towers or patrols, but he'd have scarcely noticed as he galloped. If he shouted, would anyone rush to his aid? Would they go against Bryok, the chieftain's son? Jem thought not, but he shouted for help anyway.

He faced his pursuers as they reined in their horses, still on solid ground. Bryok laughed and mimicked his cries. Night was descending swiftly, the days so short on Ergh even in this supposed spring. An icy wind from the sea whipped Jem's curls as he stood at the precipice.

There was nowhere left to run.

Chapter Twenty-One

G ALLOPING IN THE fading light, Cador crushed the reins in his fists, leaning low over Massen's back. He could imagine Austol's nose cracking, could taste the phantom spray of blood as he pummeled the traitorous prick.

Cador didn't give a shit about Austol's tearful regret and pleas for mercy. For forgiveness. Yes, after Jory had raced to find Cador and Delen, afraid that Bryok was up to something sinister, Austol had sought them out himself. Yes, he'd confessed immediately that Bryok had schemed his own plan without Tas's knowledge.

Yes, Cador still wanted to smash in Austol's face.

The four of them rode as hard as their mounts could withstand, Cador in the lead, Delen and Jory on his heels, Austol sniveling behind. Cador and Delen had strapped their short spears to their backs, and the blade of his dagger was snug against his ankle in his boot.

Cador had stopped listening when Austol had told them Bryok had taken Jem south of Rusk to the other harbor before the Cliffs of Glaw. This one was harder to access, the path down the cliffs even steeper, but it was used by fishermen sometimes.

Leaning low over Massen's neck, he praised his speed, spurring him on with promises of all the carrots Massen could eat if only he'd get Cador there in time. He didn't know what Bryok's plan was aside from kidnapping Jem earlier than Tas had planned. It didn't matter. All that mattered was getting to Jem before it was too late. Holding him in his arms, safe and alive.

He groaned aloud at the memory of Jem's horror-struck face amid the pine boughs. The betrayal etched there—honey eyes wide, that pretty mouth agape and trembling. He should have told Jem when he'd had the chance. Confessed it all and gotten Delen to cooperate after.

What a fool he was!

He squinted into the gloaming as they neared the second harbor. There were signs in the mud of recent activity, but when he peered down the cliff, he saw no one. But there—a flicker of light from farther down the coast. From the Cliffs of Glaw themselves. A fist around his heart, Cador called to the others and led the way.

"What the fuck are they doing?" Delen shouted.

He wished he could answer. Ahead, he could see torches being lit and held aloft, people on horseback—but where was Jem? He couldn't make out faces until Bryok's familiar sneer turned to him. At the base of one of the narrow finger cliffs that jutted out, Bryok hopped down from his horse and struck its backside, urging it away.

Bryok opened his arms wide, only wearing his leather vest and trousers like Cador did. "Brother! You're just in time for the ceremony."

"Where is he?" Cador didn't care what the fuck Bryok was talking about. "Jem!"

"I'm here!" Jem's voice was reedy, carried on the wind.

Relief and fear warred as Cador searched for him. For a moment, he wondered if the voice had been a ghost's and he was too late after all. Then he saw the movement out on the narrow spit of land, his eyes adjusting to the dark beyond the torchlight.

Gods! Jem stood near the finger's claw. A step in three directions would be his last. But he lived, and Cador would worship
the gods forever if Jem was returned to him safely.

Bryok blocked Cador's path. Several others still sat on
horseback, including Creeda. Cador fought the urge to leap
down, shove Bryok out of the way, and grab Jem. He had to stay
calm.

He called to Jem, "It's all right. I'm here now."

Bryok's scarred face twisted in the flickering light. "Say your
goodbyes to him, brother. We're almost ready." He looked to
the blond woman in a robe like a cleric's as she drew a circle in
the muddy soil. She'd apprenticed as a healer, Cador thought,
vaguely recalling that there'd been some upheaval and whispers
that she'd been removed from her studies.

"Hedra, please," Austol rasped, leaping down from his
mount. "It isn't right. You can't do this. We can't."

She ignored him, heaving a sack and spilling its contents
into the circle—long-dead branches of the ruined sevel trees
that the newly faithful displayed around the tribute to the gods
in Rusk. Cador tasted bile. He'd always found it unnerving
though he hadn't known why. What was this madness?

Slowly, forcing calm, he dismounted, sharing a worried
glance with Delen still on her horse. Cador, Delen, and Jory
were outnumbered to be sure. Austol couldn't be trusted despite
his pleas to Hedra. Bryok had no spear, which was an advantage.
Creeda could fight, but she wasn't a hunter. The other three
people with them unfortunately were.

"Ruan, what's going on?" Cador asked. Ruan and two more
hunters Cador had also called friends sat on their nervous
mounts. Cador held out his hands. "You know Tas guides us."

Before Ruan could answer, Bryok growled, "Fuck Tas."

It shouldn't have, but it shocked Cador. He felt for an instant like a naive boy, he and Delen always doing their parents' bidding while Bryok rebelled.

"We're done waiting," Bryok spat. The veins in his neck stood out, his hands in fists. Beyond him, Jem was still trapped. Cador forced himself to focus on his brother's snarled words.

"You and Delen may be content to sit back and wait, but if your children were dying day by day, you would not be so patient."

Delen said, "But you know we can't simply demand Ebrenn's land. We need Neuvella and Gwels as allies."

"And we will have them!" Bryok's eyes glinted in the torchlight, his voice rising. "When the queen of Neuvella sees her son's head atop the Western battlements, she will crush her enemy! *Our* enemy!"

Cador couldn't breathe. The vision Bryok's vow conjured horrified him like nothing else he could imagine. All he could do was cry, "No!" He glimpsed his horror mirrored on Jem's beautiful face before Bryok stepped closer.

"You and our sister were so determined to do Tas's bidding as always," Bryok spat. "This is still his strategy—I'm only altering it. If the boy is kidnapped, the queen will surely be worried, yes. She might join us in battle. Or she might let the clerics convince her to bargain. You know those holy fuckers will do anything to stay in control. If she receives the prince's hand, she might still bow to her enemies for his safe return. But no mother will see her child's head and *negotiate*."

"I won't let that happen," Cador vowed. "We will find another way."

"The queen will spill blood for her son," Creeda agreed.

"The clerics think they know the gods so well. But the gods demand sacrifice. They always have. For too long we denied them. They blighted our sevel trees. Now they blight our children. We will sacrifice a prince of Onan and we will have the war we need. And the gods will cheer us!"

Cador asked Bryok, "Since when do you believe in the gods?"

He shrugged. "I don't give a fuck. Let them have their delusions." He didn't seem to notice or care that his wife's spine stiffened, Creeda's jaw clenching, fury blazing in her eyes.

Bryok added, "Hedra says she can preserve the flesh. Let her do her fucking ceremony. What matters is we will return to the mainland with the prince's head and all the warriors of Ergh, and we will take Ebrenn. Take the sevels and heal our children."

"Why do you need sevels?" Jem asked.

Cador cringed, wishing Jem would stay silent and forgotten. But now Bryok's attention was back on him as he growled, "Shut your mouth!"

Austol spoke up. "Our sevel trees died some years ago. We don't know why, and they won't grow again. Some of the children who haven't cut their teeth on the fruit are stricken with this wasting disease. My sister. Bryok's son. Too many others. The healers are certain sevels are the cause and the cure. We've traded for shipments, but Ebrenn is tightfisted. It's not enough. We must control the sevel fields ourselves or the children will always be in danger."

Bryok shook with wrath, spittle flying from his lips. "Shut up! He deserves no explanation!"

Jem ignored Bryok, speaking to Austol. "Today, you..." He shook his head, and Cador could see the sorrow of yet another betrayal. Jem breathed deeply. "But why didn't you ask us for the sevels? They grow so abundantly in Ebrenn. If children are suffering, I know—"

"You know nothing!" Bryok shouted. "If the enemy knows what it is you seek, they will cling to it with their last breath. Even if we submitted to the clerics and let them indoctrinate Ergh, even if they convinced Ebrenn to send ships full of sevels, it wouldn't be enough. We must control the growth. We must make that land ours."

Jem's curls whipped around his head in a gust of sea air, the torches flickering violently. Cador longed to touch him, to carry him away from this place.

Jem stood so close to the blackness as he said, "Please. I know my mother. She will—"

"Don't make it harder for yourself, boy," Bryok snarled. "Come close and I'll make it quick."

"Your mother will avenge your murder," Creeda added. "Your sacrifice will not be in vain, I swear it."

"No!" Cador shouted. "I won't allow it. Never. *Never!*"

"You didn't give a damn what happened to him before!" Bryok's lip curled in disgust. "But now that you're fucking that pathetic piece of shit, you value him over your own people? Over your nephew's life?" He spat. "And don't deny it! I saw you in the forest. Fucking your little toy in the mud. He doesn't deserve you, brother. He's wormed his way into your favor. Turned you against us! I knew it was time to act."

Cador puffed up his chest. "I'd never deny it. Jem's my husband. I want to fuck him until we're old and gray. He hasn't turned me against anyone. He's—"

"He's nothing!" Bryok screamed. "What of Hedrok? He can no longer stand. The sickness creeps up his body without mercy. He knows his fate. He knows that all the sevels in the fucking world won't save him now. He knows it's too late for him. And you can't even bother to visit!"

Shame crashed over Cador. He couldn't deny it. He wouldn't. "I'm a coward. Seeing him suffer—it's unbearable." He should have visited his nephew every damn day. Instead he'd stayed away and tried to think of anything else. "I'm sorry." He looked between Creeda and Bryok. "Truly, I am."

Bryok rubbed a hand over his craggy face. Darkness had closed in, the torchlight flickering in shadows. "Even if it's too late for him, we will protect the unborn children from his fate."

Creeda insisted, "We don't know that it's too late for Hedrok. He's eaten many of the sevels you transported back. It might slow the disease enough. We don't know! This is why we must act." She nodded to Hedra, her thick hair whipping her cheek where the wind tore it loose from a knot. "Perform the ceremony. I have prayed with all my breath to the gods. Let them bless this sacrifice. Let it be the spark that will guarantee our war. Our salvation!"

"You would sacrifice my husband?" Cador demanded. "Even if I beg you not to?" He itched to rip his spear from its binding across his back and fight for Jem's return, but he was too aware of Ruan and the others at the periphery, and how very close Jem was to the edge of the cliffs. Jem needed him to keep his head.

A burst of panicked laughter clawed at Cador's throat. If he didn't keep his head, neither would Jem.

Think!

He had to devise a strategy like Tas would, even if it required patience. He watched Jem beyond Bryok, trapped but standing firmly, his jaw set. Even if his knees were shaking, Jem wasn't letting it show. Cador's fingers itched to touch him.

Ruan ran a hand over his graying hair in frustration. "Enough of this. You care more for this Southern prince than our children? Impossible. He is spoiled and soft and...*expendable*."

Cador nodded. "I thought so too." He looked to Jem, who watched him with wide eyes. Gaze locked with Jem's across the chasm, Cador said steadily, "He proved me wrong. He will prove you all wrong."

He spoke to Bryok. "Let us journey to the mainland now with Jem. We'll go to Tas and the queen. We'll find a way to make this work. If it's war, then let it be war. Anything but this." He beseeched his brother, who he'd tried to please for as long as he could remember drawing breath. Cador held out his hands. "Please."

The scrape of metal was Cador's answer as Bryok unsheathed his mighty sword from his back—a blade that finally severed something deep within Cador. He'd never seek Bryok's approval again. He'd never admire him. It was over.

"Oh, it will be war, brother. Trust me. Neuvella and Gwels will help us take Ebrenn, and then we'll take it all. Onan will be ours and they will be the ones to suffer!"

Unease plainly rippled through Bryok's conspirators. Ruan's lined face drew into deeper creases. "That wasn't the plan. We need Ebrenn for the sevels. We will take it for the good of Ergh." He stomped his boot. "*Our* land. We don't need the rest of it. We don't want it."

"Why not?" Bryok hissed, gripping his sword. "Why shouldn't it be ours? Why should those weaklings keep it? We can have all of Onan. All their luxuries. We struggle for every single thing here, battling the snow and ice and darkness. The endless fucking winters. While they laze in the sun and gorge on more kinds of food than we ever knew existed!"

Cador exclaimed, "You were the one scorning their luxuries at the Holy Place! Now you want them for yourself?"

"Yes! Why should we toil in the muck for every bite we eat? Why should our children?"

Creeda seethed. "Do not use our children to excuse this greed. I thought you were a righteous man. I thought you battled for our son."

"I do!" Bryok reached a hand toward her. "This is for him too. For all of our children! If you saw how they lived—how easy it is. You would want this future too. They say the gods banished us—perhaps they did! We will take back what should be ours."

Creeda shook her head sharply. "We fight for the power to prevent disease. This sickness came after the sevel trees were destroyed and would grow no more. We need the sevels to cure it. We don't need to conquer the mainland—"

"I will conquer the gods!" Bryok bellowed, spinning toward Jem.

Raising the sword.

Running along the narrow spit of cliff.

Even as Cador burst after him, he knew. Bryok was beyond his reach, his legs always regrettably longer and faster. Jem was trapped and would lose his head in a single swipe of that lethal blade—

The cry of denial tore from Cador's throat as Jem jumped into the abyss, forever gone in an instant.

Chapter Twenty-Two

G ASPING, JEM CLUNG to the side of the dred nest, his shoulders screaming. He'd asked himself what Morvoren would do and shortly thereafter leapt from the Cliffs of Glaw rather than allow his severed head to be used against his mother and start a war.

Now here he was, high on the side of a rock face hanging on by his fingernails, the icy sea crashing against rocks far below. The dred had certainly constructed its nest to last, so that was something. Jem was still in possession of his head and hands, so that was something as well.

He moaned, said hands stinging, his shoulders ready to give out after they'd been wrenched so brutally. Now he simply needed to haul himself up.

Easy.

Above, the wind carried the echo of a cry that had to be Cador's. His husband's anguish shouldn't have brought Jem such a rush of elation, but he needed every burst of energy and strength he could muster. It was a balm to the torment of knowing Cador had lied to him for so long, and for a heartbeat, Jem allowed himself to be soothed.

But only for that moment.

Gritting his teeth and praying to Morvoren—she would do him far more good than the supposed gods—he strained to pull himself to safety. If the nest gave way and he plummeted to his certain death, at least he'd have tried since that was apparently going to happen regardless.

Shoulders screeching, digging his nails into the nest's woven branches, he swung side to side. When he caught his foot over the edge of the nest, wedging his boot inside the rim, he stopped, panting.

Inch by agonizing inch, he hauled himself up, every muscle tensed and burning. He gasped in shallow breaths. He wanted to scream, but didn't have the energy—every single bit of him focused on getting into the nest.

Almost, almost…

The structure was shallow, and he rolled onto it, relief flooding him as powerfully as if he was spilling his seed. He trembled on his back, his feet sticking over the edge of the mud-sealed branches. His heartbeat filled his ears over the crash of waves far below, his chest heaving.

He was alive. Jem tasted salt, unsure if it was the sea spray carried on the vicious wind or his own tears.

When he'd tumbled from the horse and peered over the cliff's edge, he'd spotted the nest. Given the massive size of dreds and what Cador had said about sitting in one as a boy, Jem had taken his chance when Bryok rushed forward with shocking speed, that wicked blade raised, and Cador too far behind.

His small stature had worked in Jem's favor again. The dreds also built their homes with impressive craftsmanship, although he couldn't risk borrowing it for long. He squinted into the crevasse in the cliff face, not seeing any eggs or hearing hungry squawks.

Peering up, it was almost impossible to make out where the rock ended and the moonless night began. Bryok's scarred face had been terrifying in the torchlight as he'd closed in.

"Don't make it harder for yourself, boy."

As though there was some easy way to be beheaded? A strangled laugh—part sob—burbled in Jem's chest. He had no idea what ritual of Hedra's would preserve his head, but he shuddered to imagine it atop a pole.

It was madness. Would Jem's mother go to war on his behalf? He had no doubt of her love, but she was a pragmatic woman. There was no guarantee, especially if the clerics got involved. Jem supposed Bryok had little to lose—it wasn't his head, after all. And he clearly wanted war at any cost.

Over the buzz in his ears and howl of the wind, a voice echoed—Delen. "He's gone. He's gone." Regret splattered the words like blood. "Come away from there, brother."

A denial roared, close to the cliff's edge. Cador sounded like a wounded animal. Did he truly howl for Jem? Even if it could be proof of his love, it was now ensnarled with betrayal.

Terrible grief consumed Jem. Despite everything, he loved this man with a savage affection. He wanted to go to him and ease his suffering, protect him from ever hurting again. Jem wanted to shield that big body and cradle him in his arms and never let go. Yet how could he now?

He wouldn't be able to do anything until he climbed to safety. Shouts punched through the air once more, fury swirling in the cruel wind. Cador and Bryok. Jem had to move. If he stood on his own shoulders, there would be about five of him to reach the top. He could do it.

Just as Cador had said on the ship when they'd squinted up at the distant dred nest, the cliff face was marked with thin crevasses. Perfect for Jem's small hands to grip. His heart was a drum keeping time as he climbed, wedging his feet into narrow openings, reaching up, his numb fingers searching the stone.

It took a lifetime.

He was so close, but so far. A battle raged above, and even if Jem had shouted for help, no one would have heard. He clung to the rock face, wondering if he'd have been better staying put. But he ached for solid ground, and now he was halfway there and it was just as risky to descend.

So he climbed, scrabbling and desperate, his limbs on fire while his ears burned with merciless cold. The wind threatened to tear him from the side of the cliff, and terror was his hated companion as he inched upward.

Almost. Almost!

His fingers closed over the hard ground of the narrow peninsula where he'd stood. The shouts and torchlight were to his left, but he blocked it out. He was perched on a narrow ridge on the tips of his toes, his boots just fitting. One more pull and he was safe. Gods, he wanted to live!

He clenched his arms and pulled—and his fingers slipped. He clawed at the earth, his boots sliding on rock and chest ready to burst with panic. Safety was right there. He was strong enough. He could do it.

A last burst of vigor propelled him up and over, and he rolled onto the narrow finger of land. On his belly, he wriggled toward the light and the angry cries and wrestling bodies. Beyond the circle of torchlight, he hoped he was invisible in the night.

Cador had Bryok laid out on his back—at his mercy, his dagger poised to pierce Bryok's throat. Straddling his brother's larger body, Cador's chest heaved. Delen stood over them, keeping the others back.

Delen's voice was hoarse. "Jem's gone. He made a brave

choice. This won't bring him back. This will only destroy you."

Tears shone in Cador's eyes, orange flames glowing on his pale face. Jem's heart clenched to hear him say, "He is gone, and I am already destroyed."

"Go on," Bryok croaked, but it wasn't a taunt. "I can't watch my son die. Let this be my end."

Creeda didn't cry or beg—she *growled*. "You'll leave it to me, then. You'll leave it all to me. For what? For your greed. Yes, for our son, but not only him. Not only the children. You want to conquer the mainland and bend it to your rule? You'll do it alone. You've always been a spiteful coward, yet I loved you anyway." Her lip curled, and she strode forward and spat upon her husband. "You've disappointed me for the last time."

With that, she spun on her heel, mounted her steed, and galloped into the night.

On his belly in the darkness, no one even glanced Jem's way. He could hide unmoving and watch Cador end his brother. It would be easy. He was drained completely and wasn't even sure he could muster the will to whisper, let alone call out. If Bryok died, surely Jem would be safe.

Yet he saw the torment in Cador, and he rasped, "No!"

One day, Jem would have to sketch the astonishment on the gathered faces as all heads whipped to him. Cador stumbled to his feet and stared motionless, the dagger slipping from his fingers.

Pushing up to his knees, Jem nodded to the abyss, still catching his breath. "Dred nest."

A stunned smile creased Cador's face, his cheeks dimpling under his beard as he laughed and shouted all at once, running to Jem and falling to his knees to capture him in his arms. Jem clung to him, too weak to deny either of them the comfort.

Bryok snatched the dagger from the ground and lurched toward them.

Jem gasped as Cador whirled his head around, Bryok already upon them—and his hot blood sprayed their faces. Delen's spear had gone right through him and out his chest, perhaps finding his heart, for there was only a stunned moment of horror on Bryok's face before he slumped dead.

Breathing hard, Delen gritted out, "Curse you to the bottom of the Askorn Sea." She wrenched free her spear.

Bryok tumbled over the side of the cliff, swallowed by the void.

The wind howled, and the three of them were frozen in place, staring into the darkness where Bryok had disappeared.

"Bryok…" Cador shook his head, a sob escaping. "It should have been me to end him."

But Delen said, "You're too tender-hearted, brother. Best to leave it to me." Still gripping her spear, tears flooded her eyes, reflected in the torchlight. "Damn you, Bryok," she muttered.

Cador didn't seem able to speak, and Jem didn't voice his relief that Bryok was gone. As he stared into the void that would have been his own grave, he realized he was *glad* Bryok was dead. Yet he took no pleasure in this gladness, the satisfaction bitter and awful.

Delen said to him, "I'm sorry for what you've suffered. I'm sorry we deceived you so cruelly. My brother doesn't deserve you." At Cador's inarticulate sound of disagreement, she smiled wryly. "But if you'll have him, I think he loves you truly, Prince Jowan." She backed away.

How could she *smile*? And speak of love? How could Jem be expected to trust in anything they said, let alone *love*? His head spun.

He was warm in Cador's arms, but he pushed to his feet. Cador was still on his knees, and Jem couldn't resist stroking his palm over his husband's soft hair.

Cador ran his hands up and down Jem's legs as if he was making sure he was still whole. Stroking Cador's head one more time, he allowed himself a last moment of closeness, of powerful arms locked around his waist.

Then he walked away.

Cador stumbled after him, glancing back over and over as if he expected his brother to rise from the sea and take his vengeance. Jem looked back too. Better safe than sorry.

In fact, he yanked one of the torches from the earth and returned to the edge, peering over the edge of the drop, making sure the dred nest was still empty and there were no others that Bryok might have landed in by some twist of incredible luck.

He exhaled. Nothing but the empty nest, sheer rock face, and the fatal drop, though the spear wound would have surely killed him before he even hit the black, churning water. Resolutely, he walked back from the edge, shaking off Cador's reaching hand.

The others had fled except for Delen, Jory, and Austol, who approached with tears in his eyes, saying, "Jem, thank the gods you're all right."

Cador bared his teeth at Austol. "Be gone," he gritted out. "Or I'll toss you over with no regrets."

To Jem, Austol pleaded, "I'm sorry. Please believe me. Bryok was so sure this was the way. I—I—my sister—" He shook his head. "It's no excuse."

To say the very least. Jem had thought he'd made a true friend. How could he ever trust a word Austol uttered? Or Cador? In the face of Jem's silence, Austol retreated, mounting his horse in a graceful motion Jem still envied.

He shook his head. What a strange thing to think about. His mind felt oddly distant and hazy. He gazed at the abandoned circle of sevel branches, the torches that had been shoved into the ground still casting an eerie glow on the gnarled wood. He had the urge to throw the branches into the sea's abyss, yet he wasn't sure he had the vigor to even stay on his feet.

Cador was now with Delen out of earshot, standing close and speaking quietly, their expressions grim. Jem watched them blankly.

"Are you well?"

Jem blinked at Jory. He stood a few feet away, peering at him with concern. "No," Jem muttered, his own voice sounding distant. "I'm not."

"Forgive me. It was a foolish question." Jory scoffed. "I can't imagine anyone would be well after this." He ran a hand over his wild ginger hair, which had dried in a riot of waves.

Forgive. Such an innocent word. Before, Jem would have likely nodded and agreed. Now...

Jory glanced at Cador, who was back alone at the cliff's very edge, staring down into the darkness where Bryok had disappeared. Jory said, "If I'd known about any of this sooner, I would have told him to be honest with you. I swear it." He gave Jem a sad smile and retreated.

Honest.

"I swear it."

The words all seemed meaningless. Why should he believe anything Jory said either? He thought of Jory and Cador always with their heads together on the journey north from Onan, talking and laughing. He'd been jealous, but who was to say he'd been *wrong*? Even if they weren't lovers, why should Jem believe

Jory innocent in this plot?

He watched Jory and Delen mount their horses. Delen nodded to him before they rode away, but Jem didn't respond. He supposed he should be more grateful she'd killed Bryok and saved his life. Yet he thought of his hand being severed and found the terror left no room for gratitude.

"I think he loves you truly, Prince Jowan."

This from the woman who had been perfectly willing earlier that very day to see him kidnapped and maimed. A million thoughts tumbled through Jem's mind. Though he couldn't deny he'd fallen in love with Cador, it didn't mean Cador felt the same for him.

He'd probably only fucked Jem because it was convenient. Because it was a way to convince Jem to trust him until the time came. Because Jem was a willing body. A pathetic fool so eager to surrender.

The last thing he wanted to do was face this, but there was no choice. He neared Cador cautiously. "Come away from there."

Cador nodded, though he didn't move, his gaze fixed on the void. Far below, waves crashed around the rocky base of the cliff. The wind gusted. One of the torches guttered and was extinguished.

"My brother would have killed you," he said dully. "And me."

"Yes. Please, come here." Despite it all, seeing Cador so close to danger made his heart gallop.

Cador obediently walked back safely from the edge, his gaze raking over Jem. Suddenly brimming with energy, he tugged him into the torchlight and gripped his right hand. He opened Jem's fingers, displaying the brand on his palm.

"Forgive me for my treachery. I beg you." He pressed dry lips to the tusks.

Oh, how Jem wanted in that moment to give in. He wavered on his feet. He was so tired. He didn't want to fight. It would be easy to surrender once more and tell Cador he was forgiven.

Taking a fortifying breath, Jem tugged his hand free.

"Please," Cador begged. "I'm sorry. I'm so sorry. I should have told you the truth long ago."

"Yes." He crossed his arms to keep from taking Cador's outstretched hand. His whole body ached, but it was his heart that was broken. He wanted to shut his eyes and make none of it true. He wanted to wake safe at home between cool silk sheets and discover his marriage and journey was all a dream. A wonderful, terrible dream.

He kept his head high. "You wed me knowing I'd be kidnapped. Maimed. For a start."

"I didn't know you then!"

He laughed hollowly. "Is that supposed to make me feel better? That you'd subject an innocent stranger to such cruelty? Now that you *know* me, will someone else be snatched to have their hand chopped off? Their head?"

"No!" Cador pleaded, "You must believe me. I won't allow it."

"How do you know these kidnappers wouldn't have tortured me? Killed me?"

"The plan was only to—" Cador's throat worked. "The plan was only to sever your branded hand and use it to ensure your mother's rage. If my father told her everything and she declined to help us, we would have no allies on Onan. Gwels sides with your mother in all things. Ebrenn would have us at their mercy, and that king is not the merciful kind."

"Even if that's true, you lied and lied and lied." As Cador opened his mouth, Jem cut off any protest. "Omissions are lies!"

Defensive now, Cador insisted, "I was going to tell you! You agreed to wait."

A bolt of fury stiffened Jem's spine. "I didn't think it would be anything like *this*! And what will Ergh do if you win the control you crave so desperately? Will you keep the sevels all to yourself? Inflate the price so we must pay or risk Onan's children?"

Cador flinched as though Jem had slapped him. "Of course not. All children will have what they need."

"How are we to believe that? You won't trust us. Instead of coming to my mother in good faith, you plotted and schemed. Your father is there now in *my home*! Welcomed as an honored guest!"

He despised the thought of the chieftain anywhere near his mother and Santo and the rest of his family. That very minute he was ensconced in the castle, safe and warm and *lying*.

Cador insisted, "But if we trust too easily it is our very future at risk."

"As is ours! You see the conundrum."

"Yes, but…" He rubbed his drawn face. "Someone will have to be first to trust. We must—"

"*I* trusted you!" The scream tore from him, a wailing sob that left Jem unbearably hollow. He couldn't stop the hot, shameful tears that spilled down his cheeks. "I trusted you."

Face creased in sorrow, Cador reached for him, but Jem stumbled back. "My love, please."

Oh, how Jem's soul would have soared at those words only that very morning. Not even an hour ago, he'd thrilled to hear Cador's grief for him when he'd jumped off the cliff. Yet none of it seemed real now—only something he might read in one of his lost books.

Piercing barbs of his own grief hooked into him, razor sharp and inescapable. "*No.* I believed you were truthful. I gave myself to you."

He thought of their coupling and squirmed with embarrassment—with humiliation. He'd imagined himself so brave and free. Gods, the things he'd done! His skin felt too tight, and he wanted to claw at it.

He could barely whisper, "Were you laughing at me the whole time?"

"No! Never!" Cador reached for him again but let his hands drop to his sides when Jem jerked back. "Please believe me. It is my honor to have lain with you. My privilege. My joy! Before I did, I had come to realize I could never let you be taken and hurt. Could never let you be harmed at all. I would kill for you." He flung his hand toward the black sea. "I'd see my brother cut down a thousand times to keep you safe. I'd do it myself."

Jem dashed the tears from his eyes. "How can I trust you now? You were false from the moment we met." He stared down at his branded hand. Imagined the agony of it being chopped from his body like it was nothing. Like *he* was nothing.

"I beg you." Cador dropped to his knees. "I swear it. I'll never betray you again. Forgive me, my husband."

The wind ruffled Jem's hair, his heart thumping so loudly he feared it truly would shatter. He stared down at the tusks seared into his skin. Sounds and sights filled his mind—sweet kisses and laughter, Cador chewing worms for Derwa, giving Jem his furs, waiting for him in the forest to make sure he didn't get lost, fucking him the way he'd dreamed, holding him so tenderly…

His own memories were the cruelest lies.

Fisting his fingers over the brand, he met Cador's pleading

gaze. "Never."

Cador's face creased, his cry hoarse. "But you must. I can't—please!"

When he was sure his voice wouldn't break, Jem said, "We'll sail to the mainland tomorrow. We'll meet with our parents and expose Ergh's lies. I have faith in my mother to be just and fair. We'll deal with the clerics and find a way forward for Ergh's children. For all our children. If it must be war with Ebrenn, then we'll fight it. But I'm not waiting for the Feast of the Blood Moon. I'm going home."

Home.

At the very edge of Ergh, surrounded by the forbidding sea with the cold wind battering him, he ached for the warm, familiar sunshine of Neuvella. How he wished his mother were here with her calm assurances and warm embrace, the smell of her favorite lavender perfume. She was so very far away, the world between them vast and merciless.

He must be brave. He could not be the trusting fool a moment longer. He would return to the castle where life had been so easy despite his furtive desires and the yearning in his heart. How few his troubles had been! It was far, far better to return to the safety of his daydreams.

"My little prince—"

He clenched his jaw. "Don't. I was never truly yours. I will be your husband only in name, as you intended from the start."

Jem left Cador on his knees. The sea's salty bite lashed his face as the wind gusted, and he tasted drying tears. Dawn had never felt more distant, yet he marched boldly into the night's endless, lonely shadows.

Morvoren would be proud.

TO BE CONTINUED!

Will Cador win back Jem's heart?
Find out in *The Barbarian's Vow*!

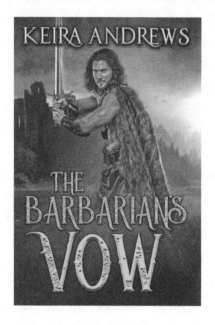

Keep reading for a sneak peek:
He claimed an innocent prince—and surrendered his heart.

T HE SHIP CRESTED a swell and dropped down the other side, and Cador couldn't quite bite back his moan. More like a shameful whimper, his empty stomach heaving, saliva filling his mouth. Jem reached out before snatching back his hand and pursing his lips.

"Press on your wrist like I showed you," he muttered.

"I'm fine." Cador stood straighter, his back to the rail, lifting his chin and speaking to Delen. "You were saying?"

She rolled her eyes. "I was saying that you two need to stop ignoring each other. There is much to discuss."

He wanted to ask her to wait until they were off the damn ship and he didn't feel quite so pathetically vulnerable. With solid ground beneath his boots, surely he'd have a clearer head. He bit his tongue. He was a mighty hunter of Ergh—he must not give in to such weakness.

Delen said, "First, we must agree on what we'll tell Tas and the queen. And when. We must be in accord." She held up a tight scroll. "I've written a message to be sent ahead. It says simply that we have returned with important matters to discuss and are traveling to Neuvella with haste. Clearly it is far too big a risk to put any other details in writing."

Cador nodded. He hated saying it, but asked, "What of our brother?"

They hadn't spoken of it by mutual, silent agreement. Bryok had met the end of Delen's spear because he'd have killed Jem— and likely Cador—otherwise. She'd had no choice. Surely Tas would understand? He was wise and fair. Wasn't he?

Cador had always thought so. He'd basked in Tas's affection and approval since he was a boy. He'd never questioned him— not even when Tas arranged Cador's marriage to Jem and planned to use Jem so cruelly. He understood Tas's fear of the clerics getting their hooks into Ergh and changing everything. The fear of revealing weakness to the mainland and losing their way of life.

But was it fair to plot and deceive? Was it right to help their sick children at any cost?

He refocused on Delen. If Cador didn't know her so well, he'd think her not bothered, but he could hear the note of tension in her voice as she answered his question.

"We can't exactly tell Tas in a letter that his son is dead with no other details. It would be too hideous." She grimaced. "Not that it will be much better face-to-face."

"No," Cador agreed. He dreaded it beyond the telling.

Jem was silent, still looking at his feet.

Delen swiftly said, "It's done and he must face it as we have. Bryok is dead, and Tas has a new heir."

Absurdly, Cador almost asked who. He blinked at her. It truly hadn't even flickered across his mind.

Delen frowned. "You're the second oldest. You'll be chieftain now."

"But I don't want to be chieftain!" He sounded like a ridiculous child. He could imagine Bryok berating him for moping over Jem and now this. He must regain control. Regain his dignity. He was a mighty hunter of Ergh, and if he was to be chieftain, he must accept it.

He discovered Jem watched him now. Was that sympathy? His heart leapt as Jem tightened his jaw, standing straighter and clasping his hands behind his back.

To Delen, Jem said, "We are in agreement on the contents of the message."

She held out the scroll. "Would you like to read it before it is sealed?"

Jem took it and scanned the short missive before nodding and handing it back.

Delen said, "We should only have to camp a night before provisions from the Holy Place arrive. Jory is our best rider, and he will be quick about it. We will travel light, aside from—" her gaze flitted to the ship's bow where Creeda hovered over Hedrok. "Well, the cart will be slower, but we can go ahead to speak to our parents. Now, as for what precisely to tell them."

"The truth," Jem said sharply.

She nodded. "Of course. But will you permit us to speak to our tas before telling your mother the...details?"

Jem's face could have been carved from stone. "By 'details,' do you mean Kenver's initial plot to kidnap me and sever my hand so it could be sent to my mother to incite a war with Ebrenn?"

Delen grimaced. "Yes, as much as we truly regret it. I'm sure our tas regrets it too."

"You can't speak for Kenver." Jem clenched his jaw. "He concocted the scheme to begin with."

She nodded. "You're right. I hope you know—"

"Don't." Jem held up a hand. "It's done and cannot be undone. Regret is useless."

In the tense silence, Cador knew the truth of those words. He'd never known such regret, and it would change nothing. He shielded his eyes from the sun, which at least was setting now.

Needing to say *something*, he blurted, "Is it always this blasted hot in summer?"

For a moment, he thought Jem would refuse to answer. Finally, he said, "No, actually. I was always told it was more temperate this far north. But it's certainly better than all that gray in Ergh."

"That's a matter of opinion," Cador grumbled.

Delen quickly said, "Let's stay focused. Prince Jowan, may we speak to our tas before confessing to the queen? I propose that Cador and I meet with him privately to discuss Bryok. Then the three of us will join you in explaining the truth to your parents. We must be united in our cause. The children are more important than anything else. Whatever our grievances may be—whatever our sins—we must stand together."

Jem seemed to consider this. "And we'll tell them the whole truth?"

"I swear it," Delen pledged solemnly.

Jem nodded.

"We'll be on land again soon, at least," she said. "You must be eager to return home, Prince Jowan."

"An understatement if ever I heard one. Yes, I am very eager to return to Neuvella permanently." Jem turned on his heel, leaving them at the bow.

Cador had no desire for small talk either, and Delen fell silent beside him. Jem rejoined Jory, picking up the dice.

Jory cast a worried look to Cador, his ginger hair wilder than ever in the sea wind and brushing his shoulders now. Cador nodded and tried to smile. Jory was a loyal friend who was completely innocent of any plotting, and at least Jem was willing to game with him. Even if it made Cador ridiculously jealous.

As the sun blessedly set, painting the sky an eerie pink, he looked to Creeda at the bow praying by Hedrok. The boy appeared to sleep, at least. Delen watched too, the pinch of her expression melting into tender concern.

Creeda had forgiven her for killing Bryok, apparently understanding that his hunger for power had surpassed redemption and Delen had only wielded her spear in necessity.

Before he could bite his tongue, Cador said, "Sometimes I think you love her."

Delen jolted, narrowing her gaze at him. "What?"

He might as well say it. "Sometimes I think you've loved her for a long time."

"And?" Her hands were fists, ready for a battle in a blink.

"And nothing." He frowned in confusion at her anger.

She glanced around and hissed, "You think I killed him for my own gain?"

It was Cador's turn to stiffen in surprise. "No!" He grasped her arm. "*Never*."

Delen exhaled loudly, the sudden fight disappearing. She nodded, looking to Creeda again. "I shouldn't," she murmured.

"Why?" He had to admit he didn't understand the appeal. But Creeda and Delen had been friends since they were girls. Perhaps there was another side to her as sweet as her singing.

Delen shook off his hand. "You know why."

"But—"

"Shall we speak of your love? How long will you shrink away and let Jem's anger fester?"

"He deserves to be angry."

"That may be, but the longer this separation lasts, the deeper the chasm between you. This talk of him never leaving Neuvella again—"

"How can you blame him after what we've done?"

Delen sighed. "I don't blame him a bit. But as I said, we must be united in our cause. You and he must be united most of all or we don't stand a chance."

"We will be."

"See to it." She gave a curt nod and strode off, disappearing into the hold.

His gaze returned to Jem as it always did. Small hands cupped, Jem tossed the dice. No secrets there. From those first moments in the Holy Place when their impending marriage was announced, Jem had revealed all.

Although he'd often tried to conceal his emotions, they were plain as day. Now it was all hurt and fury, and Cador longed to once again see his shy smiles of delight.

Resolutely, Cador faced the endless sea. He watched the waves swell, capped with frothy white as the wind increased. He inhaled the briny air that was still far too hot to be refreshing and longed to see his breath cloud in the frigid air of home. He tried to think of any damn thing but Jem.

Oh, to hear Jem's cries of passion and kiss his sweet lips. Bury his prick inside him and bring them both to ecstasy. To return to the cottage and those heady days of exploration and fucking. Even to just bake bread with him and tend the goats—perhaps nurse another hatchling like Derwa.

He never thought he would miss a bird.

In the wee hours, he rose from his pallet to piss off the rear of the ship. Meraud's second nodded to him from the helm. Snores and the sea's wet slaps on the hull were the only other sounds, the waves mercifully flattened. A breeze sent welcome goosebumps over his bare arms as he wandered to the bow.

A half moon shone high above, glinting silver on the water's surface. His heart leapt to his throat when he realized Jem was at the rail. Cador kept several feet between them but couldn't make himself leave Jem be.

For long minutes, they stood together yet apart, watching the dark horizon. It felt like an eternity as Cador waited for him to speak. To cry, to scream, to pummel him with his fists. Anything but this terrible silence.

When he could take it no longer, he pleaded in a hoarse whisper. "If you could only understand…"

"I do."

Holding his breath, Cador waited once more, a tendril of hope—

"But I hate you for it."

Cador dug his blunt fingernails into the worn rail, wanting to wrench the wood loose and smash it to smithereens. Jem was silent again, which was a relief after the ice in his voice. He was silent so long that if Cador hadn't watched him from the corner of his eye, he'd have thought himself alone. As he deserved.

"Strange how I can no longer see the stars," Jem muttered.

Cador glanced around, pathetically glad when he confirmed that, yes, Jem was speaking to him. He squinted toward Onan. The shadow of the land did indeed blend into the sky where earlier the stars had carpeted the heavens.

"Perhaps a storm approaches? Or merely clouds. We can rarely see the stars on Ergh."

"But…" Jem leaned forward, going up on his tiptoes. Cador could just make out his nose wrinkling in the remaining moonlight. "Is that…"

Will Cador win back Jem's heart?
Find out in *The Barbarian's Vow*!

Thank you so much for reading *Wed to the Barbarian*! I hope you enjoyed the first half of Jem and Cador's romance and that you'll love the thrilling conclusion in *The Barbarian's Vow*. I'd be grateful if you could take a few minutes to leave a review on Amazon, Goodreads, BookBub, social media, or wherever you like. Just a couple of sentences can really help other readers discover the book. ☺

Wishing you many happily ever afters!

Keira
<3

Join the free gay romance newsletter!

My newsletter will keep you up to date on my latest releases and news from the world of LGBTQ romance. You'll also get access to exclusive giveaways, free reads, and much more. Join the mailing list today and you're automatically entered into my monthly giveaway. Go here to sign up: subscribepage.com/KAnewsletter

Here's where you can find me online:
Website
www.keiraandrews.com
Facebook
facebook.com/keira.andrews.author
Facebook Reader Group
bit.ly/2gpTQpc
Instagram
instagram.com/keiraandrewsauthor
Goodreads
bit.ly/2k7kMj0
Amazon Author Page
amzn.to/2jWUfCL
Twitter
twitter.com/keiraandrews
BookBub
bookbub.com/authors/keira-andrews

About the Author

Keira aims for the perfect mix of character, plot, and heat in her M/M romances. She writes everything from swashbuckling pirates to heartwarming holiday escapism. Her fave tropes are enemies to lovers, age gaps, forced proximity, and passionate virgins. Although she loves delicious angst along the way, Keira guarantees happy endings!

Discover more at:

keiraandrews.com

Made in the USA
Monee, IL
24 June 2024

60585980R10198